The fiery brilliance of the [barcode] *see on the cover is created* ✄ P9-BYZ-368 *revolutionary process in which a powerful laser beam records light waves in diamond-like facets so tiny that 9,000,000 fit in a square inch. No print or photograph can match the vibrant colors and radiant glow of a hologram.*

So look for the Zebra Hologram Heart whenever you buy a historical romance. It is a shimmering reflection of our guarantee that you'll find consistent quality between the covers!

HER ANGER FUELED HIS DESIRE

"Damn you, don't laugh at me!" Caley stormed. "You've done nothing but bait and rile me and laugh at me ever since you came into town. Well, I'll be hanged if I'll put up with it any longer, do you hear?" She had no idea how much her anger heightened her beauty, nor how the sight of her provoked an even more tumultuous battle within him. "I don't want any part of you, Jake Brody!"

"Who are you trying so hard to convince, Caley?" Jake challenged in a quiet, dangerously even tone. "Me—or yourself?"

Without waiting for an answer, he swept her masterfully into his arms. Her protests were silenced by the firm, demanding pressure of his lips upon hers. Melting against him with a low moan of surrender, she raised her arms to entwine about his neck. His bronzed, naked skin felt warm and smooth and breathtakingly vibrant beneath her fingers. He kissed her long and hard, and she kissed him right back. Finally, he raised his head and gazed down into her beautiful, softly glowing eyes.

"You're mine, Caley McAlister," he decreed in a low tone simmering with passion. "You've been mine from that first day when you stood there in the street with that blasted whip in your hand, spitting fire at me." His strong arms tightened with fierce possessiveness about her trembling curves. "I think I knew it even then," he said.

**TURN TO CATHERINE CREEL — THE
REAL THING — FOR THE FINEST
IN HEART-SOARING ROMANCE!**

CAPTIVE FLAME   (2401, $3.95)
Meghan Kearney was grateful to American Devlin Monta-
gue for rescuing her from the gang of Bahamian cut-
throats. But soon the handsome yet arrogant island planter
insisted she serve his baser needs — and Meghan wondered
if she'd merely traded one kind of imprisonment for another!

TEXAS SPITFIRE   (2225, $3.95)
If fiery Dallas Brown failed to marry overbearing Ross
Kincaid, she would lose her family inheritance. But though
Dallas saw Kincaid as a low-down, shifty opportunist, the
strong-willed beauty could not deny that he made her pulse
race with an inexplicable flaming desire!

SCOUNDREL'S BRIDE   (2062, $3.95)
Though filled with disgust for the seamen overrunning her
island home, innocent Hillary Reynolds was overwhelmed
by the tanned, masculine physique of dashing Ryan Gal-
lagher. Until, in a moment of wild abandon, she offered
herself like a purring tiger to his passionate, insistent caress!

*Available wherever paperbacks are sold, or order direct from the
Publisher. Send cover price plus 50¢ per copy for mailing and
handling to Zebra Books, Dept. 2781, 475 Park Avenue South,
New York, N.Y. 10016. Residents of New York, New Jersey and
Pennsylvania must include sales tax. DO NOT SEND CASH.*

NEVADA CAPTIVE

CATHERINE CREEL

ZEBRA BOOKS
KENSINGTON PUBLISHING CORP.

ZEBRA BOOKS

are published by

Kensington Publishing Corp.
475 Park Avenue South
New York, NY 10016

Copyright © 1989 by Catherine Creel

All rights reserved. No part of this book may be repro-
duced in any form or by any means without the prior
written consent of the Publisher, excepting brief quotes
used in reviews.

First printing: October 1989

Printed in the United States of America

With love to my grandmother, Mayna Crow, whose remarkable stories made a young girl's imagination take flight.

Chapter I

Elko, Nevada . . . 1872

The six-sided star caught the sun, held it for a fleeting second in time, then set it free again.

Although wrought of the finest German silver, the badge was devoid of the fancy engraving or gold inlay coveted by most lawmen. But then, this particular emblem of unequaled frontier authority was pinned securely to the chest of a man who, some would say, had been born to the job. It was nothing more than fate that had brought him to this godforsaken town in the middle of the vast sagebrush desert. And it was nothing less than fate that would send him hurtling over the precipice of defeat if he ever betrayed the star's inescapable promise.

Jake Brody, newly appointed U.S. Marshal, stepped down from the train at last, his booted feet connecting almost soundlessly with the dust-caked boards of the platform. He lifted a hand to the snakeskin-banded Stetson on his head, gave the merest tug downward on the front brim, and allowed his penetrating, deep-green gaze to travel slowly about the Central Pacific's station and its immediate surroundings.

The station building was an unremarkable wooden structure, small and square and entirely typical of the railroad's local headquarters at every other stop along the line. A weathered sign nailed within the shadow of the roof's overhang proclaimed the name of the town in bold, bright red letters. The ticket agent, his bald and visored head bobbing on the inward side of the partially barred window, was engaged in an argument with a miner over the price of a roundtrip ticket to San Francisco. Two buxom young women clad in homemade dresses of calico whispered together and stole curious looks in the tall, handsome stranger's direction before waltzing away down the boardwalk. A trio of bearded old-timers, enthroned as usual upon wooden benches in front of the station, watched the gentle sway of the ladies' skirts and reminisced with fond half-truths about the days when they'd done a hell of a lot more than just look.

There was nothing—at first glance, anyway—to lend credence to Elko's reputation as a loud, young, and sinful place in desperate need of taming. Things seemed peaceful enough, judging from what could be seen through the cloud of smoke borne downward from the huge black locomotive by the ever-present wind.

But Jake Brody knew all too well that appearances can be deceiving . . . sometimes with deadly consequences.

It's a real, honest-to-God helltown, Brody, so watch your back, Smitty had warned him. If there was one thing he could say about Zachariah Smith, it was that the older man had never been given to exaggeration.

Jake allowed a faint smile to touch his lips at the thought of his friend. His eyes narrowed imperceptibly as he settled the hat even lower on his head and set off to begin the job he had been sent to do. The old-timers caught sight of him at last, their attention drawn to the gleaming silver star on his chest and the pearl-handled Colt .45's in the double holster buckled low on his hips. It was a well-known fact that anyone wearing two guns was either a lawman, an outlaw, or a fool—sometimes all three. But there was something about this particular man that told them he was a square-shooter all the way, a man with a purpose.

Giving a curt nod toward the trio, Jake moved silently across the platform. His long, deceptively nonchalant strides led him away from the train gathering steam to continue its westward roll to California, past the brand new Depot Hotel next door, and on toward the courthouse he knew lay at the opposite end of town. Smitty had told him everything he needed to know—or at least, everything Smitty had thought important. The rest he would have to find out on his own.

His gaze missed little as he left the station behind, and he could not help but notice the smell of freshly cut lumber filling the warm spring air: it was everywhere, mingling with the equally pungent scents of horses and cattle, food and tobacco, not to mention the ceaseless bustle of humanity. The town was fairly jumping with activity beneath the blazing noonday sun.

It was evident that the population, while predominantly male, included a healthy number of the fair sex as well as children. The latter, playing games of tag up and down the boardwalk in an exuberant celebration of freedom, or being dragged reluctantly in and out of stores by stern-faced mothers whose patience was beginning to wear perilously thin, were much the same as youngsters anywhere else. Boys clad in knickers and caps, girls attired in the same homespun dresses and slatted sunbonnets as their maternal counterparts, all were reveling in the blessed respite from school that each Saturday brought with it.

Another ghost of a smile tugged at the corners of Jake's mouth as he watched them, for he was suddenly reminded of the family he had left back home. *Home.*

His features hardened in the next instant, his green eyes darkening to jade. He had no home. The war had seen to that. Six years now . . . six long years of wandering, of traveling from one lonely frontier outpost to the next, of cursing the thieving, no-account bastards who had stolen his future. Bitterness had eventually given way to a sort of quiet resignation, though a thirst for revenge still burned deep within him.

Let it go, he sternly commanded himself. He had to keep a clear head and concentrate only on the business at hand. Nothing could be allowed to interfere. Nothing.

He turned his attention back to Elko.

Railroad tracks bisected the wide main street, along which a multitude of unpainted, false-fronted buildings had been—and were still being—erected beneath a perpetual blanket of dust. Saloons were the most prevalent type of establishment, with gambling halls providing a close second. The more proper element was also adequately represented, by way of a church, a school, a newspaper office, an impressively varied array of stores, several small hotels and boarding houses, two banks, and even an opera house. There was an unmistakable feeling of newness about everything, a circumstance which could easily be explained by an examination of the community's recent history.

Two years earlier, a disastrous fire had destroyed the first Elko, a mangy collection of tents and shanties that had now given way to a raw, rough, but ultimately permanent settlement able to boast proudly of being the biggest town between Reno and Salt Lake City. In only three short years of true existence, since that cold day in December when the transcontinental railroad had come thundering across the plains to provide it with a renewed burst of life, the windworn little metropolis had become the main crossroads for the state's burgeoning cattle country, as well as the central supply point for all of northern Nevada.

Jake knew about the town's lively past — and about its troubled present. He was possessed of an iron determination to succeed where others had failed. . . .

Aware of the many stares cast his way, he solemnly touched the brim of his hat in a polite gesture of response to the several ladies who stopped dead in their tracks when he approached. The men who took notice of him did so with even less subtlety; they reacted with narrowed eyes and frowns of suspicion, open-mouthed surprise, or unsuppressed oaths of disbelief and disapproval.

Jake had not expected to be welcomed with open arms. He seldom was.

He did not once waver in his steady progress down the boardwalk, until a fracas suddenly broke out in front of the stage office a short distance ahead. Drawing to a halt at last, he made a quick visual survey of the startling scene taking place in the street beside the already loaded stagecoach.

A young man attired in a fringed buckskin suit and a low-crowned hat had taken up a long, silver-banded whip and was at that moment snapping it threateningly near the feet of another man, thereby causing the hapless fellow to dance out of the way of the lash's fierce crackle. Laughter and taunts arose from the dozen or so men who had quickly gathered about. Loudly appreciative of the whipster's explosion of fury, they harbored little sympathy for the man who cursed and leapt wildly at each *crack*.

11

"Give 'im hell, Mac!" one of the onlookers encouraged with an ear-to-ear grin. A stocky Elkoite of indeterminate age, he looped his thumbs into the front pockets of his trousers and rocked gleefully back on his heels.

"Aim a little higher and see if his brandin' iron's as hard as his head!" another member of the crowd sang out heartily. Additional vulgar suggestions followed, all the while the whip kept snaking out in a near miss.

"You miserable, yellow-livered son of a bitch!" smoldered the young man wielding the potentially harmful weapon. His voice sounded a trifle high and immature as he spoke to his defensively hopping victim, but no one could doubt the sincerity of his anger. "I ought to flail you skinless, Joe Cottle!" he ground out with two more dangerously close snaps of the leather. "Don't you ever, *ever* raise a hand to my team again!"

"Cut it out, damn you!" the unfortunate dancer yelled hoarsely. He was not much older than his tormentor, though he was a good deal brawnier and stood two or three inches taller. "You've gone plumb loco, you little — !"

"Hell, Cottle, you're the one who's loco!" a gap-toothed cowpuncher whooped above the crowd's roar. "Anyone boneheaded enough to tangle with Mac deserves what he gets!"

Each skillful flick of the whiplash made it necessary for the man named Joe Cottle to jump backward in the street. His hat had already gone flying into the street to be trampled beyond recognition by a passing freight wagon, and sweat rolled down his face to leave muddy tracks. Finally, humiliation and outrage fired his own temper to such a level that he made a rash attempt to grab the whip.

"So help me, I'm gonna wallop the livin' daylights out of you!" he growled vengefully, lunging at his tormentor. He succeeded only in catching the very tip of the stinging cracker right across the back of his hand. With a cry of pain, he bit out a malevolent oath, lost his balance, and fell to his knees in the dirt.

A lawman's instincts prompted Jake to intervene at this point. The badge flashed in the sunlight as he stepped down from the boardwalk and moved purposefully forward to where the injured man was staggering to his feet amidst another raucous outburst of laughter.

The buckskin-clad whipster was preparing to strike again when Jake came up behind him and seized his upraised, surprisingly slender wrist in a firm grip.

"Enough," decreed Jake. His voice, low and deep timbred and offering only a faint reminder of his Texas roots, held an unmistakable note of authority.

With a sharp gasp of mingled outrage and disbelief, the young aggressor jerked his wrist free and spun about. In so doing, the wide brim of his fedora caught Jake a glancing blow on the upper arm. The hat fell backward and would have toppled to the ground if not for the braided cord which secured it about its wearer's neck.

A long, luxuriant mass of fiery auburn curls suddenly came tumbling down about the "man's" shoulders.

It was Jake's turn to be surprised. He found himself staring down into a face that was both stormy and beautiful, a face belonging not to a man at all, but to a woman who appeared to be no more than twenty years old.

A pair of wrathfully narrowed eyes, ablaze with magnificent blue-green fire, glared up at him. His own gaze was drawn irrevocably downward, to where the woman's full young breasts rose and fell rapidly beneath the soft leather of her belted tunic.

13

Her slender but well-rounded curves were all that could be desired, and more. Although tall for a woman, she was nonetheless considerably shorter than he. Indeed, the top of her head reached no higher than his chin.

His eyes gleamed with a combination of wry amusement and wholly masculine admiration while he slowly, almost mockingly, tugged the hat from his head and gave a wordless nod down at the flame-haired spitfire. He would never again mistake her for a man. *Never.*

"Why, you witless, flat-heeled bas—" the beauty in buckskin started to rage, only to break off abruptly.

Caley McAlister was both shocked and alarmed by the sudden, inexplicable current which shot through her body as she met the tall stranger's gaze. Her own eyes grew very round. She had been prepared to give the infuriating meddler a tongue-lashing that would burn his ears and send him flying for cover. Instead, she had been struck dumb. What in tarnation was the matter with her? she wondered dazedly, her head spinning and her anger forgotten for the moment.

Oblivious to the stunned, expectant silence which had fallen over the crowd, she battled to regain control of the situation. The stranger was without a doubt the most handsome, all-fired *masculine* man she had ever set eyes on. Her heart pounded crazily within her breast as she took in the sight of his rugged, warmly tanned features.

Dark brown hair, thick and streaked golden by the sun, waved slightly above the collar of a pale blue, doublebreasted cotton shirt. A belt of tooled leather was buckled at the waistband of fitted denim trousers, which in turn snugged a pair of lean, taut thighs and long, booted legs to perfection. It was obvious that the six-shooters holstered low on his hips were not merely for show; there was too much the look of use about them.

Caley swallowed hard, her face growing unaccountably warm as she blinked up at the man who had dared to interfere. His hard-muscled frame bespoke power and virility. His superior height made her feel incredibly small and vulnerable . . . and feminine. And *that* was something she hadn't felt in a long, long time.

Confused, she took an instinctive step backward. Only then did she finally take note of the silver star on the stranger's chest.

"Who—who the devil are you?" she demanded.

"The name's Brody. Jake Brody." He returned the hat to his head, a soft smile lurking about his lips as he settled it with practiced ease.

Caley, bristling anew beneath the humor in those gold-flecked green eyes that gazed down at her with such disturbing intensity, felt her cheeks flame hotter. She hastily dropped her own gaze back to the badge.

"U.S. Marshal," she read aloud. She gave a short, derisive laugh—partly to mask the inner turmoil created by his proximity. Her eyes flashed resentfully as her temper flared once more. "Well, I don't give a tinker's damn *who* you are, you've no right to meddle in my business!"

"Business?" Jake challenged, a faint, sardonic smile touching his lips. He looked past her to where Joe Cottle, having picked himself up off the ground by this time, stood leaning heavily against the stagecoach clutching his injured hand. "Whatever he's done, I don't think he deserves—"

"Why the hell should I care what you think?" interrupted Caley, her fingers clenching about the whipstock again.

It was obvious from both the fire in her eyes and the way she suddenly tensed her arm that she was

15

battling the temptation to use the whip on Jake. Several of the men watching on the boardwalk nearby smiled in anticipation. They knew all too well what sort of fury "Mac" was capable of, just as they knew better than to cross her when she was riled. And there was no doubt that she was riled now.

Caley's hotly shimmering gaze locked in silent combat with the cool steadiness of Jake's. Something she glimpsed therein caused her to draw in her breath upon a soft gasp. An involuntary shiver danced down her spine, and she was dismayed to feel her heart give a little leap of fear. She was not accustomed to being afraid.

"If you really are the law, then why don't you lock her up?" Joe Cottle demanded vengefully. He came stalking forward at last, only to stop and take a hasty, defensive step backward again when Caley rounded on him. "She—she ain't got no call to go treatin' me like she done!" he stammered out, wiping his dirt-streaked nose with the back of his good hand while shooting a wary look at his beautiful, enraged employer. His black hair was lank and greasy, and his clothes had been in dire need of laundering even before he had been sent sprawling in the street. He raised bloodshot eyes full of desperate entreaty to Jake, hoping to find an ally amidst the crowd of opposition. "I was only doin' what she told me, Marshal!"

"That's a lie, you worthless bastard!" Caley disputed with heartfelt vehemence. She advanced menacingly on him once more, her blue-green eyes blazing with righteous accusation. "I made it clear when I hired you on as the new hostler that I'd tolerate no manhandling of my animals! You accepted my terms, Joe Cottle, and yet I came out here today and caught you striking Jezebel!"

"The damned horse bit me!" he exclaimed.

16

"It was no more than you deserved!" she shot back.

"Lay into him again, Mac!" someone saw fit to interject at this point.

The silence among the crowd thus broken, another round of laughter and taunts arose to fuel the situation anew. No one seemed to pay any mind to the presence of a United States Marshal. It was as if they had already decided he was of little consequence in Elko.

Jake Brody, however, had decided differently.

With an authoritative confidence, and before Caley knew what he intended, he reached out and easily snatched the whip from her grasp. Then, while she sputtered a furiously indignant protest, he turned to Joe Cottle and advised him,

"You'd best be on your way."

Joe was not inclined to argue. He lit out without further prompting, leaving Jake to face the crowd — and Caley's wrath — alone.

"Give me that whip!" she stormed, her eyes hurtling invisible daggers at his head.

"I think I'll hang onto it for a while."

"But it's mine."

"You won't be needing it."

"Hell, man, any fool knows a Jehu ain't nothin' without a whip!" the stocky man in front of the stage office hastened to point out.

"Jehu?" echoed Jake quietly, a slight frown of puzzlement creasing his brow. He was familiar with the biblically derived term for stage driver, but he found it difficult to believe a woman, even this particular, tough-talking wildcat, could be a member of the profession. His gaze shifted momentarily to the sign above the building — *McAlister Stage and Transport Company* — before fastening upon Caley again. "You work for the line?"

"I not only work for it — I *own* it!" she answered

17

with a proud, defiant lift of her chin. "I'm Caley McAlister, and I'll be damned if I'll let you or any other man keep me from my ride! Now give me that whip! The team's been chewing leather long enough!"

It was clear she had the overwhelming support of the angered group of onlookers, for they surged forward into the street now, ringing the unwelcome stranger and the sole proprietor of the McAlister Stage and Transport Company. Never mind that she was a woman; to them, she was simply one of their own.

"Come on, give her the whip!"

"Nobody asked for you to butt in, *Marshal!*"

"Hand it over now!"

"Just because you're wearin' a badge don't give you the right to interfere with the express!"

Jake's eyes gleamed with ironic amusement at the loyalty commanded by the flame-haired beauty. Although he'd had every intention of returning her whip — at least once he had learned of her legitimate need of it — he hesitated to comply with the crowd's increasingly spirited demands. He had no desire to stir up trouble his first day in town, but he wanted to make it clear from the outset that he could not be railroaded. Experience had taught him it was best to start out the way he meant to go on.

"All right, Miss McAlister. You can have the whip," he told Caley, his deep, wonderfully resonant voice audible even above the crowd's roar.

She reached out to take it from him, but he held fast. Her eyes were full of mingled venom and mistrust as they flew back up to his.

"On one condition," he added.

"And what is *that?*" she ground out.

"We need to talk. Stop by the jail when you get back to town."

"Why the devil should I?"

"Because if you don't, I'll arrest you for disturbing the peace," he warned solemnly, though his gaze was brimming with what looked suspiciously like humor.

"Hold on now, you can't do that!" one of Caley's self-appointed champions protested emphatically.

The others began voicing their objections to Jake with just as much vigor. They contended that Mac had done nothing to warrant such rough treatment, that she had only been looking out after her own affairs as she'd always done, and that some "headbuster" fresh off the train had no right, no dangblasted right at all, to arrest anyone until he'd checked with the sheriff first! Sheriff Tickner, they went on to insist, was the law in Elko. And Ed Tickner sure as hell wouldn't let a woman be locked up in his jail.

Jake paid no mind to the arguments flying freely about. His unfathomable gaze remained fixed on Caley, and his face remained impassive as he waited for her answer.

"Well?" he prompted.

She eyed him murderously, her mind racing. On one hand, she was tempted to defy this damnably handsome intruder; on the other, she was somehow certain he would not hesitate to make good on his threat. The prospect of being jailed was a dismal one. Not only would it be a considerable blow to her pride, but she could not afford the time away from her business. There was no one else to run things.

Don't be a fool . . . he only wants to talk, she angrily reasoned with herself. What harm could there be in that? Still, it galled her to admit defeat on any level. The thought of giving this arrogant lawman even such a small victory made her see red.

In the end, however, she was forced to capitulate. But she did so with an ill grace.

"You win, damn it!" she conceded, her voice seething with fury as she met Jake's gaze.

Without a word, he held the whip out to her and she took it. Once again, something in his eyes, something she could not quite name, caused her to feel he could see a good deal more than she wanted him to. The thought made her madder than ever.

"But God help you," she cautioned him in a simmering undertone, "if you make the mistake of thinking you can run *me* or anyone else in this town!"

As if to prove her point, she uncoiled the whip, took a quick step backward, and, before Jake had guessed her intent, expertly sent the tail end of the lash cracking out to snap his hat clean off his head. It landed in the dirt near his feet.

A hearty round of applause and cheers erupted from the circle of witnesses. While the men were congratulating one another on the fact that their Mac had bested this "badge-boasting sonofabitch by the name of Jake Brody," the object of their high regard wasted little time in taking her place atop the stagecoach.

Jake's handsome features tightened into a grim mask, his gaze darkening with barely suppressed rage. Motionless and silent, he watched as Caley climbed agilely up to her seat on the right side of the coach, swiftly drew on a pair of fringed leather gloves, and lifted one slender, booted foot to the brake. She took the reins and arranged them skillfully in each hand, then made a quick but thorough perusal of the team in front of her to be certain all the hitching gear was as it should be. Beside her sat a stoic-looking fellow, also in buckskin, with a shotgun cradled in his arms.

"Let her go, Billy!" she directed the skinny, towheaded adolescent who had temporarily replaced Joe Cottle in the post of hostler. The eager Billy,

20

holding the lead span of horses, obediently dropped his hands and stepped aside, his heart swelling with pride at having played a role in the stage's departure.

With a gentle pull on the reins, Caley released the brake and shot Jake one last disdainfully triumphant look. It was the sort of look that would have wounded lesser men, but Jake Brody was feeling no pain—only a smoldering anger that made the golden flecks in his eyes glint dully. With an iron will, he held his emotions in check and resisted the urge to drag the hot-tempered young vixen down from her perch.

"Get along!" she yelled to the six impatiently snorting animals. "Keep your seats!" was for the four passengers who were knowledgeably bracing themselves in preparation for the inevitable rocking within the open-sided vehicle.

The horses lurched against their collars in unison. The bright red, fully laden Concord, a lighter mud wagon instead of a true stagecoach, pitched backward a bit before rolling forward. Amidst a rowdy sendoff provided by the onlookers, the coach picked up speed and went barrelling noisily away down the middle of the street, scattering whatever unfortunate humans or animals that happened to be in its path.

Jake stepped aside, moving out of the way with studied unhaste just in time. He turned to stare after the stagecoach—or rather, after its beautiful, unexpectedly female driver.

Caley McAlister. His eyes glowed with something other than anger as his mind repeated her name. There was no doubt about it—he would be looking forward to their talk.

Watching until she was out of sight, he finally bent and retrieved his hat. It was then that he was reminded of the way the fire-spitting hellcat had made a fool of him in front of the crowd.

"Yes sir, Marshal, I guess she gave you what for, didn't she?" one of the men still gathered on the boardwalk taunted with a broad, contemptuous grin.

"Aw, come on, Shorty, leave him alone!" another piped up. It was obvious from the crooked smile on his face that his sympathies did not exactly lie in Jake's direction, either. "Can't you see he's had enough?"

"Shut up, Ballard!" grunted Shorty, whose name thoroughly belied his size. A thickset, black-bearded giant who towered above the others, he took what he believed to be an intimidating step closer to Jake. "Could be you need to settle your business and be on your way before you get into *real* trouble, Brody."

Additional rumblings of mockery and discontent quickly followed. Neither Jake's badge nor the two guns holstered low on his hips were being shown the proper respect by these "good citizens" of Elko, for they had foolishly decided he was not a man to be reckoned with. It was a mistake they would come to regret.

"Hope you ain't plannin' to stay around too long, Marshal."

"Catchin' the next train out?"

"Sheriff Tickner'll set you straight about the way things are done here!"

Still, Jake said nothing. His gaze was suffused with a dangerous light, but his detractors took no notice of it. Negligently dusting off his hat, he lifted it to his head and strode past them, his features schooled to betray none of his displeasure. The jeers of the men followed him as he continued on his way toward the courthouse.

There were times when it took every ounce of self control he possessed to keep from offering a more

22

self-satisfying response to the difficulties that went with his job. This was one of those times.

You can thank Miss McAlister for that, he told himself dryly. His eyes now gleamed with a mixture of vengeful irritation and undeniably masculine warmth. A faint smile touched his lips.

It looked like taming Elko was going to be even more of a challenge than he had bargained for.

Chapter II

"So, you're still here." Caley's mouth curved into a brief, preoccupied smile as Billy greeted the stagecoach with a look full of hopeful expectation.

"Take care of the team for you, Miss Caley?" the sixteen-year-old offered, hurrying forward to see if she would follow through with the same tolerance she had displayed toward him earlier that same day. It wasn't often she changed her mind about anything.

Much to the boy's delight, Caley hesitated only a moment before nodding her permission.

"Thanks, Billy."

The brown and black dog who had taken the place of the man riding "shotgun" on the seat beside her clambered down to the ground. This large, scruffy-looking animal of questionable parentage, panting happily, stood at attention in the doorway of the stage office while the only human being he would tolerate for more than thirty seconds at a time performed the cautionary ritual of checking the brake, looping the reins, and dragging the empty mail pouch from beneath the driver's seat.

She had been more relieved than she cared to admit upon finding Billy waiting for her. Because of the unfortunate incident with Joe Cottle, she was now short one hostler. She told herself with an inward sigh that she should have followed her instincts and given Billy the job in the first place. After all, in spite of his youth and inexperience, he was a damn sight better with horses than that cowardly snake Joe would ever be.

"You want me to take them on around, Miss Caley?"

"I'd consider it a personal favor."

She climbed down from the stagecoach at last, her blue-green eyes shining with gratitude for his assistance while she drew off her gloves and moved to his side on the boardwalk. Lifting an affectionate hand to stroke along Jezebel's sleek, lathered neck, she reached up and drew off the dust-caked hat with her other hand, thereupon releasing the glorious tumble of thick auburn curls that had given Jake pause earlier that same day.

"Do you happen to know if Hank got off on time?" she asked the slender blond youth who was already working to free the tired animals from the harness.

"He sure did, Miss Caley. Rolled out of here more'n two hours ago."

It was half past six in the evening, and the twice weekly run to and from Bullion City had gone without a hitch. Normally, that would have been cause for celebration. But not on this particular day. *Not when there were so many other things to think about.*

"Billy?"

"Yes, ma'am?"

"I guess you know you're hired."

"Yes, ma'am." A wide grin split his freckled, boyish features.

Caley's eyes twinkled with wry amusement at his pleasure. She had long considered Billy Snyder to be a decent sort, wet behind the ears or not. It was too bad his father spent all *his* time bending his elbow over at the Senate Saloon. The boy could use a man's guidance.

"It's getting late. You'd better head for home soon as you've finished with the team," she advised her new employee, then added with a teasing half-smile, "Your ma will make my life a misery if you don't show up by nightfall."

Billy merely grinned again and turned his attention back to his task. If a willingness to perform one's duty counted for anything, Caley mused idly, he would certainly prove to be the best worker she had ever taken on. But then, he was very nearly the *only* worker she had ever taken on. Both Red Tarver and Hank Shaughnessy had been driving for the line since her father had first started it, and—up until two days ago—Dick Vanacek had been the hostler.

She mentally berated herself once more for having been careless enough to hire a shifty-eyed skunk like Joe Cottle. Not only had he been caught hitting Jezebel, but he'd made far too many mistakes when handling the gear. And his attitude had been downright surly, even from the beginning. Sometimes, she concluded with a rueful shake of her head, there was just no accounting for her own stupidity.

Heaving another disgruntled sigh, she offered Billy a few last instructions and turned to go inside. She settled a quick pat upon the dog's head when she stepped through the doorway, her gaze momentarily lighting with genuine warmth.

"Run along now and get your supper, Tripod."

With one last wag of his gargantuan tail, the animal padded away. His movements were unhurried and possessed a typically canine grace, in spite of the fact that he was missing his right hind leg. No one knew exactly how it had happened; specula-

27

tion about the lost appendage had long since died down.

Caley watched her slightly mysterious friend disappear into the waning sunlight. There was little doubt in her mind that Tripod would follow his usual custom and make straightaway for the red light and gambling district—Dobe Row, it had come to be called—where he would receive a generous outpouring of food and affection from the fallen angels who worked there. All on his own terms, of course.

A sudden weariness descended on her as she moved farther inside the dimly lit office. The headquarters of the McAlister Stage and Transport Company consisted of nothing more than a single cluttered room on the ground floor of a narrow, perennially "soon-to-be" whitewashed building wedged between the Masonic Lodge and the newspaper office in the very center of town, plus a corral and stock barn out back for the horses. While additional space could certainly be put to immediate use, business was simply too good to leave much time for enlarging or refurbishing or even straightening up. Caley's father, the late, esteemed Paddy McAlister, had still been "meaning to get around to it" when he had gone to meet his Maker six months ago.

Procrastination is a sin best not repented of till tomorrow. Paddy's only child smiled softly to herself as his whimsical, oft-repeated words echoed in her mind again. She had wisely given up trying to change him years ago.

A slight frown creased the silken smoothness of her brow as she absently scrutinized her familiar surroundings. There were no customers about so late in the day. Hank's had been the last stage, making a night run to Carlin. The next departure would take place promptly at six o'clock the following morning, which meant she had best get on with the day's final bit of business if she expected to pull herself out of bed in time to make ready.

If truth be told, it was the prospect of performing this final "business" that had her nerves strung so tight.

The frown on her face deepened. She tossed her hat to land squarely atop a peg on the wall beside the door; her aim had been perfected throughout nearly two years of practice. After pausing to make a cursory inspection of the schedule book resting open on the dusty, paper strewn counter, she headed for the staircase. She was already halfway across the room when it occurred to her that she had forgotten to close up for the night.

"You're behaving awfully damned moony all of a sudden," she muttered with a frown of self-recrimination. A handsome, ruggedly masculine face like no other swam before her eyes, but she still refused to acknowledge the origin of her disquietude.

Spinning impatiently about on her heel, she marched back to the door and shut it with a good deal more force than was necessary. The lock was turned with an equal vengeance before she trudged across the room again and up the narrow, darkened stairs to the living quarters on the second floor. Her legs felt unaccountably heavy, and so, strangely enough, did her spirits.

Reaching the top step, she opened the door and slipped quietly inside the apartment. These three small, sparsely furnished rooms above the office had been home to both her and her father since they had first come to Elko. Crowded it may have been, but she had at least been granted some measure of privacy. A bedroom all her own, plus the longed-for luxury of a real bathroom, had served to provide her with the first true feeling of permanence she had known for as far back as she could remember. The only thing lacking was a kitchen; but then, she had never been much on cooking. And she had been so thankful for Paddy's procurement of the accommodations that she dared not voice a complaint. What did it matter that all her meals had to be taken elsewhere? At least she had a decent roof over her head.

With yet another inexplicably troubled sigh, she turned to close the door behind her. No sooner had she done so when a huge white cat suddenly came flying down from his hidden perch behind the faded gingham curtains on the windowsill. He sprinted like lightning across the room and hurled himself directly at Caley's legs, his claws sinking into the soft buckskin of her trousers so that he hung suspended by his front paws a full two inches off the floor.

"Blast your hide, Shadrach!" reprimanded Caley, though she did so without a great deal of conviction. Indeed, she could not keep a smile of fond indulgence from touching her lips as she bent down and scooped the wild-eyed, unrepentant feline up in her arms. "You old scoundrel! You could at least wait until I've taken off my boots!" Her smile broadened while she cradled him closer and administered a series of brisk, affectionate strokes to the top of his head with her hand.

Supremely contented, Shadrach purred loud enough to wake the dead and settled his fat, furry body more comfortably in his owner's embrace. He was a strange-looking creature, the proud possessor of one blue eye and one green. His tail was long and thick and slightly crooked, with a kink at the very end that made him appear even more peculiar. Unlike Tripod, he was a full-time occupant of the McAlister Stage and Transport Company's headquarters, having belonged to Caley for the greater majority of his nine lifetimes.

"I suppose you'll be wanting *your* supper now, too," she remarked with mock severity. Pausing briefly to light a nearby lamp, she carried Shadrach the short distance across the room to another door. It opened onto a back staircase, which in turn led down to a wide, perpetually littered alleyway behind the row of Main Street buildings. "Well, I'm afraid you'll just have to wait until I can fetch you something from Maybelle's. In the meantime, my boy, you can go on out and make yourself useful. Try to remember you're a cat for once and hightail it after some of those mice down there. I swear, they're getting big as jackrabbits and twice as bold!"

Fully aware of her beloved pet's disdain of the sort of activities typically enjoyed by other cats—yet determined to make him embrace everything feline in spite of his high notions of himself—Caley set the reluctant warrior on the stoop outside and hurriedly closed the door before he could make a dash back inside. She could hear Shadrach's resentful *meow*, but knew it would be only a matter of seconds before something caught his interest and he scampered off to investigate. The same ritual was enacted between them practically every night. She sometimes wondered if it might not be better just to leave the cat outside as her father had always insisted upon, but she knew it wasn't any use wondering. Like it or not, she had a soft spot in her heart for the lazy, good-for-nothing animal and wouldn't dream of abandoning him to a life without her care.

A light of fond remembrance, coupled with a lingering sadness, shone in her eyes. Paddy had grumbled about Shadrach from the very beginning. . . .

The clock in the room behind her sounded the three-quarter hour, drawing her thoughts abruptly back to the present.

"Hellfire and damnation!" she breathed aloud. Her beautiful blue-green eyes sparked with renewed fire as she recalled the unpleasant duty still waiting to be discharged. She could put it off no longer; she had to get going soon or else she'd miss out on supper at Maybelle's. The widow lady who ran the boarding house and restaurant across the street was quite particular, insisting upon punctuality as well as "proper attire."

To Caley, this last was especially bothersome, for it meant she had to dispense with her buckskin and don skirts. And while wearing skirts was not exactly a rarity for her, neither was it something she did with the same willingness displayed by her more conventional counterparts.

You're a scandalous disgrace to the decent women of this town, Caley McAlister, and you'll come to no good! A soft laugh rose in her throat as she once again recalled Bertha Larrabee's words. They had been uttered in hurtful anger and disapproval, but their intended victim had merely given a defiant toss of her head and marched proudly through the group of women blocking her path. That had been more than a year ago . . . things had not changed much since then.

Directing another querulous glance toward the clock on the wall, Caley hastened to get ready. She stripped off every stitch of her clothing and padded barefoot into the bathroom. Although the cold water she bathed with made her shiver, she was nonetheless glad to wash the dust from her body. Her hair, she decided with a frown, would have to wait. She coiled it up into a knot and pinned it low on her neck, then set about making the unusually difficult decision of what to wear.

Much as she tried to ignore them, thoughts of the handsome marshal continued to plague her the whole time she was searching through the meager contents of the old, massive oak wardrobe looming in one corner of her bedroom. She was dismayed to realize her appearance suddenly mattered so much.

"You're behaving like a mush-brained female," she reproached herself in a low, slightly uneven voice. The heightened color on her cheeks gave evidence of the strange excitement which now mingled with the irritation that had been nagging at her all day.

Jake Brody had bothered her far more than she cared to admit.

Muttering an oath beneath her breath, she impatiently dragged a plain shirtwaist and sturdy cotton skirt from the wardrobe. The white longcloth chemise, drawers, and petticoat she had slipped on a few moments earlier were equally simple and unadorned. It suited her that there was none of the usual feminine frilliness about her clothing. She wore no corset; she had never owned one.

It soon became obvious, however, that she required nothing in the way of assistance when it came to her figure. While the ensemble she wore could have benefited from at least a touch of ruffling or lace, it fitted her slender, delightfully rounded curves to perfection. The narrow waistband of her skirt encircled a trim waist, while the gathered folds of dark brown calico draped gracefully over hips that were both firm and shapely. Her full young breasts were accentuated a little *too* much in her estimation; the buttons of the white muslin blouse threatened to give way at the first deep breath she drew.

She cursed the fact that she had become even more endowed since purchasing the shirtwaist some two years ago. Facing her reflection in the cracked mirror hanging above the washstand, she tugged angrily at the front of the garment in an effort to decrease the embarrassing snugness. It was no use.

She threw up her hands in an eloquent gesture of defeat before taking a seat on the edge of the bed to draw on her white cotton stockings and black, high-lacing leather boots.

Ready at last, Caley headed down the back staircase to make certain Billy had finished with the team. The sight of the horses enjoying their well-earned oats in the corral filled her with satisfaction, and she congratulated herself on finally having had the good sense to judge the boy on his merits instead of his age. Her brows knitted into a sudden frown. It was too bad she wasn't so all-fired sure of herself when it came to grown men.

With any luck he'll be gone by now, she mused hopefully, her thoughts returning with a will of their own to the town's newest arrival as she traveled between the buildings to the boardwalk out front. Either way, she'd be damned if she'd let him keep her from her supper!

The sun hung very low on the western horizon, turning the cloudless summer sky to a panorama of amber and rose. In the near distance, outlined to majestic proportion against the dwindling light of day, towered the Ruby Mountains. The low, rolling hills surrounding the town had been green in spring but were now drying into dead tones of gray and brown. Nearby was the Humboldt River, in actuality a sluggish stream once followed by pioneers heading west to the promised land of California. Its waters ran opaquely through the cottonwood brush, helpless to truly succor the sun-baked earth yet providing at least some measure of relief from the unremitting heat and dust of the desert. The wind, although diminishing with the twilight, continued to blow in from the sageland, warm and spiced and sweet as it swept across this vast, untamed country of such stark beauty.

Elko sat like a rather dubious oasis in the midst

34

of the wilderness. Far from slowing down for the coming night, it had just started gathering energy for its second life, the one that sprang into wild existence after dark. In no time at all, the saloons and gambling hells and "joy houses" would be filled to overflowing with thirsty, troublesome, woman-hungry cowboys and miners. Especially down at Dobe Row, so named because of the block and a half of adobe houses which formed that notorious red-light district, the warm summer evening would be enlivened to no end with the plunking of pianos and frequent spattering of gunshots. It was much the same night after night; it seemed that everyone had decided to pack as much living as they could into a few short hours, as though tomorrow might never come — and if it did, well, to hell with the consequences of what had come before.

With practiced ease, Caley made her way across the busy street toward the white, yellow-shuttered building with a sign out front proclaiming it to be "O'Grady's Boarding House." She paid no mind whatsoever to the trio of young men on horseback who suddenly slowed their mounts and called out to her when they were riding past. It was doubtful that they were aware of her identity; if they *had* known, they might still have filled their eyes with the sight of her, but they would never have dared offer her the sort of lewd comments usually reserved for the women in the saloons.

"Buy you a drink, honey?" one of the three offered with an unmistakable leer. He tipped his hat to her in a mocking gesture of gallantry.

"Hot damn!" another burst out. Though he was scarcely of an age to shave, his eyes raked over her with bold, wolfish appreciation. "What I wouldn't give to have me one of them gals with a round bosom and a soft white rump!"

The dark, rawboned puncher riding beside him

laughed derisively and shifted in the saddle. His own gaze devoured every sweet curve as it fastened on Caley.

"Aw hell, Farley," he drawled to his youthful companion, "you been out on the range too long to know what to do with a real, honest-to-God woman."

"No I ain't!" protested Farley, then grinned. "I just need me a little practice!"

The object of their crude impertinence did not waver in her progress. She was in all honesty too engrossed with other matters to give any thought to what was going on around her. Besides, she was too accustomed to such masculine nonsense to be affected by it; that is, unless she was of a mind to take offense. *Lord help the man who so much as looks cross-eyed at Caley McAlister when she's feeling touchy.* This bit of wisdom had once been submitted by someone who knew her well, and had come to be generally regarded as truth in the annals of Elko's brief but highly colorful history.

Caley's reverie was finally interrupted when she reached the front steps of the boarding house. The proprietress, frowning her own disapproval from the porch, greeted her with a solemn nod.

"Good thing Matt wasn't around to hear," Maybelle O'Grady remarked. She was a dark-haired widow, nearing forty but still quite comely. Her gaze moved past the other woman again to where the three horsemen still sat catching more than an eyeful atop their mounts in the middle of the street. "Vermin like them ought to be run out of town on a rail!" she pronounced feelingly. When her friend merely looked bewildered, she gave a shake of her head and changed the subject. "You're late." Her voice, surprisingly enough, held warmth instead of censure.

Caley heaved a sigh of contrition as she gathered

up-her skirts and climbed the steps.

"I know. I'm sorry, Maybelle, but—"

"Never mind. Come on in and get yourself something to eat before it's all gone. Mr. Tate's already started filling that bottomless pit he calls his belly, so I'd advise you to hurry." Her eyes alight with ironic humor, she turned and led the way through the doorway. Smiling faintly, Caley followed after her.

When the two women stepped into the lamplit dining room, they were met with the sound of voices, both male and female, engaged in a lively conversation of the incident that had the whole town abuzz. Caley was as yet blissfully ignorant about what had happened. She was soon to be enlightened.

The usual odd assortment of clientele sat at Maybelle O'Grady's table. Most of them were regulars (*irregulars*, some might have said uncharitably), but tonight's supper had brought with it the added company of a fast-talking cookstove salesman and a rather flashily attired young woman who claimed to be an actress "between engagements." Maybelle was quite choosy when it came to the kind of people who passed through her doorway. On this particular evening, the total number of diners had turned out to be unusually large. There were nine in all, including the latest arrival, whose presence was acknowledged by several nods and even a toothy smile from the infamous Mr. Tate. Caley suppressed a grimace at the sight of his greasy, overloaded mouth.

Intent only upon easing the pangs of hunger gnawing at her stomach, she took her seat at the far end of the long, linen-covered table and reached for the platter of fried chicken positioned conveniently before her. She was indifferent to the talk going on about her, until the sudden mention of an all too familiar name caused her ears to burn.

"It appears to me that Marshal Brody has set for himself a course which will in all probability prove to be unwise. I fail to see how it can benefit the man anything to engage in a battle of wills with one of our elected officials."

This came from a tall, bespectacled man by the name of James Darby Worthington III, called J.D. for short. He was seated directly across from the actress, who gazed with some interest upon his pinched, undeniably aristocratic features and thought herself fortunate indeed to be sharing a meal, however unremarkable, with such a distinguished gentleman. It wasn't often she got to break bread in the company of a "class act" like him; her masculine dinner companions were as a rule dirty, rough, and up to no good.

Caley's hand momentarily froze on the platter as she raised eyes full of surprise to J.D.'s face. She was not given the opportunity to question him about his startling observation, for the discussion was immediately taken up again by the short, balding man seated to her left.

"They say this Brody feller had the gall to march right into that jail and tell Sheriff Tickner he'd come to stay. Seems he'd already been over to the courthouse, showin' off some legal piece of paper sayin' he's been appointed right here to Elko. The way I heard it, ol' Ed jumped up and cussed the marshal out good and proper for tryin' to steal his thunder!"

George Groat gave a low chuckle before shoveling another forkful of mashed potatoes between his widely parted lips. He wasn't about to let a little thing like a potato-clogged mouth keep him from continuing.

"Yes sir," he said in between smacking chews, "I reckon there's bound to be a few fireworks before this thing's settled. Ed Tickner sure ain't one to sit back and count the buzzards while some outsider like Brody comes waltzin' in with talk of change!"

To stay, Caley was at that moment repeating to herself in stunned silence. *Jake Brody is here to stay.*

"Marshal Brody hails from Texas, you know," a spinster named Eva Hartford took pride in revealing at this point. "I happened to overhear part of his conversation with the judge this afternoon." She smiled across at J.D. while the actress beside her frowned in annoyance. Plain and on the shadowy side of youth, Eva would have been a perfect match for the confirmed bachelor—if not for the fact that he felt an uncomfortable lump in his throat every time he looked at her.

Maybelle O'Grady, meanwhile, had resumed her own place at the head of the table. She cast a benevolent eye upon the group and poured herself a cup of coffee. Her pale blue gaze twinkled with a mischievous light when it traveled back to Caley.

"A little bird told me it was none other than our own Miss McAlister who had the honor of being the first to welcome Marshal Brody to town."

Caley very nearly choked on the bite of chicken she had just forced herself to take. Coughing into her napkin, she waved away George Groat's offer of assistance and took a deep draw on the glass of water someone hurriedly provided.

"Must've been the same 'little bird' that came into the Senate a couple of hours ago," George told Maybelle with another chuckle. "It's just like that rattle-trapped Ballard to go shootin' his mouth off all over town."

"What on earth were you doing in the saloon in the middle of the day, Mr. Groat?" Eva asked with a stern frown of disapproval.

"I wish I could have been present to witness the

incident, Miss McAlister," remarked J.D., turning the talk back to Caley's highly regarded encounter with the new marshal. There were few who had not heard of it by now. "Is it true you were able to remove the man's hat from his head without doing him injury?"

"It's true," George answered for her, then laughed outright. His actions sent a small stream of potatoes spraying across the tablecloth, but he appeared not to notice. The expressions of disgust on the faces of some of his fellow diners also went unheeded. "It's true, so long as you don't count what it did to his pride!"

"I consider it quite shocking, Miss McAlister, that you would behave so shamelessly to a man in Marshal Brody's position." Eva Hartford's words were typical of an old maid schoolteacher, for the simple fact that she *was* an old maid schoolteacher. "After all, he is a guardian of the law. Why, the next thing we know, you'll be attempting to run him out of town at the point of a gun!"

Fed up with being told how *shocking* and *shameless* she was, Caley resisted the urge to tell the other woman to go to the devil. She did not, however, exercise the same restraint when it came to responding to the prophecy Eva had intended as a point-making exaggeration.

"That's not such a bad idea, Miss Hartford," she declared, her eyes narrowing while her mouth turned up into a slow, meaningful smile. "As a matter of fact, I think I'll give it a try first thing tomorrow. And you can be sure I'll let everyone know where I got the idea."

Her words achieved the desired effect. She smiled to herself in satisfaction when the schoolteacher visibly bristled and compressed her thin lips into a tight, even thinner line of displeasure.

"I hear tell this new marshal of ours is planning

40

to put up over at the Depot," the rotund Mr. Tate finally cleared his own throat enough to join in. His timing could arguably have been better.

"You heard wrong, Mr. Tate," Maybelle gently corrected. She cast another significant look toward Caley. "Marshal Brody came by this afternoon and made arrangements with me to board here. I expect he'll be moving in soon as he's finished getting things set up over at the jail."

"You don't really mean he's going to live *here*?" demanded Caley, her mouth falling open in disbelief.

"I'm afraid so."

"But he can't!" she insisted. "Hellfire and damnation, Maybelle O'Grady, have you lost your mind?"

"*Miss McAlister!*" Eva hastened to call her down. "Your language!"

"Yes, it's mine, and I'll use it whenever I damned well please!" Caley retorted hotly. She turned back to Maybelle. "Do you have any earthly idea what you're letting yourself in for? It will be too dangerous having him here!"

"Dangerous?" echoed George in puzzlement. As usual, it didn't seem to bother him that he was butting in. "Why would it be dangerous?"

"Because he'll have every blasted desperado for miles around looking to put a hole through that badge of his!" Caley predicted in dire warning.

Her beautiful face was flushed with the unexpected force of her emotions. The prospect of sitting down to supper with the handsome lawman every night made her heart quicken and sent an unfamiliar warmth racing through her veins. She didn't like the sensation one bit. Again, she tried appealing to the attractive, dark-haired widow at the other end of the table.

"I'm telling you, it won't be safe with him here! You'll find yourself awakened some night by the

41

sound of gunfire, and—"

"Well if I am," Maybelle interrupted, her opal gaze alight with wry amusement, "you can be certain I'll wait until all shots have been fired before I leave my bed to investigate. Besides," she added reasonably, "Marshal Brody looks more than capable of holding his own against anyone who might take it in mind to try and shoot it out with him."

"Oh, he's capable all right!" seconded the young cookstove salesman. He colored self-consciously when eight pairs of eyes fastened on him in surprise, but a quick recovery was his stock in trade. "Marshal Brody's reputation as a gunfighter precedes him," he explained with a knowing smile.

"What in tarnation are you talkin' about?" George demanded bluntly.

"How is it, sir, that you possess such knowledge?" J.D. questioned in a more polite manner. It was to him the salesman made a point of responding.

"I heard about Brody from a fellow passenger on the train," he began, acting as though he were about to impart great knowledge. "It was while I was traveling over from Salt Lake City last week. This big, mean-looking son of a . . . *gun*," he hastily substituted out of deference to the ladies present, "took a seat beside me and started boasting about all the places he'd been and things he'd done. I listened for a while, but soon decided I'd had enough. Well, I was just about to abandon him to his own hot wind, when he suddenly asked me where I was headed. As soon as I told him I was taking over my company's route here in Elko, his face took on the strangest look—sort of like he was in pain or something—and he said he knew of someone else who was planning to be in Elko soon."

The fancy-suited peddler, obviously enjoying all

42

the attention, paused a moment for effect. He leaned back in the chair and casually folded his arms across his chest before continuing. Since he had kept on eating while the others talked, his plate was almost empty by now.

"He told me the man of whom he spoke was on the side of the law, but that that didn't stop him from gunning down whoever got in his way. According to him, the man can't be beaten in a draw."

"And did this 'mean-looking' stranger happen to mention Marshal Brody by name?" Maybelle inquired dryly. She met Caley's troubled gaze, silently wondering at the other woman's unusual disquietude. That it had something to do with the new marshal, she had little doubt.

"No, ma'am," the salesman answered Maybelle. He gave a faint sigh of regret and shook his head. "But who else could it be?"

"Did the stranger ever give his own name?" George wanted to know.

"No. And I'm sorry to say I never asked."

"Did he say anything else about Marshal Brody?" it was Eva's turn to question. She, like the majority of the others, had already concluded that the fast-on-the-draw gunfighter in question was indeed the same tall Texan she had spied in conference with the judge at the courthouse. She felt a sudden fluttering in her stomach at the memory of the new marshal's rugged manliness. "Anything at all?" she prompted the young peddler once more.

"No, ma'am."

A lively discussion broke out amongst the diners again as they began arguing the merits and disadvantages of the country's law enforcement system. The man who had given rise to the debate declined to join in. Having lost his audience, he merely resumed his methodical attack upon the last bit of food on his plate.

Caley, meanwhile, had heard enough. Her own appetite had fled some time ago. With a hot-tempered flash of her eyes, she flung her napkin down onto the table and challenged Maybelle above the voices of the others,

"*Now* will you listen to me?"

"I'm sorry, Caley, but I can't go back on my word," the widow replied solemnly. She was about to ask her headstrong young friend to retire to the parlour with her so they could speak of the matter in private, but she never got the chance.

Without another word, Caley abruptly stood to her feet and left the table. Eva Hartford's loud exclamation of reproach for her rudeness followed her from the room. She was immediately sorry for her impulsiveness — because of Maybelle, not Eva — yet she did not turn back.

Her brisk, angry strides led her from the boarding house and back across the darkening street. It was fortunate the three rowdies who had accosted her earlier had already taken themselves over to the saloon. As Caley's father had so eloquently put it a number of times in the past, she was at present "loaded for bear and apt to go off."

Her ammunition was being stored up for a certain individual who, throughout the course of a five minutes' acquaintance, had managed to infuriate her, humiliate her, intimidate her, and worst of all, make her feel things she had never felt for any man. By thunder, she vowed umbrageously, she wasn't about to let some trigger-happy rogue get the upper hand!

If there was one thing she detested, it was an upheaval of her carefully guarded private emotions. She needed to be in control; she had been brought up to be in control. To say that she had enjoyed a childhood unlike that of other girls would be a considerable understatement. Paddy McAlister had jokingly commented on more than one occasion that she was the son he had always wanted. To the day he died, he'd had no idea how much those words had hurt . . . .

The jail, a single-story building still bearing the highly aromatic scent of the split cedar logs it had been constructed with less than a year earlier, lay on the same side of the street as the stage office. Caley was oblivious to the music and laughter and whiskey fumes drifting out to her as she marched down the boardwalk. She elbowed her way roughly past the men who tried to speak to her. No decent woman dared travel the streets alone after dark, but she refused to classify herself in either that category or the only other one open to her.

Although it took her only minutes to reach her destination, her temper had already flared to the boiling point by the time she came to a stop in front of the jail. A light was still burning inside. She peered through the front window, the fire in her blue-green eyes every bit as bright as the lamp's glow they reflected.

Her body tensed from head to toe when her searching gaze fell upon Jake Brody. He was seated behind a big wooden desk, his handsome brow furrowing in thought while he attempted to bring order out of the paperwork chaos left behind by his predecessor. His hat hung on a nail on the poster-plastered wall behind him; his shotgun stood propped upright in the corner nearby; and he had taken the liberty of removing Sheriff Tickner's personal belongings from the desk and piling them into a cardboard box on the floor.

Looks like he's already made himself at home, Caley mused resentfully. She hesitated no longer. As if charging forward to do battle, she flung open the door and swept inside.

Jake appeared not the least bit surprised by her

brusque entry. Having caught sight of her at the window, he had wondered how long it would take before she had gotten her courage up enough to come in. Now that she had, he rose unhurriedly to his feet and faced her with an unfathomable expression on his face.

"Where's Ed?" she demanded before he had a chance to speak.

"Gone."

"Gone?" Her eyes grew round with disbelief. They narrowed in suspicion immediately afterward. "Gone where?"

"I don't know," he answered truthfully.

He did not bother to add that Ed Tickner had gone storming out of the jail less than an hour ago with the stated intention to pin his badge on the first jackass he came across. The whole town would know about it by tomorrow, he realized with an inward smile of irony. It wouldn't hurt for Miss Caley McAlister to wait her turn to have a go at him for running off the sorry, "good-old-boy" bastard who had been masquerading as Elko's chief peacemaker for the past year. No matter that his own actions had been in the town's best interest — there'd be hell to pay, and well he knew it.

First things first, Jake told himself. His eyes gleamed with both pleasure and determination as they traveled over Caley. Her attire was certainly more prim and proper than before, but there was no denying she was the same fire-spitting wildcat who had been on his mind all day. She stood before him now with her beautiful head at a fiercely defiant angle and her hands balled into fists on her hips, as though she were confronting a dangerous adversary instead of a man whose sworn duty it was to uphold the law and protect the innocent.

To Caley, he *was* dangerous. She cursed the fact that he was even more devilishly attractive than she had remembered.

"Sit down, Miss McAlister," he commanded with a faint smile, the direction of his gaze indicating another chair in front of the desk. Caley remained stubbornly on her feet.

"You had no right to make me come here!" she accused.

"I told you we need to talk. Now please sit down," he reiterated calmly. Still, she did not obey.

"The only thing I have to say to you, Marshal, is that I won't let myself be ordered about by you or anyone else in this town! I am a grown woman as well as a taxpayer, and I'll be damned if—"

"*Sit down.*"

He had her attention at last. It wasn't so much what he said as the way he said it. Although his face remained perfectly inscrutable, there was something in his deep-timbred voice that made her swallow hard and fall silent. She moved stiffly over to the chair and sank down upon it.

"Thank you," Jake said with all gentlemanly politeness. A telltale glimmer of amusement danced in his green eyes, but Caley was in no mood to appreciate it. She watched as he bent his tall, powerful frame back down into the leather-upholstered swivel chair behind the desk.

"Is this going to take long?" she inquired, her voice dripping with sarcasm.

"That depends."

"On what?"

"On whether or not you cooperate." He leaned back a bit in the chair and folded his arms across his chest. His penetrating gaze fastened on Caley's stormy countenance, prompting her to bristle with annoyance.

"Cooperate? What the devil are you talking about?" she asked, her tone sharp and impatient.

Before Jake could answer, another man's voice

47

rang out from the vicinity of the barred cells in the next room.

"Is that you I hear out there, Miss Caley?"

Her eyes flickered toward the doorway connecting the two rooms of the jail. She recognized that voice. It belonged to Billy Snyder's father.

"Yes, Otis, it's me!" she called back with a deep frown.

"No fraternizing with the prisoners, Miss McAlister," Jake cautioned her, trying hard not to smile.

"What did you lock him up for?" she demanded angrily.

"He was drunk and disorderly. I expect to fill the jail with a dozen others just like him before the night's through."

"And what did Sheriff Tickner have to say about your 'expectations'?"

"I didn't ask."

"It seems to me you're taking a damn sight too many things for granted!" she opined, her eyes fairly snapping with righteous indignation.

Angry color rode high on the silken smoothness of her cheeks, while the rapid rise and fall of her breasts gave even further indication of the storm brewing within her. Had she not been so preoccupied with Jake's supposed misdeeds, she would have noticed the way his gaze, darkening with purely masculine regard, was drawn downward to where the buttoned front of her shirtwaist strained tightly across the alluring, rounded swell of her bosom.

"Blast it all," she went on to rage, warming to the task of setting him straight, "who the blazes do you think you are? You come swaggering in here like you own the place, you start ordering everyone about and—"

"Ain't you gonna get me out of here, Miss Caley?" Otis Snyder's whining, slurred plea for assistance floated out to her from where he lay sprawled

48

face down atop the cell bunk.

She scowled darkly and narrowed her eyes in his general direction, but he was mercifully spared the full brunt of her hard, quelling look due to the simple fact that he could not see it.

"Come on now, Miss Caley," the lone prisoner tried again, "get me out of here. You know my missus'll beat . . . beat hell out of me if I ain't home by mornin' . . . little woman damn near killed me last time . . ."

Jake, his mouth curving into another strangely appealing half-smile, stood and crossed to the inner doorway. Caley watched his every move. She was dismayed to experience an unaccountable lightheadedness as her eyes traveled with a will of their own across the broad, hard-muscled planes of his back and shoulders, then lower to hips and thighs that were lean and firm and were hugged to male perfection by his denim trousers.

There was nothing soft about him at all, she idly concluded. No, he had the look of someone who had spent his life out of doors, someone who had fought hard and worked hard . . . and loved hard. *Where the devil had that thought come from?*

She flushed guiltily when he closed the door and turned back to her. Avoiding his gaze for a moment, she endeavored to mask her discomfiture by launching another attack upon what she perceived to be his damnably highhanded methods.

It was impossible, however, to attack from a sitting position. Not only did she find it difficult to be "hemmed in" whenever provoked, but there was something about facing Jake Brody across a desk that made her feel as though she were a naughty schoolgirl sent to the headmaster's office for punishment. That particular humiliation had in actuality been visited upon her years ago, when her father—in a rare burst of paternal atonement—had literally dragged her into one of those fancy, high-flown young ladies' academies where she'd had no earthly hope of fitting in. As usual, she and Paddy had been on the move again after a few short months, but the memory of her treatment at the school was still painful. And she wasn't about to let any man, especially *this* one, run roughshod over her ever again.

Leaping up from the chair before her opponent in the current battle of wills could resume his seat, she held herself rigidly erect. Her flashing turquoise eyes dared Jake to protest her chosen stance.

"You've got a hell of a nerve, Marshal Brody!" she charged anew. "I don't know what's brought you to Elko, and I don't care! But we've got to get one thing straight between us here and now—keep your nose out of my business, damn it!"

"I'm here to do a job, Miss McAlister," he reminded her somberly, though a telltale gleam lit his gaze. "And if enforcing the law means I have to step on a few toes, even toes as pretty as yours, then so be it."

It was on the tip of her tongue to inquire acidly how he could be so all-fired certain her toes were not ugly as sin, but she resisted the impulse and settled instead for flinging him another murderous glare. Unscathed, he moved closer.

"I asked you to come here for two reasons," he disclosed, his dark brows knitting into a slight but nonetheless unsettling frown. Only one reason stemmed from professional responsibility; the other was purely personal and, he well knew, apt to get him into trouble in more ways than one.

Caley instinctively retreated behind the relative safety of the desk once more. She was no coward, but it didn't pay to be careless.

"And what are those reasons?" she demanded in growing exasperation.

50

With slow, measured steps he closed the gap and stood towering above her in the lamplight, their bodies separated by mere inches. They could both hear Otis snoring in the other room.

"The first, I think you already know," Jake stated quietly. The look in his deep green eyes was, at least to her way of thinking, faintly menacing.

"If I knew I wouldn't have asked!" she retorted, giving an angrily defiant toss of her head. "Either say what you've got to say, or else put a stop to this claptrap and let me get back to my—"

"Are you always this prickly?" he broke in, smiling crookedly down at her.

Taken off-guard by the teasing warmth of that smile, Caley grew uncharacteristically flustered. She colored to the roots of her auburn hair and once again sought to hide her confusion behind a firestorm of temper.

"Why, you—that's torn it!" she sputtered wrathfully. "Maybe you've got nothing better to do than sit around playing *asinine* little word games, but I have!"

She tried to push past him, but to no avail. He stood fast, an immovable force of superior height and strength and ability. His hands came up to seize her arms in a firm, familiar grip that made her catch her breath.

"Easy now," he said. His words were more of a command than a request.

Though Caley was by nature inclined to resist such authoritative manhandling, she found herself unable to do so. It seemed she had lost her voice as well as her reason, for she remained silent and motionless while gazing expectantly up at the man whose first touch upon her thinly covered flesh had sent a shiver dancing down her spine.

"If you'll stop flying off the handle at everything I say," Jake told her, "we can get this over with in

51

no time."

With a reluctance that perplexed them both, he released her. She felt a tremor of something perilously akin to fear as his gaze burned down into the widened, luminous blue-green depths of hers.

"Never take a whip to me again, Miss McAlister," he warned in a low, vibrant tone laced with steel. "And don't make the mistake of thinking I'm too much of a gentleman to repay you in kind. I'm not."

"That comes as no surprise to me, *Marshal*!" she countered hotly. Gone was the temporary paralysis of tongue and body; in its place was a vengeful fury that knew no bounds. "I've got some 'advice' of my own — dare to touch me again and I'll damned well give you double what I gave Joe Cottle!"

"I'm not a man who takes threats lightly." The glint in his eyes had grown hard, the expression on his handsome face forebodingly grim. "Don't make any unless you're prepared to back them up."

"I'm prepared all right!" she shot back, her hands clenching into fists at her sides.

"Are you?" he challenged softly.

His deep voice held an undercurrent of dangerous calm, and Caley blanched inwardly at the almost savage intensity of his gaze. But she told herself she'd be hanged before she would let Jake Brody know of her alarm. *Hanged and bait for the buzzards!*

"Go to hell!" she ground out.

Muttering a strangled oath, she abruptly gathered up her skirts and went charging past him with a vengeance. She did not bother to look back over her shoulder to observe his reaction, for her only interest at the moment lay in escaping his damnably inflaming presence.

Jake made no attempt to stop her this time. He was afraid of what he might do once he got his

52

hands on her.

Their mutual resolve was shattered, literally and figuratively, in the very next instant.

Chapter III

Following a hoarse, unintelligible shout by someone in the moonlit darkness outside, a rock suddenly
came smashing through the jail's front window.

Jake sprang into action with instinctive swiftness.
A breathless cry escaped Caley's lips when his strong
arms wrapped about her and hauled her roughly
down to the floor. He placed his body protectively
atop hers, shielding her from further danger while
his narrowed, smoldering gaze made a quick but
thorough assessment of the situation.

Caley, her own gaze wide and anxious, remained
perfectly still. Stunned by Jake's reaction, she held
her breath and listened. Nothing else happened. And
there was nothing to be heard, save the muffled
cadence of Otis Snyder's snoring and the sound of
her own heartbeat pulsing in her ears. She could see
the broken glass on the bare wooden floor across the
room, shimmering in the lamp's golden glow, and she
wondered dazedly if perhaps a shot had been fired.

Then, her eyes fell upon the rock which now rested
harmlessly in the corner near the desk. Her brow
cleared as realization dawned at last. The danger,
minimal as it had been, was obviously past.

She released an audible breath and came to life
again where she lay sprawled on her back in a tumble
of skirts and petticoats beneath Jake's hard, undeni-

ably virile frame. There was no power on earth that could make her admit how deeply affected she was by the feel of his muscular body pressing down upon the accursedly feminine softness of hers.

"You can get up now," she proclaimed in a frigid tone.

When he gave no indication of compliance, her beautiful features grew stormy. She brought her hands up to push at the broad expanse of his chest — no easy task, given the fact that his arms were locked about her like bands of iron. Still met with defeat, she glared resentfully up into his face.

"Aren't you going to go after them?" she demanded, referring to whomever was responsible for the cowardly yet time-honored attempt to scare him off. "What the hell kind of lawman are you?"

Jake did not answer. Like her, he knew the danger no longer existed. He also knew it would be useless to go in search of the culprits. This wasn't the first time he'd had a rock thrown through his window. Nor, he expected, would it be the last.

Caley was dismayed to note the strange grimness of his expression, the sudden darkening of his fathomless green gaze as it traveled over her face with bold intimacy and raked downward to linger upon the full curve of her breasts. Her struggles to be free quickly intensified.

"Get off me, damn it!"

Unaware of the battle raging within her captor, she was equally unaware of the way his desire blazed hotter with each wriggle and squirm she made. If ignorance was truly bliss, then she was soon to be both enlightened *and* plunged into heartache.

Jake Brody was a man who prided himself on self-control. After all, experience had taught him the importance of keeping a clear head. But it had not been able to teach him how to completely obliterate the needs and emotions of a healthy, hot-blooded male. The flame-haired young wildcat imprisoned beneath him had been taunting him, provoking him to madness from the very first. What he did not yet realize was that the madness would only worsen with time.

The battle was lost, at least temporarily.

With an inward groan, Jake brought his warm, firmly chiseled lips crashing down upon the parted and practically virgin sweetness of Caley's.

She stiffened in shock, her struggles abruptly ceasing. The touch of a man's lips on hers was not an altogether foreign sensation. Why, even Matt had dared to kiss her on more than one occasion, and had promptly received a kick in the shin or a punch on the arm for his troubles. She had never taken kindly to being "pawed," as she termed it, no matter what her father had long ago told her—in blunt and embarrassingly graphic terms—about the course of nature followed by men and women.

Oddly enough, however, she felt no inclination whatsoever to kick or punch the man who was kissing her now. What she felt instead was a shocking desire to kiss him back.

Jake moaned low in his throat, his arms tightening about Caley's remarkably pliant body when the kiss deepened. She gasped when his hot, velvety tongue slid between her lips to scorch the moist cavern of her mouth. The plundering invasion was not altogether unwarranted, for she had invited it, albeit unintentionally, by moving her lips in a provocative manner beneath the conquering force of his.

Her lips were not the only thing provocative about her. Briefly, she joined in the embrace with all the innocent fire being awakened within her. Her arms crept about Jake's neck, while she gave a soft moan of her own and arched her body instinctively upward into even closer contact with his. Her breasts tingled as they swept against his chest. It seemed that his hard-muscled warmth seared her flesh through the layers of their clothing. She suddenly became aware of a shameless but profound yearning to know what it was like to feel his naked skin against hers. . . .

Then, reality intruded.

"Marshal?" It was Otis Snyder again.

Caley's eyes flew open. She felt Jake tense above her.

"Marshal, they comin' to—to string me up?" Otis stammered out with a loud hiccup. His reaction to the sound of breaking glass had been slowed by the whiskey he'd imbibed all too freely, so that he now made a belated connection between himself and danger. It never occurred to him that he wasn't important enough to lynch. "Marshal?"

Suffering a sharp intake of breath, Caley tore her lips from Jake's and pushed against him with all her might.

"Get away from me, you bastard!" she hissed furiously.

This time, Jake did as she bid. With a muttered oath, he released her and climbed to his feet. She gasped again when he yanked her up beside him.

"Go back to sleep, Snyder!" he instructed the slightly panic-stricken prisoner in the adjoining room. His words were greeted by silence, leading him to believe Otis had already returned to blissful unconsciousness.

"Let go of me!" Caley demanded hotly, trying to jerk her arm free from his possessive grasp.

Her hair streamed down about her face and shoulders in a tangled, pin-strewn mass of curls, while her clothing was both dusty and disheveled. The vengeful fire burning deep within her was reflected in the magnificent, blue-green blaze of her eyes. Hating both herself and the man who had mastered her body with such humiliating ease, she did her best to resist the violent impulses which threatened to overwhelm

58

her. Her hand itched to slap his face, her knee to deliver a punishing blow to an appropriate and highly vulnerable part of his anatomy.

To Jake, she had never looked more beautiful — nor more dangerously desirable.

"I said to let me go, damn it!" she reiterated in a low, hushed tone simmering with near explosive anger. "Take your hand off me now *or lose it!*" The threat, although rashly spoken, was lent credence by the knife she brandished after swiftly extracting it from its secret hiding place in her boot.

It wasn't the sight of the cold steel that prompted Jake to relax his grip at last. No, Caley's pearl-handled dagger did not strike so much as a single chord of fear in his heart. But he finally realized how perilously close to disaster he had come. Losing his head was something he could not afford to do in his chosen line of work; self-control was essential and never to be abandoned. He knew that. He knew it better than anyone. *What was it about this red-headed wildcat that had made him forget duty and caution, as well as honor?*

He cursed silently and forced his hand back to his side as though the contact with her thinly covered flesh now burned him.

"My apologies, Miss McAlister," he intoned quietly. The light in his gaze had grown cold, the look on his face equally dispassionate.

"Your apologies be damned!" Her fingers clenched about the dagger's handle, while her face flamed with both supreme mortification and outrage. "You randy, jackass son of a bitch! If I had my whip, I'd—"

"You'd find yourself in a hell of a lot more trouble than you bargained for!" he warned in a voice that was whipcord sharp. His eyes glinting like molten steel, he commanded with unmistakable authority, "Put the knife away."

59

"Why? So you can throw me down on the floor and . . . and force another kiss on me?" she taunted with resentful sarcasm. "Or maybe you've got it in mind to do even worse than you did before?"

It was on the tip of Jake's tongue to point out that he hadn't found it necessary to do much forcing, but he wisely refrained from uttering the insult. Instead, he frowned and shook his head.

"I'll not touch you again," he promised. His frown darkened to a thunderous scowl when an inner voice told him it was a promise he could not keep. "No harm was done," he added curtly, turning away. "Let's forget what happened."

"Maybe it will be easy for you to forget, but not for me!"

Jake allowed the ghost of a smile to touch his lips as he looked back at her.

"Is that a compliment, Miss McAlister?"

That threw her. She inhaled upon a gasp, her gaze widening with disbelief as her face crimsoned anew.

"Why, you . . . you . . ." she sputtered in angry, helpless confusion.

"Come on. I'll walk you back home." He took hold of her arm as though nothing had happened and began leading her toward the door. "You shouldn't be out alone this late."

True to her own tempestuous nature, Caley resisted.

"I don't need an escort, damn it!" The feel of his warm, strong fingers closing about her arm again sounded yet another alarm in her brain. She pulled free and rounded on him with a look that would have scorched a lesser man clean through. "I've always taken care of myself and I intend to keep right on doing so! Besides, it seems to me I'll be a whole lot safer out there on the streets than in here with you!"

She gave him one last speaking glare and left the same way she had come in—with fire in her eyes and vengeful fury in her heart. The perpetual mantle of dust on the boardwalk flew in her wake.

Jake waited a moment, then followed after her. He tried telling himself he was only doing his duty, but he knew it was much more than that. *Much more.*

Caley retraced her earlier steps, storming ahead at a particularly no-nonsense pace through the groups of men loitering in front of the saloons. These crowded, rip-roaring "whiskey haunts" were a familiar obstacle and had never caused her anything more than a temporary annoyance whenever she chose to be out after sundown. Tonight, of all nights, was to be the exception.

It happened when she was in front of the town's most infamous whiskey haunt of all, the Senate Saloon. Preoccupied with thoughts of what had taken place back at the jail, she failed to react in time to avoid a collision with the man who suddenly came flying through the Senate's double swinging doors.

The force of the impact knocked the breath from her body and sent her reeling sideways against the hitching post where a baker's dozen horses waited patiently in the moonlight. She clutched at the top rail in a frantic effort to halt her stumbling descent into the street. The careless saloon patron, meanwhile, managed to steady himself with the aid of one of the doors. His bloodshot eyes lit with recognition when they fell upon the woman he had very nearly flattened.

"Well, I'll be damned!" he burst out with a grin of unabashedly lustful pleasure.

Caley had no sooner regained her balance when she found herself imprisoned by a pair of arms that were youthful but wiry. She jerked her head about to face whomever it was that valued life so little.

It was Farley, the same young puncher who, along with his two companions, had favored her with his insolent regard that afternoon. She did not remember

61

him; it wouldn't have made any difference if she had.

"Let go of me, you drunken bastard!" she raged, squirming furiously in his grasp.

"I ain't drunk!" he protested good-naturedly. "Hot damn, wait'll Buck and Hooker see what I caught me!"

To prove how delighted he was with his supposed conquest, he hugged her tighter and swung her about. She flung a string of blistering oaths at his head, her temper already well past the boiling point.

"Put me down! Put me down or so help me, I'll cut off your rooster and feed it to the buzzards!" she threatened, without success.

"Hell, honey, you won't be sayin' that once you've had yourself a good look at the size of my rooster!" boasted Farley.

Then, it was his turn to be surprised. Someone grabbed him from behind and forcefully tore him away from Caley. She gasped and watched with wide, startled eyes as the ill-mannered young cowboy was sent sprawling into the street.

"*Brody!*" she breathed in disbelief, her gaze traveling back to where Jake stood outlined against the saloon's window. His green eyes were full of such a smoldering, savage light that she paled and felt a tremor of fear shoot through her.

"On your feet!" he commanded Farley, his deep voice ringing out above the strains of revelry which were borne aloft by the cool night wind. He had already drawn his gun, having long ago learned it was a great persuader.

The younger man reddened with anger, but nonetheless did as he was told. Picking himself up out of the dust, he offered no resistance when Jake moved forward and seized his arm in a hard, punishing grip.

"Apologize to the lady," Jake directed in a dangerously low tone.

Farley cast him a mutinous look. It was on the tip

of his tongue to ask how a "lady" had come to be gallivanting about by herself after dark, but he had the good sense not to ask it. He swallowed hard and turned to Caley.

"I—I'm sorry, ma'am," he offered in obvious embarrassment. Whether his embarrassment stemmed from his own misconduct, or from the fact that he had gotten caught, Caley could not tell. But she was anxious to put an end to the whole distasteful scene.

She nodded in mute acceptance and smoothed a lock of hair from her face. Her eyes were instinctively drawn back to Jake. She was surprised when he holstered his gun and released the young cowboy with nothing more than a warning.

"It's time you called it a night," he told him. "Don't come back until you've learned better manners."

Farley reluctantly muttered an assurance that he'd do just that, then dusted himself off a bit as he headed for his horse. He was unlooping the reins from the hitching post when his two friends came pushing through the doors behind Caley.

"Hey, Farley, where you goin'?" one of them demanded with a frown. "What—" He broke off when he caught sight of Caley.

The dark, rawboned man beside him saw her at the same time. He also saw Jake. His eyes narrowed when he recalled what he had heard about Elko's new lawman. Favoring Caley with a quick look that made her even more uncomfortable, he smiled faintly and shifted his gaze back to Jake.

"What's the trouble, Marshal?"

"No trouble," Jake answered with deceptive nonchalance. Cursing the fact that Caley was in the line of fire, he could only hope Farley's companions proved to bear at least some measure of respect for the badge he was wearing.

"You ain't under arrest, are you, Farley?" the fair-haired one persisted.

"No, Hooker, I ain't!" Farley gritted, his embarrassment growing visibly worse. "Now let's just get goin'!"

"She's got somethin' to do with it, don't she?" Hooker demanded with an accusatory glare in Caley's direction. He had downed a considerable amount of liquor throughout the course of the evening, and was in an undeniably belligerent mood. "What's the matter, Farley—she try to stiff you?"

"That's enough," Jake decreed in a voice of deadly calm. "On your way or I'll lock you up."

"I could tell first time I laid eyes on her she'd be trouble!" Hooker went on in spite of the warning. "Actin' so high and mighty . . . hell, she's probably one of them two-bit gals Sadie's got workin' for her down at the—"

"Shut up, you stupid sonofabitch!" cautioned Farley in an undertone that was perfectly audible to everyone else as well. He jerked his head toward Jake, who stood surveying them with a glint in his eyes that was downright murderous. "She's the marshal's woman!"

Caley gasped, her temper blazing at his assumption. No longer content to stand quietly by and do nothing, she bent and slid the knife out of the hidden sheath she had returned it to after leaving the jail.

"Damn your hide—all of you!" she hissed, holding the weapon in plain sight as her wrathful gaze swept across the four men.

"Put it away." The order, quietly spoken, came from Jake. Caley flung him a scathing look and tossed her head in proud defiance.

"I can fight my own battles!"

"Do as I say, Miss McAlister," Jake reiterated, his voice falling to a dangerous level. At that moment, he would have gladly wrung her beautiful little neck.

"What's the matter, Marshal?" the dark-haired

man challenged with a slow, taunting smile. "You afraid she'll try to horn in your job? Come to think of it, it might not be so bad being locked up with her standing guard all night."

His hawkish gaze sought the blue-green fire of Caley's, and just for an instant, she was certain she caught a glimpse of something that ran far deeper than the sort of pesky ogling she was used to. Her eyes widened again and flew back to Jake, only to see that his handsome features had tightened. She could almost feel the fury emanating from his tall, powerful frame.

"I want the three of you out of town. *Now*," he commanded. He had not yet drawn his gun again, but there was little doubt he was fully prepared to do so if the need arose.

"We ain't done nothin', damn it!" protested Hooker, his expression growing thunderous. "We got a right to—"

"Let's get him on his horse, Buck!" Farley nervously intervened. He hastened up onto the boardwalk to pull his whiskey-emboldened cohort toward their mounts.

"I ain't goin' nowhere!" Hooker declared, jerking away. He narrowed his eyes menacingly at Jake and brought his hand down close to the gun buckled at his right hip. Farley shot the oldest of the three a frantic plea for help.

"Do somethin', Buck!"

"That's a good idea, Farley," Buck agreed smoothly. "A right good idea!"

Before Caley knew what was happening, he reached out and seized her wrist in a painful grip, then whipped her back against him. She cried out sharply as the knife clattered to the ground, but she wasted no time in mourning its loss.

Neither did Jake.

While Caley set up a violent struggle, he drew both

guns before Hooker's six-shooter had even broken leather. Farley stood gaping at the scene, for the last thing he had expected to bring back from a night out on the town was a couple of dead friends. Luckily, however, the marshal did not fire—a fact that both stunned and bewildered him.

"Let her go!" Jake directed the man who still fought with Caley.

Buck, startled to find such a tigress on his hands, swore at the inevitability of defeat. It had been his intent to use the red-haired bitch to make the lawman back down, but he hadn't been prepared for either her strength or her fierce courage. With another curse, he shoved her forcefully away, then smiled in malevolent satisfaction when she lost her balance and landed hard on her backside.

Jake's handsome features became a mask of white-hot fury as he witnessed Caley's fall. He was surprised at the way his blood boiled, surprised at the sudden, vengeful impulse to kill the man who had dared to mistreat her. No matter that his duties did not include retaliation for indignities suffered by beautiful, fire-spitting wildcats; his own instincts would not be denied.

In one swift motion, he holstered one of his guns, covered the distance between himself and Buck, and brought his fist smashing up against the other man's unguarded chin.

The force of the brain-rattling blow knocked Caley's abuser backward into the street. He crumpled down into the dirt, the lights of the saloon blurring as unconsciousness threatened to overtake him.

Caley's own eyes grew round with incredulity. Like Buck, albeit to a decidedly lesser degree, she was taken aback by Jake's unexpected outburst of violence. She was even more startled by the warning he offered Buck when the still reeling cowboy, shaking his head in an effort to clear it, finally staggered to his feet once more.

"Touch her again and you're a dead man," vowed Jake.

Then, mastering his anger with an iron will, he motioned curtly at the three troublemakers with his pearl-handled Colt.

"Mount up!"

Even Hooker offered no argument this time. It seemed he was duly chastened by just how close to eternity he had come, for he shuffled over to his horse and obediently swung up into the saddle. Farley did the same, leaving only Buck in front of the saloon near Caley. He turned and gave her a hard look as she now belatedly climbed to her feet as well.

"Someday, we'll settle this score," he ground out in a tone that was little more than a growl.

"I'll see you in hell first!" she retorted venomously. She rounded on Jake and demanded in righteous outrage, "Aren't you going to arrest them?"

"No."

"Why the devil not?" She was furious at the thought that he was going to let them off without so much as a by-your-leave. Not only had they accosted and insulted her, they had humiliated her in front of *him!* "You mean to tell me that . . . that after what they've done, you're not even going to—"

"On your horse!" Jake commanded Buck again, cutting off her heated queries. His finger tensed on the trigger of his gun as he kept a vigilant eye on all three punchers.

The lean, dark-haired man named Buck met Jake's gaze. For the merest fraction of a second, it appeared he might be entertaining the notion of resistance. Fortunately, however, he chose to ignore it. Sauntering across to where his two companions waited, he took hold of the reins Farley held out to him.

"Get going," ordered Jake.

Farley and Hooker both nodded silently, reining

about while Buck pulled himself up into the saddle. Although he might have considered avenging himself against the man who had laid him flat, the sight of Jake's well-used gun persuaded him otherwise. His dark eyes narrowed into a malignant glare that raked over Caley before returning to Jake.

"I won't forget this, damn you!" he snarled.

"Neither will I," promised Jake, his fingers tensing about the six-shooter in his hand.

Buck jerked on the reins and angrily spurred his mount forward. He rode away into the darkness, with Hooker and Farley following close behind.

Jake waited until all three troublemakers were out of sight, then slipped his weapon back into the tooled leather holster buckled low on his hips. His green eyes were full of a dangerous light when he pivoted slowly about to face Caley. But she was the one to fire the first volley.

"It's plain to see you're not going to do this town any damned good at all!" Balling her hands into tight fists, she planted them on her hips and reproached him bitterly, "You throw a harmless drunk like Otis Snyder in the hoosegow, and then you turn right around and let those beetleheaded bastards ride off scot-free! Why the hell don't you just call it quits right now and go back where you came from? Ed Tickner may not be worth his weight in buffalo chips when it comes to keeping the peace, but at least *he* wouldn't have—"

"Didn't anyone ever teach you not to cross a man with a gun?" Jake demanded grimly.

"Are you saying you would have shot me?" she retorted with biting sarcasm.

"Don't tempt me."

He began advancing upon her with slow, measured steps. Refusing to be intimidated, she bent and retrieved her knife, then slid it back into her boot. She straightened again to find Jake towering above her.

"I won't allow anyone to tell me how to do my job, Miss McAlister," he proclaimed in a quiet, resonant tone that made her heart give a sudden leap. "Not even you."

Caley was dismayed to feel her cheeks burning. His proximity made her pulse race alarmingly once more, and it was difficult for her to meet his gaze. The cacophony of music and voices blared from the saloon behind her, but she was oblivious to everything save this damnably hot-blooded man who had come into her life less than twelve hours ago and yet had already managed to twist her emotions into utter chaos. She didn't like feeling all confused and bothered, didn't like losing her grip on reality. *And reality did not include Jake Brody.*

As usual, anger was both her refuge and her ally.

"I don't give a hoot in hell about your job!" she stormed, tilting her head back in order to face him squarely. "I didn't ask for your help—as a matter of fact, the whole blasted thing got out of hand because of your interference! Once and for all, Marshal, I can take care of myself!"

"Can you?" he quipped dryly.

Ironic humor lurked in his eyes, but he suppressed the smile tugging at his lips. All traces of amusement vanished in the next instant when he noticed the torn sleeve of Caley's shirtwaist. It was a pointed reminder of what might have happened if he had not followed her. His gaze darkened as white-hot fury surged through him again. She would never know the effort it had cost him to keep from giving her assailant the beating he so richly deserved.

"It's time you were home and in bed, Miss McAlister." Cupping her elbow to provide the escort she had so fiercely claimed not to need, he cursed himself for the wicked thoughts conjured up by his words.

"Why, of all the—" she breathed, bristling anew. "I'm not a child!"

69

"So I've noticed."

Caley wasn't sure she liked the way his eyes twinkled roguishly down at her, but she went along with him just the same. She was unaccustomed to being charmed by members of the opposite sex, least of all by one she had convinced herself to dislike. Yet, here she was, feeling ridiculously light of head because Elko's new marshal—and a confounded *federal* man to boot—had apparently singled her out as his next conquest. That he'd had many, she was certain; that hell would freeze over before he'd be able to count her among them, she was equally certain.

Still, there was something oddly comforting about the feel of his strong hand guiding her through the crowd of half-drunk, woman-hungry men on the boardwalk. It had been a long time since anyone had taken care of her . . . usually, it was the other way around. Even Matt had admitted he never worried about her. There was no other woman alive, he had once said, who could handle herself in a tough situation as well as his "Mac" did.

She walked beside Jake in silence, lost in her thoughts but still very much conscious of the warmth of his fingers upon her arm. He finally released her when the two of them stood in front of the stage office, a fact for which she did not know whether to be grateful or disappointed.

"Is this where you live?" he asked, his gaze flickering up to the second floor.

"It is," she confirmed a bit defensively.

"I've got a room across the street." A brief, sardonic smile lit his face before he added, "I'm within shouting distance if you need me."

"The only shouting you'll ever hear will be when they come to run you out of town!"

"I never leave any place until I'm ready." He moved closer, prompting her to retreat until her back came up against the glass-centered door. With slow deliber-

70

ation, he braced a hand on the splintered frame just above her head and leaned forward until she could see the golden flecks in his eyes. "I don't plan to leave until this town—and everyone in it—is tamed."

"You'll not tame *me!*" She folded her arms tightly across her breasts, her fiery gaze shooting sparks up at him. "That badge you're wearing may give you the right to bully every other poor bastard around here, but I'll not let you bully me or anyone who works for me!"

"I don't want to bully you," he argued, his deep-timbred voice dropping to a near whisper that sent chills dancing down her spine.

"Then what the devil do you want to do to me?" she blurted out in exasperation.

Her face grew warm the moment the question rolled off her tongue. The situation only worsened when she spied Jake's mouth twitching. Abruptly unfolding her arms, she drew herself up to her full, indignant height of five feet seven and launched another verbal barrage before he could speak again.

"Damn you, I know your kind all too well! You think every female under the age of sixty ought to swoon dead away at your feet every blasted time you so much as cock an eyebrow at them! Well, you can go right on cocking, Jake Brody, for I sure as bloody hell won't—"

"Where did you pick up such a colorful vocabulary, Miss McAlister?" he drawled with maddening equanimity.

Caley inhaled sharply, her eyes growing very round before narrowing with another flash of anger. He was baiting her and well she knew it. But she could not help rising to it this time, not when he stood gazing down at her with what she believed to be a smugly superior look on his handsome face. Her sparkling turquoise gaze lingered upon his lips. The memory of his kiss suddenly came back to taunt her, to remind her of her own inability to resist a temptation she had never battled before.

Something within her snapped. Her temper once again ruling her head, she muttered an oath and brought her hand up to deliver a ringing slap to the rugged, clean-shaven smoothness of Jake's cheek.

She hadn't paused to consider what his reaction might be. At first, he did nothing. His gaze smoldered down into hers while she pressed instinctively back against the door and waited, wide-eyed and breathless and more than a little shocked at what she had done. Her mind screamed at her to run, to get away before it was too late, but she did not listen.

And then suddenly, it *was* too late.

"So, it's going to be like that between us, is it?" Jake remarked softly. He straightened, and Caley thought he was preparing to leave. But she was mistaken.

With alarming roughness, he seized her about the waist and yanked her up hard against him. She had no time to protest, no time to struggle, for he brought his lips crashing mercilessly down upon hers.

Holding her captive with one powerful arm, he kissed her with a fierce, demanding passion that made her head swim. His other hand swept downward along the curve of her spine, his fingers spreading urgently, possessively across her buttocks to bring her lower body into even more intimate contact with his. She gave a low moan when his hot, velvety tongue slid within her mouth to ravish its silken moistness at will. Her hands came up to push at him, but she was so overwhelmed by the sweet savagery of his embrace that she could fight with only a poor shadow of her usual spirit and defiance.

The kiss ended as abruptly as it had begun. Caley was forced to clutch at the door for support when Jake's arms left her without warning. She leaned heavily back against the quartered panes of glass, her

72

face flushed and her eyes very bright while she struggled in vain to restore order to her highly irregular breathing.

"You'll get no apology from me this time, Miss McAlister," Jake told her grimly.

Stunned, she blinked up at him. His gaze burned down into hers, making her feel that he could see clear through to where she hid the most private part of herself. Torn between the desire to give him a piece of her highly volatile mind, and the brazen urge to sway against him and plead for a continuation of his 'vengeance,' she never got the chance to do either.

The sound of breaking glass drew their attention. They both turned to watch as a man was hurtled through one of the Senate's big front windows. Tumbling end over end, he came to rest beside the row of horses in the street. His forced but remarkably harmless exit signaled the onslaught of the type of drunken brawl that was all too typical of Elko's nightlife.

"This town is hell on glass," Jake murmured with a faint smile of irony. Glancing back down at Caley, he frowned and said, "Get inside."

"*What?*" she demanded indignantly. "How dare you order me about, you arrogant sidewinder! I can stand here all night long if I want to, and there isn't a blessed thing you or anyone else can—"

"Damn it, woman, do as I say!" he ruthlessly cut her off. Emphasizing his command in the best way he knew how, he spun her about and landed a hard, insistent smack upon her backside.

He didn't even wait to see if she would obey. His long booted strides were already leading him toward the source of trouble when Caley flung about to face him again with murder in her eyes. She was so enraged she could scarcely think straight. No man had ever dared treat her as Jake Brody had just done.

Although tempted to call after him, she clamped

73

her mouth shut and simmered in silence. She hurled invisible daggers at the broad target of his retreating back, watching as he disappeared inside the saloon. For just an instant, she imagined *him* flying through the window and landing face down in the dirt. The thought made her eyes gleam with perverse delight.

With one last furious glare in Jake's direction, she whirled about and marched to the rear of the building. Shadrach was waiting for her on the back stoop. He took to yowling reproachfully when he caught sight of his tormentor/benefactress climbing the stairs.

"Did you have a bad night, too, old boy?" she murmured, heaving a disgruntled sigh as she came to a halt beside him.

In answer, he swatted at her ankle. Well acquainted with his outbursts of ill temper, she merely scooped him up and bore him inside. If she had hoped to find some consolation in the old saying "misery loves company," she was disappointed, for the cat immediately scampered off to strike his usual haughty pose in the window.

She closed the door and lifted a hand to smooth the wildly tousled auburn curls from her face. A sudden churning in her stomach reminded her of the unfinished dinner she had left behind at Maybelle's. There was nothing with which to satisfy her hunger, she realized, save for the packet of beef jerky she always kept stashed with her gear down in the office. Although the prospect of its consumption made her grimace, she told herself it was no more than she deserved after the inexcusable, lily-livered way she had let that conceited Texan lord it over her.

So, it's going to be like that between us, is it? His words came back to taunt her, fueling the fires of her anger all over again.

"No, by damn, it is not!" she adamantly dissented, her voice ringing out in the darkened silence of the three small rooms. "It most certainly is not!" Saying it aloud gave her some small measure of satisfaction — even if Jake Brody wasn't there to hear.

A well-chosen malediction rose to her lips, but she bit it back and then wondered why. Crossing to the table to light the lamp, she had just struck a match when the sound of gunfire echoed up from the streets below.

It was a common enough sound, given the fact that someone was always taking it in mind to shoot someone else in Elko. She had learned to ignore it. But this time was different. This time, she found herself plagued by the vision of a certain tall, devilishly handsome lawman shot full of holes and lying dead, or at least very near it, on the sawdust-coated floor of the Senate Saloon.

Instead of giving her pleasure, the possibility that the vision might prove true made her heart twist with alarm. She asked herself why it should matter if he had gone and gotten himself killed, but there was no answer.

A sudden, overpowering urge to see what had happened took hold of her. She turned and flew from the apartment, scurrying back down the staircase and around to the boardwalk. Fighting her way through the gathering crowd, she grew more and more anxious as she neared the saloon.

What if he *was* dead? she wondered. What if the man whose kiss still burned upon her lips had met his Maker the first day he'd come to town? Was there someone to grieve for him . . . a sweetheart or even a wife? The questions ran together in her mind, prompting her to quicken her steps until she was nearly out of breath.

She spied him a few seconds later. Very much alive and sporting no visible holes, he was emerging from the saloon with two men. He urged them forth at gunpoint, his expression quite grim and his gaze full

75

of a hard light while he pressed the menacing brunt of steel against their backs.

"Get going," he instructed in a cold, clear tone that left little doubt he meant business. "I'm sure you know the way."

Caley grasped at a post and felt relief wash over her. But relief was quickly followed by a feeling of self-loathing as she watched Jake lead his prisoners away. She cursed herself for her weakness, for caring so damned much about the welfare of a man who should by all rights mean nothing to her. *Great balls of fire, what was the matter with her?*

"Miss Caley?"

She turned to see who had called her name, then groaned inwardly when her eyes fell upon George Groat. He stood grinning at her while the crowd began to disperse for a resumption of the night's pleasures.

"What the Sam Hill you doin' out here?" asked George, but didn't bother to wait for an answer. "I thought you'd be sawin' logs by now for sure! Shoot fire, did you see that Brody character?" he remarked in admiration. "Cool as a cucumber, he was! Went chargin' right inside the Senate and broke up the set-to without anyone ever layin' a hand on him! I never seen anythin' like it!"

He stopped talking for a moment and subjected her to an uncomfortably close scrutiny.

"What's wrong, Miss Caley? You feelin' poorly?"

Her mind raced to think of an answer. The truth was simply too humiliating. Dismayed to feel her face growing warm, she managed to force a lame smile to her lips.

"No. I—I'm fine, George. Nothing's wrong."

She bristled in the next instant, musing that she didn't like being interrogated by George Groat or anyone else. The fire came back to her blue-green eyes, and she tossed her head in angry defiance.

"For heaven's sake, can't a person even go out for a walk without everyone jumping to conclusions?" she demanded.

"Conclusions?" repeated George, taken aback by her abrupt change in attitude. "I'm right sorry, Miss Caley, but I don't know what you—"

"Never mind!" she cut him off brusquely. "Good night, George!"

He frowned after her in bewilderment as she went marching back down the street. It wasn't like Miss Caley to fly at him for no reason. It wasn't like her at all. Shaking his head at the unpredictability of females in general, he pulled on his hat and ambled off to seek the relative comfort of his own bed.

Upon reaching home again, Caley slammed the door behind her and let loose with a blistering string of oaths that would have done nothing to improve her standing in the community. Shadrach took her fury in stride, sparing her only a brief, disinterested glance before settling back down upon the windowsill to watch the comings and goings of the silly humans in the world below.

Chapter IV

"All aboard!"

The usual odd assortment of passengers sallied forth from the stage office. Red Tarver, the driver on this morning's six o'clock run to Tuscarora, had just taken up the reins when he noticed the only woman traveler having difficulty. She was wrestling with her skirts in a valiant attempt to avoid exposing her ankles while climbing up into the coach. Always ready and willing to place himself at the disposal of anyone of the female persuasion—especially when she was as fair of face and form as this one was—Red gallantly jumped down to help her.

"Allow me, ma'am," he said, offering her the support of his arm. Although the aptly named jehu would not by any stretch of the imagination be called handsome, he had a certain way about him that had charmed many a woman throughout his thirty-odd years. Even Caley found his good humor to be infectious.

A stoic, gray-bearded miner dressed in a red wool shirt and patched cotton britches boarded after the prudish young lady, followed by an Eastern dandy sporting a ridiculous handlebar moustache and a stiff bowler hat that made his head resemble a large brown egg. The last two men to take their places inside the open-sided mud wagon were obviously drummers, one of them wearing a new but ill-chosen suit of the most garish plaid ever seen in Elko, and the other attired in a dark, wrinkled coat and trousers. Both carried the trademark sample case.

Once settled inside, the passengers did their best to make themselves comfortable on the narrow padded seats, but their comfort would be short-lived at best. The day's long journey would take them over some of the roughest, most bone-rattling roads known to man; the fifty miles which lay between them and their destination were considered so dangerous that only the most experienced whips could make it through. Red Tarver fell into that category.

Caley looked on while Billy handled the impatiently snorting team with gentle confidence. Her eyes, though underscored by faint, shadowy half-circles after a night of little sleep, sparkled in satisfaction when she turned away. Having already supervised the loading of the padlocked green express box, she tossed the mail pouch up to Red. She waited until he had stashed the leather sack securely beneath the driver's seat before offering a few last minute instructions.

"Mind you don't get too drunk tonight, Red," she cautioned him with a mock frown of severity. "And don't let any of those painted floozies up there in Tuscarora take advantage of you."

"Aw, hell, Miss Caley, you ain't got no call to worry on neither count," he reassured her, grinning crookedly. He usually made it a point not to curse in the presence of ladies, but it wasn't the same with Caley. It was different because *she* was different. "Tell Hank I'll be back in time to spell him on the run to Hamilton come Saturday."

"It so happens, Red Tarver, that I was planning to take that one myself!"

"No need in that," he argued. His face lit with a brief smile again. "I got me some business there."

Caley started to press him for details, but thought better of it. Drivers were notoriously close-mouthed when it came to their private lives, and Red was no exception. She knew little about him, save that he had been orphaned at the age of eleven and had made his own way in the world ever since. Mystery man or not, there wasn't a day gone by that she didn't give thanks for his cool head and steady hand. The McAlister Stage and Transport Company could never have survived without him.

Riding shotgun that day was a man by the name of Greenfield, employed by Wells Fargo to guard the express box. The exact contents of the box were known only to him and Caley, who, as the local express agent, had been required to sign a document attesting to their number, worth, and condition. She always felt uneasy whenever there was a large amount of gold on board, but she had long ago learned the importance of concealing her apprehensions. It wouldn't do to let anyone suspect just how valuable the shipment was.

"Let 'er go, Billy!" ordered Red.

The young hostler quickly complied, dropping his hands and stepping aside. The stagecoach rolled away into the crisp, pre-dawn darkness.

"You want me to hang around, Miss Caley?" Billy asked once they stood alone in front of the empty office. The streets were practically deserted at that time of day.

"No," answered Caley, shaking her head. "You go on home and get some breakfast. I don't expect Hank before five, so you needn't come back until four-thirty."

"Yes, ma'am." He gave her a deferential nod and turned to leave.

"Billy?" she detained him on a sudden impulse.

"Yes, ma'am?" Pivoting back around, he faced her with a slight frown of puzzlement.

"Is your father home yet?" *Why in blazes had she asked that?* Thinking of Otis brought to mind the man who had forced his way into her dreams last night.

"He wasn't when I left. But, me and Ma and Junie don't ever look for him until an hour or two after sunup," the slender, fair-haired youth explained solemnly. "I reckon he ain't up and about till then."

"Well, maybe with . . . with the new marshal in town, he'll be home more often from now on," she offered lamely.

"Yes, ma'am." He waited a moment to see if there was anything else she wanted, then headed down the street toward the small clapboard house he shared with his parents and a younger sister. His mother had managed to buy the house with the money she had saved from years of dressmaking. Otis Snyder, a carpenter by trade, worked only sporadically. Heaven knew there was certainly a demand for his services in the burgeoning desert metropolis, but he never stayed sober for more than a few days at a time.

Caley sighed and returned inside to the lamplit warmth of the office. Wandering across to the pot-bellied stove, she poured herself a cup of coffee. The fire crackled and hissed, chasing the chill from the cluttered room and sending shadows dancing high on the walls. Shadrach, a frequent visitor downstairs, lay curled up in a chair nearby. A faint smile touched Caley's lips as she smoothed a hand along the thickly furred softness of his back.

She moved to the desk and opened the schedule book, intending to set it to rights before taking herself over to Maybelle's for breakfast. But try as she would, she was unable to turn her thoughts away from Jake Brody.

It had been the same throughout the seemingly endless hours of the night. Every time she had drifted off to sleep, *he* had been there to taunt her, to

82

remind her of things best forgotten. There had been no escape from the memory of his kisses. Even now, the mere thought of seeing him again made her pulse race and her stomach do a strange flip-flop.

"Going to hell in a handbasket, that's what you're doing!" she muttered in furious self-recrimination.

She slammed the book shut. Shadrach awakened with a start, just in time to see his angry young owner go storming outside. Secretly delighted at the prospect of being left to catnap in peace, he closed his green eye and watched through his half-open blue one while Caley locked the door behind her and set off for the boarding house across the street.

It struck her just as she was climbing the front steps—Jake Brody might be inside at that very moment. There was every chance she would come face to face with her handsome bedeviler at Maybelle's table. She groaned inwardly and rolled her eyes heavenward. How on earth could she have forgotten that he was staying there?

"Good morning, Caley!"

She looked up to see Maybelle smiling at her from the doorway. Musing that she couldn't very well turn tail and run now, she managed a weak smile in response.

"Morning, Maybelle." She determinedly squared her shoulders and raised her head high, sweeping across the threshold without another word.

"You're looking mighty thoughtful this morning," the widow remarked dryly. She moved to the edge of the porch to empty the dustpan in her hand, then followed Caley back inside and closed the door. "Anything wrong?"

"Wrong?" echoed Caley, dismayed to feel herself flushing guiltily. She hastened to deny it while her gaze scanned the surrounding area for the one boarder she wished to avoid. "No, nothing's wrong! Why do you ask?"

"Well, for one thing," Maybelle answered with a glimmer of fond merriment in her brown eyes, "you're half an hour too early for breakfast. Not that I mind having your company, but—"

"Maybe I ought to skip breakfast this morning!" Caley suggested. It came out sounding like a childish retort, which was not at all what she'd intended. She tried to smooth things over by smiling apologetically and explaining with at least half truthfulness, "I'm sorry, Maybelle, but it's just that I . . . well, I didn't get much sleep last night and I was up early seeing Red off. I guess I lost track of time."

"Good heavens, you know you're always welcome here, Caley McAlister!" the other woman declared. She linked her arm through Caley's and began leading her down the hallway. "Besides, I've already made one exception to the rule, and I don't suppose the world will come to a sudden end if I make another."

"Exception?"

Caley had no time to question her further, for they had reached the dining room. Her turquoise gaze made a quick, encompassing sweep—and lit upon Jake Brody.

"I've brought you some company, Marshal," Maybelle announced brightly.

Jake stood from his seat at the table. His eyes literally danced with a combination of amusement and desire when they met Caley's.

"This is an unexpected pleasure, Miss McAlister," he told her with all gentlemanly politeness. She was not fooled.

"Is it?" she snapped. She could feel the warm color rising to her face and knew herself damned.

"Miss McAlister is going to have her breakfast early as well," their hostess went on to proclaim, urging Caley down into the chair directly across from Jake's.

"I'm really not very hungry—" Caley tried to pro-

84

test.

"Nonsense," Maybelle brusquely cut her off. She smiled to soften her words and said, "I 'd best go on out to the kitchen and see if Jerusha's put more biscuits in to bake. I expect there'll be a stampede once the folks upstairs get a good whiff of my coffee."

Watching her leave, Caley was sorely tempted to bolt from the room in the opposite direction. She could feel Jake's eyes upon her as he resumed his seat, and she suddenly wished she had worn something other than the form-fitting red calico dress. Like the rest of her wardrobe, it had definitely seen better days. She offered up a silent prayer for Maybelle's prediction of a stampede to prove true without delay.

"Sleep well last night?" Jake asked her, a teasing note in his deep voice.

"What business is it of yours how I slept?" she retorted, making no attempt at civility. It dismayed her to no end to find herself thinking that he was even more damnably attractive than she had remembered. The vivid memory of what it had felt like being in his arms flashed into her mind, prompting her to clench her teeth and mentally consign him to the devil.

But she would not admit defeat so easily. Maybelle had offered her breakfast, and breakfast she would have! Holding her body stiffly erect, she snatched up the napkin beside her plate and placed it in her lap. Her lips were compressed into a tight, thin line of displeasure when she reached for the large bowl of scrambled eggs. Jake, whether by design or accident, reached for it at the same time, so that her fingers brushed against the strong warmth of his. She inhaled sharply and drew her hand back as if the contact had burned her.

"Care for some eggs, Miss McAlister?" he offered

with a faint smile of irony.

"No, Marshal Brody, I do not!" she ground out. Flinging him a defiantly scathing look, she seized the platter of ham instead and forked two slices onto her plate. Her eyes blazed and narrowed when she heard Jake's quiet chuckle. "What the devil is so funny?" she demanded in angry resentment.

"Are you always this difficult to get along with before you've had your coffee?"

"I suppose a man like you isn't used to being around women who have gumption!"

"I've known one or two," he countered smoothly, though his eyes still brimmed with roguish humor. "But never any with as much gumption as you. It seems you got more than your fair share."

"And you just can't bear it, can you?" she shot back. She picked up her knife and set about attacking the ham as though it were still alive. "You just can't bear the thought of not being able to . . . to *enslave* me like you probably did all the others!"

"Why are the details of my love life so fascinating to you, Miss McAlister?" he challenged in a low, wonderfully resonant tone.

Her eyes, ablaze with blue-green fire, flew up to meet his again. He was smiling softly across at her, his rugged, sun-bronzed features appearing even more tanned above the unbuttoned collar of his white shirt. She found herself staring at his firmly chiseled lips, remembering all too well how they had moved with such sensuous persuasion upon hers. . . .

No, damn it, no! Swallowing hard, she forced herself back to reality.

"Don't flatter yourself!" she countered acidly. "You can go around bedding every blasted thing in skirts for all I care!" To add emphasis to her declaration of disinterest, she stabbed a piece of ham and raised it to her mouth. It gave her a certain amount of off-kilter pleasure to pretend it was Jake Brody she was chewing to bits.

"Why don't we call a truce?" he suddenly put forth, his smile deepening. The sight of it made the coldness around Caley's heart melt, though she would never own up to any such thing. "I plan to be in town for a long while yet," he continued, "and if we go on rubbing each other the wrong way, there's no telling—"

"I don't intend for us to 'rub' each other any way at all!" she hotly maintained. "If I were a man, you'd never have dared to treat me the way you did last night!"

"You're right," he surprised her by agreeing. His piercing, deep green gaze traveled over her with a bold intimacy that took her breath away. "But not for the reasons you imply."

His remark sent the warm color flying to her cheeks once more. She hastily looked back down to her plate, uncertain as to what she should say or do next. On the one hand, she was reluctant to stir up any further sparks between them; on the other, she would have liked nothing more than to tell him exactly what she thought of the way he kept needling her. No man had ever gotten to her the way this one did—*and in only one day's time*, an inner voice gleefully pointed out.

The solution to her present dilemma arrived in the form of Maybelle, who returned from the kitchen just then bearing a fresh pot of coffee.

"Why, Caley," remarked the brunette, noting her friend's scarcely touched food, "I guess you meant it when you said you weren't hungry." She filled Jake's cup with the dark, aromatic brew and casually mentioned, "Most of the ladies at my table eat like half-starved birds. Not Miss McAlister." She beamed an affectionate smile in the younger woman's direction. "Her appetite puts theirs to shame."

Caley groaned inwardly at the compliment. It

didn't help matters any when she glimpsed the light of unholy amusement in Jake's eyes. Visibly bristling, she raised her own cup of coffee to her lips. The hot liquid burned her tongue, but she wasn't about to give any indication of it.

"What are you doing up so early, Marshal?" she questioned him in a tone laced with sarcasm. "I would have thought you'd sleep in till noon or after, seeing as how you no doubt spent all night filling the jail!"

"Half the night," he corrected her, leaning back a bit in his chair. He took another drink before adding, "But you're right about the jail being full."

"It's high time someone did something about the wildness that goes on around here after dark!" This came from Maybelle, who had moved to take a seat at the head of the table.

"My sentiments exactly, Mrs. O'Grady," said Jake. With an easy, masculine grace, he drew his tall frame upright and nodded down at both women. "If you ladies will excuse me, I've got work to do."

"Dinner's at twelve if you're able to get away," Maybelle informed him.

"Thanks. I'll keep that in mind." He then looked to Caley. "By the way, Miss McAlister, it might interest you to know I've got a man claiming to be a friend of yours locked up."

"A friend of mine?" she repeated, her silken brow creasing into a frown. "What are you talking about? If this has something to do with Otis Snyder—"

"His name's Griffin," he interrupted. "Matt Griffin. He said you'd vouch for him." He studied her reaction closely, cursing himself for the surge of jealousy which shot through him.

"*Matt?*" Her eyes grew round with stunned disbelief. "You mean to tell me you actually arrested Matt Griffin?"

"I do, and I did."

"But you can't do that!" she adamantly protested, leaping to her feet now as well. "Hell's bells, you beef-witted son of a bitch, don't you know anything?"

"Caley!" Maybelle reprimanded sharply. Far from achieving the desired effect, her words only spurred the angry young redhead onward.

"Isaiah Griffin is one of the most important men in the county!" stormed Caley. "You can damn sure bet he isn't going to stand by and do nothing while some pissant federal man throws his son behind bars!"

"I don't intend to ask his permission," Jake decreed quietly. His gaze was suffused with a dull glow, and his expression had grown forebodingly grim. "Matt Griffin will be treated the same as any other lawbreaker."

With another curt, wordless nod down at Maybelle, he left the table and headed toward the doorway. Caley went after him.

"Just what *are* the charges against Matt?" she demanded. A gasp broke from her lips when he abruptly rounded on her, and she felt a tiny knot of fear tightening in her stomach at the almost savage gleam in his eyes.

"Drunk and disorderly, like everyone else," he replied tersely.

"Well then, I'll pay his bail!"

"No need. He'll be released this morning."

"Why the hell didn't you just tell me that in the beginning?" She was surprised to observe a wry smile tugging at his lips.

"Because I'm a pissant federal man who does things his own way," he drawled.

He turned his back on her and set off once more, pausing briefly in the entrance foyer to lift his hat down from the mirrored hall tree. Caley watched as he strode outside and closed the door behind him.

"Caley McAlister, what on earth has gotten into you?" scolded Maybelle, bustling forward now. "You know good and well I don't allow rough language in this house!"

"I warned you he'd be nothing but trouble!" Caley pointed out, whirling to face her. "You saw for yourself how—"

"Marshal Brody appears to me to be a perfect gentleman!" the widow rushed to his defense. "And even if he weren't, you've no right to behave so rudely to one of my boarders!"

"I have more right than you can guess!" Her beautiful face crimsoned anew at the thought of what she had endured at Jake Brody's hands. She threw up her own hands in an eloquent gesture of exasperation. "Great balls of fire, Maybelle, don't you see what's bound to happen? He'll get himself killed if he doesn't wise up and—"

"Why should it matter so much to you?" the older woman probed, her eyes narrowing in suspicion. "He's little more than a stranger. In all the time I've known you, I've never seen you take an interest in any man. Except Matt, of course," she amended thoughtfully. "And I'm not sure that counts."

"What do you mean 'you're not sure it counts'?" Caley demanded with a slightly affronted air.

"I mean, my dear," said Maybelle in a more gentle manner, "that Matt Griffin has been telling everyone for years that the two of you are going to be married someday, but I've not seen any desire on your part to lead him to the altar. If I were you, I'd have roped and hogtied that man and dragged him there!"

"Well you *aren't* me, and I haven't been ready—" she started to offer an excuse, only to break off and flare up again. "What in tarnation does that have to do with Jake Brody?"

"I don't know. I'm just trying to find out why you flew off the handle at him like that. What is it,

Caley? What's the matter?"

"Oh . . . you wouldn't understand," she murmured with a disconsolate sigh. Once again, her anger had fled as rapidly as it had blazed to life. She pressed her fingertips against her temples and dropped her arms back to her sides. "I've got to get back to the office."

"Surely you can sit down and finish your breakfast first," Maybelle told her with a conciliatory smile.

"No, I'm afraid I can't. I'm sorry, Maybelle. I . . . I'll be in for supper as usual."

She reached out to lightly grip the older woman's arm for a moment, then turned and hurried from the house. The rising sun had set the cloudless sky aglow. Its radiance promised another twelve hours of relentless, scorching heat for the awakening town. There were a few brave souls to be seen parading about on the streets by this time, and Caley mused sourly that their bellies were probably full in preparation for the long day ahead.

If this keeps up, you'll be nothing but skin and bones, she told herself. Twice now, Jake Brody had been the cause of her going hungry; twice now, she had left Maybelle's table in a flurry of ill temper. She didn't know who deserved the most blame.

Recalling Jake's news about Matt, she felt a sharp, inexplicable pang of loneliness. Maybelle's words had hit closer to home than she cared to admit. . . .

There was plenty of paperwork to be done at the office, and plenty of errands to be run around town, which meant her mind was kept mercifully occupied throughout the remainder of the morning. Noon was fast approaching when she heard the familiar clarion call of the train whistle. It was generally acknowledged that the sound, coming as it did at all hours of the night and day, was responsible for the town's inordinately high birth rate. The thought made her mouth curve into a rueful little smile.

"What the hell's got you looking all moony-eyed?" a masculine voice reached out to her from the doorway.

Startled, Caley jumped up from her seat behind the desk. The bottle of ink she had been using rolled off the edge, clattering to the floor and sending a spray of the indelible black liquid all over the tops of her boots.

"Damn you, Matt Griffin, now see what you've done!" she cried reproachfully, her eyes flashing across at him as she lifted her skirts above her ankles.

The object of her wrath merely gave a low chuckle and tipped his hat farther back upon his head.

"I figured you'd be all riled up about last week," he remarked lazily, referring to the fact that he had not been to see her in a while. He stepped inside, his boots adding to the layer of dust which always caked the floor. To Caley's way of thinking, it had long ago taken on a life of its own.

"Riled up? Quite the contrary," she denied with a proud toss of her auburn curls. "At least not until you showed up!" She grabbed a piece of toweling stuffed behind the counter and bent down to impatiently wipe the ink from her boots.

"Come on now, Mac, that's no way to treat me after I rode all the way into town just to see you," said Matt, grinning broadly. Blond and blue-eyed and standing at six feet even, he was attractive in a sort of "bad boy" way. He could ride and rope with the best of them, could hold his liquor almost as well as the tough old man who had sired him. His reputation as a hellraiser was well known—*and* well earned.

"You're lying through your teeth," accused Caley, though without any real malice. "I happen to know you spent the night in jail!"

Straightening again, she tossed the ink-stained cloth back down behind the counter and planted her hands on her hips to confront the fair-haired cowboy with the obvious error of his ways. She proceeded to light into him but good, as if he were Billy's age instead of a grown man some five years older than herself.

"You couldn't have wanted to see me too awful much, you mule-brained idiot, not if you had time to go and get yourself roaring drunk! And on top of that, you were arrested for it! Are you looking to follow Otis Snyder's example? 'Drunk and disorderly,' I believe the charges were, and—"

"I guess you heard all this from that smooth-talking bastard over at the jail, didn't you?" Matt ground out, his previous good humor replaced by a sudden, highly explosive fury. Stalking forward, he took hold of Caley's arms and demanded with harsh insistence, "Did Brody come by here last night to tell you I was locked up? By damn, if he came running to you—"

"He didn't come running to me!" She jerked away and folded her arms indignantly across her breasts. "Although he might have done so, since you made a point of spilling my name to him! What blasted good did you think that would do?"

"Hell, Mac, I was drunk!"

"And I just naturally come to mind when you're drunk, is that it?" she retorted with bitter sarcasm. Her beautiful face flushed with an anger she did not fully understand, she narrowed her eyes up at him and feelingly proclaimed, "Well let me tell you something, Matt Griffin. If you can't stop behaving like some spoiled, wet-behind-the-ears boy, don't bother thinking of me at all! I have better things to do than worry about you getting yourself thrown in the damned pokey! You're lucky the new marshal didn't leave you there to rot. He's not like Ed Tickner, you know—he'd just as soon shoot you as look at you!" she concluded, knowing full well it was an idle threat.

93

"What the hell makes you such an expert on this sonofabitch Brody?" growled Matt. "He only got into town yesterday!"

"Maybe so, but he's already made it clear he plans to make some changes around here!"

"Is that a fact?" Something in her voice made him eye her suspiciously. "How is it you know what his plans are? I heard some talk at the saloon last night about the two of you having some kind of set-to, but I didn't put much salt in it. Seems I was wrong!"

"As usual!" she countered tartly. Pushing past him, she marched to the window and turned her fiery gaze outward. She was unprepared for the way Matt, grinding out a curse, suddenly grabbed her and spun her back around to face him.

"What happened between you and the marshal?" he bit out. His blue eyes gleamed with a feral light, and his youthful, rough-hewn features had taken on a look that boded ill for any man who dared tangle with his woman.

"Nothing! And take your hands off me, you—"

"You'd better not be lying to me!" he warned, his fingers digging mercilessly into her soft flesh. He lowered his head so that his face was mere inches from her own. "If I thought for one minute he—"

"Blast your hide, I told you nothing happened!" she reiterated in a voice that was fairly choked with anger.

Wrenching away from him again, she balled her right hand into a fist and hit him square on the jaw. He cursed and took an involuntary step backward, then stood fingering the reddened spot on his face while leveling a resentful glare at Caley.

"What the hell did you do that for?"

"You know damned good and well!" she shot back. Her color high and her eyes still ablaze, she furiously raked a wayward strand of hair from her forehead. "You've no right to . . . to *interrogate* me

94

as though I owed you an explanation! I won't put up with that from anyone, not even you! And I'll be hanged if I'll let you manhandle me ever again! You don't own me, Matt Griffin!"

"Not yet," he allowed with a dark scowl, "but I will someday!"

"Don't be so sure!"

"What the devil's that supposed to mean?"

"Exactly what it sounds like!"

She spun about and resumed her seat at the desk, practically throwing herself into the chair while struggling to regain control over her raging emotions. As her anger began to evaporate, she began to feel heartsore about what had taken place. It always pained her to quarrel with Matt, and yet neither of them could seem to help flaring up whenever they were together of late. Things had changed . . . and she didn't know why.

Watching her, Matt waged a battle with his own feelings. There were times when he longed for the old Caley, the wild, free-spirited girl who had been as good a friend and companion as any man. Yet, there were other times when he wanted her to be all woman, times when he found himself wishing she could be a little more like the women down at Dobe Row. His eyes glinted hotly at the thought of her lying all soft and sweet for him on one of those big brass beds Miss Sadie kept in her "special" rooms. . . .

Cursing again, he bent and swept his hat up off the floor.

"When's the next stage due back in?" he asked Caley, his voice tight as he fought down a surge of pure, unbridled lust.

"Five o'clock," she answered dully. Staring down at the papers before her, she was blissfully unaware of the way Matt's gaze virtually devoured her. Tears swam in her eyes, but she blinked them back with a

95

vengeance. "Hank's bringing in an important ship-ment from Carlin," she added in an effort to sound composed. "I'll rest a lot easier when—when he shows up."

"Aw hell, Mac, let's just forget what was said," Matt suggested, giving a heavy sigh and slapping his hat against his leg. "Why don't you ride on out to the ranch with me? You can get back in plenty of time. Besides," he confided with a sudden, disarming grin, "Pa's been chewing on me but good for not bringing you out last week."

"I'm sorry, Matt," she declined, shaking her head. "Not today."

"Then how about Saturday?" he persisted. He moved forward and leaned an arm on top of the counter, his eyes full of a warmth Caley neither suspected nor desired. "You're not taking the run yourself, are you?"

"No." She released a long, pent-up breath and finally looked up at him. "All right," she capitulated, smiling faintly. "Tell your father I'll be out on Satur-day."

"He'll be glad to hear it." He raised his hat to his head and tugged the brim low in front. "I'll be by for you after breakfast."

She nodded wordlessly. Her gaze met his at last, and she was perplexed by the strong feeling of uneasi-ness which suddenly crept over her. She thought for a moment that Matt was going to say something else, but he did not. He merely turned and strode from the office, his boots sounding out his departure on the dusty wooden planks outside.

Caley's eyes were clouded with mingled distress and confusion as she stared after the man who had been her friend since childhood. Why, oh why had she flown at him that way? she lamented with a sigh. Mentally shaking herself, she picked up the pen again. She did her best to put the disturbing incident

96

from her mind and get on with her work—but without much success. Matt's accusatory words continued to echo in her brain, just as memories of her own tempestuous behavior came back to haunt her over and over again.

Finally, after finding it impossible to concentrate for any worthwhile length of time, she abandoned her efforts and set off to perform the last of her errands. Anything, she decided, was better than staying cooped up in the office and being alone with her chaotic thoughts.

Shading her eyes against the sun's brightness as she stepped through the doorway, she reached hastily back inside for her hat. It had belonged to her father and bore no resemblance at all to the befeathered, beribboned headgear selected by most young women her age, but she loved its broad-brimmed floppiness and never climbed atop a stagecoach without it. She liked to credit both the hat and her custom-made whip with her good fortune as a driver—they were the closest things to lucky charms she had ever possessed—although there was no denying she'd never have been able to handle the reins without benefit of her father's expert guidance and instruction.

Locking the door behind her, she headed straight-away toward Elko's "Chinatown," a small collection of ramshackle buildings down near the red-light district. Here could be found the town's small but industrious population of Chinese immigrants, made up mostly of railroad laborers who had remained behind to start a new life. A number of women and children had joined the men in the past few months, so that the place was finally beginning to take on a much-needed air of respectability. None of these "foreigners" seemed to mind the fact that they were living within a stone's throw of a present-day Sodom and Gomorrah; if they did mind, they chose not to speak of their dissatisfaction. There was enough bigotry and resentment being harbored against them already.

Entire families participated in the running of the laundries and restaurants and teahouses. Caley had grown quite fond of a certain Mr. Ling and his wife and four sons, all of whom helped to operate the laundry begun by him over a year and a half ago. He had worked hard for many months, living quite simply and saving nearly every penny he earned in order to bring his family to Elko. The eldest of his sons was not yet ten, while the youngest, named Chu, was five. It was he who opened the door to admit Caley.

"Good afternoon, Chu," she told him politely, stepping into the tiny, curtain-walled front room that smelled strongly of lye soap and vinegar. Greeted as she always was with the traditional bow, she returned it by lowering her head and bending forward at the waist. She straightened again and smiled down at the solemn, raven-haired little boy. "Will you please tell your father I've come for my laundry?"

He said nothing, but nodded in response and scampered back to the rear of the building where the actual washing and pressing was done. Caley could hear the child speaking to his father, though she had no earthly idea what he was saying. All four boys loved to show off their newly acquired English when exploring about the town, but Chinese was still the customary language in the home.

Mr. Ling himself came hurrying forward a brief instant later. He pushed through the curtains and bowed to Caley, his face lighting with a smile of genuine warmth.

"Good day to you, Miss Caley!" On his tongue, her name became two separate and distinct syllables — *Kay Lee*. "I have your laundry, I have it here!" he announced eagerly, handing her the folded clothing wrapped in brown paper.

He stood only an inch or two above five feet in

height, and he wore his hair braided into a single pigtail that hung down to the middle of his back. His attire was much the same as the others who shared his Oriental heritage—a plain black tunic and pants, a brimless black cap, and black cloth shoes.

"Thank you, Mr. Ling," replied Caley. She took the packet from him and warned with mock severity, "I brought along plenty of money this time, so don't you go telling me I don't owe you anything!"

"But you are my friend, Miss Caley!" he protested, vigorously shaking his head. "I do not forget your kindness to me!"

"I am glad of that, but you still must allow me to pay you. You'll never get rich if you keep refusing your customers' money!" she scolded with a teasing smile.

"Ah, but I do not try to get rich," Mr. Ling told her in all seriousness. His eyes met hers, and she could have sworn she glimpsed a mischievous twinkle in their dark brown depths. "To be rich with money brings only trouble. Do you not think it is better to be rich with love?"

"Why, I—I suppose so," she murmured with sudden difficulty, embarrassed to feel herself coloring. Mr. Ling was instantly contrite.

"Please to forgive me, Miss Caley!" he begged, his features crestfallen. "I do not wish to cause you unhappiness!"

"You've caused me no unhappiness, Mr. Ling," she assured him while managing a quick smile. Reaching into the pocket of her dress, she withdrew a generous payment for the work he had done and pressed it into his unwilling hand. "There! Now let's have no more talk about your being beholden to me. I expect to be treated the same as anyone else!"

"Ah, but that is not possible!" he retorted, his eyes crinkling with laughter.

Caley found his good humor irresistible. The smile

which rose to her lips this time was completely voluntary.

"Please tell Mrs. Ling I'll send that mail-order firebox of hers over just as soon as it comes in." She pushed open the door. Sunlight spilled into the warm, steamy room, and the sound of children's laughter was carried inside on the woodsmoke-scented breeze. "There's a run due in from Carlin this afternoon." Even with the advent of the railroad, it still cost less to arrange for goods to arrive by stage.

"I will tell her," declared Mr. Ling. He bowed again and lifted his hand in farewell. "You must come soon, Miss Caley, and share a humble meal with my family and myself!"

Promising that she would do just that, Caley took her leave. She set off for home once more, walking with long, sure strides that carried her back up the street and past the row of adobe buildings where she knew for a fact all sorts of wickedness took place day and night.

She had once sneaked inside *Miss Sadie's* to witness the debauchery firsthand. Although she had been seized with a natural curiosity to know what went on in such "dens of iniquity," the true reason she had done it was to get even with Matt for a remark he had made about the women on Dobe Row being a damn sight prettier than any of Elko's respectable females. She had desired nothing more than to be able to tell him he was wrong.

Her adventure had not been too terribly difficult to achieve, for she had dressed in her buckskins and tucked her long hair up beneath her hat, but it had been an adventure all the same. No one had even noticed her. The town's leading brothel, its ground floor saloon crowded and smoke-filled and reeking with the smell of rotgut and cheap perfume, had proven a disappointment in more ways than one. She had expected to find plush red carpets and crystal chandeliers; what she had found instead were filth-laden bare floors and dirty oil lamps casting a dim, mercifully inadequate glow over the corrupt proceedings.

The majority of the fallen angels, lounging about in various stages of undress, had obviously been lacking in any real enthusiasm. Some of them might have been considered pretty, but they had hidden their natural beauty underneath a thick layer of powder and rouge. The whole atmosphere, in spite of the forced laughter and gay music and open displays of bedroom behavior, had been one of quiet desperation.

Recalling that night, Caley mused that she was fortunate to have spent only five minutes inside the place. She had never told Matt. From then on, however, instead of looking upon the women there with contempt, she had pitied them.

But pity or no pity, she didn't take kindly to hearing that Matt continued to frequent *Miss Sadie's*. The thought of him being fawned over by one of those painted "sisters of sorrow" brought more pain to her pride than it did to her heart. It galled her mightily to realize that the man everyone expected her to marry suffered little or no guilt over being faithless. While it was true they were not officially betrothed, she had still hoped he would quit sowing so many wild oats as he grew older. How could she know for certain he would not go hightailing it back to Dobe Row once they were man and wife?

Frowning darkly, she was about to quicken her steps again when she spied Tripod making his way toward her. He skillfully dodged the wagon wheels and horses' hooves as he ambled across the busy street, his gigantic tail wagging and his tongue hanging out to be coated with dust before he drew it back in again.

"So, you big old scoundrel, did you get enough to

101

eat last night?" asked Caley in a soft tone brimming with affection.

She knelt down to ruffle the thick, brown and black fur about the dog's head. He panted happily and wagged his tail harder, as if he considered her the most wonderful thing in the world. Caley's brow cleared at the sight of his pleasure, and her beautiful face wore an ironic half-smile when she rose to her feet again.

"Walk me home?" she suggested, then was pleased when Tripod silently agreed by leading the way.

She followed, making no effort to keep the hem of her red calico skirts up out of the dirt. The absence of boardwalks in the red-light district did not trouble her, though it was a common complaint among the patrons that there was no relief from the sea of mud whenever it rained. The town fathers apparently did not consider it their duty to provide any extra conveniences for the people there — "let them conduct the devil's business in the swill where it belongs" was a typical reply to the problem.

Caley tightened the strings of her hat when a sudden gust of wind threatened to send it flying. Tripod, padding easily along beside her, never slowed his pace.

"Afternoon, Mac!" someone called out.

She acknowledged Will Ballard's presence with a nod as he went riding past. Several other men offered her a friendly wave or a word of greeting. The women, as usual, merely stared. Although she secretly desired their good favor, she refused to admit feeling anything for them but scorn. After all, she mused with a defiant toss of her head, *they* would never know the freedom she possessed, would never know the pleasure to be gained from driving a six-horse team hellbent for leather across the countryside or simply dressing for comfort instead of torturing themselves with layer upon layer of suffocating frills.

No, her life was far superior to theirs. Far superior.

"It's hotter than hell," she murmured to herself, flinging a disgruntled look up at the relentlessly blazing sun. If only it would rain. . . .

Suddenly, she heard a deep-timbred voice unlike any of the others calling her name. Drawing to an abrupt halt, she whirled about just in time to see Jake Brody sauntering bold-as-you-please out of *Miss Sadie's*.

Chapter V

"I might have known he'd find his way *there!*" Caley muttered beneath her breath.

Her blue-green eyes kindling with an emotion she either could not or would not recognize, she spun back around and set off again. But Jake Brody was not a man so easily ignored. His long, booted strides allowed him to overtake her without employing much haste at all.

"What's your hurry?" he demanded, his hand closing about her arm and forcing her to stop.

"None of your business!" she retorted hotly. She jerked free, her magnificent, fire-spitting gaze daring him to touch her again. "Haven't you got better things to do than to go about accosting the citizens? No, don't bother answering that—I can *see* you've got better things to do!" she charged, giving a furious, pointed nod toward the adobe building he had just exited. Even in broad daylight, there were more than half a dozen horses tied to the hitching post out front.

A smile played about Jake's lips, and his eyes gleamed with sudden comprehension.

"You mean Miss Sadie's place," he drawled, casting a brief, deceptively casual look in that direction. He reached up and tugged the hat from his head. The sunlight danced on his dark brown hair, setting it afire with glints of red and gold. "Well now, Miss McAlister, I'm afraid my job makes it necessary for me to associate with—"

"I'll just bet it does!" she derisively cut him off. "But you don't have to explain anything to me, Marshal Brody, for I don't give a damn!"

"Don't you?" he challenged, his voice dropping to a level meant for her ears only. All traces of amusement vanished, and his gaze darkened as it traveled slowly over her stormy countenance. "I never allow pleasure to interfere with business, Miss McAlister. But if I did, the last place I'd look to find that pleasure would be at Miss Sadie's place."

Warm color crept over her, and she was dismayed to realize that she was trembling from head to toe. *What the devil had he meant by that remark?*

She hastily averted her gaze, breathing an inward sigh of relief that she had something else upon which to fasten it—Tripod. He had paused a short distance ahead and now waited patiently for her to make use of his escort again. Jake's eyes brimmed with amusement when they fell upon the dog.

"Friend of yours?" he asked Caley.

"Yes!"

"What happened to his leg?"

"How the devil should I know?" She whipped off her own hat and proclaimed irritably, "If you've nothing more 'fascinating' to discuss, then I'll be on my way!"

"Is it true you're going to marry Matt Griffin?" he startled her by demanding.

There was something deadly serious about the way he asked it. Caley, her wide and luminous gaze meeting the piercing green intensity of his, felt a small, unaccountable tremor of fear course through her. She swallowed a sudden lump in her throat.

"I fail to see how that's any of your—" she started

to protest, only to break off with an audible gasp when his handsome features grew thunderous.

"Damn it, woman, answer me!" he ordered curtly. He took a menacing step closer. "Is it true?"

"No!" she blurted out, then furiously amended, "I mean—yes! Yes it is! I *am* going to marry Matt Griffin!" It sounded like she was trying to convince herself as well as him, but she was far too provoked at the moment to think about that.

"Like hell you are!" Jake ground out.

His gaze burned down into hers, and she was painfully aware of the fact that she was trembling again. She tried telling herself it was from anger— nothing more.

"Why, you arrogant, overbearing bastard!" she fumed, battling the temptation to haul off and hit him just as she'd done to Matt earlier. *This man would probably hit you back*, an inner voice cautioned smugly. Her eyes flashed and narrowed at the thought. "Once and for all, Jake Brody, you have no blasted right to tell me what to do! I don't need you or anyone else to run my life for me!"

"What you need, you little wildcat, is a man who isn't afraid to stand up to you," he said quietly.

"Oh, and I suppose you think *you're* the man for the job, is that it?" she challenged sarcastically.

"Maybe," he replied with maddening aplomb.

Caley's eyes grew very round. Her heart pounding fiercely within her breast, she was alarmed to find herself unable to think of a suitably scathing retort. She never used to be at a loss for words; quite the contrary. But that was before Jake Brody came along. Fate, she mused bitterly, must have thrown him at her as punishment for some misdeed or another. Yet surely she hadn't done anything so bad as to deserve *this*?

"A word of warning about your 'fiance'," Jake declared grimly, fighting back the urge to grab her and kiss her right there in front of the whole damned town. He cursed himself for the fire in his blood . . . and for the longing in his heart. "Griffin's trouble, Miss McAlister. Take my advice and keep away from him."

"Trouble?" she echoed in surprise, then visibly bristled again. "I don't know what the blazes you're talking about! Why, I've known Matt Griffin since long before my father and I came to Elko, and I—"

"And you're going to marry him," he finished for her in a low, level tone that belied the jealousy raging within him. His eyes were suffused with a dangerous light as he told her, "You'll be making a big mistake if you do."

"And how is it you've come to know Matt so well? You'd never even met him before last night! Hellfire and damnation, how can you possibly learn so much about *anyone* in that piddling amount of time?"

"With some people, that's all it takes." That was true enough, thought Jake. But Smitty had filled him in on Griffin, and a lot of others, back in St. Louis. He smiled inwardly, wondering how good old Smitty could have neglected to make any mention of Elko's most intriguing resident—the beautiful, flame-haired hellion glaring so fierily up at him right now. The thought of her marrying Matt Griffin, or any man for that matter, caused his gaze to smolder with raw emotion. "I know what I'm talking about, Miss McAlister," he insisted evenly. "I've seen his kind before, more times than I care to remember."

"And I've seen yours!" she countered with no lack of spirit. She angrily folded her arms across her chest and gave a short, humorless laugh. "Oh yes, Marshal Brody, I'm all too familiar with men like you . . . men who think it's their God-given right to control everything and everyone around them! Do you think you're the first to come in here and try to change things? Well you're not, not by a long shot! I'll give *you* a word of warning—get out of town before you end up on Boot Hill with all the others!"

She pushed past him to join Tripod again. Although tempted to steal a glance back at Jake, she determinedly kept her eyes fixed straight ahead. She spoke a few soft words to the dog and bestowed a quick pat upon his scruffy head before setting off once more.

Just then, the sound of a woman's scream pierced the hot, moistureless air.

Caley, instinctively tensing in alarm, spun about. Her startled gaze sought Jake's, but he had reacted without hesitation and was already on his way back to *Miss Sadie's*. Following a sudden impulse, Caley took off after him.

The scream had come from one of the rooms on the second floor. Jake drew his gun and entered the building with caution. The saloon was far from crowded at that time of day; only two men stood drinking at the bar, both of whom had propped one booted foot negligently up on the tarnished brass rail along the bottom, while three others sat enjoying the company of "hostesses" at small wooden tables that had been broken and repaired so many times the legs were absurdly uneven.

None of the people in the dimly lit room appeared to find anything unusual about the shrill outcry which had just sounded above. They viewed Jake with equal disinterest as he stepped inside and raised his fathomless green gaze toward the stairs.

"Back so soon, Marshal?" the buxom, brassy-haired woman behind the bar asked with a mockingly seductive smile. It was Miss Sadie herself. "I thought you'd had your say." She poured herself a generous shot of whiskey and sent Jake a look that was both challenging and full of scorn. "But then again, maybe you've changed your mind about my offer—"

Another scream rang out. Jake's features tightened, and his fingers clenched about his gun. He headed up the stairs to investigate, hurrying as much as he dared. His boots connected softly with the worn, dirty carpet on the steps, and his eyes hastily scanned the narrow landing while he moved ever closer to the source of the trouble.

There was little doubt in his mind what was going on — many a time in the past he had found it necessary to intervene when a cowboy, usually liquored up and meaner than hell, decided to vent his unwarranted fury on one of the soiled doves. The sight of their injuries, sometimes fatal, never failed to sicken him. It always required every ounce of self-control he possessed to refrain from giving the cowardly bastards the same cruel treatment they had given the women.

His eyes glinted with vengeful fury as he approached a closed door at the far end of the upstairs hallway. He could hear a woman's pitiful sobs coming from within the room, could hear a man muttering a string of vile curses and staggering drunkenly against the furniture.

Reaching for the doorknob, Jake tried it and found it locked. Yet another scream rent the stale, smoke-scented air, and the unmistakable sound of flesh striking flesh prompted him to take action without further delay.

He lifted a foot and kicked at the door, splintering it clear of the frame with a loud crash. The man inside the room whirled about, leaving the bleeding, half-naked woman he had been beating to crumple into a heap on the floor. Jake leveled his pistol at her assailant.

"Hold it right there!" he ordered tersely. "Step away from her and put your hands up. You're under arrest."

The young, wild-eyed puncher, either too drunk or just too plain stupid to know any better, made the mistake of going for his own gun. He had done no more than grip the handle when Jake fired. . . .

Caley, meanwhile, had burst through the swinging double doors of the saloon downstairs. She gasped in alarm when the shot rang out. *Dear God, he's gone and gotten himself killed*! she thought, then was shocked at the sharp twinge of pain she felt. She started for the staircase, only to feel someone's hand gripping her arm.

"I'll see to it, Miss Caley." The man who spoke was Dan Mitchelson, Ed Tickner's deputy. He had been sitting at one of the tables, but had offered no assistance to Jake.

"Why the devil did you let him go up there alone?" demanded Caley, her tone furious and accusing. She yanked her arm free and turned back to the staircase, just in time to see Jake hauling his prisoner none too gently down the steps.

"Move aside, Miss McAlister," he commanded quietly.

The fight had gone all out of the young hellraiser he prodded onward. Caley's eyes widened with surprise when she noticed the spreading stain of crimson on the sleeve of the man's shirt.

"You shot him," she murmured, stating the obvious as she obeyed and stepped aside.

"I winged him," Jake corrected her with the ghost of a smile. "If I had shot him, he'd be dead." He led the prisoner toward the doorway, remarking to Miss Sadie over his shoulder, "I warned you. Once more and I'll close you down."

"You can't do that!" the amply endowed blonde protested. She bustled forward in a flurry of silk and satin, planting herself right square in Jake's path. "I've got friends in high places, Marshal, don't think I haven't! You go making trouble for me and you'll be sorry! No one closes me down, do you hear? No one!"

Suddenly, the man at the nearest end of the bar launched an unexpected strike upon Jake from behind. He lifted the bottle in his hand and prepared to bring it smashing down against the back of Jake's head. There was no time for Caley or anyone else to raise a warning, no time for Jake to avoid what seemed to be inevitable.

It was Dan Mitchelson who saved him. Acting on instinct, the deputy lunged forward and knocked Jake's would-be attacker to the floor. He grappled with the man for a few moments before finally subduing him with a well-placed blow to the chin. Then, breathing heavily, he climbed to his feet again and met Jake's gaze.

"Thought you . . . you could use some help," he said.

"Thanks," Jake offered solemnly. His eyes fell upon the badge still pinned to Dan's vest. "Are you one of Ed Tickner's men?"

"I was," replied Dan. Of medium height and build, he was a remarkably even-tempered young man with a true sense of justice that his former boss had often ridiculed. He frowned and nodded curtly toward Jake. "But I'm out of a job now."

"Not anymore."

"What are you talking about?"

"Any objections to working for me?" It wasn't just gratitude that prompted him to make the offer. He knew all about each and every one of Sheriff Tickner's deputies. There had been many, and none of them had lasted long.

"You want me to be your deputy?" Dan asked in disbelief. "But, I thought—"

"You thought wrong," Jake told him, smiling faintly. "Get cleaned up and report to the jail."

"Yes sir!" said Dan, scarcely able to believe his good fortune. Five minutes ago, he had thought himself the most miserable, put-upon man on the

112

face of the earth. And now, he was about to be become a Deputy U.S. Marshal. His eyes aglow with excitement, he hurried out of the saloon to follow his new employer's instructions.

Miss Sadie had no choice but to move aside as Jake led his prisoner out into the brilliant sunshine. Caley, unable to resist flashing the angry blonde a triumphant little smile, followed close behind. She caught up with Jake and stole a look at his inscrutable features from beneath her eyelashes.

"Hiring Dan is the first smart thing you've done since you got here," she pronounced dryly.

"That's high praise indeed, coming from you," he drawled. He had holstered his gun, but kept a firm grip on the passive young cowboy's arm. Although he intended to charge the man with attempted murder, he knew how reluctant juries were to convict anyone for beating up the sort of women found in Miss Sadie's place.

"Don't ever let me catch you in that part of town again," he suddenly warned Caley, his eyes glinting like cold steel.

"*What?*" she breathed, her mouth falling open in stunned astonishment. "Why, of all the—"

"You might have been killed, damn it!"

"And so might you!" she pointed out. "Hell's bells, the next thing I know, you'll be telling me it's too dangerous to drive the stagecoach and that I should sit at home with my sewing like other women!"

"That's not a bad idea." His gaze twinkled with roguish amusement before he sobered again. "I mean it, Caley. Stay away from Dobe Row."

"I'll go where I please! And I never gave you permission to call me that!"

"It's your name, isn't it?"

"Of course it is, but that doesn't—"

"Would you rather I called you 'Mac' like Matt Griffin does?" he then asked, his deep voice holding

113

a noticeable edge.

"You leave Matt Griffin out of this!" she demanded as her temper flared anew. "I've known him for more than ten years, and he can call me anything he wants!" That wasn't quite true, but it helped make for a more convincing argument.

"It doesn't suit you," Jake decreed bluntly. "And I think you know as well as I do that we've come too far for me to keep calling you 'Miss McAlister'."

"We've not *come* any distance at all!" she asserted with considerable vehemence. "And we're damned sure not *going* to, either!"

She suddenly had the distinct impression that, if not for the fact that it was necessary for him to maintain his firm grip on the half-conscious prisoner, Jake Brody would gladly have laid hands upon her.

It was this particular, unsettling thought that prompted her to whirl away from him and go striding angrily across the street. She sought refuge in her office once more, where she was only too happy to remain until a half hour before the stage was due in. By that time, she was congratulating herself on having managed to push a certain tall, devastatingly handsome Texan to the back of her mind. It would suit her well if she never set eyes on him again!

"You want me to go on out back, Miss Caley?" asked Billy when he came round at the appointed hour of four-thirty.

Rising from her seat at the desk, Caley frowned a bit at the tenseness of her muscles. She nodded at the boy in the doorway and brought a hand up to rub gently at the back of her neck.

"Yes, Billy. We got a load of hay in today. And you'll need to be sure and give the horses fresh water. I noticed that the trough is getting a mite too green," she finished, her mouth curving into a brief, crooked smile.

"Yes, ma'am." With his usual eagerness, he took

114

himself off to the stables at the rear of the building.

Caley released a faint sigh and wandered over to the window. She gazed outward upon the neverending whirl of activity that was Elko's main street, musing absently that there'd be no recognizing the town in another year or two. It had changed so much in the past six months alone. . . .

"Miss Caley!" It was Billy again. He suddenly materialized in the front doorway, announcing in a voice that was full of boyish excitement, "Miss Caley, the stage is coming!"

"Well, for heaven's sake!" she breathed, hurrying outside to see for herself. "Hank's never made it in this far ahead of schedule!"

Her own eyes soon provided her with the startling evidence. Sure enough, there was Hank Shaughnessy, driving the coach lickety-split down the street as though the very devil himself was giving chase. Humans and animals made a frantic scramble to remove themselves from its path, scattering like so many chickens as the furiously spinning wheels churned up a thick cloud of dust.

Caley's pulse raced with sudden alarm. It wasn't at all like Hank, usually the most imperturbable of men and the most conscientious of whips, to come barreling in like that. *Something was wrong.*

She hastened forward as he pulled the team to a halt. Her trepidation increased tenfold when she saw the look on his face.

"What is it, Hank?" she demanded anxiously.

"We been robbed, Miss Caley!" he proclaimed hoarsely. "Happened not five miles out of town! They got the whole damned shipment!" He quickly secured the brake, handed the reins to Billy, and climbed down to give his stunned employer further bad news. "Them bastards shot the express man! He's lyin' inside with a bullet hole in his shoulder!"

"Dear God!" she whispered in horror, her eyes

flying to the stagecoach. Someone had jerked the canvas curtains to one side, and she could hear what sounded suspiciously like a child crying.

"The passengers are pretty shook up!" Hank told her, hurrying now to help them out of the coach. "And we got a young'un in there that's sick as a dog from all the commotion!"

Caley sprang into action alongside him. A crowd was gathering on the boardwalk by the time the first passenger disembarked. Two men, one woman, and a boy of perhaps four were assisted into the office, where they sank wearily down upon the benches and were grateful for Caley's offer of the coffee and sandwiches Maybelle's cook had brought over a short time earlier. Outside, a couple of the onlookers helped Hank lift the injured guard out of the coach. Someone had already gone running for the doctor— and for the marshal.

Jake and his new deputy arrived on the scene in a matter of minutes, making their way swiftly through the crowd. Dan remained outside to have a word with Hank, while Jake wasted little time in finding Caley. He caught sight of her across the cramped and noisy interior of the office. She had just hurried forward with a damp cloth, and he watched as she knelt to press it gently upon the forehead of the pale, frightened little boy being cradled in his mother's arms.

"There now," Caley murmured to the child in a soothing tone of voice. "You're safe now. No one's going to hurt you."

Her blue-green eyes were full of compassion, and there was a look of such tenderness upon her face that Jake's fierce gaze softened as he crossed the room to her side.

"Miss McAlister?"

"Yes?" she responded, so preoccupied with her concern for the child that she did not realize who had spoken her name. When she turned her head and saw that it was Jake who stood looming over her, she frowned and hastily rose to her feet. "I suppose you've heard?" she asked, though it was in truth more of an accusation than a question.

"I have," he confirmed with a slight furrowing of his own brow. "I need to get some information from you."

"What kind of information?"

"Over here," he insisted. Taking her arm, he led her back behind the counter where they could have a bit more privacy. "This isn't the line's first robbery, is it?" he began. His deep, resonant voice was strangely comforting in the midst of all the pandemonium.

"The first? No," answered Caley, shaking her head. "There was one other, last year when my father was still alive. But . . . well, they didn't get away with much. It was coming in on a run from Highland. Some of the mines around there had just shut down, so there wasn't as much gold as usual."

"How much was on today's stage?"

"I can't tell you that!" she replied with an angry flash of her eyes. Folding her arms beneath her breasts, she lifted her chin to a stubborn angle and declared, "As the local representative for Wells, Fargo and Company, it is my sworn duty to—"

"Your *duty*," Jake masterfully cut her off, "is to cooperate with the authorities. Now how much gold was on that stage?"

Although reluctant to disclose the information he sought, Caley realized she had very little choice in the matter. He was, after all, she reminded herself, a United States Marshal. And then there was the simple, undeniable fact that he was the only lawman in Elko. No one else around at the moment had the power to arrest the road agents—if and when they were caught, of course.

"I was told to expect twenty-five thousand", she finally revealed, making no effort to conceal her displeasure at having to do so. "I can't swear to the exact amount; the line office in Carlin will have to do that. You'll have to ask Hank how much mail he was carrying."

"My deputy's taking care of that."

"Well then, what are you waiting for?" she demanded, her gaze bridling with indignation. "Why aren't you already on your way after those thieving sons of bitches? Hellfire and damnation, they could be in the next county by now and here you stand—"

"It's called 'investigating', Miss McAlister," he informed her with a mocking half-smile. His eyes, however, seared relentlessly down into hers. "I'll find them," he vowed. "But I'll do it my way."

He touched a finger to the front brim of his hat and turned away. Caley stared after him, her pulse racing as she watched his long, sure strides lead him back outside. *I'll find them*, his words still burned in her ears. It struck her once more that he was a man who would stop at nothing to get what he wanted. Nothing.

Musing that she didn't know whether to be relieved or alarmed that Jake Brody was on the case, she returned to the task of seeing that the passengers were made as comfortable as possible. She knew that all but one of them would be putting up over at the Depot Hotel for the night to await the next westbound run in the morning. Although stagecoach travel was not nearly so fast or smooth as going by train, it was still the only means most folks could afford. In today's case, unfortunately, it had proven to be a hazardous means indeed.

A short time later, Caley took herself off to the telegraph office to notify the Wells, Fargo headquarters in California of the robbery. She would also have to let them know that one of their men had been wounded while in the line of duty. The doctor had said that the guard, a man by the name of Adams,

118

stood a pretty good chance of recovery, but he had then secretly confided to Caley that there was a slim possibility the patient would lose his arm before it was all over.

Her beautiful eyes sparked with a blaze of renewed fury when she recalled what Hank had told her about the incident. Neither he nor the express man had been able to move fast enough to prevent the three masked bandits from seizing the shipment.

"Adams raised his shotgun soon as his eyes lit on those bastards," Hank had explained, pulling at one end of his thick brown mustache while his gray eyes narrowed into mere slits. "But they'd come out of nowhere and gotten the draw on us both before we knew what the hell was going on. They didn't give no warning—just shot Adams and ordered me to throw down the box and the mail."

Knowing full well that Hank would have given his very life to ensure the safety of his passengers, Caley offered up a silent prayer of thanks for the fact that the robbers had not made any move toward the coach itself. Hank Shaughnessy was not only one of the best drivers in all of Nevada, he was her friend. She shuddered to think of him lying dead out there in the windswept desert.

Her spirits low and her head aching, she plodded wearily back to the office. Not even the sight of Tripod snoozing on the boardwalk out front could cheer her much. She paused to absently smooth a hand along his back, then stepped inside to find Billy waiting for her in the otherwise empty room.

"Hank said to tell you he's gone on home, Miss Caley. And Dan Mitchelson's in charge over at the jail until Marshal Brody gets back. He wanted you to know in case you need—"

"Back?" she echoed with a frown, instinctively focusing on that one word.

"Yes, ma'am. Marshal Brody's gone off to try and

119

find out who robbed the stage. He didn't take no one with him, neither!" added Billy, his boyish features alight with admiration. "Dan Mitchelson said he— Marshal Brody, I mean—that he's used to working alone and that there's none better when it comes to tracking down killers and robbers and all kinds of desperadoes!"

"And how does Dan Mitchelson know so much about the man who only hired him four hours ago?" she inquired dryly.

"I don't rightly know," the slender, towheaded youth admitted, his brows drawing together for a moment. He smiled again and gave a quick shrug of his shoulders. "Maybe he asked him."

"I don't think that's very likely," Caley opined as she started gathering up the cups and other paraphernalia scattered about the room. "Jake Brody may be the most all-fired *cocksure* man I've ever known, but he isn't one to reveal much of himself." Her turquoise gaze clouded with a combination of resentment and confusion at the thought, but she staunchly pushed it aside and told her young hostler, "You might as well go home, too, Billy. There's nothing more to be done around here till morning."

"Yes, ma'am." He headed for the doorway, but pivoted about to ask on impulse, "Do you think he'll find the men who did it, Miss Caley?" He was surprised to see the way she suddenly tensed.

"I can only hope so," she replied, dumping the whole mess in her arms atop the desk. Somehow, the thought of him coming face to face with the sort of men who'd shoot someone in cold blood made her breath catch in her throat.

"Good night, Miss Caley. See you in the morning!" Billy called out cheerfully as he finally went on his way. To him, the whole thing had been a source of untold excitement, one he would never forget.

"Good night, Billy," Caley murmured after him.

She sank down into the chair and closed her eyes. But there was no respite from her troubled thoughts . . . no escape from the truth. Heaven help her, she was worried about the man she had vowed to hate. And though she tried telling herself that her concern was nothing more than what she would have felt for any other human being, she could not deny the strange heaviness of her heart.

At that same moment, Jake was drawing his mount to a halt a few miles outside of Elko. Darkness would soon be closing in, but for now, the low, rolling hills of the stark summer landscape were turned to gold as the sun emitted its last burst of brilliance for the day. A lone jackrabbit, startled by the human intruding into its silent desert world, bolted into the sagebrush ahead of Jake, zigzagging in long, frightened leaps. Its frantic flight stirred up a pair of mourning doves, whose sudden beating of wings in turn provoked a thick, furious swarming of mammoth horseflies.

Jake swung agilely down from the saddle, maintaining a loose grip on the reins while his horse followed obediently after him. He stood at the spot described by Hank as the scene of the crime. His piercing green gaze took note of the way the road cut straight up across a particularly steep rise in the land before curving sharply back around to the left. According to Hank, the robbers had blocked the route just beyond the curve, as if they'd been well aware of the fact that the driver would already have slowed down the team's pace in order to keep the stagecoach from turning over.

They knew what they were doing, that's for damn sure! he recalled Hank saying. He was inclined to agree.

Bending his tall frame downward, he surveyed the telltale marks left behind in the dust. The wind had not yet erased them. He could clearly make out the coach's path, as well as the hoofprints of the six horses drawing it. Searching a short distance away from the road, he also found the prints of the road agents' horses. Their tracks led away from the hill and down into the narrow valley, toward the brackish, virtually useless waters of the Humboldt River.

Soon thereafter, he came across the green express box. Too heavy to take along, it had been abandoned and now lay near the crest of the hill. The lock had been shot off and the box emptied of its valuable contents. There was no sign of the mail packet.

He straightened again and was about to turn away, when his attention was caught by a sudden flash of light. Looking down, he saw a small silver object resting at the base of a creosote bush. He picked it up and lay it flat in the palm of his hand to examine it closely.

It was the rowel of a spur. How it had broken off was a mystery, but there was nothing mysterious about its cruel purpose. It had obviously been part of what was known as a "Mexican" spur, for its edges were sharp and pointed, instead of blunted like those favored by most cowboys. Whoever had lost it wasn't too concerned about the pain it would inflict upon a horse.

Jake's rugged, sun-bronzed features tightened, his eyes smoldering with grim determination. He closed his hand about the rowel and settled his hat upon his head once more.

Although his duty to uphold the law made him want to see the bastards brought to justice, he could not deny that there was more to it than that. They had robbed a stagecoach belonging to Caley McAlister. For that reason alone, he would have hunted them down.

Damn it, man, she belongs to another! a voice in the back of his mind saw fit to remind him.

"Not yet," he dissented in a low, husky tone. "Not

122

by a long shot."

His gaze burning hotter than ever, he mounted up and rode toward Carlin.

Chapter VI

Caley awoke with a start.

"What the—" she murmured drowsily, tossing back the covers and sliding from the bed. She pushed the tumbling auburn curls from her face and padded out into the other room.

A blinding flash of white suddenly streaked directly across her path, forcing a loud gasp from her lips as her pulse leapt in alarm.

"Shadrach!" she scolded, placing a hand over her wildly pounding heart. "Damn it, cat, you scared the hell out of me!" She subjected him to a furious glare in the darkness, but could not tell whether it had the least effect at all.

The knock, loud and insistent, sounded downstairs again.

Finally realizing what had awakened her, Caley hastened to toss a wrapper about her nightgown-clad shoulders. She did not bother slipping on shoes before she raced down the stairs to see what was going on. Once in the office, she grabbed up the shotgun she kept behind the counter, then approached the front door, where she could make out a man's tall form through the glass.

"Who is it?" she called out.

"Marshal Brody," came the startling answer. "Open up, Miss McAlister."

Good heavens, it's him! The color flew to her cheeks, and she felt an involuntary shiver dance down her spine. Hesitating no longer, she unlocked the door and flung it open.

"What is it?" she demanded breathlessly. "Did you find the—"

"Inside," he cautioned, his eyes gleaming down at her in the moonlit darkness.

Moving aside, she allowed him to enter and closed the door. She leaned the shotgun in the corner, belted her plain blue cotton wrapper at the waist, and turned back to face Jake. Instead of telling her straight out what he had come to tell her, he threw the bolt on the door and pulled the shade. He had just struck a match to light the lamp when the clock in the apartment upstairs chimed the ungodly hour of two.

"Well?" Caley prodded with growing impatience. "Have you found the men who robbed my stage?"

"No," he admitted quietly.

"Well then, what the devil are you doing here at this time of night?" She had no idea how young and lovely and desirable she looked, standing there with her bright hair cascading softly down about her and her bare feet visible beneath the hemline of her white cotton nightgown.

"I've been to Carlin and back. I thought you might like to know some of the gold has already turned up." His gaze darkened to jade as it raked over her adorable dishabille. He cursed the fire in his loins, cursed doubly the way his heart moved at the sight of her.

"How do you know that?" she asked with a frown of disbelief. "Gold is gold. There's no way you can be sure it's part of my shipment."

"Yes there is." He reached into his shirt pocket and withdrew a twenty-dollar gold piece. Holding it out to her, he explained, "The Wells, Fargo agent in

126

Carlin noticed this and two others like it when he was filling the box yesterday. He made mention of them when I questioned him a few hours ago."

Caley took it from him and moved closer to the lamp's glow. She noticed that the coin was badly discolored, an unusual sight indeed given the fact that it was solid gold. She knew gold was rarely affected by anything.

"What on earth could have marked it like this?" she wondered aloud.

"Acid, most likely," he replied, taking the piece of evidence back from her and returning it to the safekeeping of his pocket. "The important thing is, it was already like that when it headed out with the rest of the gold aboard your stagecoach. Whoever stole the shipment has obviously been in the Senate Saloon tonight."

"You found this at the Senate?" Her eyes widened in surprise, then blazed with vengeful fury at the thought of the robbers living it up right there in Elko while the man they had shot lay fighting for his life only a little farther down the street.

"The bartender took note of it and set it aside for the owner to take a look at later," Jake told her, a faint smile of irony touching his lips. "He wasn't too happy about surrendering a twenty-dollar gold piece as evidence. And he can't seem to remember who gave it to him."

"By damn," seethed Caley, "I'll kill them myself if I ever find out who they are!"

"No you won't," he calmly insisted. "They'll get the fair trial they're entitled to under the law."

"The only thing those bastards are 'entitled' to is the biggest necktie party this town has ever seen!"

"You don't mean that." He was gazing down at her with such somber intensity that she took an instinctive step backward. "In spite of the tough act you put on, Caley McAlister, you've a soft heart."

"I have not!" she denied, then blushed at both the lie and the childish vehemence with which she proclaimed it.

"And that's not the only thing about you that's soft," he added as though she had not spoken at all.

He slowly closed the distance between them again, his eyes suffused with a warm glow and his handsome face wearing a strangely unfathomable expression that set off a warning signal in Caley's brain. She caught her breath on a soft gasp and retreated until her back came up against the counter.

"When are you going to stop pretending you're a man?" Jake challenged in a low, vibrant tone that made her pulse leap wildly.

Feeling scorched by the warmth emanating from his powerfully muscled hardness, she muttered an oath and tried to push past him. His strong fingers closed about her shoulders, holding her captive while his gaze burned down into hers.

"You're a woman, Caley. It's time someone made you remember that."

"Is that so?" she countered scornfully. "And I suppose you're volunteering for the job?"

"Maybe," he replied without smiling, though his eyes were full of an intoxicating mixture of warmth and amusement and—*God help her*—desire.

Fiercely determined to resist the manly charm she was so sure he'd used on countless other women, she gave a proud, defiant toss of her head and brought her hands up to push him away.

"Why, you conceited Texas jackass! I don't need anyone to remind me of anything, and even if I did, you'd be the last man on earth I'd call upon to do it!"

She broke free and took refuge behind the counter—as if even that formidable barrier would make any difference to a man like Jake Brody. Standing there like a beautiful young tigress preparing to defend herself against a hungry predator, she would not for one moment acknowledge the liquid fire racing through her own veins.

"Good night, *Marshal*!" she announced pointedly. "Thanks for the information, but the next time you want to talk to me, you can damned well do it in the daytime! Now get out of here!" she finished, emphasizing her demand with a curt nod toward the door. "Go on, get out!" She jerked the edges of her wrapper more closely about her and waited to see if Jake would comply.

He did not.

"Damn it, woman, I've had enough of these games between us!" he ground out, the light in his eyes boding ill for the flame-haired spitfire who had captivated him with her beauty and taunted him with her spirit at every turn.

"I don't know what you're talking about!"

"Don't you?"

He rounded the corner of the counter now, prompting Caley to inhale sharply and make a desperate flight toward the stairs. He caught her easily, his hands seizing her arms in a grip that was firm and yet surprisingly gentle. She struggled, but he was in no mood to let her go.

"There's something between us, Caley," he asserted, shaking her a little as he forced her about to face him. "I don't know what the hell it is, but it's there just the same. And it's high time we both stopped denying it!"

"No!" she cried, twisting futilely in his grasp. "Take your blasted hands off me and get out!"

"Not until I've made you admit you feel it, too!"

With that, he fiercely swept her up against him and captured her lips with his own. He proceeded to kiss her quite thoroughly, his warm mouth conquering the moist sweetness of hers while his arms tightened possessively about her slender, beguilingly curved softness. She fought him as best she could — but her best simply wasn't good enough. Balling her hands into fists, she could only manage to beat at his back with a disgusting weakness that made her suffer a sharp pang of self-loathing. At the same time, however, a low moan of surrender rose in her throat.

Jake showed her no mercy. His hands swept downward, his fingers curling tightly, urgently about the shapely roundness of her buttocks while his hot, velvety tongue slipped between her parted lips. She gasped when her thighs, protected only by two thin layers of cotton, came into contact with the undeniable evidence of his manhood. Her eyes flew open in startlement, her heart pounding in growing alarm as well as excitement.

Dear Lord, did Jake Brody mean to ravish her right there and then? she wondered dazedly. The possibility that he did set up a veritable whirlwind of conflicting emotions within her.

Before she could do anything more than push feebly against him, she was literally swept off her feet. The spell was temporarily broken when his mouth relinquished the well-conquered softness of hers. She knew she should be thankful for the reprieve — so why then did she feel so terribly disappointed?

But, as she soon discovered, Jake was not through with her yet. While she was striving to recover her voice, he took a seat in the chair and settled her upon his lap. His hard, sinewy arms imprisoned her there when she tried to rise.

"No!" she protested breathlessly. Her cheeks flamed at the shocking intimacy of her position. Confusion joined with passion's glow to set her beautiful eyes afire. "Let me go, damn you!" she choked out, panic bringing a return of her defiance.

Jake's only response was to entangle a hand in the

luxuriant thickness of her auburn curls and bring his lips down upon hers once more. He kept one arm locked about her hips, his fingers digging into the soft flesh of her wriggling bottom as his kisses once again forced her into submission.

Try as she would, Caley could not find the strength to resist him. She had never been kissed the way Jake Brody kissed her. She had certainly never been kissed while sitting half-naked on a man's lap in the middle of the night. The experience was far from being unpleasant; she was in truth aghast to find herself enjoying it so much. But no matter how much the inner voice of reason screamed at her to put a stop to the sweet madness, she found herself melting against her devilishly handsome tormentor, returning his kisses with an ever-increasing willingness that both amazed and frightened her.

Jake felt his own passions blazing dangerously near the point of no return. He wanted the beautiful wildcat in his arms more than he'd ever wanted any woman, wanted to kiss and caress her until she begged for mercy . . . until she burned for him every damned bit as much as he burned for her. Right or wrong, she was in his blood. Right or wrong, he was going to make her realize that she could belong to no other. *She was his!*

Caley was left gasping for breath when he suddenly tore his lips from hers and trailed a fiery path downward to where her pulse beat so wildly at the base of her throat. She clutched at his shoulders for support as he brought his hand around to untie the belt at her waist. He impatiently tugged the front of her wrapper free, then unbuttoned her prim white nightgown with such swift dexterity that, somewhere in the benumbed recesses of her mind, she wondered how he had acquired this remarkable expertise at getting women out of their clothes.

She drew in another audible breath when the

cool, lamplit air touched her feverish skin. Jake swept aside the liberated edges of her nightgown, baring the upper portion of her breasts. She cried out softly when he lowered his head and pressed a series of warm, tantalizing kisses upon her naked flesh.

Her hips squirmed restlessly atop his granite-hard thighs and her eyes swept closed as wave after wave of near painful ecstasy washed over her. Her fingers curled almost convulsively about his shoulders, her head falling back so that her long hair cascaded down her back like a shimmering, fiery red curtain.

Jake's hand came up to close upon one of her breasts. His masterful touch seared her through the thin cotton, and she bit at her lower lip to suppress a moan when he caressed her full, rose-tipped flesh with a demanding yet gentle passion. His mouth soon replaced his hand—her eyes flew open when it suddenly closed about her breast. She shivered deliciously when she felt the moist heat of his tongue flicking across her nipple, and she gasped again when his lips tenderly suckled her breast through the flimsy barrier of her nightgown.

Just when she was certain she could bear no more of the exquisite torture, his mouth returned to roam ardently across the flushed smoothness of her face. His fingers delved into her glorious tresses once more, and it was only a mercifully brief instant before his lips captured hers in a kiss that was even more rapturously intoxicating than its predecessors.

Swept away by sensations she had never known to exist, Caley felt her head spinning. There was such a fierce, unfamiliar yearning deep inside her that she found herself alternately wanting to cry for a release from the splendid agony, and beg for it to never stop. It was all happening with such wild impetuosity, there was no time to think, no time to consider how she was going to hate herself after letting Jake

Brody do the things he was doing to her.

She was scarcely aware of the moment when he pulled the folds of her nightgown and wrapper upward. She wore no undergarments. Jake seized full advantage of her delectable nakedness, his hand smoothing upward along the satiny curve of her thigh. She blushed to the very roots of her hair when his fingers stroked appreciatively over her bare bottom. Squirming anew, she lifted a hand to push at his arm in a halfhearted protest.

Her objection achieved results, but not those she had intended. As her father would have put it, she went "from the frying pan to the fire." Instead of sparing her further embarrassment, Jake trailed his hand purposefully back across her hips and around to the flat, silken planes of her abdomen. Then, his fingers crept downward . . .

Caley inhaled sharply, her whole body tensing when he touched her at the very core of her womanhood. The most powerful surge of pleasure she had ever known coursed through her body like wildfire. *Heaven help her, what was happening?*

Frightened, she tore her lips from Jake's. She arched her back in a desperate attempt to prevent his wickedly evocative caress, but she succeeded only in allowing him even greater access to her soft, trembling charms. He slipped one arm about her waist and urged her farther upward, his lips branding the conveniently placed fullness of her breasts while his other hand traveled back down to the triangle of silky auburn curls between her thighs.

Caley struggled to escape the inevitable. She was shocked to feel her legs parting of their own accord. In spite of her battle against her own accursedly feminine weakness, she clung to Jake as if she were drowning, her breath coming in soft gasps and every inch of her body tingling. The spark of desire which had been kindled within her now blazed to a white-hot flame. She made one last valiant effort to fight against passion's sweet fury, but it was too late. A breathless cry broke from her lips as, suddenly, the flame shattered into a thousand tiny stars.

Miraculously, Jake was the one who called a halt to the madness.

The darkness of character which is in every man told him that the woman in his arms was ripe for the taking, that he'd be worse than a fool if he didn't seize this opportunity. But it was no use. No damned use at all.

In the end, it wasn't just honor or duty that prompted him to set her free before he had made her his. It was something else . . . something else he could not quite put a name to but was there all the same. Never, in all the years since he had become a man, had he found himself backing down from the sort of challenge she presented — at least not when things had gone this far. Why the devil was it so different with this woman?

You know the reason, an inner voice remarked sagely. *You've known from the very first.*

With an inward groan, Jake forced himself to release her. The supreme effort of will it cost him was reflected by the abrupt darkening of his eyes, but the only thing Caley took note of was the almost savage expression on his handsome face.

It suddenly occurred to her that he hadn't really wanted to ravish her at all. His kisses and caresses had probably stemmed from nothing more than a desire to exert his will over her, to show her the truth of his male superiority. Yes, by damn, she fumed in stormy-eyed silence as her rage took flight, Jake Brody had used her own blasted femininity against her! He had humiliated her for his own enjoyment — and for that, she would never forgive him.

"Let go of me, you rakehelling son of a bitch!"

134

she demanded wrathfully.

She pushed at him with such violence that she slipped off his lap and would have toppled to the floor if not for his arms catching her in time. But she was not of a mind to feel grateful.

"Don't touch me, damn you! Don't ever touch me again!" She jerked away from him and rose unsteadily to her feet, her eyes blazing their magnificent blue-green fire and her hair streaming down about her in a tangled mass of equally fiery curls. Masking her pain with anger, she furiously tied the wrapper about her again and declared in a tremulous voice, "I hate you, Jake Brody! Now get out of my office before I forget I'm only a poor, helpless *woman* and give you worse than you'd get from any man!"

Jake had risen to his own feet by now and stood gazing steadily down at her. He couldn't blame her for being angry; he couldn't even blame himself for having lost his head. She was enough to tempt a saint — *and heaven knew he was no saint.*

"I'll go," he agreed in a quiet, resonant tone that made her shiver anew in the lamplit coolness. He picked up his hat and lifted it to his head. "But I'll be back."

"You come back and you're a dead man!" threatened Caley, folding her arms across her breasts. She was surprised to glimpse the faint smile playing about his lips.

"There are some who'd say I've already bitten the dust," he drawled enigmatically. He tugged the front brim of his hat lower and subjected her to one last long, smoldering look. "Good night, Caley McAlister."

"Go to hell!"

Resisting the temptation to grab her again and kiss the fire out of her, Jake swore silently and headed for the door. Caley glared at the broad

135

target of his retreating back, her gaze bright with unshed tears as she watched him leave.

The instant the door closed behind him, she hurried forward to throw the lock. *Do you really think that would stop him*? a little voice inside her taunted.

"Shut up!" she hissed aloud.

She whirled away from the door with a vengeance, blew out the lamp, and flew back up the stairs. Once safely ensconced in the tiny quarters above, she threw herself face down upon the bed. She pounded at the unresisting softness of her pillow — secretly wishing it was Jake Brody's handsome face — and wept hot, bitter tears that would no longer be denied.

Shadrach's curiosity was aroused by the sounds of her distress. He took it upon himself to offer some measure of consolation. His one green eye and one blue gleaming, he approached the bed, took a flying leap upward, and landed in the middle of Caley's back. She gasped and rolled over.

"Oh Shadrach!" she murmured brokenly, catching the large white feline up in her arms. She clutched him to her bosom while the tears continued to roll unheeded down her flushed cheeks. "What am I going to do? What the devil am I going to do?" she asked in a hoarse whisper. Her arms tightened about the cat as she sat up and began to rock gently back and forth.

Shadrach gave a loud rumble of protest. Scrambling free, he leapt down from the bed and returned to his favorite perch in the window. Caley was alone in her misery then . . . alone to curse herself over and over again for her weakness . . . alone to wonder why her heart ached so terribly.

Two days later, she went out riding with Matt as

planned. They headed away from Elko just before nine o'clock on that cool Saturday morning, their horses lively in the brisk, sagescented air and the clouds above offering a hopeful promise of rain later in the day.

"Heard any more about the robbery?" asked Matt once they were well away from town.

"No," Caley replied, shaking her head.

Her eyes clouded with the sudden pain of remembrance. She had neither seen nor spoken to Jake Brody since the night he had humiliated her—though he had been in her mind with damnable frequency. She was naturally curious to know what sort of progress he was making in his investigation, but she stubbornly refused to seek him out.

"What about the guard?" Matt then asked. "Is he going to make it?"

"Yes, thank God," she answered with an audible sigh of relief. "Doc says his arm's healing just fine. He'd have been dead if those bastards had aimed an inch lower." Her gaze kindled with renewed fury at the thought of the robbers. Close on the heels of that thought came one of Jake. "I just hope he catches them!"

"Who? Brody?" His mouth curved into a smile of pure contempt. "That sonofabitch couldn't find his own butt in a dust storm!"

"What makes you say that?" demanded Caley, her voice holding an inexplicable note of defensiveness. She tightened her hold on the reins and shifted in the saddle. "From what I've heard, Marshal Brody has a lot of experience. And he damn sure knows how to handle a gun!"

"Yeah, well from what *I've* heard, he likes to shoot first and ask questions later," Matt scoffed with a dark frown.

"That's a bunch of claptrap!" she proclaimed in disgust.

"Is it?" he shot back, raking the hat from his blond head and slamming it down against his denim-clad thigh. "Could be you don't want to hear the truth about him! Damn it, Mac, don't tell me you've been taken in by that holier-than-thou act he puts on!"

"I've not been 'taken in' by any blasted thing!" she adamantly denied, then fell silent while the lie echoed in her brain. She turned her troubled gaze upon the towering, snow-topped peaks of the Ruby Mountains in the near distance while the memory of those few, wickedly pleasurable moments she had spent in the lawman's arms came back to haunt her once more.

Matt's blue eyes glittered hotly as they moved over his beautiful riding companion. She had chosen to wear her buckskins that day, perhaps because she knew damned good and well how much his father disapproved of women parading about in trousers. She had always taken pleasure in defying authority of any kind; that was one of the first things he'd learned about her. And whereas he used to be enchanted by her rebellious, headstrong nature, he had found himself wishing more and more of late that she could be a bit less peculiar in her behavior. Particularly where the new marshal was concerned.

"Whatever your opinion of the man," said Caley, unable to leave the subject of Jake Brody behind just yet, "you can't deny that he's got things stirred up around here! He's gone and hired Dan Mitchelson as his deputy, and George Groat told me only yesterday that the whole town's talking about how he fills the jail every night—without killing anyone, I might add. And it looks like even Ed Tickner's decided not to cause trouble for him!"

"That's what you think," muttered Matt. He gave a short, malevolent laugh. "It might interest you to know old Ed's been rounding up a mob to run

138

Brody out of town. And there's no shortage of volunteers."

"*What*?" Caley gasped in wide-eyed startlement. She reined to a sudden halt and watched as Matt did the same. "Good heavens, you don't mean they're actually going to—"

"What the hell difference does it make to you?" he challenged tersely, his own eyes narrowing in suspicion. "You still seem to be taking a damn sight too much interest in Brody's welfare!"

"But he's a federal man!" she hastened to point out, ignoring the bitterly jealous accusation he leveled at her. "If they try and do anything to him, the governor will have their hides!"

"Not if my father's one of them," Matt offered with smug assurance. He raised the hat to his head again and smiled at Caley. "He and the governor go way back, remember?"

"Yes, but—"

"But nothing," he cut her off. "If Pa takes it in mind to see Brody tarred and feathered—or worse—then you know as well as I do there's no one going to stop him!"

"You're wrong, Matt! There are a lot of people in Elko who won't just stand by and do nothing, even if it is Isaiah Griffin who's calling the shots!"

"Are you one of them? Are you willing to side with that bastard against your own friends?"

Caley bristled at the reproach in his voice. She also took considerable exception to the way he kept grilling her about Jake Brody. There was no doubt he suspected something; but what the hell was there to suspect?

"I might be!" she finally retorted, her eyes flashing beneath the broad, floppy brim of her hat.

"You don't mean that!"

"How do you know what I mean?" It was her turn to fling some charges. "You hardly ever come around anymore, and I can't even remember the last time you rode into town without first heading over to *Miss Sadie's*!"

"That's none of your business!" he growled, his attractive features growing surly.

"It is if I'm going to be your wife!" Her words lacked conviction, but Matt didn't seem to notice.

"Well if you're going to sound like a wife, then you might as well start *acting* like one, too!"

Before Caley could ask him what he meant, his arm shot out to clamp about her waist. She was practically yanked out of the saddle as his lips came crashing down upon the startled softness of hers.

Although her first instinct was to resist the way she always did, she forced herself to rest passively against him. Somewhere in the back of her mind, it occurred to her that she needed to know if Matt's kisses could set her afire the way Jake Brody's did.

Alas, they did not.

There was no answering passion within her, none of the wild, desperate yearning she had felt when Jake had kissed her. With Matt, she felt nothing but a sharp pang of disappointment.

How could this be true? she asked herself numbly. She and Matt Griffin had shared a special bond for years, a bond which they had both always believed would someday lead to an even deeper one. Why then was the touch of his lips upon hers so unpleasurable?

God help her, but she could think only of the dashing Texas rogue who had showed her, for the first time, what it truly meant to be a woman. . . .

"Damn it, Mac, when are you going to marry me?" Matt demanded once his mouth left off its highly practiced yet ultimately dissatisfying conquest of hers. His tone was tinged with a certain huskiness that gave evidence of his growing frustration. "When the hell are you going to stop torturing me this way?"

"Torturing you?" Caley echoed in bewilderment. She pulled away and lowered her hips to the curve of the saddle once more, her face warm with guilty color. "I—I don't know what you're talking about." Her fingers trembled as they gathered up a tighter hold on the reins.

"Like hell you don't!" he ground out, his eyes blazing with raw emotion. "I want you, damn it! I've been patient long enough!"

His words struck fear in Caley's heart. She frantically searched for a way to smooth things over, to turn the conversation away from such dangerous ground.

"Oh Matt, please," she implored him, though her voice held an undeniable edge. "Let's not quarrel any more!"

"You can't run away from me forever," he warned grimly. His gaze was full of barely controlled violence as it bored across into the wide, luminous depths of hers. "Sooner or later, I'm going to get tired of waiting. And then, by damn, I'm going to take you!"

He angrily spurred his horse into a sudden gallop, leaving Caley to waver indecisively between going after him and returning to town. She heaved a long, disconsolate sigh before finally choosing the former. There was nothing to gain by taking the coward's way out.

Some time later, after she and Matt had fallen into an uneasy truce, she was surprised to see a flock of sheep grazing contentedly atop one of the low, rolling hills in the distance. It was a common enough sight elsewhere in the spring and summer months; that was when vast numbers of the animals were being moved eastward to the railheads. A few small "farm" flocks had even been established near Elko this past year, but this part of the county had

141

always been reserved for cattle. And itinerant operators were never welcome.

"I didn't know there were any sheepherders this side of town," remarked Caley, turning to Matt with a frown.

"Sheepherders?" He followed the direction of her gaze, then bit out a blistering oath. "Those dirty Bascos know better than to come this far out!"

"Why do you keep calling them that?" Her frown deepened into one of intense annoyance. She knew very little about the Basques, other than the fact that they had come from a faraway, mountainous region between Spain and France. Most folks took them for Spaniards, and it seemed they had a natural talent for raising sheep. Either that, or they had simply taken on the jobs no one else wanted. Whatever the case, she hated to hear anyone deride them.

"Because that's what they are!" insisted Matt. "Someone needs to teach them once and for all that they can't come tramping in here like they owned the place. Hell, we'll be overrun with the stinking bastards if we don't put a stop to it!" He jerked on the reins and said, "Come on!"

"What are you going to do?"

"I'm going to run them off!"

Caley breathed a curse of her own and reined about to follow him again. She knew all too well what a damnably foul mood he was in—*she* was the one who had put him in it—and she was worried that his temper would boil over at the least little provocation from the herders.

As it turned out, she had good reason to worry.

Matt heard the sheepmen's dog bark a warning as he went thundering down upon them. His face set in a grim mask of determination, he rode straight through the flock of sheep. Their loud, bleating cries of protest rose in the dust-choked air while they scattered out of his path.

142

Caley topped the hill in Matt's furious wake. She gazed down upon the small sunlit camp below, her trepidation growing when she took note of the two young boys flying toward the familiar, straight-sided type of wagon that was favored by the nomads of the plains. It was the only home most herders knew for years on end.

A woman of perhaps twenty, clad in a white blouse and a bright red skirt, stepped down from the wagon and protectively gathered the boys close. The two men who had been tending the sheep hurried down the hill to the camp. They got there just as Matt drew his mount to a halt in front of the wagon.

"You're on Griffin land, damn it!" he snarled. "Now pack up and get the hell out of here!"

Caley drew up beside him, her mind racing to think of a way to prevent disaster. She was painfully conscious of the five pairs of eyes upon hers. Taking note of the fact that neither one of the men was armed, she waited for them to speak. when they did not, she hastened to intervene.

"This is open range, Matt!" she reminded him in an undertone laced with steel. "Please, let's just go!" She laid a hand upon his arm, but he shook it off and flung her a hot, quelling look.

"Stay out of this!" he ordered harshly, then turned back to the solemn-faced people who stood before him without any trace of fear. "You heard what I said—get the hell off my land!"

Still, none of the Basques spoke. Whether it was from defiance, or from a very real ignorance of English, Caley could not tell. She was surprised when, after several long moments, the pretty, raven-haired woman finally exchanged a quiet word with the older man and took a step forward.

"You are Mr. Griffin?" she asked Matt. Her voice was soft and melodious, and her words bespoke a more than passing knowledge of her adopted country's language.

"That's right!" he shot back.

"My father wishes me to tell you we have done nothing wrong."

"Why doesn't he tell me himself?" Matt demanded contemptuously.

"I will ask him."

She proceeded to do just that, while Matt fumed in hard-eyed impatience. Caley could not help but admire the young woman's calm behavior, and she prayed that the blaze of Matt's temper would lessen a bit in the face of it.

The gray-haired man reached up to tug the black beret from his head. Like the younger man beside him, he was dressed in a gathered white shirt tucked into full black trousers. He fixed Matt with a steady, fathomless gaze while his daughter put the question to him. When he answered her, he did so in his own language.

"My father says we are on free land," she then translated. She raised her head proudly, her dark eyes glistening. "And I tell you we know this to be true."

"Do you now?" sneered Matt. "Well, you black-eyed little bitch—"

"Damn you, Matt Griffin, you have no right to speak to her like that!" protested Caley, her own temper flaring in righteous indignation. "This has gone far enough! Either you ride out of here with me right now, or so help me, *I'll never speak to you again*!"

Her threat was not an idle one, and Matt knew it. He knew better than anyone how stubborn and unyielding she could be when it came to such things. Once, he had made the mistake of calling her bluff; he didn't want to make that mistake again. But neither did he want to let her think she

144

could run roughshod over him. It was time she learned who was boss.

"Aw hell, they're not worth it!" he muttered, his lips curling into another sneer. "Let's go."

Caley thought she detected a strange glint of purpose lurking in his gaze, but she nonetheless offered the sheepherders a weak, apologetic smile and reined her horse about. She had ridden only to the crest of the hill again when she realized Matt had lingered behind.

"Matt?"

Drawing to an abrupt halt, she jerked her head about to see that Matt had uncoiled his rope. She called out to him, but he paid her no mind.

With a skill and swiftness borne of much practice, he swung the lariat above his head and roped the water barrel lashed securely to the wagon. He then looped one end of the lariat about his saddlehorn, spurred his mount onward, and brought the lightweight vehicle toppling over on its side with a splintering crash.

Caley's eyes were shooting furious, blue-green sparks as she rode back down the hill. The object of her wrath, however, spared her only a passing glance before rounding on the family of Basques once more.

"You'll get worse next time!" he threatened. "Now get those stinking woolies out of here and don't come back!"

"*Matt Griffin—*" Caley stormed, only to clench her teeth as he went galloping past her without a word. She was fairly quaking with the force of her anger, but she managed to advise the young woman, "I'm sorry! Maybe you'd better do as he says before there's any more trouble!"

"The family of Bertrand Larronde does not run from trouble!" the raven-haired beauty proclaimed feelingly. Her dark eyes were full of unquenchable

145

fire as she glared after Matt. "And we do not frighten so easily as Mr. Griffin believes!"

Caley, gazing down upon the scene of destruction in helpless rage, could think of nothing further to say. She muttered a curse underneath her breath and urged her horse about to follow Matt's burning trail once more.

If not for the fact that Isaiah was expecting her, she would have gladly headed back to town right there and then. As it was, she intended to give Isaiah's beloved eldest son the tongue-lashing of his life. She caught up with him just before the sprawling headquarters of the Griffin ranch came into view.

"Have you gone plumb loco?" she charged furiously, her mount keeping pace with his. He had certainly done things in the past that had gotten her dander up, but she couldn't recall ever having been as angry with him as she was at this very moment. "Damn it all to hell, Matt Griffin!" she raged. "That was without a doubt the meanest, most low-down stunt you've ever pulled!"

"Don't go laying into me, Mac!" he warned tersely. His eyes narrowed into mere slits as he shot her a glowering look. "I'm not of a mind to hear it!"

"Well you'd damn well better *get* into the mind!" she parried, too infuriated to lend credence to his warning. "Are you so lily-livered that you've got to make war on unarmed men . . . on women and children, for heaven's sake? Those people haven't done anything to you! They're just trying to—"

"Why is it you're always standing against me now?" Matt reproached in a tight voice brimming with hurt. "There was a time when you wouldn't have been so quick to judge me!"

"Maybe so, but that was back when we were children! Things are different now!"

"Why? Why are they different?" His gaze became suffused with a savage light as he answered for her, "It's because of the marshal, isn't it?"

"I don't know what the devil you're talking about!" she denied hotly, the telltale color flying to her cheeks.

"Don't you?" Matt lashed back. "You've not been the same since Brody showed up! I've been a damned idiot, Mac. I tried telling myself there was nothing between the two of you. But now, I'm beginning to see —"

"There isn't anything to see!" she cried in a burst of thorough exasperation. "No one else is to blame for what's wrong between you and me! And if anyone else *were* to blame, it sure as hell wouldn't be Jake Brody!"

"It better not be!" he ground out. There was a look of such deadly calculation on his face that Caley's pulse leapt in alarm. "Because if I ever find out the two of you played me for a fool, I'll kill him. So help me God, I'll kill him with my bare hands!"

"Don't talk like that!"

"I mean it, Mac," he reiterated, his eyes glinting dully now as they met hers. "You're mine. You've always been mine. Just remember that."

Before she could set him straight once and for all about the question of her "ownership," he spurred his horse away from hers again and went thundering down the hill to the ranch. Her emotions were in utter chaos as she stared after him.

You've not been the same since Brody showed up, he had said. It was true. Heaven help her, but it was all too true. . . .

"Caley!"

Startled from her painful reverie, she looked up to see Isaiah Griffin hailing her from the front porch of the main house. It wouldn't do to let him suspect

147

anything was wrong, she told herself. She didn't want to upset him; neither did she want to be the recipient of his advice. He had always been like a second father to her, and the tough old cattle baron took full advantage of that position whenever he could.

Releasing a long sigh, Caley forced a smile to her lips and swung down from the saddle to walk down the hill. Jake Brody's handsome face swam before her eyes every step of the way.

Chapter VII

"We've missed you around here lately, Caley," said Maybelle, greeting her at the front door of the boarding house. Her eyes twinkled while a wry smile tugged at her lips. "I was beginning to think maybe you'd found some cooking you liked better."

"There's not much possibility of that in this town," Caley replied with a dramatic sigh. Returning the widow's smile, she stepped inside and accompanied her to the lamplit dining room.

The regulars were already there, still talking about the one subject Caley would have given her eye teeth to avoid. It was hopeless; the minute she sat down, George Groat started in.

"Did you hear what the new marshal's done now, Miss Caley? He's gone and posted a notice in all the saloons, saying all guns have got to be left at the door!" George laughed heartily at the preposterous notion of unarmed cowboys. "There's no way on God's green earth he'll make it work!"

"I wouldn't be so certain of that, Mr. Groat," opined Eva Hartford. She beamed J.D. Worthington III what she believed to be a winning smile, then turned a stern, schoolteacherly eye upon George once more. "While there will naturally be some resistance to his plan, I cannot help but think—"

"Resistance?" George broke in rudely. He nudged Caley with his elbow and gave her a knowing wink. "You might say that!"

"It won't wash," mumbled the forever chewing Mr. Tate.

"What was that, Mr. Tate?" asked Maybelle, her pale blue eyes twinkling again.

"I said it won't wash," he obligingly repeated, swallowing at last. "No man's gonna give up his guns. More likely, Marshal Brody'll find himself shot full of holes."

"What a perfectly dreadful thing to say!" Eva was quick to admonish him.

"Perhaps, but it is a consideration," J.D. interjected. His high, aristocratic forehead creased into a frown of thoughtfulness. "If the marshal were present at this moment, I do believe he would say much the same."

"Where is the marshal, anyhow?" George wondered aloud, shooting a quick glance back over his shoulder.

"I'm afraid Marshal Brody won't be joining us for supper," explained Maybelle. Her gaze shifted to Caley. "Seeing as how it's Saturday night, he thought it would be better to stay on the job. Heaven knows, things always get entirely too rowdy on a Saturday around here. Some folks seem to think the good Lord created the week's end for the sole purpose of raising Cain."

"*I* shall spend the entire evening in the parlour," Eva announced to no one in particular. "Venturing out on the streets would be utter madness. Why, I might very well be accosted by one of those inebriated ruffians!"

"Not likely," Mr. Tate contended through a mouthful of beef stew. His ungallant remark earned him a scathing glare from the plain, pinch-featured

150

spinster across the table.

"Did Red Tarver make it in with the stage all right?" George asked Caley at a sudden thought.

"Yes," she replied a bit absently, then cleared her throat and relegated thoughts of Jake to the back of her mind. "Thank God, nothing happened."

"I would be curious to know what Marshal Brody's investigation of the robbery has yielded thus far," said J.D. He, too, looked to Caley. "Has he revealed any of his findings to you, Miss McAlister?"

"No," she lied, then was dismayed to feel the warm, guilty color rising to her face. Great balls of fire, she mused with an inward groan, every time she tried to forget the night she had played wanton in Jake Brody's arms, someone saw fit to remind her of it! She'd go stark, raving mad if this kept up. They'd have to put her away for sure.

"You mean he hasn't told you anything at all yet?" George questioned in disbelief. "I heard Wells, Fargo isn't even going to send one of those fancy detectives out here to look into it like they usually do. Seems they've decided to let Marshal Brody handle it by himself."

"Have they?" She felt a twinge of angry resentment, for she had received no notification of their decision. "Well, I've not even spoken to the marshal since the day before yesterday," she went on to declare with outward calm, determined to finish her supper. "And I have no idea what he's been up to as far as the robbery's concerned."

For some reason, she was reluctant to let anyone know about the gold coin Jake had found. It wasn't as if its discovery was a secret; the bartender knew about it. But the man had apparently chosen not to share his knowledge. Either that, or Jake had warned him against doing so.

151

"Did you go out to the ranch with Matt today?" Maybelle next asked her in all innocence.

"You know I did," Caley replied evenly. "You waved at us this morning, remember?"

"Oh yes, of course. Well then, did you enjoy your ride?"

"Yes." She hastily lowered her gaze toward her plate and pushed the food about with her fork.

"And did you find Matt's father in good health?" Maybelle persisted.

"In perfect health. As always." She couldn't help smiling a little at that, for Isaiah Griffin was strong as a bull and twice as ornery. The smile quickly faded when she recalled that it was Matt's brother, Ned, who had ridden back to town with her. Matt had already taken himself off again.

"Your father was an old friend of Isaiah Griffin's, wasn't he?" queried J.D.

"Yes," she answered, nodding her head. "The two of them knew one another even before I was born. Isaiah helped my father start his first stage line back in California."

"Is that why you and your father chose to make Elko your home?" Eva was determined not to be left out of the conversation. "Because Mr. Griffin was here?"

"That's the main reason, I suppose," Caley told her. "That, and the fact that Elko presented a good opportunity for business. And Lord knows, my father was never one to pass up an opportunity," she added, her eyes clouding with the memories of so many other towns and other dreams that didn't quite pan out.

"When are you and that young fellow of yours finally going to get hitched?" George asked teasingly.

"Matt Griffin needs a wife to keep him from

152

raising so much hell," Mr. Tate piped up before Caley could answer.

"I should think any decent woman would think twice before tying herself to such a scoundrel!" Eva offered with severe condemnation. "Why, he and all the other men who frequent that . . . that *den of iniquity* down there should be ashamed of themselves!"

"Would you like some cornbread, Caley?" Maybelle hastened to intervene at this point. She alone took note of the telltale shadow crossing the younger woman's features.

"No, thank you," Caley responded in a low, tight voice. Striving to maintain control over her perilously rising temper, she forced herself to ignore Eva Hartford and take another bite of the stew.

"There's going to be a dance over at the lodge tonight, isn't there, Mr. Worthington?" Maybelle inquired with a polite smile in his direction.

"Yes, Mrs. O'Grady. We are hoping for a record attendance."

"A dance?" Eva repeated in surprise. "Why have I not heard of it?"

"I don't know, Miss Hartford," J.D. took it upon himself to answer. "Perhaps it was because we only began advertising it in the *Independent* a few days ago."

"Are you planning to attend, Mr. Worthington?"

"Yes, Miss Hartford, I am." He could tell that she was waiting for him to say more. Squirming a bit uncomfortably in his seat, he reached for the platter of cornbread.

"Are you going alone, Mr. Worthington?" Eva probed further.

"No, Miss Hartford. I . . . I am escorting Miss DuMonde."

"DuMonde?" George butted in as he was wont to

153

do. "Say, isn't that the pretty little actress who was here a couple of days back?"

"Yes, Mr. Groat," confirmed J.D, avoiding Eva Hartford's bitterly accusing gaze. "Miss DuMonde will be appearing in a production of *A Case for Divorce* at the Opera Hall next week. She has taken lodgings with the rest of the troupe at the Depot Hotel."

"That reminds me," said George, starting off on one of his infamous stories again. This one turned out to be mercifully short. "I'll never forget that time last year," he reminisced with a broad grin, "before they finally wised up and nailed down the boards of the stage over there at the Opera Hall. This one actor, a big sonofagun named Harrison, got himself so caught up yelling his lines like a banshee, he plumb forgot about the built-in booby-trap. One of those boards came right up and slapped him square in the nose. That was the biggest laugh he got all night!"

Caley, having heard the story many times before, smiled weakly and finished her stew. She was relieved to escape the boarding house shortly thereafter. Although she was in truth quite fond of Maybelle's "regulars," she was finding it increasingly difficult to tolerate their company. They asked too many questions—and knew too blessed much about her private life.

Private life, her mind repeated. What private life? She lived all alone with an ill-tempered old cat in three tiny rooms, with nothing better to do in the evenings than go to bed early or curl up next to the window and watch the world pass her by. By damn, that was some private life all right, she reflected dourly. She might as well be Eva Hartford.

Her eyes traveled with a will of their own toward the jail as she crossed the street. Darkness was falling, and she could well imagine that the marshal and his deputy were steeling themselves for a typically rough night in Elko. Miners and cowboys from miles around would come spilling into town, drinking hard and gambling hard and saying to hell with tomorrow. It was always the same.

She frowned when she recalled what George Groat had said about Jake's new proclamation forbidding guns in the saloons. Did he truly think it was possible to enforce that rule? Though she hated to admit it, her heart twisted painfully at the thought of Mr. Tate's dire prophecy coming to pass. How could two men bring order to a whole town full of—*full of men like Matt Griffin*? that inner voice finished for her.

Twilight had brought with it another promise of rain. She breathed deeply of the rapidly cooling air, tossing a glance overhead toward the rumbling, dark gray clouds. In more ways than one, they were an omen of what lay ahead.

Trapped in that dream world that exists between sleep and wakefulness, Caley tried to convince herself the sound was only another clap of thunder. Lightning had been streaking across the sky ever since she had taken herself off to bed more than an hour ago; thunder had been answering.

The heavens had opened up at last, releasing a cloudburst upon the grateful, sun-baked land. Rain drummed steadily on the roof, lulling her back to sleep until the sound cut through the storm and prompted her to sit bolt upright in the bed. Her eyes flew open as her mind fixed upon the cause for her sudden, instinctive alarm.

A gunshot! That particular sound in itself would have been relatively unimportant, had it not been for the fact that it was accompanied by the shrill whinnying of terrified horses.

"Dear God, the horses!" breathed Caley.

She flung back the covers and scrambled out of bed, tossing her wrapper about her shoulders as she hurried to the back door of the apartment. The rain stung against her face when she stepped outside, but she paid it no mind. Her one thought was to see to the animals.

A whole volley of gunfire erupted before she reached the bottom of the stairs, and her throat constricted in dismay when she realized that the shots were coming from the building next to hers. It was the lodge, hardly the usual place for raising hell. She remembered about the dance taking place there that night, then wondered dazedly what could have gone wrong.

Whatever it was, she told herself in growing fury, no one had the right to go shooting off their blasted guns and frightening her horses! Her bare feet sank in the mud as she raced across to the corral. She tried soothing the panic-stricken animals prancing restlessly about, but they backed away in fear every time another shot rang out. To make matters worse, thunder rumbled down upon the earth to join the man-made commotion.

Caley's temper blazed. She did not pause to consider the wisdom of her actions; she rashly allowed impulse to lead her. Spinning about, she flew back up the rain-slicked steps, dashed through her living quarters to the inner stairway, and rushed down to the office to fetch her shotgun. Her blue-green eyes were full of vengeful fire as she then set a course for the building next door.

She was soaked to the skin by the time she approached the lodge's doorway. Her wet hair streamed down about her shoulders, her nightgown and wrapper clung suggestively to her supple curves, and raindrops glistened on the flushed, stormy beauty of her countenance. Too enraged to notice the scandalous state of her appearance, she pushed her way determinedly through the group of onlookers assembled in the doorway and burst into the crowded room.

The sight which met her eyes was an astonishing one. What had begun as a wholesome, old-fashioned social event had deteriorated into an all-out melee when a band of drunken revelers had suddenly come pouring in from outside. Lured on by the sounds of music and laughter—not to mention a glimpse of pretty women whirling about in a rustle of petticoats—the punchers had resisted the efforts of the bravest lodge members to evict them. Guns had been drawn, and the whiskey-loaded intruders had proceeded to make merry by shooting holes in the punched tin ceiling.

They were still doing it when Caley paused for a moment to size up the situation. Several of the ladies took to screaming as the troublemakers fired off another round. There was apparently such confusion that no one had thought to send for help, and none of the men had come armed to what was supposed to have been a simple dance.

Caley was an unlikely savior. Looking more like a drowned kitten than an avenging tigress, she nevertheless showed she meant business by aiming her shotgun toward the bullet-ridden ceiling and adding an ear-splitting blast to the din.

An abrupt silence fell over the crowd. All eyes turned to fasten in startled disbelief upon the beautiful young woman, dripping wet and clad only in her nightclothes, who stood leveling a shotgun directly at those responsible for the havoc.

"Clear out, damn it!" she ordered in loud, ringing

157

tones.

"Well I'll be—" one of the cowboys muttered, his bloodshot eyes wide with incredulity.

"It's an angel!" another whispered hoarsely. "A redheaded angel!" There was little doubt he had downed too many glasses of whiskey.

"An angel from hell, you mean!" the most sober of the hellraisers pronounced in disgust.

"I said to clear out!" Caley reiterated, settling the gun's polished wooden stock more securely against her shoulder. "Do it now before this thing goes off!"

The other men and women in the room waited in silent, breathless anticipation to see whether the cowboys would test Caley's mettle. J.D. Worthington III stood only a few feet away from her. He knew, as did many another, that she would not hesitate to shoot if necessary.

The five young intruders began to argue amongst themselves as the long, agonizing seconds ticked by.

"Drop her, Mick! Shoot her right now and let's get back to the party!"

"Naw, don't kill her! Hell, look at her! She's too damn pretty to kill!"

"Shut up, you stupid bastards! Don't you know any better than to argue with a woman holdin' a gun on you?"

"I say we rush her!"

"You do that, and you'll be the first to go down!" Caley promised the one who had made that ill-advised suggestion. It was beginning to look like things were at a standstill—and heaven help her, but she didn't know how to put an end to it.

The matter was literally taken out of her hands in the next instant.

Before anyone could shout a warning, a slack-jawed young giant came up from behind and grabbed her. She fought him with all her might, but

158

he easily wrenched the shotgun from her grasp and sent her sprawling down onto the floor. Her heart pounding in fear, she hastily scrambled back to her knees and found herself staring up into the barrel of her own gun.

"What do you want me to do with her, Mick?" It was obvious now that he was with the others.

"Please, haven't you done enough?" J.D. stepped forward to make a desperate appeal on her behalf. "You're welcome to stay, if only—"

"Pipe down, you ugly bastard!" growled the man holding the gun on Caley. He backhanded her would-be champion across the face. J.D. staggered backward, landing heavily against the wall.

Caley was on the verge of throwing herself against J.D.'s assailant in a courageous yet hopeless attempt to get her gun back, when her fiery gaze was caught by a sudden movement on the staircase in the far corner.

Jake!

Her pulse leapt in mingled relief and alarm at the sight of his handsome face. She quickly made note of the fact that none of the troublemakers had seen him yet. Holding her breath, she watched from the corner of her eye as he moved slowly down the stairs and positioned his tall frame half within an inner doorway.

"Hold it right there!" he called out to the six young punchers.

He was prepared when two of them opened fire. Pulling back out of the way, he waited until they had emptied their guns, then brought his own six-shooters into view. At that same moment, Dan Mitchelson got the drop on them from the front doorway.

"Throw your guns down and put your hands up!" the deputy shouted, his guns shaking a bit before he

159

got a firm grip on his excitement.

A loud murmur arose from the crowd when the six men reluctantly obeyed. Even the one who still had possession of Caley's shotgun evidently decided the risk wasn't worth it; he grew very red in the face and lowered the gun to the floor.

J.D. was the first to reach Caley. He helped her to her feet and gallantly took off his coat to place about her shoulders. The next thing she knew, she was surrounded by a mob of grateful, overly solicitous women who bombarded her with a chattering string of questions and comments and general "fussing over" that made her head spin.

All of a sudden, Jake was there to rescue her. He had charged Dan and several of the lodge members with the duty of transporting the six prisoners to the jail. His one purpose now was to deal with Caley.

Striding through the crowd, he gazed impassively down at her. His fathomless, deep green eyes traveled over her rainsoaked dishabille before returning to fasten with penetrating steadiness upon her face. The way he looked at her made her blush to the very roots of her wet auburn hair. Painfully aware of the fact that all eyes in the room were upon her and the tall, quiet man who had just saved her life, she suddenly found herself wishing the floor would open up and swallow her whole.

Then, without a word, Jake took her arm and led her away. She wisely chose not to resist. The murmur of the crowd they left behind increased to a veritable roar as they moved outside and down the muddy boardwalk. The silence hung heavily between them, the strange tension building with each passing second. By the time they reached the front door of the stage office, Caley could bear it no longer. She pulled free and took a proud, defensive stance before him.

"You don't have to worry about me, Marshal! I'm quite all right! You can go—"

"Get inside," he commanded in a low voice of almost deadly calm.

"What?" she blurted out, her eyes growing very round.

"Get inside."

He was obviously in no mood to tolerate any defiance on her part. Normally, she would have told him to go to the devil. But, she rationalized inwardly, she was too tired and wet and flat-out miserable to argue with him.

"All right," she agreed, drawing herself rigidly erect. The rebellious expression on her beautiful face only served to heighten the fury simmering within Jake. "But you can't stay long," she insisted with a frown. "I'm taking tomorrow's run and I've got to get some sleep."

She preceded him into the darkened room, hurrying across to light the lamp. A shiver ran down her spine as she struck a match, but she could not honestly say whether it was from cold or fear.

As he had done before, Jake moved to lock the door and draw the shades. His actions made Caley's eyes widen with growing apprehension.

"There's no need for that!" she told him.

He disregarded her protest and followed through. When he turned to face her, she was standing back near the staircase, clutching J.D.'s coat about her and looking like she was ready to bolt at the slightest advance. She silently cursed herself for a coward; she had only minutes ago faced up to five armed men, and yet she found her courage fleeing as she waited for Jake Brody to do nothing more than speak.

Nothing more? it then occurred to her to wonder. Her heart took to pounding quite erratically.

161

"Damn it, woman, I could wring your little neck!" Jake finally ground out, causing her to start in alarm. His handsome face was thunderous, his gaze smoldering with a rage that even he did not fully understand. "Where the hell did you get the idea it was up to *you* to keep the peace around here? You've done a lot of stupid things, Caley McAlister, but I would have thought even you had more sense than to go charging into a room full of—"

"Stupid things?" she echoed, her eyes kindling with an answering fury. Anger brought with it a return of her usual indomitable spirit. "Why, you arrogant, bullheaded—" she fumed. She broke off and marched forward to confront him head on, furiously sweeping a lock of wet hair from her flushed and stormy countenance. "It so happens I went over there to put a stop to the commotion because it was scaring the hell out of my horses! I didn't know there were going to be five drunken bastards shooting up the place! No one else seemed to be doing anything about it, and—"

"And you might damned well have been killed!" he pointed out in a voice that was whipcord sharp. His gaze burned down into hers. It was all he could do to keep his hands off her; in that moment, he would have gladly done her bodily harm. "If Dan and I hadn't come along when we did—"

"I'd have handled it without your help!" she retorted, knowing it was a perfectly irrational claim to make but unable to hold it back. She folded her arms across her breasts and lifted her chin to an even more proudly defiant angle. "*You* were nowhere in sight when the trouble began!"

Glimpsing the barely controlled violence in his eyes, she gasped and took a hasty step backward.

"We were down at Dobe Row when we heard the

shots," he explained in a low, dangerously even tone. "We got there as soon as we could!"

"You were at *Miss Sadie's*, I suppose?" she inquired with biting sarcasm. "Did you have a good time?"

"So help me, you little wildcat—"

"How the devil was I to know where you were?" she demanded indignantly, choosing not to let him answer the unfounded charges she had just thrown at him. "I'm used to looking after myself and my own, Jake Brody, which is precisely what I was doing tonight! And I'll be hanged if I'm going to stand here another blasted minute and listen to you rake me over the coals for having the guts to do what I thought was right!"

"You didn't think, damn it!" he opined ruthlessly.

Caley opened her mouth to tell him exactly what he could do with his opinions, but thought better of it. She flung him one last speaking glare, then spun about on her bare heel and headed for the stairs. Surprisingly enough, Jake did not try and stop her. She had already reached the door to her rooms before she heard his footfall on the steps. She whirled to find him towering ominously above her.

"What the blazes do you think you're doing?" she demanded in breathless, wide-eyed disbelief.

His only response was to seize her arm in a none too gentle grip and propel her forcefully inside the apartment. A flash of lightning chased away the darkness for a brief instant, allowing her wide, frightened gaze to meet the piercing intensity of his.

"Let go of me and get out of here!" she ordered, mustering a show of bravado that belied the very real alarm racing through her. "You have no right—"

"I have every right, damn it!" he decreed angrily. His strong arms wrapped about her, drawing her

163

close to his hard warmth. "I went through hell when I saw that bastard holding a gun on you! If you ever do anything like that again, I swear I'll beat that pretty bottom of yours till you can't sit for a week!"

"You wouldn't dare!"

"I would, Caley," he warned quietly, his deep, wonderfully resonant voice sending a tremor through her. "I'll do whatever it takes to keep you from danger!"

"Let go of me!" She brought her hands up to push against him, but his arms only tightened about her until she could scarcely breathe. *Dear God, was it going to happen again*? "NO!" she cried hoarsely, her struggles intensifying as hot tears of defeat gathered in her eyes. "I hate you, Jake Brody! I hate you!"

"Call it what you will," he murmured, his head lowering relentlessly toward hers. "But know that you're mine!"

His lips captured hers in a kiss that was at once demanding and yet strangely gentle in its insistence, a kiss that she could literally feel down to her very toes. The heat of his powerful, undeniably virile body scorched her trembling curves. She moaned low in her throat and swayed against him in unspoken surrender, every square inch of her coming to life as it had never done before fate threw this handsome lawman in her path.

Gone was all thought of what had happened before, of the humiliation and burning desire for revenge she had felt the last time he had held her in his arms. There was only Jake . . . only his splendid, fiercely intoxicating mastery of her newly awakened passions . . . only this sweet blaze of desire coursing through her body like wildfire.

His hands suddenly came up to tug J.D.'s coat from about her shoulders. She shivered as the cool air swept across her damply clad softness, but she was soon warmed by Jake's inflaming touch. With wholly masculine impatience, he swept aside the edges of her wrapper and sent it sliding downward to join the borrowed coat on the floor. The thin white fabric of her nightgown was virtually transparent as a result of the soaking it had received, but the darkness which cloaked the room ensured that her maidenly modesty would not find itself betrayed.

But then, Jake's rapturous assault upon her senses had driven all thought of modesty clean out of her head. She trembled when his strong arm slipped about her waist to pull her close again. His other hand stroked downward to clasp her about the buttocks, his warm fingers branding her firmly rounded flesh as he pressed her lower body to the hard, searing warmth of his.

His mouth left off its sensuous conquest of hers long enough to roam across her face, then down along the slender, graceful column of her neck. She drew in her breath upon a sharp gasp when he suddenly, and quite without warning, brought his hands up to the top edge of her nightgown and sent the buttons flying with a single yank downward. The fabric gave way with a rending tear, baring her breasts for his pleasure . . . and hers.

His arm clamped about her waist again and lifted her higher in his tenderly savage embrace. A soft, breathless cry broke from her lips when his mouth wandered hungrily across her naked breasts. His hand closed about one of the satiny, rose-tipped globes while his lips bestowed their hot, moist tribute upon the other.

Caley stifled a moan and clung weakly to the broad strength of his shoulders. Her head fell back, her long, wet auburn tresses streaming down about her as her full young breasts were caressed with a skill and urgency that left her gasping for breath. By the time Jake's lips returned to claim hers once more, she felt as though she would faint with the sheer, mesmerizing pleasure of it all.

Jake knew himself lost. Liquid fire coursed through his veins, and his body burned to possess the woman who delighted him with her passion and stirred his heart as no one else had ever done. . . .

But a sudden clap of thunder brought him crashing back to reality. He later wondered if Providence had sent it to remind him of his duty.

Tearing his lips from Caley's, he seized both of her arms and set her almost roughly away from him.

"Damn it, woman, no more!" he ground out.

Caley stared up at him in the storm-tossed darkness, her whole body aching and an awful pain gripping her heart. She choked back hot, bitter tears, believing that she had once again allowed herself to be humiliated by a man who wanted only to torment her.

"We can't go on this way, Caley," Jake told her more calmly, though his voice still sounded raw with emotion. "I want you too damned much to keep holding back."

"Holding back?" she echoed in bewilderment, her own voice tremulous. She was too hurt, too full of confusion at the moment to feel either angry or embarrassed.

"I told you once before I'm only human," he reminded her with a faint smile of irony.

His eyes glinted dully as they moved over the white, shadowy form of the woman before him. He gave an inward groan at the thought of what he had almost done. Still burning for her, he cursed himself anew for allowing his personal feelings to interfere

166

with his job. *Damn her as well*, he thought, but knew he didn't mean it. For better or worse, she was in his blood—and he might as well face up to the fact that she was there to stay.

"I've got to go," he announced quietly. Another brief, mocking smile touched his lips. "Someone else might take it in mind to shoot up the town." He took a step toward her again, but she backed away. His green eyes clouded with mingled remorse and pain. "I'm sorry, Caley. I didn't intend to let things go this far."

"Didn't you?" she countered, swiping angrily at a tear. The temporary numbness had worn off, and in its place came the inevitable flood of furious self-reproach. But outwardly, her anger was reserved for the man who seemed to take perverse satisfaction in bringing her to the point of shameless abandon. "Damn you, Jake Brody, just go! Get out of here and leave me alone!"

"Caley—"

"No!" she cried hotly. "I don't want to listen to you! I—I don't want to see you ever again!"

"Well you're going to," he vowed. There was a certain vibrancy in his tone that made her pulse race again. "As a matter of fact," he added as he crossed unhurriedly to the doorway and turned back to her, "you're going to see a hell of a lot more of me—and soon."

"What's *that* supposed to mean?"

"You're a great one for thinking. You figure it out."

With that, he was gone.

Caley waited until she heard the front door opening and closing again before flying back downstairs. She locked the door, then turned to lean weakly against it.

Jake's last words still rang in her ears. She caught

167

her lower lip between her teeth, her cheeks flaming as she thought about what had just happened. A sudden shiver coursed down her spine, and her bright, troubled gaze dropped to the front of her nightgown. The torn fabric was a painful reminder of Jake's smoldering determination and her own inability to fight it.

To make matters worse, the image of Matt Griffin charged unbidden into the forefront of her mind. She remembered all too clearly what he had said about playing him for a fool with the new marshal. Had she really betrayed him? Or was she simply betraying herself?

"Dear God, what am I going to do?" she implored in a ragged whisper. "What in tarnation am I going to do?"

Elsewhere that same night, less than an hour after Caley had returned to the lonely comfort of her bed, the man who had claimed her for his own years ago rode out into the rainswept night to complete a bit of unfinished business. His brother Ned rode with him, as did three other men from the Griffin ranch, all of them intent upon one purpose—running the Basque sheepherders off the land Isaiah Griffin had commanded must be kept "fresh" for cattle. Open range or not, Isaiah had told his sons, the interlopers had to be taught a lesson. And just like they always did, Isaiah's sons had set off to do his bidding.

"I don't like this, Matt. I don't like it one bit!" Ned Griffin confessed to his older brother as they neared the herders' camp.

"Aw hell, Ned, we're not going to hurt them! We're just going to put a little scare in them," Matt assured him with a low, malevolent chuckle. "After we've finished with these damned wooly-tenders, they won't think twice about lighting out for the other side of the county!"

"Yeah, but I remember what happened the last time you put a 'little scare' in someone. And I'm not going to be part of anything like—"

"You'll do as you're told, damn it!" snarled Matt.

Although the two of them were brothers, there was little love lost between them. They resembled one another physically, but their temperaments were as different as day and night. Younger by three years, Ned was possessed of a generous heart and a sense of justice that would not be denied; peculiar indeed, given the fact that both his father and brother were hotheaded rascals who believed the only right way of doing things was their own. They had frequently ridiculed him for being different, for being a "yellow-bellied sky pilot," as they liked to put it—"sky pilot" being a popular, rather derogatory name for a missionary or preacher. He sometimes asked himself why he stayed.

"No one forced you to come along!" Matt reminded him with a sneer.

"You know why I came." His blue eyes, so much like his brother's and yet full of a warmer glow, narrowed as he cast a look overhead at the star-studded sky. The storm had passed, leaving the desert landscape bathed in moonlight and the air filled with the pleasant scent of rain and sagebrush. "Someone's got to make sure you keep a lid on that temper of yours." His youthful features, far less rakishly attractive than his brother's, tightened in anger when the other man gave a derisive snort of laughter.

"You taking on the job?" Matt challenged in a voice laced with sarcasm, then grew deadly serious. "I'm warning you, Ned—don't get in my way. Don't ever make the mistake of crossing me again!"

"You're not above the law, Matt. You can't go around pistol-whipping men like Roy Shelby just because they have the guts to stand up to you. It's a good thing I came along when I did," he pointed out with a deep frown of remembrance. "If Shelby had died, you'd be facing a charge of murder right now."

"Ed Tickner wouldn't have charged me with a damned thing!" Matt declared with swaggering confidence. "Besides, that stupid bastard got no more than he deserved! He'd been warned plenty of times about watering his herd on our land!"

"You know as well as I do that the spring doesn't legally belong to us!" argued Ned.

"Maybe not, but we control it! And out here, that's all that matters!" Matt concluded, abruptly spurring his horse farther ahead.

Ned had no choice but to follow. *Someday*, he promised himself. Someday he'd find the courage to leave Elko and never look back.

The five horsemen reached the Basque family's camp soon thereafter. The young woman and the children had already gone to sleep in the hastily repaired wagon, leaving Bertrand Larronde and his son to stand watch over the flock. A fire burned in the middle of the camp, its flames dancing brightly beneath the endless night sky. The sheep had settled themselves peacefully to wait for the dawn, and even the dog lay in quiet repose nearby.

Matt gave the signal. He and the three hired hands rode swiftly down the hill, setting up a loud, blood-curdling cry that caused the two sheepherders beside the fire to leap to their feet in alarm. As before, the Basques were unarmed, and thus could do nothing but watch in mute horror as Matt took aim and fired directly into the flock of sheep. The men with him obediently followed his lead. The shots rang out in rapid succession while the bleating cries of the helpless, panic-stricken animals rose in the night air.

"No!" Ned yelled in furious disbelief. "No, damn you, no!"

He spurred his own mount forward to put a stop to the senseless killing. Just as he reached the camp, the young woman came stumbling out of the wagon with a rifle in her hands. Clad in a white nightgown, she had thrown a brightly colored shawl about her shoulders, and her unbound raven tresses streamed down her back while she raised the gun toward Matt.

Ned, catching sight of her, felt his heart stand still. He made a split second decision. Whether it was to save his brother's life, or to prevent the vengeful slaughter of the sheepherders, he couldn't have said. There wasn't time to think.

"*No, don't!*" he cried hoarsely, at the same time jerking on the reins and hurtling himself from the saddle.

He knocked the young woman to the ground, one of his hands grasping the rifle while his other arm clamped about her waist. The two of them landed heavily beside the wagon and rolled together toward the wheel. Ned's body pressed the young woman's down into the soft, muddy earth as he came to rest atop her.

"Elena!" he heard one of the Basque men shouting.

"Hold it right there, you dirty basco!" Matt bit out, holding his gun on the sheepmen now. "And don't pretend you don't know what the hell I'm saying!"

Ned stared down into the stormy features of the woman lying beneath him. His eyes widened in surprise at her unexpected beauty. The firelight played across her face, allowing him a captivating glimpse of her dark, fiery gaze and a mouth that was full and soft and inviting.

"Elena! Elena!" a childish voice called out above the piercing echo of gunfire.

Startled, Ned looked up to see two very young boys scrambling down from the wagon. They bravely threw themselves upon him, their tiny fists pummeling his back. Unscathed by their fierce but ineffectual blows, he climbed to his feet and pulled Elena up with him. She jerked away and gathered the boys close to her.

"Cowards!" she spat at Ned. "You are nothing but a *zakhurra*—you and the others!"

"What's the matter, little brother, she too much woman for you?" Matt taunted with a scornful laugh. He still sat astride his horse, and he tossed a lazily interested glance toward his brother before shifting his feral gaze back to the two sheepherders. "You've got till morning to move out! If I come back and find you here after sunup, I'll burn your wagon and kill every damned one of your sheep!"

Although the shooting had mercifully stopped by now, the hired hands had not yet finished their dirty work. Matt gave a curt nod. The three acted promptly upon his signal. Spurring their mounts, they thundered through the frantically scurrying flock of sheep, whooping loudly and waving their hats. They soon disappeared over the hill, scattering the animals far and wide across the moonlit desert. The herders would now be left with the almost impossible task of rounding the sheep up again.

"Damn you, Matt, *enough!*" Ned desperately tried to intervene, but his protest fell on deaf ears. It was always the same.

"Clear out!" Matt snarled to the stoic, silently

172

rage-filled Basques once more. He looked to Ned. "You coming? Or would you rather stay out here and roll around in the mud some more with your *senorita*?" he asked derisively.

Ned's features tightened into a grim mask of fury. Without a word, he crossed to where his own well-trained mount waited near the campfire. He swung up in the saddle, clutched the reins in one hand, and turned back to where Elena stood so proudly erect with the boys' small arms wrapped about her waist.

"I'm sorry. I'll be back!" he promised, his gaze full of genuine remorse.

Matt gave a snort of disgust, then reined about and rode away. Ned, tearing his eyes away from the raven-haired young beauty whose dark gaze seemed to cut right through him, forced himself to ride after his brother.

Elena pulled away from the children and flew to where the rifle lay half-buried in the mud. She snatched up the gun, raised it to her shoulder, and took aim.

"*Ez, Elena, ez!*" her father hastily cried out for her to stop.

But his warning was not necessary. She could not pull the trigger.

Elena Larronde cursed herself for her lack of *sendotasuna*, for lacking the strength of character every Basque woman is taught to cultivate from an early age. In the turbulent depths of her mind burned the image of the young man the other had called "little brother."

Hot tears started to her eyes at last. She lowered the rifle and raised a trembling hand to smooth the tangled, mudcaked ebony tresses from her face. The two young boys, her late sister's children, raced ahead to their grandfather and uncle.

"Come," said Bertrand Larronde, his remarkably steady voice betraying little of the anger boiling within him. "We have much work to do."

A short time later, Ned Griffin finally found the courage he had been praying for. The incident at the sheepherders' camp had, for him, been the last straw. Leaving his horse tied in front of the ranch house, he strode purposefully inside to his room and began gathering up a few of his things. His eyes glinted with a dull light as he stuffed the clothing into his saddlebags. It was time, he told himself, time he stood on his own two feet.

With that one thought in mind, he returned outside and prepared to mount up. Matt's voice, brimming with disdainful sarcasm, sounded behind him.

"Going somewhere?"

"Tell Pa I'll be back out in a couple of days to collect the rest of my gear," Ned replied somberly. He swung up into the saddle and gazed down at his brother in the moonlit darkness. "You've gone too far this time, Matt. You and Pa both."

"I don't know what the hell you're talking about," his brother drawled with mocking unconcern.

"You can't count on Ed Tickner to cover up for you anymore. From what I hear of the new marshal, he's not a worthless puppet like Ed. He's not going to dance whenever Isaiah Griffin pulls the strings," Ned predicted bitterly.

"You taking a stand against us?" Matt demanded, his gaze glittering hotly now. "Because if you are, you'll get just what the others get!"

"Save your threats, big brother." He reined about and tossed back over his shoulder, "You and Pa can find me in Elko if you need me for anything."

"Need you? Hell, we won't need for you a damned thing!" Matt countered scornfully. "Go on, damn you, go on and keep going!"

First Caley and now his own brother, he thought, watching Ned disappear over the hill. Damn it all, everything was going wrong . . . and most of it could be blamed on Jake Brody.

Brody, he rasped inwardly, his eyes suffused with hatred's dark, menacing glow. The time had come to do something about that sonofabitch. Then, he told himself, then he'd show everyone that Matt Griffin was a force to be reckoned with. And Caley would be his at last.

Chapter VIII

"Any trouble, Miss Caley?" asked Billy, taking the reins from her. Tripod, apparently choosing not to linger that afternoon, scampered away as soon as his three huge paws hit the ground.

"No." Caley climbed down from the stagecoach and pulled off her hat, freeing the luxuriant mass of auburn curls she had twisted up beneath it. "But then again, the run *was* only up to Dinner Station and back," she added, smiling faintly.

The place she referred to was a bleak, two-story stone structure flanked by several small outbuildings some twenty miles north of Elko. This famous — or infamous, depending upon one's opinion of the food — stage station served as a meal stop for stage travelers bound for either Tuscarora or Mountain City, or even farther westward.

On this particular Sunday, Caley had made only a "half run," due to the fact that there was no express box to be transported and the lone passenger had specifically requested to break the trip to Mountain City into two days instead of the usual one. This had presented no problem, since another stage, with Hank sitting as jehu, was scheduled to head up along that same route the following day.

"Things seem to be slowin' down a bit since the

robbery, don't they, Miss Caley?"

"I'm afraid so, Billy," she admitted with a sigh. She drew off her leather gloves and turned her pensive gaze up the street toward the jail. Reluctant to follow through on her intent, she released another sigh and told Billy, "I've got to speak to Marshal Brody. Do me a favor and keep an eye on things till I get back, will you?"

"Yes, ma'am!" the young hostler agreed without hesitation. "Take all the time you need, Miss Caley!"

Her mouth curved into a warmly lit smile at his neverwaning enthusiasm. She moved to the doorway of the office, negligently tossed her hat and gloves inside, and set a course for the jail. The whip remained in her hand, though she had retained possession of it quite without design. Her boots sounded out a brisk cadence on the boardwalk as she went — and her heart seemed to echo every step with a pounding that rang in her ears.

The events of the previous night were a burning memory she had been trying, without success, to forget ever since she had pulled herself out of bed at the crack of dawn. Sleep had not come easily; neither had awakening. It had required three cups of strong black coffee to get her fired up for the day's job. Once she had settled herself atop the stage, however, instinct had taken over and provided her with the necessary control of the reins. But she had been continually plagued by visions of both Jake and Matt . . . although, in truth, Jake's face had been the one rising before her most often.

She hated like the very devil having to seek him out. The thought of being in the same room with him sent a whirl of mixed emotions coursing through her.

"Afternoon, Mac," a thickset, black-bearded gi-

178

ant of a man hailed her as she marched past him without speaking. She stopped and turned back with a slight, preoccupied frown.

"Oh . . . hello, Shorty." Her fingers tightened about the whipstock. She had never liked being called *Mac* by anyone but Matt. And she had damn sure never liked Shorty.

"Where you headin' in such a hurry?" he probed, flashing her a grin that revealed jagged yellow teeth. He edged a bit too close for her taste. Battling the urge to tell him to back off in no uncertain terms, she pivoted about and continued on her way.

"See you later, Shorty," she murmured coldly.

He stared after her for a moment, then muttered something about the addlepated nature of females and took himself inside the saloon. Even on a late Sunday afternoon, the place was doing a bang-up business, dispensing drinks with such intriguing names as "Muldoon," "Dashaway," "Milk Punch," and a vast array of others. The names didn't matter. As long as the glasses were full and the women friendly, the saloon's patrons were satisfied to throw their money down.

Caley had always thought it said a lot about the town, the fact that there were more people in the whiskey palaces on Sunday than in church. Of course, she herself had only been down to the new, whitewashed frame chapel a couple of times since services had been held there; she'd have gone a lot more often if sharp-tongued busybodies like Bertha Larrabee hadn't made such a point of informing her what was wrong with her appearance, her attitude, and her life in general. Still, she knew it was cowardly to let them keep her away. Her father would probably have told her to "charge right in there and show those fussed-up old biddies the

179

stuff McAlisters are made of." But then, her father wasn't around to prod her any longer. . . .

Reaching the jail, she opened the door without knocking and stepped inside. Jake and Dan were both there, the two of them engaged in a low-voiced discussion regarding the six young punchers who had been arrested the night before and still sat behind bars in the other room. Marshal and deputy glanced up in unison as Caley stood surveying them with a troubled light in her eyes and a warm flush stinging her cheeks.

"I need to talk to you," she told Jake in a determinedly even tone of voice. Dan cleared his throat and retrieved his hat from atop the desk.

"I think maybe now's a good time for me to take that supper break you promised me, Marshal Brody," his deputy announced with a crooked smile.

"I'm glad to see I hired a man with some sense," was Jake's way of giving his consent.

"Miss McAlister," said Dan, nodding politely at her before he left and closed the door behind him.

"I—I just wanted you to know I found another one of those coins!" Caley blurted out as soon as Dan was gone. She reached into the pocket of her buckskin trousers and withdrew the gold coin bearing the same peculiar markings as the one Jake had showed her.

"Where did you find it?" he asked quietly, taking it from her.

"Dinner Station. I just got back. I thought I should let you know right away."

"I see. And you brought that along for protection?" he then queried, his gaze brimming with wry amusement as it dropped to the whip in her hand. Her color deepened.

"No, blast it!" she denied irritably. She had

known it was a mistake to come. What had happened between them was something that could not be forgotten . . . well, at least not any time soon, she amended silently. Her blue-green eyes turning fiery, she drew herself even more loftily erect and declared with admirable composure, "That's all I had to say. You can add the coin to your collection of evidence—provided you *have* a collection of evidence."

"I have," he confirmed.

"Don't you think I have a right to know what it is?"

"Maybe. But I'm not ready to tell you yet."

"Why the devil *not*?" she demanded, bristling anew.

"Because, Caley McAlister," he replied, moving slowly around the desk to tower above her, "I never reveal anything until I'm good and ready."

His words had an ominous ring to them, but all Caley noticed was the way his deep green eyes traveled with such bold intimacy over her upturned face—that, and the way her whole body grew warm beneath his gaze. She felt herself becoming dangerously lightheaded at his proximity.

"I—I have to be going," she faltered in a small, breathless voice.

"Count yourself lucky," he told her as the merest ghost of a smile played about his lips. "If not for the fact that there are no shades on the windows, I'd give you a proper goodbye—the kind we give back in Texas."

"I don't give a damn how you do things back in Texas!" retorted Caley, her eyes blazing at his audacity. "And the lack of shades didn't stop you before!" she added, referring to the first kiss he had forced upon her right there in that very jailhouse. She regretted the words as soon as they were

181

out of her mouth.

"Is that a dare, wildcat?" Jake challenged softly.

She swallowed hard and tried her damnedest not to think about how wickedly enchanting it had been to be in his arms. Her gaze dropped with a will of its own to his firm, chiseled mouth . . . the same mouth that had ravished hers with such fierce, demanding passion . . . the same warm lips that had roamed so hungrily over her naked breasts. . . .

Suddenly, the door was flung open. Caley started guiltily and whirled about. Her eyes widened with startlement when they fell upon the young Basque woman from the sheepherders' camp.

"I—I must speak with the sheriff!" Elena proclaimed in obvious distress.

"I'm Marshal Brody," said Jake, striding forward with a frown of concern. "What is it?"

"My name is Elena Larronde, and we need your help!" Elena told him. She glanced at Caley, her dark eyes lighting with recognition. "You are Mr. Griffin's friend!" Her features tightened in anger and suspicion when she accused, "But perhaps you know of this already!"

"Know of what?" Caley responded in bewilderment.

"They came last night!" Elena explained, turning back to Jake. "They were Mr. Griffin's men. He was with them. They killed many of our sheep, and he told us he would return to kill the rest if we did not leave at once!"

"Matt Griffin—the man I was with yesterday did this?" Caley asked in stunned disbelief. She had known he was angry about the sheepmen, but she had never really believed he would do anything so contemptible.

"He did!" confirmed Elena, her eyes narrowing

182

in a blaze of renewed fury before she looked back to Jake again in desperate entreaty. "My father has said we must not speak of it to anyone. He is a proud man and would be very angry if he knew I had come to you for help. We have spent all night driving our sheep closer to town, but still, I am afraid—"

"You were right to come to me, Miss Larronde," Jake assured her quietly. His handsome face had become a mask of grim determination, and his eyes smoldered with a dangerous light as he took up his hat.

"What are you going to do?" Caley demanded, her pulses racing in alarm.

"I'm going to arrest Matt Griffin."

"*What*? Why, you can't do that!" she protested quite vigorously, reaching out to grasp his arm. "Hellfire and damnation, if you go riding out to the Griffin ranch and try to arrest Matt, you'll never get out of there alive!"

"I appreciate your concern for my welfare, Miss McAlister," he declared with a faint, mocking smile, then grew forebodingly solemn again. "But my job is to uphold the law. And Matt Griffin is no different from anyone else who breaks it." He faced Elena and promised her, "I'll see that you're repaid for the loss of your sheep, Miss Larronde."

"But I—I do not wish for you to be harmed, Marshal Brody!" the raven-haired young beauty exclaimed anxiously. It had just now dawned on her that, because of her own desire to see justice done, this man's life would be in jeopardy. "There has been enough violence, enough hatred. What they have done is not worth—"

"She's right!" Caley interjected, still trying to make him see reason. "What the hell good is it going to do anyone if you go riding off half-cocked and get yourself shot full of holes?"

"I'm never 'half-cocked'," he reassured her, his mouth curving into another brief, sardonic smile. He put on his hat and headed for the door. "When Dan gets back, tell him where I've gone."

"I'm not going to tell him a blasted thing!" Caley retorted fierily. She pushed past him and got to the door first, spinning about to add with a spirited toss of her head, "Because I'm coming with you!"

"Like hell you are," Jake disputed with an angry, tight-lipped expression.

"You can't stop me!" she insisted stubbornly. "I can ride wherever I damned well please—and if I please to ride out to the Griffin ranch, there's nothing you can do about it!"

"No, Caley," he decreed in a low voice charged with emotion, none of it pleasurable. "You're not going. Now get out of my way."

"You can ride off without me, but I'll still follow!"

"Damn it, woman—"

"Damn it, yourself!" she shot back, her luminous turquoise gaze locked into silent combat with the smoldering green depths of his. "I've known the Griffins a long time. They'll be far less likely to listen to you than to me!" she pointed out. "And besides, I'm partly to blame for what happened! I was with Matt when he first threatened the herders yesterday. I thought he was bluffing . . . but if he really is guilty of attacking their camp, then I'd better be there to make sure he doesn't try anything stupid!"

"I won't have you in the middle of this," Jake ground out.

"I'm already in the middle of it! And I *am* coming with you!" To Elena, she tossed out, "Tell Deputy Mitchelson where we've gone!"

Abruptly turning away, she marched outside to unloop the reins of Dan's horse from the hitching post. Jake muttered a savage oath beneath his breath, cast Elena a look of helpless rage, and strode angrily outside.

"If I had any sense, I'd lock you up and throw away the key," he told Caley in a fury-laced tone of voice.

"Hah! If you had any sense, you'd quit arguing and admit you could use my help!" She mounted up and watched as he did the same.

"I'm curious to know one thing," he said, his gaze burning across into hers again. "Who are you trying to protect—Matt Griffin or me?"

"Both!"

"I thought you hated me," he ungallantly reminded her.

"I do!" she insisted, lifting her chin. Her voice held a note of defensiveness when she clarified, "But that still doesn't mean I want to see you cut down for trying to do your job!"

"I'm glad we got that straight." His eyes brimmed with ironic humor as well as fury now.

"So am I!"

Tugging on the reins, she urged her borrowed mount away from the boardwalk and rode off down the street. Jake, cursing himself for a damned fool, followed in her dust-swirled wake.

Few words passed between them on the way out to the ranch. Caley stole a look at her unwilling companion now and then, only to note that his ruggedly handsome features looked every bit as grim and forbidding as before. She found herself making a mental comparison of the two men in her life—not that she'd actually own up to Jake Brody being in her life, of course. He and Matt were so very different, she mused, both in personality and looks . . . and otherwise.

Oh, but it's the otherwise that'll get you every time, an inner voice taunted her. She blushed at the sudden, painfully vivid memory of the way she had melted in the lawman's arms last night. Great balls of fire, she swore inwardly, when had she become such a shameless hussy? She had certainly never been one before; far from it. The next thing you knew, she'd be acting just like those scarlet angels down at Miss Sadie's, letting Jake Brody do whatever he pleased with her. The prospect was not a pleasant one—*or was it*?

"What happened yesterday?" Jake suddenly asked.

"Yesterday?" Startled from her shocking reverie, she colored and shifted uncomfortably in the saddle.

"When you and Griffin were at the Larrondes' camp."

"Nothing, really," she answered, finding it difficult to meet his gaze. "Matt . . . well, he was angry at finding them on his grazing land. He told them to move out."

"Why didn't you tell me about it?"

"Because there was nothing to tell! Matt's always had a short fuse, but he usually simmers down in a little while. For heaven's sake, I never thought he'd really *do* anything!"

"I warned you about him, Caley. Now maybe you'll believe me when I tell you he's trouble."

"Why are you so all-fired anxious for me to stay away from Matt Griffin?" she demanded.

"I have my reasons," he replied enigmatically, his eyes narrowing a bit as he settled his hat lower on his head.

Caley decided not to press him further. They were soon bearing down on the sprawling head-

186

quarters of the Griffin ranch, where they spied the patriarch himself striding from one of the barns to the house. Isaiah's tall, gray-haired form was easily identifiable in the waning sunlight. He was an imposing figure, what with his proud, almost regal bearing and his life-honed swarthy features fixed in a perpetual scowl.

"Let me do the talking!" Caley instructed Jake as they slowed their mounts to a walk.

"No. It's my job. I'll handle it," he decreed, his low, deep-timbred voice edged with undeniable authority.

"But—"

"Do as I say, Caley."

She had no time to argue, for they were within earshot of Isaiah now. The rancher, still lusty and vigorous in spite of being in the twilight of his life, had stopped and turned to face the two approaching riders in front of the house. His steely gaze lit with initial pleasure when it fell on Caley, then darkened when it was caught by the silver badge shining on Jake's chest.

"Caley," said Isaiah, nodding up at her while pointedly ignoring the man beside her. "What brings you out here this late in the day?"

"I'm sorry, Isaiah, but the—Marshal Brody needs to have a word with Matt!" she stammered out in a rush.

"Matt's not here," he declared with his usual gruffness.

"Where is he, Mr. Griffin?" asked Jake. The eyes of the two men met, and it was immediately understood between them that they were adversaries. Each had fully expected it to be so.

"Don't know," replied Isaiah. "He's been gone since sunup." That was partly true. "What's this about?" he then demanded of Jake, his thick, salt-

and-pepper brows drawing together in a frown of intense displeasure.

"There was some trouble last night at the sheepherders' camp!" Caley hastened to reveal, earning her a sharply quelling look from Jake. She disregarded it and continued, "Matt and some of your men have been accused of killing off part of their flock, Isaiah. That, and threatening to do worse!"

"Is that true?" The older man's gaze sliced back to Jake for confirmation.

"It's true."

"How do you know my son's involved?"

"There were witnesses."

"You talking about those bascos?" asked Isaiah, only to twist his mouth in a gesture of disgust. "Damn it, man, you can't mean to take their word over Matt's! Hell, those tramp sheepers would say anything if they thought it'd get them what they wanted!"

"That's for a jury to decide, Mr. Griffin," Jake proclaimed calmly, though his eyes were suffused with a dull glow. "Now where can I find him?"

"I wouldn't tell you even if I knew!" the other man growled. "Besides, you're wasting your time. Matt and Ned were both right here at the ranch with me last night. All night long!"

"You can swear to that in court."

Isaiah's face reddened with anger. He climbed to the top step of the porch and rounded on Jake with a furious glare.

"We protect our own out here, *Marshal*, and I'll be damned if I'm going to let you lock my boy up on some trumped-up charge brought by a bunch of dirty immigrants! I don't know who the hell you think you're dealing with, but you'd better get it through that thick skull of yours right now—no one calls me or mine a liar and gets away with it!

No one stirs up trouble for the Griffins and lives to tell about it!"

"Isaiah, please just—" Caley tried reasoning with him in vain.

"I let it ride the first time you threw him in jail," he continued, his hostile gaze locking with Jake's. "I let it ride because I figured you hadn't had time to learn the lay of the land around here. But you've got no excuses now! Take my advice and get out while you can, Brody. Your days are numbered if you stay in Elko!"

"Threatening a federal peace officer is a serious offense, Mr. Griffin," Jake told him with a faint smile. His expression grew deadly somber when he warned, "Don't ever make the mistake of doing it again."

"Get off my land!" Isaiah roared, his temper exploding. "Get off before I throw you off!"

"Tell your son it'll go easier on him if he gives himself up," said Jake. Although tempted to remain and conduct a search of the premises, he told himself he had to bide his time. Patience truly was a virtue when it came to his line of work. "I'll send you an accounting of the sheepherders' losses. Take *my* advice and cover them." He touched a finger to the front brim of his hat in what the older man judged to be a mocking gesture of respect, then turned to Caley. "Are you coming, Miss McAlister?" It was more of a command than a question, and they both knew it.

"She's staying right here!" Isaiah answered for her.

Caley, recalling what Jake had said earlier about her being in the middle, found herself precisely that. Torn between loyalty to an old friend and an inexplicable desire to remain with the very man she had professed to despise, she wavered on the edge of uncertainty. The decision was not an easy one to make; she sensed that there was a whole lot more to it than the simple choice of riding back to town or staying at the ranch.

"I'm sorry, Isaiah," she finally declared, her bright gaze full of contrition. "But I've got to get back."

"You shouldn't have come with him, Caley. I never thought I'd live to see the day Paddy McAlister's girl threw in with the likes of *him*!" accused Isaiah, jabbing a finger in Jake's direction.

"I haven't thrown in with him!" she hastened to deny. "And I came along because I thought it might do some good for me to be here, not because I was looking to rile you! Blast it all, Isaiah Griffin, you should know better than anyone that I call my own shots!"

"I used to think that," the self-made cattle baron allowed tersely. "But nowadays, I'm not so sure!" He had known something was wrong between her and Matt. And when he had pressed his son for details, Brody's name had come up. The possibility that Caley might be letting her head get turned made him hate the marshal all the more. "Get going, the both of you!" he ground out. Without waiting to see if they obeyed, he spun about on his booted heel and stalked furiously into the house.

"Come on," Jake said quietly.

Caley, feeling sick inside, released a long, disconsolate sigh and reined about. She was relieved that Jake didn't try to make conversation as they rode away, for she was too upset to think straight at the moment. Isaiah's remarks had cut her to the core. A wave of mingled guilt and misery washed over her, and she had to fight the impulse to turn around and go tearing back to beg the tough old rancher's forgiveness.

She and Jake hadn't traveled more than a couple of miles when it happened.

One moment, she was engrossed in her troubled thoughts; the next, she was startled by the loud report of a gunshot. Her whole body tensing in alarm, she jerked on the reins and suddenly felt herself being dragged down from her horse.

Jake, reacting with his usual lightning-quick speed, literally threw her to the ground and placed his body protectively atop hers. Lying face down in the dirt, she raised her head in a desperate attempt to see what was going on.

"Be still, damn it!" Jake whispered stridently. He had drawn his gun, and his smoldering gaze raked over the wild, rolling countryside for any sign of who had fired the shot. There was none.

Caley held her breath and waited. She could hear nothing but the sound of her own heart pounding in her ears, and the quiet whinnying of the horses. For what seemed like an eternity, she lay there with Jake's hard body pressing hers down into the soft earth.

"Do—do you see anything?" she finally asked him, her voice low and tremulous.

"No. Whoever it was, I think they've gone."

He holstered his gun and climbed to his feet, then reached down to pull Caley up as well. She stifled a moan as feeling returned to her body, for her muscles ached as a result of the rough treatment they had just suffered.

"Are you all right?" Jake asked, frowning as his gaze flickered up and down the disheveled, buckskin-clad length of her.

"I'm fine!" she breathed. She raised a hand to sweep the tangled mass of fiery curls from her face. "Are you?" Her eyes fell upon the bright red stain spreading across the front of his shirt. "Why, you've been hit!" she exclaimed.

"It's nothing. Come on." He seized her arm in a firm grip and began pulling her along with him to where their two mounts stood pawing impatiently at the ground.

"What do you mean 'it's nothing'?" she demanded in wide-eyed disbelief. "You've been shot! You'd better let me have a look—"

"The bullet just nicked me," he assured her with an ill grace. "Now shut up and get on your horse!" His hands grasped her about the waist, lifting her up to the saddle while her gaze sparked with anger.

"You muleheaded idiot, you might bleed to death before we get to town!"

"Maybe so, but I'll be damned if I'm going to hang around out here and let someone use us for target practice!"

He mounted up and brought his hat slapping down upon the sleek rump of Caley's borrowed horse. The startled animal took off, racing back toward Elko while Jake's own horse followed close behind.

Darkness had already fallen by the time they drew to a halt in front of the jail. Caley swung down from the saddle, hastily looped the reins about the hitching post, and hurried to Jake's side.

"I'll fetch the doctor!" she told him, only to find herself detained by the warm touch of his hand upon her arm.

"There's no need for that," he insisted.

"Of course there's a need!"

"For once, Caley McAlister, do as I say." A crooked smile tugged at his lips, and his eyes glowed with such teasing warmth that Caley felt her stomach doing a strange flip-flop.

"All right," she reluctantly agreed. "But if you won't have the doctor, then you'll have to let *me*

192

have a look at it!" she declared with an obstinate tilt of her head.

"It's a deal."

She preceded him across the boardwalk and into the lamplit confines of the jail. The front room was empty, although Dan had left a note saying he'd be back after making the hourly round about town.

"Take off your shirt," Caley ordered Jake, watching as he closed the door and tossed his hat to land atop the desk.

"With pleasure," he drawled, then added, "After I've checked the cells."

Taking up the keys, he unlocked the door to the other room and stepped through the doorway. Caley could hear masculine voices raised in anger, and she idly wondered if Otis Snyder's was one of them. Jake reappeared less than a minute later, closing the door again and returning the keys to the top drawer of the desk.

"Your shirt is soaked with blood!" Caley pointed out accusingly. "Now sit down, damn it, and let me see what I can do before you keel over!"

"I've never keeled over in my life."

"There's a first time for everything!"

She moved to the small cabinet in the corner and took out the bandages and bottle of iodine she knew Ed Tickner kept there. Jake bent his tall frame into the chair and unbuttoned his shirt. He was just drawing it off when Caley turned back to face him.

She very nearly dropped the iodine. The sight of his naked, powerfully muscled upper body made her cheeks grow rosy and her legs grow weak. His bronze skin gleamed in the lamplight, his chest broad and lightly matted with dark brown hair, his strong, sinewy arms looking as though they could easily crush the life from a man's body—or a woman's.

"Another inch or two north, and Isaiah Griffin would have gotten his wish," he remarked dryly, glancing down at the wound just below his ribs. He dropped the bloodstained cotton shirt to the floor and met Caley's gaze once more.

"Isaiah Griffin?" she echoed in bafflement. Her brow cleared as realization dawned on her. "Surely you don't think Isaiah had anything to do with—"

"It's a possibility," was all he would reveal.

"Well, it's a harebrained one!" she pronounced indignantly. She marched forward and set the bottle down on the desk with considerable more force than was necessary. "Hell's bells, Isaiah may be a lot of things, but he isn't stupid!"

"Even smart men can become stupid when their whole way of life is threatened."

"What the devil are you talking about?"

"It's called 'progress,' Caley," he explained. "But men like Isaiah Griffin don't want things to change. They've controlled the range for so long, they view settlement—and the law order that goes along with it—as an invasion."

"That's nonsense!" she scoffed, angrily pulling the cork out of the bottle. "Isaiah just doesn't want to see men bringing sheep into cattle country, and he—"

"It isn't only the sheep. It's the railroad, the town, the people . . . everything. The very things that brought him here in the first place are now threatening to encroach upon this little kingdom he's built for himself. He'll go down fighting," predicted Jake, a note of admiration creeping into his voice. "But he'll go down just the same."

"And you're the one who's going to make sure he does, is that it?" she challenged bitterly. She poured some of the iodine onto a bandage and prepared to cleanse his wound.

"I'm not here to bring anyone down," he replied, his handsome brow creasing into a frown.

"Well you sure could've fooled me," she murmured.

Bending over him, she gently touched the bandage to his torn flesh. He tensed at the sting of the iodine, but offered no complaint as she swabbed at the spot where the unknown assailant's bullet had mercifully just grazed him. Her long, flame-colored curls tumbled down across her shoulders to tease lightly at his bare chest and arms. His green eyes darkened to jade, the familiar liquid fire racing through his veins because of her nearness. More than anything in the world, he wanted to pull her down upon his lap and bury his face in her hair . . . to kiss her sweet lips until she begged for mercy . . . to make her forget all about Matt Griffin and admit that she was *his*.

"It bled a lot, but I've always heard that keeps the poison out," remarked Caley, straightening again. She refused to meet his gaze and busied herself with folding another bandage. "You're one lucky son of a bitch."

"Am I?"

"Now hold still while I get this in place," she instructed with amazing equanimity. Holding the folded bandage over the wound, she wrapped another long length of the clean cotton about Jake's ribs and secured it with a knot in the front. She stood back to inspect her handiwork with a critical eye. "I won't say it's the prettiest fix-up I've ever seen, but I guess it'll do."

"Had a lot of experience at this sort of thing, have you?" asked Jake, his gaze alight with roguish warmth as he watched her cork the bottle of iodine

195

again.

"Some," she answered evasively. Still far more affected by his half-nakedness than she cared to acknowledge, she was about to gather up the extra bandages when her eyes fell upon a jagged scar running horizontally across his side. "What happened there?" she blurted out, impulsively smoothing a finger along his bronzed, hard-muscled flesh.

"Bayonet." Groaning inwardly at the way her touch made his loins burn, he forced himself to refrain from grabbing her and saying to hell with the consequences.

"The war?" she then asked.

"Yes."

"You fought for the Confederacy, I suppose?" Her voice held an undercurrent of disapprobation.

"I did," he answered without any sign of having taken offense.

She said nothing else on the subject. But, as she started to turn away again, another scar caught her attention. Blissfully unaware of the battle she had set to raging within Jake, she reached out and touched him again.

"And this?" she queried, referring to what looked suspiciously like the mark of a bullet on his left shoulder.

"Texas." *Damn it, he couldn't take much more of this.*

"Texas?" she echoed in surprise. Her widened eyes finally traveled up to his face, and she was even more startled by the smoldering look contained within those magnificent, deep green orbs of his. Dismayed to feel a sudden and quite delectable tremor course through her, she quickly pulled her hand away and sought to cover her nervousness by making idle conversation again. "Was it a jealous husband?" she questioned archly.

196

"Hardly," he quipped with a faint smile of irony. It was difficult for him to keep a clear head with her so close. He watched as she began rolling up the leftover strips of cotton. His eyes were drawn to where her full breasts rose and fell beneath the soft, clinging leather of her fringed tunic. With another inward groan, he looked back up to the proud beauty of her face. "It was a long time ago," he went on to elaborate in a low, vibrant tone that made Caley's heart pound all the harder. "Back when I rode with the Rangers. I was little more than a kid—full of myself and looking for a fight, I suppose."

"You haven't changed much," she retorted. The sound of his quiet chuckle provoked a lightheadedness that threatened to send her swaying against him. Never in her life had she wanted to touch a man as she found herself wanting to touch him . . . wanting to smooth her hands over his lean muscles . . . wanting to feel her own woman's body crushed to the powerful, utterly masculine hardness of his.

"I've got some other scars," he told her, a wicked gleam dancing in his eyes now. "But they'll have to wait until we're alone."

Caley blushed fierily and whirled away. Jake's hand shot out to seize her wrist.

"I didn't take you for a coward, Caley McAlister."

"I'm not a coward!" she denied in an angry flash of spirit.

She wrenched free and carried the iodine and bandages back to the cabinet in the corner. Jake's eyes followed her every movement, brimming with passion's fire as they took in the sight of her gently swaying hips hugged to alluring perfection by the fitted buckskin trousers. The silken auburn tresses, reaching to her waist, shimmered to and fro across her back with each step she took.

Muttering a savage curse beneath his breath, Jake stood and turned the lamp's flame even higher.

"Why didn't you go back to Texas?" Caley suddenly asked, closing the cabinet doors and turning to face him again. Her eyes grew very round, for he looked even more devilishly appealing when standing.

"I did. But it wasn't the same after the war." He unbuckled his holster and lowered it to the top of the desk.

"Were you a lawman there, too?" She suddenly found herself curious to know everything she could about him, to know what kind of life he had led before coming to Elko. *And*, heaven help her, to know if there really had been an endless string of other women who had found him as damnably hard to resist as she did.

"I was a rancher," he confided, his gaze hardening at the painful memories he now called forth. "My father died while I was away fighting. I went back to help my brother with the ranch."

"Did you . . . did you settle down while you were there?"

"Settle down?"

"You know what I mean, confound it!" she maintained, her eyes flashing in annoyance.

"If you're asking whether or not I ever married, the answer is no," he told her with only the merest hint of a smile playing about his lips. "There's never been anyone like that in my life." *Until now*, he added silently.

"Oh come on, Marshal," she responded in a mixture of sarcasm and disbelief, "surely not even one of those pretty little Texas belles?"

198

"Not a one of them."

"Then why did you leave?" she next asked him, at the same time asking herself why she should feel so damned pleased at learning he had remained unattached.

"Like I said—it wasn't the same as before." His eyes met and locked with hers before he added in a resonant voice that was scarcely more than a whisper, "But Texas will always be home."

"At least you have a home," she murmured, her gaze falling before the steady, penetrating intensity of his. Folding her arms across her breasts, she wandered to the window and gazed outward upon the night-cloaked street. "We never lived in one place long enough for it to feel like home. I guess Elko's the closest I've ever come." She released a sigh and absently swept a wayward strand of hair from her face, her eyes clouding when she revealed, "I don't even know if I've got family somewhere. My father never spoke of his past much, except to remind me that we were descended from Irish royalty or some such poppycock. My mother's folks lived back East—Pennsylvania, I think. But I don't know for sure. She died when I was very young."

"You've always pretty much looked after yourself, haven't you?" asked Jake, his heart twisting at the thought of the lonely young girl she must have been.

"Yes, and I've done a damned good job of it, too!" she declared, raising her head defiantly.

"So much so that you're afraid to let anyone get close to you."

"I'm not afraid of anything!" She spun about and closed the distance between them in three long, angry strides. Her hands gripped the edge of the desk as she told him, "I'm not like the other women you've known, Jake Brody! I'm not some frail, meek little bundle of submission who will flatter your ego and feed your pride!"

"You think that's what I want?" His eyes were full of tender, loving amusement as he smiled softly down at her. "You don't have to tell me you're different. Anyone can see that. Hell, I noticed it right away."

"Damn you, don't laugh at me!" she stormed. "You've done nothing but . . . bait me and rile me and . . . and *laugh* at me ever since you came to town! Well, I'll be hanged if I'll put up with it any longer, do you hear?" Drawing herself rigidly erect, she cast him a narrow, furiously scathing look that was intended to chill him to the bone. She had no idea how much her anger heightened her beauty, nor how the sight of her provoked an even more tumultuous battle within Jake. "I don't want any part of you, Jake Brody! I wish to God that bullet *had* been an inch or two farther north!" She knew she didn't truly mean this last bit, but she was too infuriated to take it back.

"Who are you trying so hard to convince, Caley?" Jake challenged in a quiet, dangerously even tone. "Me — or yourself?"

Without waiting for an answer, he came around the desk and swept her masterfully into his arms. She inhaled upon a sharp gasp, her protests silenced by the firm, demanding pressure of his lips upon hers. Melting against him with a low moan of surrender, she raised her arms to entwine about his neck. His bronzed, naked skin felt warm and smooth and breathtakingly vibrant beneath her fingers. He kissed her long and hard, and she kissed him right back.

Finally, he raised his head and gazed down into her beautiful, softly glowing eyes.

"You're mine, Caley McAlister," he decreed in a

low tone simmering with passion. "You've been mine from that first day when you stood there in the street with that blasted whip in your hand, spitting fire at me." His strong arms tightened with fierce possessiveness about her trembling curves. "I think I knew it even then."

Caley felt the barriers she had long ago erected about her heart tumbling. Still, she was not one to be conquered so easily.

"I'm not yours! I'm not yours or any other man's!" she denied hotly, her eyes kindling again as she struggled within his forceful grasp. "But if I did belong to someone, it would be to Matt Griffin!" Angered beyond all reason, she took her defiance one step farther—one step too far, if she had but known. "As a matter of fact, I'm going to marry Matt Griffin and there's not a damned thing you can do about it!" she proclaimed recklessly. A sharp, breathless cry escaped her lips when Jake suddenly yanked her up hard against him.

"You're going to marry *me* you little hellcat!" he commanded hoarsely, his gaze full of a savage light as it burned down into hers. His handsome face wore a grim, unmistakably relentless expression that left little doubt as to his determination to be her master.

"Marry you?" Caley echoed in shocked amazement, her eyes growing round as saucers.

"Yes, damn you, you're going to marry me!" he reiterated with none of a lover's usual gentleness.

"Why, I—I'd as soon bed down with a rattlesnake!" she retorted in a flash of scornful bravado.

"Like it or not, you'll bed down with me." His mouth curved into a slow, teasing smile when he added huskily, "But I think you'll like it."

To prove his point in the most effective way known to a virile, flesh-and-blood man like him-

201

self, he claimed her lips with his own once more. His words echoed throughout the turbulent recesses of Caley's mind, but the wild, sweet ecstasy wrought by his kiss sent all rational thought flying. . . .

"Oh, I — I'm sorry!" Dan Mitchelson stammered out from the doorway a few long, exquisitely agonizing moments later. "I didn't mean to barge in on anything!"

The sound of his voice broke the spell.

Caley's eyes flew open. Her face flaming in embarrassment, she pushed against Jake with all her might. He released her, but he took his own sweet time about it. And even then, he retained possession of her hand.

"Come on in, Dan," Jake instructed his deputy. "You can be the first to congratulate us."

"Congratulate you?" Dan echoed in bewilderment. His eyes traveled swiftly over Caley's blushing countenance and his boss's tall, half-naked frame. His eyes filled with comprehension just about the time Jake offered a startling explanation.

"Miss McAlister and I are going to be married."

"*What*?" gasped Caley, rounding on him in furious disbelief. "The hell we are!"

She jerked her hand free and stalked to the door. A thoroughly bemused Dan removed himself from her path, but she drew to a halt before reaching the doorway and spun back around to fling her "fiance" a fiery, downright murderous glare.

"I wouldn't marry you if you were the last man on earth, Jake Brody!" she bit out.

"From here on out, I'm the first *and* last," he countered, his low, deep-timbred voice laced with steel. "Get used to the idea."

"Why, you—" she sputtered in wrathful indignation. Giving a toss of her flame-colored tresses, she marched forward and snatched up the whip she had left coiled atop the cabinet. Her fingers curled about the whipstock as she flung about to face Jake again. "Come near me again, and I swear I'll turn you into a gelding!"

"You might regret that once we're married," he drawled, his green eyes smoldering with an irresistible combination of humor and desire and something else he had not yet put a name to.

Caley, her own eyes shooting lethal, blue-green sparks, leveled a blistering curse at his handsome head and finally stormed out of the jail. Dan stared after her a moment before closing the door and meeting Jake's gaze.

"If you don't mind my saying so, Marshal," the young deputy remarked hesitantly, "Well . . . Miss McAlister doesn't seem too awful keen on the notion of matrimony."

"You're looking at the man who's going to change her mind," Jake vowed quietly. Then, changing the subject, he filled Dan in on the situation with Matt Griffin and the sheepherders.

It was only a matter of time now, he told himself, before all hell broke loose.

Chapter IX

Three days, thought Caley, her silken brow creasing into a frown of displeasure. It had been three whole days since she had last spoken to Jake Brody.

He had been in her thoughts with damnable frequency. And she had caught a glimpse of him several times as his long, easy strides carried him about town. But, he had not sought her out since the night she had bandaged his wound. Not even once.

According to what Maybelle had told her, he was taking most of his meals down at the jail. She had been avoiding Maybelle's table all the same, cursing herself for a coward yet unable to reconcile her tightly strung emotions with her usual bold resolve. To make matters worse, she had not heard from Matt, either.

"What the devil's going on?" she murmured aloud, her troubled gaze meeting its reflected counterpart in the mirror hanging above the washstand. She had braided her hair for a change, and now pinned up the two thick plaits so that they would stay securely beneath her hat. "Men!" she fumed, jabbing the last pin in with a vengeance.

Heaving a sigh, she mentally consigned both Jake Brody and Matt Griffin to the devil for at least the hundredth time in the past seventy-two hours, whirled away from the mirror, and caught up Shadrach on her way downstairs. He struggled in her grasp, but she held tight until they reached the office, at which time the ornery, independent-minded cat went scampering away to make a nuisance of himself among the six passengers waiting to climb aboard the stage to Tuscarora.

"Mornin', Miss Caley!" Red Tarver called out when he saw her. He sauntered across from the doorway and swept the hat from his head. "You don't look none the worse for wear!" he remarked gallantly, referring to the rough weather she had encountered the day before.

"Good morning, Red," she responded with a warm smile of gratitude. "Thanks for opening up this morning."

"I wish you'd let me take your run today," he told her with a worried frown. "The roads are bound to be a mite rough. And after that storm you ran into—"

"I appreciate the offer, but as you said, I'm none the worse for wear. It would take a hell of a lot more than a little rain to make me cry uncle. Besides," she added, buckling a leather belt about her slender waist and taking up her gloves, "seeing as how you went and got yourself married, you might as well take all the runs to Hamilton so you can see the happy bride now and then!"

"It's too soon to tell if she's gonna be happy or not," he declared, releasing a sigh and shaking his head for effect. His eyes lit with playful humor. "But I'll give it my best shot, Miss Caley."

"You do that," she retorted dryly, casting him a

look of mock sternness before moving past him to fetch her hat. She pulled it down low on her head while her gaze made a quick, encompassing sweep of the crowded office.

All the passengers that day were of the male persuasion, a circumstance she viewed with mixed emotions. Men were usually better travelers than women on a long haul such as the one they'd be making today; of course, there were always exceptions. And there was no denying that members of her own sex were as a rule more resourceful when it came to handling trouble. They might cry and scream and make a lot of noise in general, but by damn, they'd be there when it counted.

She strolled outside to find Billy checking the harness one last time. Musing that he was doing the work of two men twice his size, she made a mental note to give him a raise just as soon as she got back that evening.

"She's all ready, Miss Caley!" the slender youth announced with a note of pride in his voice.

"Thanks, Billy."

She climbed up to take her place in the driver's seat atop the coach. Red brought her the mail pouch, which she proceeded to stash beneath the seat. It puzzled her that there was still no sign of the express man, for she had been notified by telegram that she'd be transporting a large shipment of gold on the return trip. Perhaps, she mused, a guard would be waiting for her in Tuscarora.

"There'll be a new man riding shotgun with you today," Red told her, as if he'd read her thoughts. There was something strange about the way he said it, too.

"A new man?" she probed for more information,

narrowing her eyes down at him.

"Now don't go gettin' a burr under your saddle, Miss Caley," the other driver cautioned amiably. "You can take my word for it — he's a trustworthy sonofagun and a real squareshooter to boot."

"Who is it, Red?" she asked in growing suspicion.

"Marshal Brody," came the answer, but not from Red.

Caley jerked her head around at the sound of his voice. She watched in stunned disbelief as Jake strode unhurriedly forward along the boardwalk and came to stand beside the stagecoach.

"What the hell are *you* doing here?" she ground out, dismayed to feel the warm color rising to her face.

"I've been assigned to ride along with you," he replied with maddening calm.

Without another word, he thrust his shotgun into Caley's unwilling hands, hoisted himself upward, and sat down close beside her. She visibly bristled and edged her hips as far away from his as the narrow wooden seat would permit.

"What do you mean, 'assigned'?" she demanded testily, pushing the gun back at him.

"Let's just say the head office thought it advisable for me to come."

"Are you talking about Wells, Fargo?"

"Maybe," was all he would reveal. His reticence — not to mention his highly unsettling presence — served to add fuel to the fire already simmering within her.

"*I'm* the driver on this run, Jake Brody, and I'll be damned if I'm going to go all the way to Tuscarora and back with you sitting there —"

"Then let one of the other drivers do it," he

208

suggested with a faint smile.

His gaze met hers, and she could have sworn she glimpsed an unspoken challenge within the fathomless green, gold-flecked depths of his. Once again, it seemed she had forgotten how incredibly handsome he was—and how infuriatingly stubborn.

"All right, damn it!" she capitulated with an ill grace.

Making no attempt whatsoever at civility, she gathered up the reins and in so doing elbowed the man beside her sharply in the side. His rugged, sun-bronzed features tightened, but he said nothing. The second time she did it, however, his hand shot out to seize her wrist in a none too gentle grip that gave evidence of his own flaring temper.

"Easy, wildcat," he warned quietly.

"Just stay the hell out of my way!" she parried, pulling free. The fringe on her buckskin suit danced wildly about as she shifted on the seat again and lifted a booted foot to the top edge of the boards.

"You ever been to Tuscarora, Marshal?" Red asked casually, managing to keep a straight face in spite of the absurdity of the situation.

"No."

"Well, I don't rightly know if it's possible, but there are some who say Tuscarora's even more the devil's own playground than Elko. Watch yourself," Red offered by way of a little friendly advice.

"Thanks," said Jake, giving a curt nod down at him.

"All aboard!" Caley's voice rang out in the brisk morning air.

The six passengers hurried from the office and took their places inside the coach, settling themselves as best they could while Caley scanned the hitching gear and glanced down to check the position of the long leather straps in her hands. This last ritual was unnecessary, for like any jehu worth his salt, she could feel the reins at all times, even through the protection of her gloves, and drove more by instinct than anything else.

"Let 'er go, Billy!" she shouted the familiar command to the hostler.

Billy obeyed and stepped back out of the way. The six horses took off, pulling against their collars in perfect unison. The stage leapt into motion. Jake, cradling the shotgun across his lap with one hand, gripped the back of the seat with the other and watched as Caley maneuvered the reins with a light touch that bespoke inborn ability as well as practice.

The fully loaded mud wagon rolled northward out of Elko. Low on the eastern horizon hung the rising sun, as if gathering courage to face the day ahead. Caley felt much the same way.

She tried to forget about the man sitting beside her, but there was no earthly way she could. Fate had played a cruel trick on her—that was for damned sure. Of all the men who could have ridden shotgun on her run that day, why the blazes did Jake Brody have to be the one?

His proposal of marriage, or rather, his *decree* of marriage, had caused her no end of anger and confusion and troubled dreams. She told herself that he couldn't possibly have meant it. He had said nothing about harboring a "tender affection" for her. Neither had Matt, come to think of it, but then Matt had never been one for spilling his heart out to anyone. And she had certainly never asked him to.

No, she concluded bitterly, it was all clear to her

210

now. Jake Brody was a man who was accustomed to getting what he wanted. She had resisted him, and he couldn't stand it. The arrogant Texas scoundrel just couldn't stand it. He wanted nothing more than to conquer her, to carve another notch in his belt. The thought left her feeling more miserable than ever.

The first portion of the journey passed without incident. Leading up through the steep, barren hills into Dobe Canyon, the road followed the same route used by freighters and stockmen heading to and from the mining boomtowns. The rains of the previous day had soaked the heavy clay and left it muddy, but the road was still quite passable, and, in certain spots, even more easily traversed than when dry.

By the time Caley eased the team to a halt at Dinner Station, it was nearly noon and the passengers were glad to have the chance to stretch their legs. They filed into the stone building for a meal that cost fifty cents and would in all probability leave them satisfied.

Jake climbed down and reached back up for Caley. She pointedly ignored his outstretched hand, choosing instead to descend from the other side. After checking to make sure the team was given water and oats by the station's hostler, she tugged the hat from her head and set off toward the main building.

"Sooner or later, we're going to have to talk," she heard Jake remark behind her. She stopped dead in her tracks and whirled to confront him.

"We've nothing to say to one another, Marshal Brody," she contended with icy composure. She was tempted to add that since he hadn't seen fit to speak more than a dozen words to her these past several hours, she sure as hell wasn't in the mood to listen to him now. Her eyes flashing, she declared, "We leave again in half an hour. If you want to eat or 'pick daisies' or anything else, you'd better get to it!"

Jake's mouth twitched at her charming metaphor for a visit to the outhouse. Clutching the shotgun in one hand, he followed her into a large, dimly lit room filled with rough-hewn benches and tables and the appetizing aroma of the "three B's", as they were often called on the frontier—bacon, beans, and biscuits.

The stage pulled out again right on schedule. Climbing to a low pass in the Independence Range, the road ran along jagged ridges blanketed with grass and sagebrush. The going was much slower now, and it was necessary for Caley to concentrate almost exclusively on her driving as she urged the team farther and farther into the rugged, wildly beautiful reaches of northern Nevada. Around the horizon spread a land that was unbelievable in its magnitude. In the southwest the distant valley of the Humboldt appeared to be nothing more than a dirty gray patch, while in the southeast the snow-covered peaks of the Rubies seemed to be reaching for the very heavens themselves.

Inside the coach, most of the passengers were enduring the constant and sometimes violent pitching motion quite well; others were suffering their own private hell. One of the men was a crusty old miner who would now and then turn to the open window and release a thick stream of amber liquid under considerable pressure. Although his fellow travelers instinctively pulled away from that side, the wind was merciful and carried the spray of tobacco away from the coach. Another man, a mineral assayer by trade, had the misfortune to feel his dinner making itself known with each jolt and lurch. The young cowboy seated opposite made it a point to keep his brand new, fancy leather boots out of the way.

On the seat above, Jake watched the young woman beside him. His heart swelled with pride for her beauty, her spirit, and her expertise at a job few women would have either the courage or the desire to take on. He was always ready to lend a hand should she need it, but she never did. His few attempts at conversation were rebuffed.

The long trip provided him with plenty of time in which to think about this flame-haired spitfire who, whether she was ready to admit it or not, was all woman . . . about his feelings for her . . . about their future together. He had never been given to a lot of introspection or soul-searching; he had always been a man of action instead of words. But he knew he was willing to do whatever it took to make Caley his own. *Whatever it took.*

Finally, the high country mining town of Tuscarora came into view. The first thing Jake noticed as they neared the infamous community was its cemetery, where white headstones and simple carved boards were conspicuous against the brown, sagebrush-dotted earth. It was a chilling sight, a stark reminder of man's inescapable destiny. Noticeable on a hill above the rip-roaring camp of several thousand, was the tall, red brick stack of the new smelter. Progress had even crept this far north.

The wheels of the stagecoach rolled directly across a little stream of cold water; there was an abundance of good water in Tuscarora, a rarity for Nevada's mining towns. But water was not foremost on the minds of its inhabitants, at least not if all the stories Jake had heard were true. It was said that the population, mostly male, imbibed ten times more whiskey than water. Saloons were certainly plentiful, as were brothels and gaming halls and even a number of opium dens. The town had a sheriff—a *real* sheriff, Dan Mitchelson had confided to Jake—who did his best to keep peace amidst the miners, Chinese laborers, gamblers, merchants, freighters, and assorted other characters.

Caley guided the team down Tuscarora's thickly congested main street and tugged gently on the reins as the coach rolled up before the local stage office. A man came bustling forward to assist the passengers, their muscles cramped and aching, from the mud wagon, while the hostler wasted no time in changing out the horses.

After setting the brake and securing the reins, Caley tugged off her gloves and prepared to climb down. Jake didn't wait to offer his hand this time—he seized her arm in a firm grip and virtually hauled her down to stand beside him on the muddy boardwalk.

"Let go of me, damn it!" she hissed, angrily trying to pull away. He held fast.

"I've got to pay a visit to the sheriff. When do we pull out again?"

"As soon as everything's loaded up!"

"I'll be back in five minutes," he promised. Releasing her at last, he gazed solemnly down into her stormy, fiery-eyed countenance. There was a hint of devilment lurking in his own gaze when he instructed, "Just make sure you don't leave without me."

"The stage waits for no one!" she insisted, yet

knew full well that she couldn't leave him behind. He was the designated guard for the express box, and she needed the business from Wells, Fargo too much to jeopardize the safe transport of the shipment. So, even though she would have liked nothing better than to conveniently "lose" her shotgun man, she told herself that her personal feelings would have to be set aside. *Later,* she vowed silently. Once the job was done, she'd make him understand once and for all that she wanted none of him.

"They won't load the box until you're here," she admitted reluctantly, "so make it quick!" She gave a curt nod over her shoulder. "The jail's that way!"

"Much obliged." A faint smile touched his lips before he strode away.

Caley stared after him a moment, then marched inside the office. She was surprised to learn there would be no passengers on the return trip. The prospect of being all alone with Jake Brody for the next several hours was highly unsettling.

Five minutes turned into ten. She was waiting impatiently beside the coach when she spied Jake. He towered above most of the other men moving along the boardwalk; he was also a damn sight more handsome. Breathing an oath, Caley whirled about and prepared to hoist herself up to the driver's seat.

"Well now," a familiar, gravelly voice sounded behind her, "if it ain't Miss Caley McAlister, come to Tuscarora to show us all what a hell of a little whip she is!"

She turned to face Ed Tickner. Her blue-green eyes were devoid of warmth as they flickered over him, for she had never considered him a friend. Far from it.

215

"What are you doing here, Ed?" she asked with a tightlipped frown.

"Just visitin'," he drawled, giving her a broad, rather insolent grin. The grin faded when his eyes shifted to fall upon Jake. His features hardened with angry displeasure as the marshal drew closer. "I see you brought along that dirty rebel bastard!" In truth, he had noticed Jake when the stagecoach pulled up.

Caley was taken aback by the hatred in his voice. Jake, reaching them mere seconds later, met her troubled gaze before turning his attention to Elko's former sheriff. His eyes glinted coldly down at the man he had only a few days ago forced out of office.

"Tickner," he said, giving him a curt nod.

"Your time's comin', Brody!" Ed Tickner spat at him. Though he would not by any stretch of the imagination be considered attractive, his coarse, unshaven features looked even more repulsive than usual. "Yes sir, by damn, you'll be on your way out soon!"

"Come on," Jake spoke quietly to Caley, taking her arm. The other man, however, would not be ignored.

"We'll see who has the last laugh, Brody! We'll see who ends up runnin' things in Elko!"

Caley took her place upon the driver's seat and looked back down to where Jake had turned to face Tickner again. She took note of the dangerously grim expression on Jake's face, and the menacing scowl on Ed Tickner's. Waiting breathlessly to see what would happen, she found herself offering up a silent prayer on Jake's behalf.

"You don't scare me none, you four-flushin' sonofabitch!" snarled Ed. "I ain't without friends, and I damn sure ain't without friends who'll back me against *you!*"

"I told you before, Tickner," Jake reiterated in a low tone edged with barely controlled fury, "if you've got any complaints, come by the jail. This is neither the time nor the place to discuss—"

"Hell, there's no need to 'discuss' a damn thing, Marshal!" the shorter, heavier man broke in. He gave a grunt of laughter all of a sudden, his eyes lighting with malignant humor and, oddly enough, triumph. "You and your little redheaded sidekick there go on your way! I'll bide my time, just like I been doin'!" With that bold, cryptic statement, he tipped his hat mockingly to Caley and swaggered away up the street.

"Ed Tickner always was a mangy, no-account polecat!" Caley muttered as she jerked on her gloves. "But he doesn't have enough guts to do more than shoot his mouth off!"

"Men like him are full of surprises," remarked Jake, meeting her eyes for a moment before turning about to supervise the loading of the express box.

They set off for Elko again soon thereafter. Ed Tickner watched them go.

His eyes followed the stagecoach as it rumbled away and disappeared around a bend in the road. He knew it might have been a bit risky to show his face the way he'd done, but he told himself it had been worth it all the same. It had been worth it to stand there and let Brody know he'd made a mistake in treating him like dirt. He'd settle that score all right, settle it good and proper.

Tipping his hat farther back upon his head, Elko's former "arm of the law" emerged from the shadows and rounded the corner of the building to join the endless flow of humanity along Tuscarora's main street.

Caley was relieved to spot the familiar buildings of Dinner Station in the near distance. Coming down out of the high country was always more exhausting than going up, for she was required to apply just the right amount of brake and couldn't afford to make even a simple error in judgment. One mistake, and the coach would go toppling off the narrow, twisting, rock-strewn road to smash into bits in the canyon below. The responsibility could be quite overwhelming if she allowed herself to think about it much.

Her nerves were also strung tight as a result of Jake's disturbing presence beside her. Although she couldn't deny he had been a perfect gentleman and had not distracted her with conversation or complaints or anything else, she had nevertheless remained acutely conscious of him at all times.

Great balls of fire, how could she not be? she reflected irritably. Try as she would to despise and resist him, she could not for the life of her manage to forget him. More than once that day, she had caught herself remembering their last fiery encounter and the startling words he had spoken. Every time they had accidentally bumped against one another atop the rocking, bouncing stagecoach, she had heaped a thousand silent curses upon his head as well as her own.

It was late in the afternoon by the time they pulled up in front of the midway station. Caley started off for the hot meal she knew would be waiting, but she stopped and turned back toward the stage when she realized Jake had not yet made

218

a move to follow after her.

"Aren't you coming?" she asked, her brows knitting into a slight frown of puzzlement.

"No."

"Why not?"

"Because, Miss McAlister," he informed her in a voice brimming with wry amusement, "I can't leave the shipment unguarded."

"Oh for heaven's sake, who in tarnation's going to steal it out *here?*" she demanded in exasperation as she dragged her hat from her head. "It's impossible for anyone to—"

"Nothing's impossible. And we can't afford to take any chances." He shifted on the seat, negligently lifting a booted foot to the board and tugging the front brim of his hat lower.

He was right, and she knew it. But that still didn't mean she liked being told how to do her job.

"Then go hungry, damn it!" she ground out, her eyes hurtling invisible daggers at his handsome head before she stormed inside the building. She could have sworn she heard a low chuckle behind her.

Leaving Dinner Station a scant quarter of an hour later, they headed back through rolling, wildflower-strewn country where range cattle grazed peacefully beneath the cloudless blue sky. As always, the Ruby Mountains were like a magnificent, snow-topped beacon in the distance.

The stage was still nearly two hours away from its final destination when Caley's eyes suddenly detected movement in the road ahead. She knew Jake saw it, too, for she felt him tense beside her.

But it was already too late.

Five armed men, their heads covered by hats and

219

the lower half of their faces hidden behind brightly colored kerchiefs, materialized to block the coach's path. A loud gasp broke from Caley's lips as she tugged on the reins in alarm.

"Hellfire and damnation!" she breathed, coming half off the seat in an effort to stop the team in time. She later mused that she should have kept right on going and run the bastards down. But then again, hindsight is hardly ever wrong.

Jake said nothing, but sat in deadly and silent calm beside her. If she had chanced to look at him just then, she would have observed the savage, intensely purposeful gleam in his eyes and known that something was afoot.

"Halt and throw down the box!" one of the men yelled in a strange, raspy tone of voice while the shrilly protesting horses slowed to a reluctant halt.

To Caley, it looked as if the worst was inevitable. The road agents, however, had not counted on Jake Brody.

Everything happened with such dizzying swiftness after that, there was no time to think—only act, or *react*, as Caley was forced to do.

"Get down!" Jake thundered at her, flinging her bodily to the floorboards with one hand while raising his shotgun and firing a deafening blast with the other. He wounded two of the masked men and sent the other three scurrying for cover.

The frightened animals harnessed to the stage bolted, causing the mud wagon to give a violent lurch before flying forward in the wake of the frantically plunging team. The surprised, would-be robbers dove behind some of the large rocks on either side of the road.

Caley, holding on for dear life, somehow managed to retain possession of the reins. She staggered up to her knees on the floorboards, while Jake emptied the other barrel of his shotgun in the direction of the road agents. He then drew his two six-shooters and kept on firing.

Still determined to gain control of the express box, the three men jumped on their horses and gave chase, returning Jake's fire with a vengeance. The sound of gunshots filled the air, and bullets whizzed by in a terrifying series of near misses.

"*Jake!*" Caley screamed when he bit out a curse and momentarily clapped a hand to his arm.

"Keep going!" he roared above the ear-splitting din. He reloaded one of the Colts and took aim again.

The wild flight continued, with Caley driving like she had never driven before and Jake ignoring the blood streaming down his arm as he gave the robbers a taste of good old-fashioned Texas grit. He had never given up on a job and he sure as hell wasn't going to do so now.

They reached a long stretch of straight road. Jake was finally able to steady his aim and shoot with more accuracy. One of the three pursuing bandits howled in pain and went crashing to the ground as the lawman's bullet found its mark. The last two men called it quits at that point, jerking their mounts to a halt and glaring after the stagecoach with frustrated, bloodthirsty menace in their eyes.

The horses continued their mad dash across the rugged landscape. But Caley and Jake were not, unfortunately, in the clear yet. Just when it began to look as if they were safely away with the shipment of gold, disaster visited them in another form.

They had put a good five miles between them-

221

selves and the road agents when it happened. Caley, driving the team down a steep grade, reached for the brake to slow the stage's pace around the curves she knew lay ahead.

The brake lever broke off in her hand.

She was nearly thrown from the seat, but Jake caught her. Her horror-filled gaze dropped to the horses as the coach began an unchecked downhill run. The animals alone could not hold back a wagon on a downgrade if it already had momentum, and the driver who tried to pull up and stop the team would in all likelihood find himself left with injured or dead horses as well as a wrecked coach.

"Dear God!" Caley put forth in a ragged whisper. Facing one of the predicaments most feared by stage drivers, she desperately sought to guide the team around the first curve. Her reinsmanship was the best it had ever been—but even then, the situation was hopeless.

"Let go!" commanded Jake, clamping an arm about her waist and yanking her toward him.

"No! No, I can't!" she shouted in defiance, refusing to admit defeat.

"Damn it, Caley, I'm not going to let you kill yourself! *Now let go!*"

She was not given the chance to argue. The moment the coach reached the curve and started to lean precariously to one side, Jake yelled at her to jump. He hauled her along with him, the two of them sailing through the air to land with such force upon the rain-soaked ground that the breath was knocked from their bodies.

Behind them, the stagecoach tumbled over onto its side with a loud crash. The force of the strain broke the hitch loose and sent a thick cloud of dust spiralling heavenward. The team of six horses, leaving the wrecked coach behind, instinctively galloped down the road toward the comforts waiting for them in Elko.

Jake had maneuvered so that he took the brunt of the fall. He rolled over and over with Caley until they came to rest at the foot of the hill. They lay there with their bodies entwined for several long moments, both of them stunned and thankful to be alive.

Jake was the first to stir. He braced his hands on either side of Caley and pushed himself upward a bit to peer anxiously down into her face.

"Are you all right?" he asked, his voice taut with worry.

"Yes. Yes, I—I'm all right!" she assured him breathlessly, then grimaced at a sudden pain and added, "At least, I *think* I am."

"Lie still," he commanded. Kneeling beside her, he made a quick but thorough examination of her limbs. "You've no broken bones, thank God."

"What about you?" Still shaken, she raised up on one elbow and caught sight of his blood-soaked sleeve. "You're wounded!" she exclaimed, then suddenly remembered how it had happened. She sat up so fast it made her head swim. Her eyes sparked with furious, vengeful fire as she declared, "Those bastards shot you!"

"I know," Jake quipped dryly. Unbending his tall frame, he rose to his feet and reached down to pull her up beside him.

"I've got a medical kit in the stage! Just let me—"

"No. It can wait."

"What do you mean 'it can wait'?" she demanded, jerking her hand from the strong, warm

223

grasp of his. "Don't tell me it doesn't hurt!"

"It hurts like hell," he confessed with a faint smile of irony. "But those men might be coming this way. And we've got to be ready for them if they do."

His words struck fear in her heart. Her wide, luminous gaze traveled up the hill to where the coach lay on its side beside the road.

"Dear God, we're stranded out here!" she breathed in dismay.

"For now. But once the horses make it back to Elko, the whole town will be out looking for us."

"Do you really think so?" she asked with a frown of uncertainty.

"Isn't that what they usually do?" he challenged in a light, mocking tone.

"How the hell should I know?" she retorted, her usual indomitable spirit reviving with a passion. "Nothing like this has ever happened to me before!"

"Come on." Taking her hand again, he began pulling her along with him up the hill. He paused to retrieve his guns, then moved forward with Caley to inspect the damage to the coach.

"At least she's still in one piece," muttered Caley, her gaze clouding as it flickered over the battered mud wagon. The wheels on the underside had been smashed to bits, and several items lay strewn about on the ground.

She bent and lifted the mail pouch from beside the splintered hitch, while Jake checked to make certain the express box was intact. It was.

"I'm sorry this happened, Caley." He found his shotgun and began reloading it, trying to ignore the burning pain in his arm.

"So am I!" She didn't know why she felt angry

with him, but she was angry all the same.

"My job was to guard the shipment. Even if I had let them take it, there was still a possibility they'd have killed us both."

"We damn near got killed anyway!" she pointed out reproachfully.

She ducked inside the coach and came out with a bag full of supplies that had been stashed beneath one of the seats. Inside were blankets and food and a few other things, kept handy should an emergency arise. This was the first time one had—at least on one of *her* runs.

Standing on the other side of the coach, Jake watched her rummaging angrily through the canvas bag. His blood boiled with white-hot rage at the thought of the men who were responsible for endangering her life, and his heart twisted at the realization that she might have been seriously injured or even killed as a result of his own actions. He had reacted with his usual obedience to duty, but that same duty had very nearly cost him the one thing in life he held dear.

"No more arguments!" said Caley, marching toward him now with the small medical kit in her hands. "I'm going to bandage that arm of yours, Jake Brody, whether you like it or not!"

"I didn't know you cared so much, Miss McAlister," he drawled, a teasing light dancing in his green eyes in spite of the gravity of the situation.

"I don't!" Her face had taken on that look of proud rebellion he knew so well. "I just don't want to be stuck out here in the middle of nowhere with a blasted dead man for company!"

She avoided his gaze while she set to work unbuttoning his shirt and easing it carefully off him. Leaning back against the coach, he gritted his teeth against the pain. He never once offered a complaint, not even when she cleansed the wound with an antiseptic that made him feel like he'd been set afire.

"I'll bet you enjoyed that, didn't you?" he challenged once she had finished with the swabbing and began folding a strip of cloth into a bandage.

"You've been lucky again," she noted with a frown, disregarding his attempt to bait her.

"Have I?" His fathomless, warmly glowing eyes were fastened on her face, but she still obstinately refused to look at him.

"The bullet cut straight across and missed the bone." She pressed the bandage to the wound and wrapped strips of the cloth about his upper arm.

"This is starting to become a habit with us, isn't it, wildcat?" he remarked in a low, wonderfully vibrant tone.

Caley finally raised her eyes to his face, only to feel her legs grow weak. A soft smile touched his lips, and his gaze was suffused with a strangely tender light that made her want to melt against him. She hastened to cover her disquietude by looking away and setting the medical kit to rights once more.

"You don't really think those men will come after us, do you?" she asked in a small voice.

"No, I don't," Jake was able to reply truthfully. "I don't think they want to run the risk of being seen by anyone. But it never pays to try and second guess men like that." He drew himself up to his full height and cast a look overhead at the sky. "It will be dark soon. We'd better get a fire going."

"There's a canteen and . . . and a packet of beef jerky in the bag," she murmured, unable to tear her traitorous gaze away from the bronzed, hard-muscled expanse she remembered all too well. It seemed that one of them was always half-naked when they were alone together.

"Good," he responded, flashing her another smile that brought warm color to her cheeks. "Then we won't starve while we wait. It could take all night, you know."

"All night?" Her eyes grew enormous in the delicate oval of her face as very real alarm shot through her.

"Don't worry. We'll be all right," he assured her, mistakenly believing that her trepidation stemmed from sources other than himself. He smiled briefly again and added, "I've been in worse spots. And I haven't lost a fight yet."

"Is that so? Well it could just be that your memory's a bit rusty!" Caley suggested in willful disloyalty.

Hellfire and damnation, she swore inwardly, how was she going to manage to be alone with him for the next several hours without—no, she couldn't allow herself to think about it. If she thought about it, she'd be a goner for sure. And anyway, Jake Brody wasn't the kind of man to take advantage of the situation. *Want to bet?* that tiny voice in the back of her mind parried gleefully.

Jake, telling himself there'd be plenty of time for talk later, turned away and began his preparations for the fire. Wood might be scarce, but sagebrush was plentiful and burned well, even if it did do it a bit pungently. In no time at all, he had achieved a bright, comforting blaze beside the overturned stagecoach.

Caley added more brush to the fire before spreading one of the blankets on the damp ground and taking a seat. The sun had already disappeared

227

behind the ridges of the surrounding mountains, thereby loosing a chill to spread upon the shadowed land. As if to signal the coming night, a coyote howled mournfully in the distance.

"It gets awfully cold out here after dark," she told Jake, her eyes moving with a will of their own again over his bare, powerfully formed upper body. She pulled the other blanket from the bag and thrust it toward him. "Here. Take this. I'll be hanged if I'm going to sit here and watch you freeze to death!"

"For someone who claims to despise me, you sure take a lot of pains to keep me this side of hell," he quipped, his gaze brimming with wry amusement as he took the blanket from her.

"Right now, Jake Brody, you're my responsibility!" she proclaimed defensively.

"How do you figure that?"

"You were riding shotgun on *my* stage, weren't you? That means I'll be held accountable for your safety!"

"And what about your own safety?" he demanded, tossing the blanket down beside her. "Damn it, woman, you'd have been killed if I hadn't made you jump."

His eyes glinted dully at the memory, his handsome features tightening as he lowered himself to the ground and rested the shotgun across his knees. Caley, bristling at the censure in his deep voice, edged farther away. She picked up a stick and poked at the fire, her long, unpinned braids swinging forward with each angry movement.

"I never give up on anything!" she declared by way of excuse.

"Neither do I," he countered tersely. His hand shot out to close about her wrist. "I don't want

228

you hauling any more shipments, Caley. It's too dangerous. What happened today proves it."

"Why the devil should I care what *you* want?" she retorted indignantly. "You've no right to order me about! Hell's bells, if I want to take on every blasted shipment in the state, you can't stop me!"

She tried to pull free, but drew in a sharp breath as she was suddenly and quite forcefully yanked back across the blanket. Coming up hard against Jake's naked chest, she gasped again and was dismayed to feel a tremor shake her.

"I have a right!" he ground out, his gaze burning down into the wide, startled depths of hers. "You're mine, Caley McAlister, and you'll do as I say. I won't have my wife tearing all over the countryside and getting shot at by a bunch of mean-spirited bastards who—"

"*Your wife?*" she raged. "There you go again with that ridiculous—"

"It's the truth," he ruthlessly cut her off. "And if you weren't so damned stubborn, you'd admit it." He released her wrist and stood again, clutching the shotgun in one hand.

"Where are you going?" she demanded, glaring up at him in fiery-eyed resentment.

"To the top of that bluff." He gave a curt nod back toward the spot where the road first started its curving descent. "I thought I'd check to make certain we weren't about to have company." Frowning down at her, he resisted the impulse to press a kiss upon her parted, damnably sweet lips. "Stay here," he ordered in a voice that let her know he'd brook no defiance.

"I had every intention of doing so!" she insisted, jabbing the stick into the midst of the dancing flames again.

229

She couldn't keep her eyes from following him as he strode away. The way he moved, with that easy, masculine confidence of his, made her heart beat faster. It occurred to her that if she could choose who to be stranded with out in the wilds all night long, Jake Brody was not a bad choice at all. In truth, no one else even came to mind. . . .

Flushing guiltily, she heaved a sigh and reached for the packet of jerky. She lifted a strip of it to her mouth, biting into the dried, salted beef that was as tough as rawhide and tearing off a small piece of it with her teeth.

A gunshot rang out.

Caley nearly choked on the jerky. She spit it out and scrambled to her feet, her hand moving instinctively toward the coiled whip beside her. She grabbed it and started flying up the rock-rimmed stage road, her one thought to help Jake.

Tormented by visions of him lying dead or dying, she was shocked to observe him making his way down from the bluff. His actions displayed no sign of either haste or alarm, and he certainly appeared to be unharmed. When he reached the road, she could see that he carried something in addition to the shotgun now. It was a rattlesnake, its head severed from its body by a single shot from one of Jake's revolvers.

"I'm not much on jerky," he explained, drawing closer. "These make good eating once you—"

"You scared the hell out of me!" she stormed, her turquoise eyes blazing. "Why, I thought you were . . . I thought those . . ." Her voice trailed away as she watched a slow smile spread across his handsome face.

"It's nice to know you were willing to come to my rescue," he said, glancing significantly down at

230

the whip in her hand.

"I won't make that mistake again!" she bit out, her face flaming in wrathful embarrassment. She whirled and stalked back to the fire, flinging the whip down and fighting back a sudden, inexplicable wave of tears.

Jake cursed himself for a fool. Striding forward, he set the dead snake and shotgun atop the coach. He moved to stand behind Caley, forcing her about to face him with gentle firmness. She resisted his efforts, but his hands closed upon her arms to hold her captive.

"I'm sorry, Caley," he told her in a low, vibrant tone. All traces of amusement had vanished, and his eyes were full of contrition. "It was stupid of me."

"Yes, it was, damn you!" she vehemently agreed, raising her own furious gaze to the compassionate warmth of his. He cursed himself all the more when he saw the tears glistening in her eyes. "You should have known I'd think the worst! You—you should have—have—"

She broke off and choked back a sob. Though she despised herself for her weakness, the tears would no longer be denied. They spilled over from her lashes to course down the flushed smoothness of her cheeks.

Suddenly, Jake's arms were about her. He pulled her against him, holding her gently while she cried in a sorely needed emotional release. Always before, he had held her in passion; now, there was only a wonderful sense of security, a feeling of caring and warmth that reached down to her very soul. She would never have believed that a man so strong and fiercely resolute could be capable of such tenderness. No one had ever given her comfort the way he was doing . . . no one had ever made her feel so utterly feminine and glad of it.

Finally, the stormtide of weeping subsided. Caley raised her head and gratefully accepted the handkerchief Jake pressed into her hand.

"I hate weepy females," she murmured, blotting the last of her tears.

"You were entitled to cry, wildcat," he pronounced softly. "It's been a rough day, to say the least."

"And it's getting colder by the minute!" she observed. Feeling self-conscious now, she pulled away from him and turned to put more brush on the fire.

Jake, trying his damnedest to ignore the fire in his blood, muttered a silent oath and forced himself to turn away as well. It was going to be a long night. . . .

Chapter X

"Caley. It's all right, Caley. I'm here."

Jake's voice penetrated the sweet mantle of her dream. At first, she resisted the compelling resonance of that voice, preferring to linger in unconsciousness rather than awaken to the known dangers of reality. Finally, however, her eyelids fluttered open and she found herself gazing up into the same, ruggedly handsome features which had dominated her restless slumber.

"Jake?" she whispered. Her sleep-drugged gaze cleared, and she saw that he was kneeling beside her on the ground. "What is it?" she asked in bewilderment. "What—"

"You were dreaming," he explained, smiling softly down at her in the firelit darkness.

He didn't add that she had called his name several times, nor that she had done so in a voice full of desperate longing. The sound of it had stirred his heart . . . and sent the familiar liquid fire racing through his veins. He wanted her so much it hurt, yet he couldn't allow himself to touch her. Both the time and the place were wrong, and he knew it. Still, that didn't keep him from thinking about what it would be like once she was

233

his.

Soon, Caley McAlister, he vowed silently. *Soon.*

"Dreaming?" Caley echoed with a frown. She sat up, her eyes moving to the blaze which still crackled and danced beneath the endless night sky. "What time is it?" she wondered aloud, drawing the blanket more closely about her as cold air swept down from the mountains.

"About midnight, I'd say," replied Jake. He wore a blanket draped about his own bare shoulders, and his holster remained buckled low on his hips in defensive readiness.

"Midnight!" she breathed, her gaze widening in alarm. "They should have found us by now!"

"They'll be along soon," he calmly reassured her. "Besides, if they haven't shown up by first light, we'll strike out on our own."

"But it's miles back to town!"

"We can stay out here if you prefer. Come to think of it, that might not be such a bad idea after all." His eyes brimmed with ironic humor, and a crooked smile played about his lips as he stood and moved to put more brush on the fire. "It might do us a lot of good to be alone out here for a few days."

"You mean it might do *you* a lot of good!" she retorted, watching while he shrugged off the blanket and negligently rearranged the burning pile of brush with a stick.

"You know, given the chance, I could make you forget how much you despise me," he declared in all seriousness, though his green eyes continued to twinkle quite roguishly. "As a matter of fact, I could make you forget a lot of things."

"Why, you conceited bas—"

"That reminds me," he cut her off with madden-

234

ing equanimity. "You can talk to me however you like when we're alone—provided I get the same privilege, of course. But it won't do for the wife of a United States Marshal to go around swearing at her husband in public."

"I'm not going to *be* the wife of a United States Marshal, damn it!" she denied hotly.

She jerked the blanket farther upward and then was annoyed to see that she had succeeded only in uncovering the lower half of her body. With a sigh of disgruntlement, she climbed abruptly to her feet and extended her hands toward the fire's warmth. She could feel Jake's eyes on her. She could also feel the way her body sought to betray her by trembling from head to toe.

"Have you heard from Matt Griffin?" Jake suddenly demanded.

"No!" she answered with unnecessary vehemence. "No, I—I haven't. Why do you ask?"

"He seems to have disappeared."

"Well I haven't seen him!"

Studying her reaction closely, he was satisfied that she was telling the truth. It was difficult for him to remain objective when it came to Griffin—for more reasons than one.

"How did you ever get mixed up with a man like that?" he asked as he straightened and faced her across the fire.

"I told you before, we grew up together," replied Caley, raising her head defensively. "And there's nothing wrong with the kind of man he is!"

"No, not if you ignore the fact that he's been terrorizing the countryside for the past two years."

"Terrorizing the countryside?" she repeated in scornful disbelief. "I don't know what you're talking about!"

"What about the sheepherders?" challenged Jake. His eyes darkened, and his rugged features became grim. "That's just the latest, Caley. He's made a habit of seeking revenge against anyone who dares to cross him."

"He was wrong to do what he did to Elena and her family," she allowed reluctantly. "But that doesn't mean he's as bad as you're trying to make him out to be!"

"The fact is, you don't want to know the truth," he charged in a low, tight voice. In two angry strides, he had come around the fire to tower ominously above her, his gaze burning down into hers with near savage intensity. "It's time you faced up to it, Caley. It's time you stopped being so damned stubborn and saw things for what they were!"

"You're against him because of me, aren't you?" she shot back with an accusatory glare. "Do you really think it would make any difference?" Her beautiful eyes sparked and blazed, and two bright spots of color rode high on her cheeks. "Well I'm telling you right here and now that it wouldn't!" she declared quite feelingly. "It wouldn't make any difference at all! Even if Matt Griffin wasn't standing between us, I'd still have none of *you*, Jake Brody!"

"Oh, you'll have me all right, you redheaded hellion," he vowed with dangerous calm. "What's more, you'll like it."

For Caley, that was the last straw. Her temper, always ready to explode whenever Jake was around, flared beyond control. Muttering a particularly unladylike curse, she whirled about and snatched up her whip.

Jake reached for her, but he was too late to

236

prevent her from drawing back her arm and bringing the lash snapping forward. The end of it caught him on the bronzed hardness of his bare back, just below his right shoulder blade. He did not utter a sound at the searing pain, but merely clenched his teeth and gave his beautiful, headstrong tormentor a look that was full of barely controlled violence.

Caley was immediately aghast at what she had done. She gazed up at Jake in breathless, wide-eyed expectation for several long moments. The whipstock slipped from her grasp as she gave a small, strangled cry and whirled to flee.

There was never any hope of escaping him. He caught her about the waist with his uninjured arm and yanked her roughly back against him. She fought him like a veritable tigress — fighting herself as well, if truth be told. Kicking and squirming within his relentless grasp, she tried in desperation to pry away the arm clamped like a band of iron about her waist.

Her elbow suddenly slammed back against Jake's bandaged wound. He ground out a curse and momentarily relaxed his grip. Caley took full advantage of his pain, breaking free and darting back toward the fire.

A loud gasp broke from her lips when she felt the lower edge of her buckskin tunic being seized. Tugging on it with all her might, she was dismayed to hear the sound of the soft leather giving way at the seams. She felt a rush of cool air on her skin, but she had no time to lament the damage to her much worn and much beloved garment, for Jake grabbed her about the waist again.

"*No!* No, damn you, no!" she cried hoarsely.

Struggling with even more vehemence than before, she suffered a sharp intake of breath when he suddenly flung her down atop one of the blankets and imprisoned her body there with his own. She was both shocked and enraged by her position, lying as she was on her back with the whole virile length of Jake Brody's hardness pressing intimately down upon her. His hands gripped her wrists to force her arms above her head, while his long, powerfully muscled legs ensured that she was unable to kick free.

"I warned you before Caley," he said, his deep voice laced with desire as well as fury.

Refusing to meet his gaze, she furiously twisted her head to and fro upon the blanket as she continued to struggle. But it was no use. His lips came crashing down upon hers, fierce and hotly demanding and all too provocative.

A scream of helpless anger and defeat rose in her throat, only to become almost instantly transformed into a moan of passion's sweet surrender. Jake's wildly intoxicating kiss set her afire and made her forget any thought of further resistance. The next thing she knew, her wrists were being released and she was clutching with rapturous fervency at the smooth, granite-hard shoulders of the man she had only moments ago sought to escape.

The kiss deepened, Jake's tongue thrusting between her parted lips to explore the moist cavern of her mouth while his warm, strong hands delved within the gaping side seams of her tunic to close possessively upon the soft, rose-tipped roundness of her full young breasts . . .

Once again, however, fate intervened to prevent the natural course of things.

The sound of approaching hoofbeats called an abrupt halt to their tempestuous embrace. Jake was on his feet like a shot, jerking Caley up as well and shoving her unceremoniously toward the overturned stagecoach.

"Get down and stay down!" he commanded, at the same time drawing both of his pearl-handled revolvers.

Caley was too dazed to argue. She stumbled over to the coach and dropped to her knees beside it, her widened gaze flying up to where more than half a dozen riders were bearing down upon them from one of the southward hills. Her pulse leapt in alarm, but a wave of relief washed over her in the next instant when she recognized several faces in the group of horsemen. She climbed to her feet and hurried back to stand with Jake at the fire.

"We were beginning to think you'd never show!" she called out as the men drew their mounts to a halt.

"You all right, Miss Caley?" Red asked worriedly, swinging down from the saddle.

"I'm fine!" she assured him, her eyes moving to where Hank and the others were dismounting as well.

Dan Mitchelson was there, along with J.D. Worthington III, George Groat, Billy Snyder and even, miraculously enough, a sober Otis Snyder.

"Sorry it took so long, Marshal," offered Dan. "Tarver and Shaughnessy were both late getting in with their runs, and young Billy here had a hell of a time finding me."

"Think nothing of it," Jake responded with deceptive nonchalance. He didn't know whether to be grateful for their timing—or to curse it.

"What happened?" Dan then asked, eyeing the wrecked coach and his boss's bandaged arm.

"Road agents."

"Road agents?" Billy's eyes shone with excitement. "Did you kill them, Marshal?"

"Maybe," he answered with a faint smile. "I didn't hang around to make sure. Two of them were still in the saddle when they gave up the chase."

"I don't guess there's any need to ask if they got the shipment," Dan remarked wryly.

"They didn't!" Caley intervened at this point. "And we'd have made it back to town if I hadn't lost my brake lever while coming around the downside of that blasted curve!" she added, nodding toward the road.

"We figured it had to be somethin' like that," said Hank, "seein' as how the team wasn't draggin' the hitch."

"We were afraid we'd find you dead for sure, Miss Caley!" Billy confessed with a boyish grin. His father was a thin, balding, silent figure beside him. Otis sent her a kindly look that let her know he, too, was glad the worst case hadn't been borne out.

J.D. and George came forward now. Caley was puzzled by the somber looks on their faces; she was absolutely thunderstruck when they turned to Jake and uttered the words that would seal her fate.

"I should hope, Marshal Brody, that you intend to behave in an honorable manner toward Miss McAlister," declared J.D. with stern formality.

"Yes sirree, looks like we got here just in the nick of time!" George remarked bluntly, narrowing his eyes at Jake's bare chest. "If you're half the man we think you are, Marshal, you'll do right by our Miss Caley just as soon as we get back to town!"

"What the devil are you two talking about?" Caley demanded, her bright gaze moving from one man to the other.

"Now, Miss Caley, don't you worry none," George told her with an almost paternal, indulgent air that sent her into further confusion. "We ain't about to tell anyone what we saw."

"What you saw?" she echoed, her eyes growing very round. *Good heavens*, she thought with dawning dismay, *surely they hadn't*—

"I am afraid, Miss McAlister, that we witnessed the . . . well, shall we say, the 'incident' with Marshal Brody from the top of the hill," J.D. confirmed her worst fears, a dull flush of embarrassment rising to his aristocratic features. "Quite unintentionally, of course."

She crimsoned to the very roots of her auburn hair. Her eyes flew to Jake. A strange smile was playing about his lips, and there was a noticeable gleam contained within the magnificent, fathomless green depths of his gaze. Suddenly, she felt like a caged animal.

"This is ridiculous!" she insisted quite adamantly, turning back to J.D. and George. "Whatever you think you saw, it—it doesn't matter!"

"I'm afraid it does, Miss McAlister," J.D. disagreed with his usual regard for propriety. "You are, after all, an unmarried young lady, and you and Marshal Brody have spent the better part of a night alone together under highly intimate conditions. For that reason alone, your reputation will no doubt have already suffered damage beyond repair."

"I don't give a hoot in hell about my reputation!" she countered, growing more enraged with each passing second.

241

"Maybe not, but you can bet the other ladies in town will pounce on this like a skunk on a cabbage!" George hastened to point out to her. "Why, they're liable to tar and feather the marshal here and run you clean out of business!"

"Why, they—they couldn't do that!" She shifted her wide, troubled gaze in a silent appeal to Red and Hank, who stood looking a bit uncomfortable themselves.

"Well now, I didn't want to be the one to break it to you, Miss Caley," Red disclosed with obvious reluctance. "But, fact is, there's already been a heap of talk about you and the marshal. It didn't help matters none when word got around that he was ridin' shotgun with you all the way to Tuscarora and back."

"That wasn't my idea, confound it!" she reminded him in profound exasperation. "And what the blazes was I supposed to do after the horses ran off? Hell's bells, there wasn't any way I could avoid being—"

"Miss McAlister and I had already decided to make it legal," Jake broke in to proclaim with maddening calm. He took one of the blankets and draped it about her shoulders as solicitously as any lover.

"Make it legal?" she seethed indignantly.

"That's the right of it," Jake's deputy seconded with admirable loyalty. "I found out about it myself some three or four days ago," he told Caley's self-appointed champions of morality.

"Is that so, Miss Caley?" George asked her, his voice full of hope.

"NO!" she denied in a loud, ringing voice. She flung Jake a murderous glare and bent to retrieve her whip. Her hand curled about its silver-banded stock as she drew herself rigidly erect, and it was obvious she was fighting back the impulse to use it again. "I'm not going to marry Marshal Brody! I'm not going to marry anyone!"

"I can think of one other man who'll be right sorry to hear that," drawled Hank, exchanging a quick look with Red. There was little doubt he was referring to Matt Griffin.

"Well, if you are indeed willing to take Miss McAlister to wife," J.D. told Jake, casting a dubious glance toward Caley, "I suppose that will put an end to any vicious rumors circulating about the town."

"Miss McAlister doesn't *want* to be taken to wife," Caley ground out with her turquoise eyes ablaze, "and she damned sure doesn't want to stand here and listen to this . . . this . . . *claptrap* any longer!"

She stormed away to fetch the mail pouch from the coach. The nine men looked at one another in silent, wholly masculine understanding, as if to say there was no way on God's green earth to figure out the workings of the female mind.

To make matters worse, Caley was forced to ride double with Jake. Billy gallantly offered her his horse and moved to share a mount with his father, leaving her what appeared to be the much-needed luxury of being alone with her thoughts during the trip homeward. She had already swung up into the saddle when she glanced up and saw her "betrothed" striding purposefully toward her.

"What the hell do you think you're doing?" she demanded in a low, simmering tone.

"Exactly what it looks like." Disregarding the scathing look she cast him, he mounted up behind her and took control of the reins.

243

"You're crazy if you think I'm going to let you—" she started to protest.

"You're damn right I'm crazy," Jake murmured close to her ear. "Crazy for not beating some sense into you when I had the chance!"

She gasped as he suddenly wrapped a sinewy arm about her waist and pulled her back against him. There was no further opportunity to tell him just what she thought of him at the moment, for he abruptly urged the horse into a gallop. The others followed, riding back across the starlit desert to the turbulent oasis that was Elko.

It was late in the morning by the time Caley finally dragged herself out of bed. When she had bathed and dressed, she went downstairs to find that both Hank and Red had already taken the day's runs. There was a note waiting for her on top of the counter, in which Red explained how they had wanted to let her sleep, and that they'd be back before nightfall. Touched by their thoughtfulness, she smiled to herself and tossed the note to the desk. Her smile faded when she noticed that the front door was closed and locked. There was no sign of Billy.

"That's odd," she murmured, her cotton skirts gently rustling as she crossed to the window and gazed outward. She raised a hand to reposition one of the pins in her upswept curls, her silken brow creasing into an even deeper frown when she pondered the reason for Billy's absence.

It wasn't like him not to be there at that time of day. Perhaps he had been every bit as exhausted as herself, she mused. Last night had certainly been long and difficult enough to exhaust anyone. *Don't*

244

start, she then sternly cautioned herself. If she started thinking about it all again, she'd never stop and then the whole blasted day would be ruined.

Her brow cleared and her eyes widened in surprise when she suddenly caught sight of her young hostler across the street. She hurriedly opened the door.

"Billy!" she called his name, stepping outside onto the boardwalk. "Billy Snyder!"

For a moment, it looked as if he would keep on going, even though she was certain he had heard her. He raised his head at long last, however, and made his way across the street.

"Billy, what is it? What's wrong?" Caley asked, genuinely concerned when she took note of the troubled look on his lightly freckled countenance.

"Nothing, ma'am," he murmured, his gaze falling before hers as he swept off his hat and clasped it to his chest with both hands.

"Well then why weren't you here? I mean, I certainly don't mind if you finish your work and want to leave early. It's just that you're usually here until—"

"It's Ma, Miss Caley!" he finally burst out.

"Is your mother unwell, Billy?"

"No, it's not that." He reddened and looked away again.

"Then what is it?" she probed gently, expecting to hear that his father had gotten into some kind of trouble.

"She won't let me work for you no more, Miss Caley!" It all came pouring out in a rush of misery now. "Pa got drunk and let it slip to her about— about what happened last night, and she says I can't work for you no more! She says I'm to stay clear of both you and your horses, and that it

245

wouldn't be fittin' for me to—" He broke off and appeared to be on the verge of tears.

"I see." She was more hurt than she cared to admit. Hurt and angry and sick at heart.

"You know *I* don't feel that way, Miss Caley!" Billy declared with fervent sincerity. "Why, I think you're just about the finest woman who ever lived, and I'd lay right down and die if you asked me to! But . . . well, Ma's got her own ideas about things, and there's no talkin' to her when she gets in one of these moods," he finished with a heavy sigh.

"I understand, Billy," she told him, managing a weak smile. She lightly gripped his arm with her hand. "You run along now. Maybe your mother will change her mind if we give her some time."

"Do you really think she might?" he asked hopefully.

"I think there's a good chance of it," she assured him, though her voice lacked conviction. "But try not to worry about it. I'll keep the job open for a while, and I—I'll manage somehow until we work this out."

"Thanks, Miss Caley." Appearing somewhat consoled, he lifted the hat to his head and turned to be on his way again.

Caley stared after him as he strode back across the street. Her eyes clouded with unhappiness at what he had just told her, and she released a long, disconsolate sigh. It was hard to believe that Susan Snyder, usually the most fair-minded of women, would display such intolerance toward her.

Your reputation will no doubt have already suffered damage beyond repair, J.D.'s warning came back to haunt her.

"It doesn't matter," she murmured aloud. "It just plain doesn't matter!" She whirled back inside and

246

closed the door.

Things only got worse after that.

Bertha Larrabee, that paragon of virtue herself, came bustling into the office just after noon. Looking every bit like a large, frilled-up hen, she let Caley know in no uncertain terms that the women of the town were up in arms over her scandalous behavior.

"I'd hardly call that news!" Caley retorted sarcastically. She kept right on with her work, sparing Bertha only a disinterested glance as she stood behind the counter and made an entry in the schedule book. "Since when haven't you and all the others disapproved of me?"

"Whatever else we may have thought of you, Caley McAlister, we did not believe you to be completely devoid of morals—until now, that is!" the plump, brown-haired matron pronounced with a glowering look of condemnation. "I am older than you, and therefore wiser in the ways of the world. You must allow me to advise you. I would be remiss in my duty as a Christian if I did not tell you that it is all over town how you and the new marshal spent the night alone together!"

"We didn't spend the night 'alone,' blast it!" denied Caley, though she wondered why she even bothered. "The truth of the matter is," she declared with exaggerated patience, "that Ja—Marshal Brody and I were stranded for a few hours following an accident! I fail to see what all the fuss is about, and I sure as hell—"

"Susan Snyder has told me the truth of the matter!" Bertha rumbled.

"Susan Snyder?" So, she thought resentfully, the tongues have already been set to wagging. Well, then so be it. She didn't care. By damn, *she didn't*

247

care!

"Yes, and you should know that there will no longer be a place for you in this town—unless you intend to take up residence in Dobe Row, that is! Indeed, I shudder to think what Matt Griffin will say when he hears of your disgrace!" Bertha unwisely continued. "Why, everyone knows the two of you—"

"OUT!" Caley ordered, her eyes full of blue-green fire. She was fairly quaking with the force of her anger. "Take your 'Christian duty' and your 'well-meaning advice' and get the hell out of my office!"

"Why, how dare you!" gasped Bertha, obviously much affronted. Her face had gone all red, and her ample bosom heaved beneath the overly strained bodice of her plum calico gown.

"I said get out!" reiterated Caley. To emphasize her wishes, she marched to the door and flung it open.

"I knew all along you'd come to no good!" the older woman said acidly. "I knew you had the very devil himself in you the first moment I laid eyes on you! You with your unnatural ways and your man's trousers and your vile language! You mark my words, Caley McAlister—you will most assuredly reap what you sow!"

Flinging her one last smugly triumphant glare, Bertha went sailing through the doorway like the superior being she considered herself to be.

Caley slammed the door and leaned weakly back against it. First Billy's mother and now Bertha Larrabee, she mused with a frown. How many others would take it upon themselves to judge her? Great balls of fire, she wasn't even guilty! Well, she amended as her cheeks grew warm, at least not to the extent they all seemed to believe.

Feeling more and more as if she were lost in a nightmare, she straightened and opened the door again. Her stomach was making its emptiness known. She had not had anything to eat since—

"No, don't think about it!" she reminded herself once more. Holding her head proudly erect, she traveled across the street to Maybelle's. Instead of climbing the front steps, however, she made her way around to the kitchen door at the rear of the house. The last thing she wanted to do right now was face the regulars. She could imagine all too well how they'd bombard her with questions and advice and more good intentions than she could bear. And the thought of being in the same room with J.D. and George almost ruined her appetite.

Minutes later, she returned to the office with a sandwich and a glass of milk provided by Maybelle's cook. She cursed herself for being so faint-spirited, but nevertheless sought refuge in the privacy of her rooms upstairs. There, at least, she could forget about the rest of the world for a while.

Shadrach was less than a comfort to her. Even he seemed to have taken it into mind to punish her for some real or imagined transgression. After greeting her with a particularly forceful swipe at her foot, he scampered away to dive underneath the bed.

"All right then, stay there, you sour old furball!" muttered Caley. She heaved another sigh and sat down to eat her dinner in lonely, troubled silence.

Her loneliness, at least, was about to come to an end . . .

It was shortly past five o'clock when she began pacing aimlessly about. She was running out of things to do — or rather, things she wanted to do. The schedule book was in order for the first time in months, the office had lost a remarkable amount of clutter, and even the apartment upstairs looked like a different place. She had purposely kept herself occupied for the space of several hours, but still, her spirits were low and her mind in turmoil. No amount of work would dispel the strangely restless mood which had fallen over her.

She had just wandered back to the desk for the fifth time in as many minutes when the front door swung open. Jake Brody's tall, muscular frame suddenly filled the doorway.

"*You!*" breathed Caley, her eyes sparking with several conflicting emotions. "What the devil are you doing here?" She instinctively stepped behind the protective barrier of the counter.

"We've got some business to take care of," Jake informed her quietly. There was a look about him that sent a tremor of alarm coursing through her.

"What business?" she demanded in visible mistrust.

"You'll find out," was all he would say. Tugging the hat from his head, he sauntered forward and allowed his penetrating gaze to travel slowly over her face. "You look a bit tired."

"Well what the blazes do you expect?" she retorted, bristling. "I had a rough night — *remember?*"

"I remember a lot of things." Although his expression was perfectly solemn, his eyes were aglow with tender amusement. He stepped around the counter and took her arm in a firm but gentle grip. "Come on. It's getting late."

"I'm not going anywhere with you!" she defiantly insisted, pulling free. "I don't know what this 'business' of yours is, but I'm not about to —"

"It's important, Caley," he told her with a slight frown. "And it can't wait."

"Then why don't you tell me what it is?" She tried to ignore the wild racing of her heart.

"Because there isn't time." He raised the hat to his head again and gave her a soft, thoroughly captivating smile that made her melt inside. "There's someone waiting to talk to us."

"Who?"

"You'll find out."

This time, she did not resist when he took her arm and began leading her toward the door. She was nonplussed by his mysterious behavior, and more than a little apprehensive. Stealing a look up at him, she saw that his handsome face was inscrutable. His eyes were gleaming with a strange light of determination.

"Where are we going?" she asked once they were outside.

"Not far."

"Damn you, Jake Brody, why won't you tell me what all of this is about?" She glanced surreptitiously up at him once more.

His rugged features appeared tan and healthy above the collar of his clean white shirt, and the six-pointed star pinned to his chest was an outward testament to the air of authority that was his by nature. On this particular day, however, there was something different about him, something Caley could not quite put a name to but was there all the same.

"I'll bet you were hell on surprises as a kid," he remarked with another brief smile.

"I'm not sure what you mean by that," she said, eyeing him narrowly. "But I hate surprises and I've certainly had enough of *this* one!"

"Patience, wildcat," he drawled.

"Stop calling me that!" she shot back.

Becoming increasingly conscious of the curious stares they were attracting as they headed southward along the boardwalk, she couldn't help but wonder how many of the people watching them would attach undue significance to their being seen together. It seemed they were destined to fuel rumors, she mused irritably, then wondered why no one had ever made such a commotion over her and Matt Griffin.

Where there's smoke, there's fire, she recalled the old saying. There had been no smoke with Matt — nor any fire, either, she admitted to herself at long last.

"Here we are," Jake finally announced, leading her across to the front steps of a small, whitewashed building set off the road a bit.

"But — this is the church!" she pointed out unnecessarily.

"I know."

"Well, what the hell kind of business — "

"For once, Caley McAlister, don't ask questions," he told her, his gaze alight with a damnably irresistible combination of humor and warmth. A smile tugged at the corners of his mouth before he added, "And try not to swear once we're inside. It wouldn't do to show a lack of respect."

Casting him a look that was anything but reverent, she jerked her arm from his grasp and preceded him into the quaint little chapel. The sunlight was streaming in through the real stained glass windows, donated by a miner who had struck it rich on a claim nearby, and the room was filled with the pleasant aroma of the lemon oil and beeswax which had been used to polish the two

252

dozen wooden pews.

Caley was surprised to see both Maybelle O'Grady and Dan Mitchelson standing together before the altar. She came to an abrupt halt and rounded on Jake.

"What's going on?" she demanded, out of all patience now. "What are Maybelle and Dan doing here?"

"They're part of the business I was talking about," he replied calmly.

"Once and for all, what *is* the business?"

"A wedding."

"A wedding?" she echoed. While her eyes grew round with incredulity, Jake took her arm again and propelled her to the front of the church. She turned her startled gaze upon a smiling Maybelle and asked, "Why didn't you tell me you were planning to marry Dan?"

"Marry Dan?" It was Maybelle's turn to look surprised. "Good heavens, I'm not marrying anyone!"

"Then who . . . what . . ." Her voice trailed away as she looked back to Jake for an explanation. He didn't say a word, but just stood there with a strange half-smile on his face and a tenderly roguish gleam in his eyes.

The truth struck her like a bolt of lightning.

"No!" she breathed in stunned disbelief, slowly shaking her head as if to prevent what had been inevitable from the very first.

"You mean you didn't tell her?" Maybelle asked Jake in a low tone edged with disapproval.

"I thought it might sting her pride a little to be carried kicking and screaming to her own wedding," he offered wryly.

"There isn't going to be any wedding!" stormed

Caley, her eyes blazing wrathfully up at him. "I told you before, Jake Brody — I wouldn't marry you if you were the last man on earth!"

"She did say that," Dan recalled, trying his best to suppress an unholy grin.

"You're going to marry me, Caley. You have no choice," decreed Jake, all traces of amusement disappearing from his smoldering green gaze. "The preacher will be here any minute now."

"I'll be damned if I'm going to let you —"

"You'll be damned if you don't," he cut her off in a voice that was whipcord sharp. "The whole town's talking about the two of us. This is the only way to put a stop to it."

"Let them talk! Do you think I care what anybody thinks of me?"

"Yes, I do," he answered somberly. "I think you care a lot more than you'd ever admit. But I'm not marrying you because of the talk. We both know that."

"The only thing *I* know is that I'm getting the hell out of here!" she declared, her voice rising on a shrill note as panic raced within her.

She spun about to flee, but Jake was not to be denied. Reaching out to capture her hand with the warm, relentless strength of his, he easily pulled her along with him to the altar. The matron of honor and best man — notified by Jake of the impending nuptials only that morning — looked on in mutual worriment as he disregarded his unwilling bride's vehement struggles and held her there to wait for the preacher.

"It's time to stop fighting it, Caley," he said in a low, vibrant tone. "We couldn't go on the way we were any longer. It's time to face the truth and get on with things."

"You can't force me to do this!" she defied with as much bravado as she could muster under the circumstances. Trying in vain to free her hand, she looked to Dan and Maybelle in desperate, furious entreaty. "Hellfire and damnation, aren't the two of you going to do anything?"

"I'm sorry, Caley," replied Maybelle, "but I . . . well, I think it would be best if you did as Marshal Brody says."

"*What?*" Flabbergasted by the widow's betrayal, she ceased her struggles for a moment. "I thought you were my friend, Maybelle O'Grady, and yet here you are, telling me—"

"I am your friend! But anyone with eyes could see how you and the marshal struck sparks every time you were in the same room! And you might as well know that I think he's a far sight better man for you than Matt Griffin!"

"That's the right of it," Dan eagerly lent his support to the older woman's views. "You don't want to be mixed up with Griffin anymore, Miss Caley. He's a bad one."

"Matt Griffin has nothing to do with this!" fumed Caley. "And I don't—"

She broke off with a sharp gasp when the side door to the chapel opened and the new preacher hastened forward to take his place before the "happy" couple. His dark hair was wet and slicked back from his forehead, and his black serge coat and trousers bore signs of a puzzling dampness as well.

"Please forgive me for being late!" he apologized. He beamed a paternal smile at all four members of the wedding party, in spite of the fact that he was younger than three of them. "I was called upon to baptize someone down at the river.

255

And when the Spirit moves, I've got to move, too!" he added with a quiet chuckle of appreciation for his own cleverness.

"I was tricked into coming here!" exclaimed Caley. "And you might as well go on back to your baptizing, because there damn sure isn't going to be any wedding!"

She resumed her struggles, though not with her usual rough-and-tumbleness. Still a bit stiff and sore as a result of having been thrown from the stagecoach, she felt a dull ache with each twist and tug. It gave her no small amount of perverse satisfaction at that moment to think that Jake, what with his shot-up arm, was probably hurting a hell of a lot more than she was.

The young preacher, meanwhile, was shocked by her highly unconventional behavior. He frowned in stern disapproval and looked back to Jake.

"*Now* I understand what you were talking about, Marshal Brody. You were quite right not to delay the matter."

"Let's get on with it, Parson," decreed Jake, appearing not the least bit perturbed by his bride's all too visible reluctance.

"I hope you fully appreciate the marshal's willingness to do his duty, Miss McAlister!" the clergyman couldn't resist lecturing to someone so obviously in need of it. "There is no more honorable state than marriage, and—"

"I'm not going to let you get away with this, Jake Brody!" hissed Caley. Her fiery gaze sliced back to the preacher again. "There's got to be some kind of rule that keeps you from marrying someone against their will!"

"The only rules I follow are God's rules," he declared with dutiful piety. "Since Marshal Brody has already explained both the urgency and necessity of the situation to me, I would advise you, my dear Miss McAlister, to submit without further resistance. The sacred institution of marriage is not to be embraced with anything but prayerful consideration and thankfulness."

That said, he got down to business. He opened the small book in his hands, the leather still smelling brand new and the pages crackling fresh, and found the place he had marked earlier.

"I'm only going to do this once, Caley McAlister, so stand still and listen up," commanded Jake, slipping his good arm about her waist and drawing her possessively against him.

They were standing in the reverse of the traditional wedding pose, but it was only a minor detail and not one worth protesting — particularly under the present difficult circumstances. Maybelle took her place at Caley's side, while Dan moved to Jake's.

This can't be happening, Caley thought dazedly. But it was. Almost before she knew it, the preacher had gotten to the "better or worse" part and was looking expectantly to her for a response.

Her eyes flew up to Jake's face. He turned his head and gave her a look that sent a warm, thoroughly delicious shiver dancing down her spine. Still, she had never been one to admit defeat so easily.

"I most certainly — " she started to adamantly deny, her gaze kindling anew.

"She does," Jake took the liberty of answering for her.

The young parson continued. Caley's eyes brew round as saucers, her mouth falling open in stunned disbelief.

"Wait just a blessed minute!" she protested, feeling as if caught up in a whirlwind. "I didn't—"

"What God hath joined together, let not man put asunder," the preacher finished with eyes raising heavenward.

Caley felt perilously lightheaded all of a sudden. Jake gathered her close and pressed a gentle, sweetly compelling kiss upon her startled lips. She swayed against him, only to find herself released an all too brief moment later. Her senses still reeling, she was dimly aware of Maybelle and Dan offering their heartfelt congratulations, of the parson adding his own best wishes for a fruitful union, and of her new husband leading her from the church.

Once outside, she blinked at the sun's brightness and heard Dan telling Jake he'd hold down the fort if he wanted to call it quits a bit early, seeing as how it was his wedding day and all.

"I'll be along in a minute," Jake told him.

"You sure about that?" asked Dan, his gaze moving significantly toward a still silent Caley.

"Come on, Deputy," Maybelle intervened. She slipped her hand about his arm and cast a knowing smile at the newlyweds. "You can walk me back."

Too much the gentleman to refuse, Dan set off with the attractive widow at his side. Jake stood alone with his bride in front of the church, his green eyes aglow as he raised his hat to his head.

"I'll move my things over from Mrs. O'Grady's later."

"Move your things?" Caley echoed in bewilderment. The numbness was finally beginning to wear off. *Dear Lord, what had she done?*

"To your place." A wry smile tugged at his mouth. "My room at the boarding house isn't big enough for the two of us."

"What the devil are you—" she started to demand, only to break off as realization sunk in. Her eyes grew very wide, then narrowed and blazed with defiance. "No! Oh no you don't! Absolutely not! You're not about to—"

"Oh, but I am," he insisted in a low tone laced with steel. "You're my wife now, Caley."

"I don't want to be your wife!" she stormed, her beautiful face flushed quite becomingly. Her breasts rose and fell angrily beneath the square-necked bodice of her plain, pale blue cotton gown. "Damn you, Jake Brody, you may have forced me to go through with that poor excuse for a wedding, but I'll be hanged if I'll let you ramrod me into your bed!"

"It will be *your* bed," he pointed out, again with a disarmingly roguish light in his eyes, "and there won't be any need for ramrodding." He tugged the front brim of his hat lower and promised with maddening equanimity, "I'll be home before dark, Mrs. Brody."

Caley was left to stew in helpless fury as he turned and strode away. She glared at the broad target of his retreating back. If looks could kill, she would have most assuredly been a widow right there and then.

Mrs. Brody. The name burned in her ears.

Swearing roundly, she whirled about and made her way across the busy street. She tried not to think about the fact that it would be dark soon. . . .

Chapter XI

Night fell, and still there was no sign of Jake.

Caley stood alone at the window upstairs, her mind drifting back over the past few hours. Hank and Red had completed their runs without incident, both of them pulling in within an hour of each other. She had been glad of the fact that Billy's absence had left her with so much work to be done. After unhitching the teams and seeing to the horses' needs and making sure the coaches were in order for the next day's runs, she had almost been too tired to think about what had happened. Almost.

Releasing a heavy sigh, she turned away from the window and wandered to the rocking chair again. She sank down upon it, absently scrutinizing the half-finished plate of food on a nearby table. Maybelle had brought it over a couple of hours earlier. Although she had wondered if Jake had gotten his supper, too, she hadn't allowed herself to ask. Maybelle had tried talking to her, of course, but she had stubbornly refused to listen. She regretted that now, just as she regretted ever having left her bed that morning.

She leaned back in the chair and closed her eyes.

But there was no respite from her troubled thoughts, no escape from the foreboding *tick, tick, tick* of the clock in the corner. Each passing second brought her that much closer. . . . well, to whatever was going to happen between her and Jake Brody.

She had toyed with the idea of leaving town, but was simply too proud to turn tail and run. Besides, she couldn't stay away forever; she had a business to run, didn't she? It had also occurred to her that she could try locking all the doors and barricading herself in the apartment, but she knew without a doubt that her new husband wouldn't let anything, especially a locked door, stand in his way. He had to be the most all-fired *determined* man she had ever met, she mused resentfully.

But she wasn't about to surrender without a fight. No, by damn, Jake Brody had finally met his match!

Bolstering her courage with this thought, she stood and padded barefoot to the window once more. Moonlight shone pale and silvery on the never ending bustle of the street below, and a cool, woodsmoke-scented breeze swept upward to tease at the faded gingham curtains. She drew in a slightly ragged breath, her beautiful face taking on a faraway look.

The sound of someone knocking on the door downstairs startled her from her disturbing reverie. *Jake.* Her heart leapt in her throat, and she was dismayed to feel herself trembling like any other bride on her wedding night. Except she was not like other brides — whereas they had at least been granted the choice of being wedded and bedded, she had been forced into marriage with a man who was still little more than a stranger.

262

The knock sounded again, more insistently than before. *The time has come,* thought Caley. She frowned and finally stirred herself into action. Catching up a lamp with one hand, she made her way slowly down the narrow staircase and across the dark confines of the office. Her fingers shook a little as she reached for the doorknob, but she squared her shoulders and proudly lifted her head, as if she were preparing to meet her executioner instead of a tall, devilishly handsome Texan whose very touch set her afire.

But it wasn't Jake who stood grinning down at her when she opened the door. It was Matt Griffin.

"What took you so long?" he complained good-naturedly.

"Great balls of fire, what are *you* doing here?" she demanded in breathless, wide-eyed astonishment.

"I came to see you. Just now got into town."

Without being invited, he sauntered past her and into the room. He walked with a slight limp, but Caley was too preoccupied with other thoughts to notice. She hastily closed the door, her pulse racing and her gaze full of consternation. The last thing she needed right now was to have Jake arrive and find Matt alone with her.

"You can't stay here, Matt!"

"I wasn't planning to," he replied with a frown. "Hell, Mac, aren't you glad to see me? It's been a while." He smiled then and lazily tipped his hat back upon his blond head. "I'd have been in before now, but there was that business with those damned basco wooly-tenders. My father took care of it for me. A little bit of money always did go a long way toward settling things." His spurs jingled softly as he began advancing on her. "And since

I'm no longer a wanted man, you and me are going to make up for some lost time," he promised.

"No! Oh Matt, you — you've got to leave!" she stammered anxiously, her hand closing about the doorknob again.

"What's wrong, Mac?" He studied her face closely, his eyes narrowing. "I heard someone tried to hold up the stage yesterday. You didn't get hurt, did you?"

"No, I'm fine!" she hastened to assure him, then wondered if he had also heard about how she and Jake had been stranded together last night. She didn't think so; if he had, she told herself, he would have mentioned it right off. And it was obvious he didn't know of her marriage yet. *Her marriage.* She shuddered to think how he would react when he found out. "I'll explain everything to you later! Please just go!" She flung the door open again and pushed insistently on Matt's arm.

"What the hell's going on?" he demanded in growing suspicion. He jerked his arm away and rounded on her, his blue eyes glinting hotly. "Why are you trying so hard to get rid of me?"

"Because, I —" Breaking off, she muttered a curse and moved away to set the lamp on top of the counter. When she turned to face Matt again, she folded her arms tightly across her chest and blurted out the truth. "Because I'm married, damn it!"

"Married?" he repeated, scowling in disbelief. "What kind of trick —"

"It's no trick, Matt! And it happened only a few hours ago!" she revealed, bracing herself for the storm she knew to be forthcoming. "I'm married, I tell you!"

"You're lying!" he gritted between clenched teeth,

264

stalking forward and seizing her arms in a cruel, punishing grip. His face had become a mask of almost savage fury. "Tell me you're lying, Mac!"

"I only wish I were!" she declared miserably. Hot tears glistened in her eyes. She felt sick at heart and terribly guilty about her betrayal of all the plans they had made throughout the past ten years. In that moment, she wasn't sure who she hated most — herself, or Jake Brody.

"Tell me his name," Matt ordered in a tone of simmering violence.

"It doesn't matter!"

"It does to me!" He yanked her up hard against him, his gaze searing mercilessly down into hers. "Who is he?"

"Brody!" she cried, knowing he'd find out sooner or later. "Jake Brody!"

"No!" he muttered. Shaking his head in a furious denial of the truth, he fixed Caley with a hard, vengeful look and ground out, *"Not him!"*

"I — I didn't mean for it to happen, Matt!" she tried desperately to explain. "If there was only some way I could make you understand, some way I could —"

"I'll kill him! By damn, I'll kill the bastard!" he vowed, then ruthlessly demanded of Caley, "Has he had you yet, Mac? Has he?"

She stared up at him in stunned, silent anguish, her throat constricting painfully and her whole body trembling. Another loud gasp was forced from her lips when he yanked her close again.

"Tell me the truth, damn you!"

"No! Dear God, Matt, you —" she choked out.

"Take your hands off my wife."

Caley inhaled sharply, her eyes flying to the doorway while Matt's fingers tensed upon her

265

arms. Jake stood gazing across at them with a deadly calm that belied the white-hot fury raging within him. His eyes narrowed imperceptibly as he waited for Matt's reaction.

He was ready when it came.

While Caley stared back at him in mute horror, Matt's hand inched downward. He suddenly flung her away from him, spinning about and going for his gun at the same time. The chance to fire never came.

"Drop it," Jake ordered quietly, his own six-shooter leveled at the other man.

Matt hesitated. No one had ever gotten the draw on him before. Filled with a hatred so intense it made him reckless, he tightened his grip upon the handle of his gun.

"Please, Matt, don't!" implored Caley.

Her words were like a knife twisting in Jake's heart. Mistakenly believing that they signified a concern for Matt's safety alone, he tried not to let his emotions cloud his judgment. Still, jealousy burned within him as he recalled the intimate scene he had just interrupted, and he realized that he would gladly kill Matt Griffin if given the chance.

But it was not to be. Not yet. Whether it was because of cowardice or a simple acceptance of the other man's superior prowess, Matt finally backed down. Caley felt giddy with relief when he slipped his gun back into its holster.

"Next time, you thieving son of a bitch!" he promised Jake, his voice raspy and malevolent. His feral gaze shot back to Caley. "This isn't finished between you and me yet, Mac. You know it isn't!"

She swallowed hard, watching as he strode un-hurriedly to the door. Jake moved aside to let him pass, but not before issuing a warning of his own.

266

"Stay away from my wife, Griffin." His eyes were smoldering, his rugged features dangerously grim. "Come near her again, and you're a dead man."

"You'll pay for this, Brody!" snarled Matt. "No one takes what belongs to me and gets away with it. *No one!*"

Then, he was gone.

With quiet deliberation, Jake retrieved the canvas bag he had left outside, closed the door, and locked it. He turned to face Caley. She flushed guiltily, her gaze falling beneath the piercing intensity of his.

"I—I didn't know Matt was coming!" she faltered.

"No. I don't guess you did." Though his voice was scarcely more than a whisper, it held an undercurrent of raw emotion.

Caley raised her eyes again, her heart pounding fiercely within her breast while Jake tossed the bag onto one of the benches against the wall. He took off his hat and hung it beside hers. The lamplit air was filled with tension. She sought to think of a way to break the awful silence stretching between them.

"You said you'd be here before dark!" she reminded him accusingly, then could have bitten her tongue. It sounded like she had been on pins and needles while awaiting his arrival. She *had,* of course, but didn't want him to know it.

"I was detained," he offered with a studied evenness. His expression became even more tight-lipped when he added, "It didn't look like you were too damned lonely."

"I told you I didn't know Matt was coming!" She lifted her chin in an angry, defensive gesture and crossed her arms against her breasts again. "But it's

267

just as well that he did!"

"Is it?" He advanced on her at last, closing the distance between them with deceptive unhaste. "How do you figure that?"

"It was only right that he heard about . . . about our so-called marriage from me!" She felt small and vulnerable and incredibly feminine with him towering above her. His gaze burned down into hers, and she could literally feel the heat emanating from his virile, hard-muscled body. Swallowing a sudden lump in her throat, she forced herself to confront him squarely. "You can't blame him for being hurt and angry!" she insisted, rushing to Matt's defense now. "After all, he and I were once—"

"That doesn't matter anymore!" Jake cut her off tersely, his green eyes darkening to jade. His handsome face looked quite thunderous, and he spoke with a controlled violence that sent a tremor of fear through Caley. "You're my wife. You'll do as I say from here on out. And I'm telling you to stay away from Griffin!"

"I take no orders from you!" she countered hotly, her own eyes shooting blue-green sparks. She unfolded her arms and planted her hands on her hips. "None of this was *my* idea! What's more, you might as well know right here and now that I've no blasted intention of letting things go any farther! I may have lost my head down there at the church today, but that's not going to happen again!"

"You think not?" he challenged, his low, deep-timbred voice causing her pulses to leap in alarm.

"No! I mean, yes! Damn it, I want you to get out of here and leave me in peace!" she stormed. Her temper flaring to a perilous level indeed, she marched across to the bench and snatched up the canvas bag. "Take your things and go on back to Maybelle's where you belong!" she instructed wrathfully, pivoting to face him again. "What happened today was a mistake!"

"The only mistake was mine," Jake replied in a cold, clear tone that was in direct contrast to the fire in his blood. He moved slowly toward her, his face inscrutable but his eyes filled with a foreboding, almost savage gleam. "I should have said to hell with everything else and brought you back here right after the wedding. Yes, by damn, I should have carried you upstairs and done what I've been wanting to do since the first day we met!"

Caley blushed fierily. Breathing an oath, she flung the bag at Jake.

"GET OUT!" she cried in a voice quavering with fury.

She tried to push past him, but he dropped the bag and seized her arm. A loud gasp of startlement escaped her lips when he suddenly yanked her back, spun her about, and sent her flying face down over his broad shoulder.

"The time has come, *Mrs. Brody,*" he ground out as he clamped an arm about her knees, "for the honeymoon to begin!" He bore her purposefully toward the staircase.

"No! No, damn you, put me down!" she raged, kicking and squirming furiously, her hands doubling into fists to pound at his back. "I hate you, Jake Brody! I hate you, and I'll be damned if—"

She broke off with a strangled cry of indignation when he brought his hand up and gave her wriggling backside a hard, punishing whack.

"Keep still!" he commanded sharply.

"Why, you thickheaded, overbearing son of a—" she fumed, obviously still far from chastened.

"Quiet!" His large hand found its conveniently placed target again.

"*Ooooh!*" Caley growled in outrage.

She clutched desperately at the corner of the stairway, but was unable to prevent Jake from climbing up the steps. He conveyed his furiously unwilling burden into the dimly lit apartment and kicked the door shut behind him with his heel. Setting Caley on her feet, he calmly began unbuttoning his shirt.

"What the devil do you think you're doing?" she demanded, her beautiful face quite flushed and her whole body atremble with anger and apprehension and no small amount of excitement.

"Exactly what it looks like," he drawled.

While Caley stared at him in mingled uncertainty and disbelief, he drew off the shirt and tossed it across the rocking chair, then took a seat and tugged off his boots and socks.

"This has gone far enough, damn it!" she seethed when he stood again and started to unfasten his trousers.

She whirled and made a frantic dash for the back door, only to cry out when Jake caught her about the waist and lifted her bodily. Trying in vain to pry his arm loose, she suddenly found herself being hauled toward the bedroom.

"Let me go! You—you can't do this!" she sputtered in growing panic.

"I can and will!" her new husband vowed. "I mean to tame you, my wild, fire-spitting bride. And I'll drive all thought of Matt Griffin from your head, once and for all!"

She suffered a sharp intake of breath as she was tossed unceremoniously atop the quilt-covered bed. Landing with a bounce that set the ancient springs to creaking, she scrambled to her knees and saw that Jake's eyes were suffused with a light that could best be described as tenderly wolfish.

"You can undress in privacy this once if you like," he offered, his voice low and wonderfully vibrant. "Or I'll be glad to lend a hand."

"Go to hell, you bastard!" she shot back with a proud, defiant toss of her head. The hairpins had long since come loose, and her thick, luxuriant auburn tresses streamed down about her face and shoulders in glorious disarray.

"All right then. Have it your way."

Her eyes flew wide when he reached for her. She murmured another breathless protest and twisted about to go bouncing off the opposite side of the bed. Her feet hit the floor at the same moment Jake entangled a hand within the fullness of her skirts.

"Let go!" she cried vehemently, tugging with all her might.

Her efforts succeeded only in making the button fly off and the edges of the waistband slide open. She gasped in dismay, clutching at the bottom half of her two-piece gown, but ultimately abandoning it to Jake's possession. He was left grasping the skirt when she managed to extricate herself from its pale blue folds.

"It's no use, Caley," he told her, his green eyes full of loving amusement as well as desire. He watched while she edged toward the window. "Don't you think it's about time—"

"No!" she denied, obstinately shaking her head. "So help me, Jake Brody, I'll never forgive you if you do this!"

"You'll never forgive me if I don't!" he parried with a frown. He flung the skirt aside and began advancing on her again.

Caley started in alarm, her eyes searching desperately for any avenue of escape. But there was none. She was trapped. Trapped with a man—with a *husband,* damn it!—who possessed the unnerving ability to make her forget everything and everyone else whenever he took her in his arms. It scared the hell out of her, the way he could bend her to his will so easily. She wasn't used to losing control . . . to feeling the things only he could make her feel . . . to having her heart touched as it had never been touched before. For the first time in her life, she was truly frightened.

"Stay away from me!" she choked out.

She whirled about and retraced her steps, her one thought to get away before it was too late. Jake was there in a flash, tumbling her down upon the bed with him. She cursed and pulled away, but he grabbed her petticoat and gave a merciless yank upon it. The delicate fabric tore loose with an audible *rip.* He sent the petticoat floating downward to join her skirt on the floor.

"Why, you miserable, green-eyed devil!" she bit out reproachfully, anger overpowering fear once more.

"Had enough?" he challenged with a faint, unrepentant smile at the absurdity of the situation. He sobered again and told her, "You're only making it harder on the both of us." He had fully expected her to rant and rave a little, but somehow, he mused wryly, he hadn't envisioned a wedding night quite like this.

"Then give up!" she hissed.

With a renewed vengeance, she kicked and squirmed and struck out at him like a beautiful, wild-eyed tigress. He was equally determined. His

272

hands moved to the front of her bodice, and he did not hesitate before literally tearing it apart from top to bottom. The buttons flew every which way. While Caley twisted furiously up onto her knees again, he jerked the bodice free and added it to the growing heap of discarded clothing. She was left clad in nothing more than a thin white cotton chemise and drawers.

"I mean to have you, Caley," decreed Jake, his hand capturing hers before she could slide from the bed. "You're my wife. Now stop fighting and—"

"Never!" she proclaimed dramatically, though she was already weakening.

She struck out at him once more, flailing at his naked chest as he tried to draw her close. A shadow of pain crossed the rugged perfection of his features when she caught him a glancing blow on his injured, still bandaged arm. Her eyes momentarily clouded with remorse, but she pushed all thought of guilt aside and wrenched herself from his grasp. She got as far as the door.

Suddenly, his hands were upon her again. With a wholly masculine impatience that quite took her breath away, he picked her up, tossed her back upon the bed, and untied the strings of her drawers. She fought him as best she could, but he merely rolled her onto her stomach and lifted her hips. Yanking the undergarment downward, he bared her firm, shapely derriere to his burning gaze.

Caley's face flamed in shocked embarrassment as she felt a rush of cool air upon her naked flesh. She immediately rolled to her back again, but only made it easier for Jake to pull the drawers all the way off. They, too, took their place on the floor.

She sat up and hastily tugged the hemline of her

273

chemise down over her nakedness, but Jake would not allow her even this last bit of maidenly modesty. He stripped the chemise from her trembling body. His penetrating gaze raked boldly, hungrily over her exposed charms while she crimsoned and tried in vain to cover herself with the quilt. Pulling her to her knees on the bed, he slipped an arm about her waist and cupped her chin with his other hand.

"You're mine, Caley!" he whispered hoarsely. "Damn it, you're mine!"

She fought him with what little strength she had left—but she knew the battle was lost the instant his lips came crashing down upon hers.

He kissed her with an impassioned thoroughness, his mouth conquering hers while he lowered her back to the bed. She shivered when his powerful, lightly matted chest came into contact with her bare breasts. Still branding her lips with his own, he expertly stripped off his trousers with one hand and enveloped her within the warm circle of his arms again, bearing her backward to the quilt.

She inhaled sharply, her eyes flying wide when he placed the whole length of his virile, hard-muscled body atop her womanly softness. Her naked flesh felt scorched by his. She squirmed beneath him, but he merely tightened his arms about her and suddenly rolled to his back.

Caley's moan of protest turned to one of irrevocable surrender as Jake's warm, velvety tongue thrust between her lips to plunder the sweetness of her mouth. She kissed him back with an innocent seductiveness that both delighted and inflamed him. He groaned inwardly and struggled to maintain control of his own raging, undeniably masculine needs. His strong hands swept downward, smoothing along the slender curve of her back to clasp her buttocks with fierce possessiveness and urge her farther upward atop his searing hardness.

She gasped again when his mouth left hers to roam hungrily across the satiny globes of her breasts. Her fingers threaded almost convulsively within his thick, sun-streaked hair, and she suppressed a breathless cry of pleasure when his lips captured one of the rose-tipped peaks. His tongue flicked across the nipple with tantalizing lightness while his mouth gently suckled.

Her eyes swept closed as she felt herself being assaulted by the most wickedly rapturous sensations she had ever known. Jake's mouth soon transferred its moist, highly provocative caress to her other breast, his warm fingers clasping the firm mounds of her bottom with even more impassioned urgency. She caught her lower lip between her teeth and instinctively arched her back, her hands moving to clutch at the bronzed strength of his shoulders while he continued his delectable adoration of her full young breasts.

Then, rolling so that he was atop her again, he reclaimed her parted lips in a hot, wildly intoxicating kiss that demanded a response. She moaned softly and entwined her arms about the corded muscles of his neck, her whole body trembling with passion's fire beneath the magnificent hardness of his. The fire blazed hotter and hotter when one of his hands trailed a fiery path across her hip to the triangle of silken auburn curls between her thighs.

She tensed at the first touch of his fingers upon the delicate pink flesh. He immediately set up a gentle yet riotously compelling motion that caused her legs to part wider and her hips to strain upward. A deep, almost painful yearning seized her in its grip. She clung to her devilishly skillful tormentor as if she were drowning and he the only means by which she could be saved.

Finally, Jake could stand no more. Sliding his large hand beneath her buttocks, he positioned himself above her. Caley's eyes flew wide again when she felt his throbbing hardness between her legs. She pushed feebly against him, but he would not be denied. He swallowed her breathless cry of pain when his manhood sheathed to the hilt within the honeyed warmth of her feminine passage.

His lips releasing hers at last, he stared down into the flushed beauty of her countenance. His hands clasped her hips, masterfully tutoring them into the slow, captivating rhythm of his. She clung to him again as pain was replaced by pleasure, as his loving possession intensified and sent their mutual passions soaring heavenward. When fulfillment came, it was sweet and savage and ultimately satisfying . . . a promise of what lay ahead.

Lying together in the aftermath of that first, tempestuous union, neither of them spoke. Now was not the time for words. Jake rolled to his back in the wildly rumpled bed, gathering his bride's pliant, well-loved body close to his. He cradled her head upon his shoulder and kept an arm draped possessively across her slender waist. His green eyes were full of tenderness, warmth, and no small amount of wholly masculine triumph.

Caley, meanwhile, was stunned by what had just happened — stunned and yet filled with a sense of completeness and contentment that was positively indecent. *So that's what all the fuss is about,* she thought in wonderment. Now she understood why so many women, swept away by uncontrollable passion, were tumbled into bed by men all too willing to take advantage of their temporary madness. By damn, she mused while blushing rosily, any pangs of guilt suffered afterward were well worth it. *At least when Jake Brody was the one doing the tumbling,* she then thought, her whole body feeling more vibrantly alive than ever before.

Releasing a long sigh, she closed her eyes and allowed herself to be held captive against her husband's hard warmth. Later, she told herself drowsily as her thoughts drifted back to the way he had literally torn the clothes off her, later she would let him know she was not to be treated so rudely . . .

Except for the soft lamplight spilling in from the other room, the bed was still bathed in darkness. Caley sat up and turned her head to look down at the man sleeping peacefully beside her. He lay upon his back, his nakedness fully exposed to her curious gaze. She grew quite warm, her eyes widening as they traveled over his powerful, undeniably male frame.

She had never seen a man in the altogether before, at least not a man like *him*. Once, while she had been driving past the Elko Hot Hole just south of town, she had caught a glimpse of some men frolicking in the hot springs there. They, too, had been naked. But, she went on to recall, although they had possessed all the right "equipment." they had certainly looked nothing like Jake Brody.

Her face flamed at the wicked turn of her thoughts. She forced her gaze away from Jake and slipped carefully from the bed. Snatching up her chemise, she pulled it on and padded from the room, her bare feet moving soundlessly across the wooden floor as she headed into the bathroom.

Emerging a short time later, she crossed to the window in the main room and raised her eyes toward the starlit sky. Her silken brow creased into a troubled frown while her eyes became clouded with confusion. She breathed a rather halfhearted oath before turning away and moving back toward the bedroom.

She wavered indecisively in the doorway, her pride battling with her emotions once more. Torn between the desire to resume her place in the bed, and the urge to hold herself aloof from the arrogant, infuriating man who had turned her entire world upside-down, she had not yet made a decision when her ears suddenly detected the distinct sound of a cat's meow at the back door.

"Shadrach!" she whispered, realizing that she had put him out earlier and then completely forgotten about him.

Hurrying to the door, she opened it and watched as the angry feline shot inside. He was on his way to his usual perch in the window when, apparently sensing a strange human's presence, he drew to an abrupt halt. His one blue eye and one green narrowed, and the fur on his back stood up when he started inching stealthily toward the bedroom.

Too late, Caley moved to stop him. He had already pounced atop the bed and was preparing to swat at Jake's prone body when she reached the doorway.

"Shadrach!" she called out in a stern undertone. "Get down from there, you old rascal!"

He paid her no mind, of course, and went right on with his swatting. His claws came out, and he made a vengeful swipe at the tall usurper's naked hip.

Jake ground out a curse and came bolt upright in the bed. Shadrach, a mass of hissing and spitting fury, went flying off the bed and scampered back into the other room. Caley pressed a hand to her mouth in a futile attempt to suppress a laugh.

"What the—" muttered Jake. The thunderous look on his face cleared, and his eyes gleamed with ironic humor when they met the unrepentant sparkle of Caley's. "Blast it, woman, you set that cat on me again, and I'll wring both your necks," he threatened with a mock scowl.

"I guess he just doesn't want to share me with anyone!" she declared with a spirited toss of her head, coloring beneath the warmth in his gaze.

"I can't say I blame him."

His eyes darkened as they took in the bewitching sight of her dishabille. Her beautiful face, looking as proudly defiant as ever, was framed by a shimmering mass of tousled auburn curls. Outlined by the lamp's soft golden glow behind her, each alluring curve of her body was all too apparent beneath the thin cotton of her chemise.

"Come back to bed, Mrs. Brody," Jake commanded in a quiet, splendidly resonant tone that made her knees weaken.

"When hell freezes over!" she retorted, folding her arms across her thinly covered breasts. The hemline of her chemise rode up to the middle of her thighs.

"Are we going to have to go through this every night?" he challenged with a sardonic half-smile. "Come morning, we'll both be too worn out to be much use." Musing with an inward smile of irony that they were likely to be that way anyway, he left the bed and rose leisurely to his feet—every magnificent, full-of-vitality inch of him.

Caley's eyes moved with a will of their own to where his manhood sprang from a tight cluster of dark brown curls between his granite-hard thighs. She swallowed hard and instinctively retreated a step, her cheeks flaming and her pulse racing.

"Haven't you . . . done enough?" she demanded weakly.

"I've only just started." He began advancing upon her now. There was a wickedly purposeful gleam in his eyes that sent a tremor of mingled alarm and excitement coursing through her. "We're going to take it slow and easy this time," he decreed in a low voice brimming with the promise of passion.

"I'm not going to take it any way at all!" insisted Caley, still backing away. "You may have *ravished* me once, Jake Brody, but I'll be—"

"Ravished?" A crooked smile tugged at the corners of his mouth, and his eyes twinkled with roguish amusement. "You can call it whatever you like, you little hellion, so long as you understand I mean to keep on doing it every chance I get."

"Touch me again, you conceited bastard, and I'll make you sorry you were ever born!"

Her hands curled into fists at her sides, and her fiery turquoise gaze swept about the room as she tried in desperation to think of a way to keep him at a distance. It went entirely against her nature to admit defeat—but, heaven help her, what a glorious defeat it had been! Realizing that more of the same was in store for her, she groaned inwardly and tried not to be so very much aware of Jake's compelling nakedness.

Finally, she scurried around the rocking chair and positioned herself behind its woefully inadequate protection. Her hands grasped the carved sides of the chair while she cast her new husband a look full of helpless anger and confusion.

"It won't do you any good to fight," he proclaimed calmly. "We're married now. And it's time you learned who's boss of this outfit."

"I—I'll get a divorce!" she rashly threatened at a sudden thought.

"Like hell you will!" he ground out, his voice whipcord sharp and his eyes glinting harshly. "You're my wife, Caley. Don't ever make the mistake of forgetting it."

His words contained a not so subtle threat that prompted her own gaze to kindle anew. Her temper flaring, she colored hotly and flung another murderous glare at his handsome head. They faced one another like two combatants—one quietly determined, the other so besieged by conflicting emotions she could scarcely see straight. Shadrach was a disinterested, lazy-eyed witness to this scene of "marital discord" from where he lay curled up on the window sill.

Jake finally grew weary of his bride's defiance. His hand shot out, seizing her wrist in an iron grip and pulling her from behind the rocking chair. She suffered a sharp intake of breath as he suddenly swept her up in his arms and carried her back to the bedroom.

"You have no right to—" she protested in a small, breathless voice.

"I have every right."

"Why?" she demanded resentfully, struggling in vain. "Because you forced me to stand before a preacher and—"

"I didn't have to force you as much as you like to think," he pointed out with unchivalrous honesty. "But yes, I have the right because I'm your

281

husband." He lowered her to the bed and watched as she hastily pushed herself up into a sitting position. A soft smile played about his lips when he added in a mellow, deep-timbred voice that washed over her in the lamplit darkness, "And I have the right because I love you."

Caley stared up at him in startled disbelief. Her eyes grew very wide. *Had he really said what she thought he'd said?* Her mouth fell open, and she was too dazed to utter a protest when he reached down to tug the chemise from her body again.

"You—you don't mean that!" she stammered, beset by confusion once more. "You're just saying that because you think it'll make things easier on you!" Bristling again, she yanked the edge of the quilt upward to shield herself from his burning, boldly possessive gaze. "That's what men do, isn't it?" she demanded with bitter sarcasm. "Hell yes, they think if they just let those three little words roll off their lying, conniving tongues, they'll succeed in making any woman toss up her skirts and say, 'Take me, I'm yours'! Well, it doesn't work that way with me, Jake Brody, and—"

"Damn it, woman, shut up."

"*What?*" she breathed, highly indignant.

"You heard me." Taking a seat on the edge of the bed, he yanked the quilt away from her and brought her naked body into shockingly intimate contact with his once more. "Believe what you will," he murmured, his expression forebodingly grim. "But we both know I don't need lies to take you!"

Her gasp of outrage was lost against the demanding pressure of his mouth. He kissed her with a fierce, yet strangely tender insistence that took her breath away and provoked a wealth of sensations—all of them wildly pleasurable—deep within her. Realizing full well that she'd probably hate herself in the morning, she was still unable to prevent her arms from stealing up about his neck. She swayed against him in unspoken surrender, reveling in the feel of his hard warmth against her trembling softness. For better or for worse, she could not resist this masterful, hot-blooded lawman who had claimed her for his own.

True to his word, he made love to her this time with a gentle and tantalizing unhaste that drove her nearly mindless with desire. He turned her upon her stomach and swept her long hair aside, his lips searing provocatively downward from the back of her neck to her shoulders, along the sweet curve of her spine, and lower still to the alluring roundness of her derriere.

She clutched at the pillow beneath her head while her hips moved restlessly beneath his warm, wickedly audacious kisses. She blushed to the very roots of her titian locks when she felt his teeth bestow a light playful nip upon the bare shapeliness of her bottom before he continued his downward exploration.

Already beyond the realm of truly coherent thought, Caley voiced no objections when he urged her to her back. His mouth immediately returned to its hotly mesmerizing task, capturing her lips in another soul-stirring kiss before roaming across the flushed beauty of her face and teasing at her ear. Shivering when his tongue dipped within the delicate curl of flesh, she smoothed her hands across his back and whispered his name.

His mouth trailed fierily, purposefully downward, until at last claiming the rose-tipped fullness of her bosom. A series of low, breathless moans were elicited from her while his lips and hands and tongue paid loving tribute to her breasts. Her fingers tensed upon his shoulders, and she was perilously near to begging for mercy when he finally transferred his attentions to the rest of her lush curves. His lips followed an evocative, imaginary path downward . . .

Jake!" she gasped.

She suffered another sharp intake of breath when he finally brought his powerful frame down upon her trembling softness once more. One of his hands returned to its scorching possession of her breasts, while the other smoothed down across her hip.

"Caley," he murmured huskily close to her ear, his fingers strong yet gentle as they sought the tiny rose of femininity between her thighs. "My beautiful Caley." His voice sent chills down her spine and provoked a wild leaping of her pulse, making her clasp him tighter.

Certain she could bear no more of such ecstasy, she cried out with pleasure, not pain, when his throbbing manhood sheathed within her. She met his thrusts with an equal fire, her hands curling tightly upon his shoulders while her hips obeyed the sweet mastery of his.

Riding the crest of passion like the two vibrant, spirited individuals they were, they reached the very pinnacle of earthly delight in almost perfect unison. The second union of their hours-old marriage had proven even more intense and fulfilling than the first, so much so that Caley felt as though she had somehow lost part of herself . . . and gained part of Jake.

Plagued by this highly unsettling thought, she tried to pull away from him. He would not let her go.

"What's the matter, Mrs. Brody?" he queried in a soft, teasing tone as he lay back and imprisoned her against him. "Didn't you like lesson number two?"

"NO!" she lied.

"Yes you did," he contradicted, a tenderly crooked smile tugging at his lips. His fingers curled about her naked hip while his eyes filled with a warm glow of supreme satisfaction. "So did I."

"Of course you did!" she retorted, inexplicably angry once more. "You've probably given 'lessons' to hundreds of women!"

"Hundreds?" His mouth twitched again.

"Yes, blast your hide," she seethed, her eyes flashing with an emotion she refused to acknowledge, "and I'll bet you told all of them what you told me!" Pushing up on one elbow, she turned her stormy gaze upon her husband's damnably handsome countenance. "How many of *them* did you promise to marry if they'd let you—"

"None," he answered truthfully. His features had grown quite solemn, and the look in his eyes made her tremble anew. "I've never loved anyone before. And I never lied about the way I felt."

"Until now, you mean!" she countered, trying in vain to pull free again. A sharp gasp broke from her lips when he suddenly yanked her all the way atop him.

"Damn it, Caley, why else would I marry you?" he demanded, his features taut with anger. His gaze burned relentlessly into hers. "It wasn't in my plans to fall in love with you. Hell, that's the last thing I wanted!"

"Why, you—" she started to rage indignantly.

"But it happened just the same," he went on as if she had not even spoken. "In spite of my plans, in spite of everything, it happened." He relaxed his grip on her a bit and lifted a hand to entangle within the tangled mass of flame-colored tresses. "I could have taken you before now. God knows how much I wanted to. But it had to be right. And it had to be forever."

"What about Matt Griffin?" she then challenged, still obstinately refusing to believe him. Having guarded her heart for so long, she wasn't at all certain how to stop.

"What about him?" Jake parried tersely. His green eyes darkened to jade, and his expression became one of tightlipped displeasure.

"I was supposed to marry him, that's what!"

"You never loved Griffin."

"How the hell would *you* know?" she demanded, struggling again. "You don't know anything about me, Jake Brody, and you—"

"I know you better than you think!" he cut her off. He seized her arms and imprisoned them behind her back. "Griffin had his chance; he waited too long. But that doesn't matter now, and I'll be damned if I'm going to let you think it does! Body and soul, you belong to me, Caley. Till death do us part, remember?"

"I'll kill you myself if you don't let go of me!"

"I told you before, wildcat—don't make threats unless you intend to carry them out." Amusement had crept into his smoldering gaze, and it was soon joined by desire as a result of his bride's furious squirming atop him.

"I'll carry it out all right, you—"

She found herself silenced quite effectively when he pulled her head down and captured her lips with the firm warmth of his own. He rolled so that she was beneath him again.

286

"But you can't . . . that is, we just . . ." she faltered when he finally allowed her to draw breath.

"And we will again," he promised in a low voice brimming with an irresistible mixture of passion and humor and love. "I'm going to make sure this night is one you'll never forget."

Above all else, Jake Brody was a man of his word . . .

Chapter XII

Caley awakened to find her new husband gone. Dismayed to observe the bright sunlight streaming in through the window, she breathed a curse, flung back the covers, and scrambled from the bed. Shadrach waited in ambush in the other room. He seized his opportunity when she emerged and headed straightway toward the bathroom.

"Not now, Shadrach!" she muttered, impatiently reaching down to pry his paws from about her ankle. She relented enough to give him a quick pat on the head before disappearing into the bathroom and closing the door.

Later, after she had bathed and dressed and repeatedly bemoaned the fact that she was sore in places she hadn't even known to exist before, she cast a troubled look at the bed. She blushed fierily as memories of the long, passion-filled night came flooding back to remind her, with painful clarity, of the defeat she had "suffered" at Jake Brody's hands.

Four defeats, to be precise, an inner voice generously added them up for her.

"Hellfire and damnation!" she ground out. Jabbing the last pin into her hair, she took herself

289

downstairs.

Neither Red nor Hank were there, but Billy was. Her eyes widened in surprise when she caught sight of him sweeping the top layer of dust from the office floor.

"Billy! What on earth are you doing here?" she asked, moving away from the staircase.

"My ma said I could come, Miss Caley!" he hastened to assure her. His own eyes were alight with pleasure, and he colored faintly when he explained, "It's all over town about you and the marshal gettin' married."

"It is?" It was her turn to color.

"Yes, ma'am. And Ma said your bein' married made it all right for me to come back to work." His gaze fell before hers, and he appeared to be wrestling with something for a moment. "I . . . well, I'm right glad for you and the marshal, Miss Caley," he finally declared. In truth, his heart was feeling a bit sore, for he had entertained boyish notions about the day when he'd be old enough to marry her himself. Still, if he couldn't have her, Marshal Brody was the next best thing. "Reckon I'll have to get used to callin' you Mrs. Brody now!" he commented with a broad grin.

"Miss Caley will do just fine," she insisted, frowning. Her brow cleared in the next instant when she told him earnestly, "I'm glad you're back, Billy." Turning away to check the schedule book, she groaned inwardly at the young hostler's next words.

"The marshal said we was to let you sleep in. He said you'd probably be feelin' a mite tuckered this mornin'."

"Did he?" she managed to respond, albeit with a telltale unsteadiness to her voice. Dismayed to feel her face flaming anew, she kept her back turned to Billy and seemed to take great fascination in the book lying open on the counter before her. Billy resumed his sweeping.

"I expect you'll be gettin' a lot of visitors today," he remarked idly.

"Visitors?"

"Yes, ma'am." He swept the accumulated mountain of dust out the front door, thinking it would gather little notice on the already well-coated boardwalk. "My ma said there's nothin' like a weddin' to bring out the best in folks."

"I hardly think that applies to my situation," Caley replied dryly.

No sooner were the words out of her mouth when, much to her surprise, she turned about again and saw that Bertha Larrabee stood in the doorway shaking the dust from her full skirts and frowning reproachfully at Billy for having sent it there.

"Watch what you're doing, Billy Snyder!" the plump matron scolded with the privilege of her age.

"Yes, ma'am." Hastily setting the broom aside, he looked to his beautiful young employer. "Think I'll go on out back and see to the horses." He made good on his escape, leaving Caley alone with her chief detractor among the town's female population.

"What is it now, Mrs. Larrabee?" she asked wearily.

"There's no use in beating about the bush, so I'll get right to the point!" proclaimed Bertha. She swept haughtily inside, scattering more dust in her path. "I've heard about your marriage. I'm sure everyone has by now. You should have told me

291

what you were planning to do when I came to see you yesterday! But, even though you made the mistake of putting the cart before the horse, so to speak, I'm not the kind of person who holds another person's past against them."

Stepping forward, she grabbed Caley's unsuspecting hand and sandwiched it between both of her large, gloved ones. The merest glimmer of warmth lit the gray coldness of her eyes.

"I wish you well, Mrs. Brody," she declared somberly, "you and your husband both. Heaven knows, you've a difficult road ahead of you. But, God willing, you'll make the best of things."

Caley's own eyes grew wide with incredulity. Bertha Larrabee, the same woman who had criticized, ostracized and flat-out antagonized her for the past two years, was now actually offering her felicitations. Great balls of fire, she thought dazedly, it was beyond belief.

"I hope to see the two of you in church come Sunday," Bertha concluded as she straightened her bonnet and bustled imperiously toward the doorway again. "Your husband is by trade a man of violence; it would do him no end of good to listen to the parson's sermons and have the Lord's guidance. You could certainly use some of that guidance yourself." She turned and gave Caley a nod, "Good day to you, Mrs. Brody," then was gone.

Stunned, Caley stared after the formidable Mrs. Larrabee. It amazed her to realize that, simply because she had married Jake—or any other man, she supposed—she had gained respectability. Would the same have held true, she mused while her eyes shone with ironic mirth, if she had been one of the women down on Dobe Row and had managed to rope one of the lovesick young punchers into holy matrimony? Apparently so, at least under Bertha Larrabee's criteria.

She sighed, her thoughts drawn irrevocably to her new husband. A tingling warmth stole over her again, and she was more than a little dismayed to find herself counting the hours till nightfall.

"You *are* shameless!" she muttered in a burst of self-recrimination. "Shameless and crazy and—" Breaking off, she compressed her lips into a tight, thin line, shot a look full of anger and entreaty heavenward, and spun about to get on with the day's work. Marriage or no marriage, she was determined that her life would remain the same.

Her next visitor was every bit as unexpected as the first. He materialized in the doorway less than an hour after Bertha's departure, sweeping the hat from his dark blond head and fastening his intelligent, light blue gaze upon Caley. She was at present conducting business with another one of those plaid-suited drummers wishing to book passage to the ripe pickings of Tuscarora.

"The stage leaves at six o'clock sharp," she told the drummer, taking his money and entering his name in the book.

"Six o'clock?" he echoed with a frown. "Isn't there another stage—"

"No. There's only one. You miss it, and there won't be another until Tuesday." She smiled to lessen the severity of her words, and suddenly caught sight of the man watching her from the doorway. "Ned Griffin!" she exclaimed, her eyes sparkling in genuine pleasure. She hastened from around the counter to greet him with a warm, affectionate hug and demand, "Where the devil have you been keeping yourself?"

"I finally did it, Caley. I finally up and left." He

293

hugged her back and smiled down at her like the brother he considered himself to be. "I've been working over at Peterman's the past week."

"You *left?*" she repeated in startled disbelief. "Oh Ned, what—"

"I'm still waiting for my ticket," said the drummer, not at all hesitant to interrupt the touching scene being enacted before him.

Caley frowned in exasperation, but nonetheless hurried back to ticket the line's future passenger and send him on his way. She closed the door after him and immediately fired a barrage of questions at Ned.

"What happened? For heaven's sake, did you and Matt get into it again? And how come you haven't been in to see me before now?"

"Matt's got nothing to do with it, not really," Ned answered solemnly. "I just finally got a bellyful of things and decided I'd waited long enough to strike out on my own. I ran into Peterman here in town the next day. He gave me a job as foreman on his ranch. I haven't been back since, else I'd have told you. Besides," he added with a rueful smile, "I figured you'd probably hear about it from Matt."

"Well I wonder why he didn't mention—" she started to reflect aloud, but left the sentence unfinished when she recalled how there hadn't been much time for talk the last time they had been together. Her throat constricted painfully at the memory.

"You've seen him?" At her silent nod, he asked, "When?"

"Yesterday. Last night, to be exact. He . . . he came by to let me know the charges against him had been dropped."

"Yeah, I heard they'd been paid off." His eyes glinted dully, and the young Basque woman's image drifted across his mind again like it had done so frequently throughout the past week. "You know, I was with him the night he paid that little 'visit' to the sheepherders' camp. Like a damn fool, I thought I could do some good."

"You were there?" she asked in surprise. "Then why didn't you stop him?"

"You know Matt. There *is* no stopping him when he gets his mind set on something."

It was true. She knew it better than anyone. Just like she knew he would never forgive her for her betrayal of his love.

Her eyes clouded at this last thought. Matt had never said he loved her. Like everything else, it had always just been understood between them. . . .

"What about your father?" she asked Ned, forcing her attention back to the subject at hand. "How is he taking it?"

"You mean my leaving?" He gave a short, humorless laugh. "He's probably glad to be rid of me. Hell, Caley, you know I've never been what he wanted. I couldn't be like Matt, and he didn't want me being any other way."

"Oh Ned," she sighed disconsolately. Her heart ached for them all, but most especially for the sensitive young man before her. He had always been different. And in truth, she had always known there would come a time when he'd have to leave. "I don't suppose you've tried talking to Isaiah about any of this?" she suggested, all the while knowing it was hopeless.

"Since when has Isaiah Griffin been willing to listen to anyone but himself?" Ned pointed out with another sad smile of irony. "No, it's best this way. He'll stay riled for a while. But you never can tell. Maybe, given a little time, he'll realize that we're a hell of a lot better off with some distance between us."

"So you're just going to stay on at Peterman's?" she challenged, folding her arms beneath her breasts. "Damn it, Ned, there's no future in tending another man's cattle! You've got to get a stake somewhere and start building your own spread. Think of the future—there's no way on God's green earth you'll be able to support a family on that little bit of chicken feed Peterman pays his hands. You *do* want to get married someday, don't you?"

"I've given it some thought," he confessed, breaking into a real grin now. His face reddened slightly, and his eyes glowed with secret pleasure. "But that's still a long way off yet."

"It can happen sooner than you think," murmured Caley. She shifted her gaze down toward her high-laced boots while guilty color stained her own cheeks.

"You mean you and Matt?"

"No. I mean me and . . . and Marshal Brody."

"Marshal Brody?" He had seen the new marshal only once, a day or two after Matt had gotten himself thrown in jail. But he had certainly heard a lot of talk about the man from his brother and father—none of it good. "What's going on between you and Brody?" he demanded with a frown.

Caley muttered an inward curse. Taking a deep breath, she determinedly raised her eyes to Ned's again and revealed the startling truth.

"The marshal and I are married. We have been since yesterday."

"*Married?*" Obviously taken aback, he tightened his grip on his hat and asked, "That came about

296

all of a sudden, didn't it? How the hell did it happen?"

"I don't know!" Whirling about, she paced angrily back to the window. "I can't explain it to you, Ned. It—it just happened!"

"Does Matt know?" he asked quietly, his thoughts following the natural course of things.

"Yes." Her beautiful eyes were full of anguish when she turned around again. "He didn't take it too well. Who can blame him? I've never seen him so hurt and angry and—" She swallowed a sudden lump in her throat before declaring brokenly, "Oh Ned, I didn't mean to hurt him!" Hot tears glistened in her turquoise gaze, and she was glad for the support of Ned's arms about her as she flew into his welcoming embrace.

"It's all right, Caley," he murmured in a low, soothing tone. In all the years he had known her, this was only the second time he'd seen her cry. Loving her as he did, he found himself seized with the vengeful desire to make whoever was responsible for her pain pay for hurting her. "Matt will get over it," he tried reassuring her.

"No he won't," she insisted, shaking her head against his chest. "And I'll never forgive myself for doing this to him!"

"He did it to himself! Damn it, Caley, if he hadn't dragged his feet these past two years, you'd have been married to *him* by now. He's got no one to blame but himself."

"But that was my fault as much as his!" She drew away and dashed impatiently at her tears. "Don't you see? I was the one who let herself get . . . I was the one who . . ." None of this was making sense, even to her. "Everything was fine until Brody came to town!" she blurted out.

297

"No it wasn't," Ned disagreed honestly. "Things haven't been the same between you and Matt since way back before Paddy died. I could tell. So could my father."

"I don't suppose it matters anymore now, does it?" she concluded, her voice edged with bitterness. No amount of tears or talk would change things. Releasing a long, ragged sigh, she said, "I'm sorry, Ned. I didn't mean to go all to pieces on you like that."

"You can go all to pieces on me any time," he offered with a crooked grin. "But that new husband of yours might not take too kindly to it." Sobering, he studied her face closely. "Is he good to you, Caley?" he demanded. "Because, if he's not, you've only to—"

"No!" She colored and explained, "I mean, yes, he's good to me." She was tempted to say more, but decided against it. There was no use in telling Ned that her marriage wasn't what he thought. Well, it *was*, but not in the usual sense. Nothing about her marriage was in the usual sense!

"I'm glad to hear it," replied Ned, apparently satisfied. He raised the hat to his head and started slowly toward the doorway. Caley walked with him.

"You'll come and see me the next time you're in town, won't you?"

"Nothing could stop me," he promised. "Besides, I'd like to meet the marshal and tell him what a lucky man he is." He turned and subjected her to one last long, searching look. "If you need me for anything, Caley, anything at all, you know where to find me." Recalling that he had said the same thing to Matt once, he felt a twinge of pain.

"Thank you, Ned. You—you really are the best!" She hugged him close again, then smiled and remarked teasingly, "I always knew I should have set my sights on you instead of Matt."

"If you had, I would never have let anyone else take you from me," he replied in all seriousness. "Never."

He brushed her cheek with his lips before striding away, leaving her to fight back another wave of tears. There were times, thought Caley, when fate played cruel tricks on everyone. It had certainly played one on Ned by making him Isaiah Griffin's son.

Ned, meanwhile, had set a course for the jail. Determined to speak to Marshal Brody and ascertain for himself whether or not the man was even half good enough for Caley, he was too engrossed in his thoughts at first to take notice of the young woman pulling her mount to a halt in front of the mercantile. He had already passed the store before he raised his head and cast a glance up at the cloud-choked summer sky.

Then he saw *her*. She swung down from the saddle, her full, bright red skirts swirling about her legs. Her raven tresses were tied back with a red ribbon, and her long-sleeved white blouse had a low, rounded neckline which was gathered just above the swelling curve of her breasts. She was even more beautiful than Ned had remembered.

"Miss Larronde?"

Elena started at the sound of her name. Her gaze swept hastily about, only to widen with surprise when it fell upon Ned. He stepped down from the boardwalk, tugging the hat from his head and giving her a rather tentative smile that made her pulses quicken alarmingly.

"How do you know my name?" she demanded with a proud composure that belied the tempest within her. She remembered all too well the feel of his lean, muscular body upon hers, and the kindness in his eyes that awful night.

"It wasn't hard to find out," he replied. "I'm Ned Griffin."

"I know."

"You do?" It was his turn to be surprised when he glimpsed the light of mischief in her sparkling brown eyes.

"It was not hard to find out," she countered innocently.

She looped the reins about the hitching post and gathered up her skirts to step onto the boardwalk. Ned gallantly offered her his hand. She declined to take it, however, choosing instead to make her way without assistance.

"I've been meaning to ride back out and look in on you and your family," Ned remarked apologetically. Standing before her, he couldn't help noticing that she was a full head shorter than himself. "I'd have been out there before now," he added, "but when I heard my father—"

"You do not have to explain to me, Mr. Griffin," Elena interrupted with a frown, looking away. "I know you must do as your father says."

"Not any longer." He was pleased when her eyes flew back up to meet his again. "I don't work for my father any more, Miss Larronde."

"Then where—" she started to question, only to chide herself for her boldness. Her father would be very angry if he knew she had stopped to talk to anyone; his temper would know no bounds if he knew she had stopped to talk to *this* man.

"I've got a job on a ranch about five miles the other side of town," he supplied. "The pay's not much, but it . . . well, it's a start."

Their gazes met and locked, and neither of them spoke for several long moments. They were completely oblivious to the ceaseless flow of people on the boardwalk, oblivious as well to the sights and sounds emphasizing the fact that another week had ended. Finally, Ned gently cleared his throat.

"What about you?" he asked. "I mean, what about your family? Are they getting along all right?"

"Yes." Elena nodded and raised a hand to brush a stray lock of hair from her face. "We, too, are not far from town. My father and my brother, they must keep the sheep moving." Her lips curved into an unintentionally captivating smile. "The boys are much too little to help, but they are happy to try. I have come to buy them new shoes," she explained, glancing toward the mercantile.

Ned couldn't take his eyes off her. She wasn't like any of the women he'd met before. But it was more than that. He had known it from the very first, when she had come flying out of that wagon with her hair streaming behind her like a black silk banner and her big brown eyes snapping with the light of battle. He had known it then.

"I—I must go now, Mr. Griffin," she told him, coloring faintly beneath his steady blue gaze.

"Maybe I should hang around and ride back with you," he suggested on a sudden impulse. His eyes made a quick, encompassing sweep of the crowded street. "Seeing as how it's a Saturday and all, you really shouldn't be out alone like this. I can see that you get home all right and then—"

"No!" Her color deepened. "I do not wish to be rude," she apologized, her gaze falling before his, "but my father would not allow it."

"Because of what happened?" he asked with a

301

touch of bitterness.

"No. Because . . . because you are not *Euskaldunak*." She raised her eyes to his once more, and he could see that they were full of sadness. "Because you are not Basque."

"But you're in America now," he argued, frowning. "Things are different here."

"No, they are not." She shook her head. "Not for us. My father says we must keep the old ways. We must remain Basque." Forcing herself to turn away at last, she murmured, "Goodbye, Mr. Griffin," and disappeared inside the store.

Ned battled the urge to go after her. He was enough like the other Griffins to get his mind set on something and vow to make it his—but he was not enough like them to take it by force.

With Elena Larronde's face burning in his mind, he continued on his way toward the jail. He knew how to be patient. And he knew how to hope. Some things, not even his father and brother had been able to take away from him.

Caley gathered her courage about her and swept inside the dining room. They were all there, just as she'd known they would be, waiting to pounce.

"Well, well, so the 'blushing bride' emerges at last," Eva Hartford remarked sourly.

"Missed you at breakfast," mumbled Mr. Tate, eyeing her briefly before resuming his attack upon the plate of beef stew and cornbread. "Saw your husband, though."

"Caley! I was hoping you'd come," said Maybelle, rising from the table to welcome her young friend with a warm embrace. "You're not still angry with me, are you?" she whispered in her ear.

"It wasn't your fault," Caley pronounced with a sigh. She drew away and cautioned with a faint smile of irony, "But don't go asking me any questions."

"Good day to you, Mrs. Brody," declared J.D. when she took her seat across from him. "I should like to offer you my warmest and sincerest congratulations upon your marriage." His bespectacled gaze shone with kindness, and contained not even a hint of condemnation.

"Thank you, J.D," she replied, then gasped in surprise when George suddenly wrapped an arm about her shoulders.

"Mrs. Brody!" he repeated her name with a chuckle. "Yes sir, I like the sound of that! And the marshal's a damn lucky son of a—"

"Mr. Groat!" rebuked Eva.

"*Gun!*" George finished triumphantly. He leaned over and gave Caley a hearty kiss upon her cheek before releasing her. "I heard about it over at the Senate last night. Guess who else was over there bendin' an elbow?"

"We haven't the slightest bit of interest in hearing about your latest dissipation, George Groat!" Eva insisted in her best spinsterly manner.

"It was Matt Griffin!" George revealed anyway. "He damn near tore the place apart when some stupid bastard made the mistake of askin' what he thought about the marshal's gettin' married, and—"

"Please, Mr. Groat, you know good and well I don't allow that kind of talk at my table!" Maybelle hastened to intervene. She cast a worried glance at Caley, who had paled and now sat staring fixedly at her empty plate. "You've not yet told us about the play, Mr. Worthington," she said, turning to J.D. in an attempt to steer the conversation onto safer ground.

"I am happy to report that it was quite successful, Mrs. O'Grady." There was an undeniable note of pride in his voice when he added, "Miss DuMonde's performance received a great deal of applause from the audience. She was also given extremely favorable mention in the latest edition of the *Independent*."

"Miss DuMonde will be leaving soon, I suppose?" Eva queried with a pointed raising of her eyebrows.

"Perhaps," J.D. answered enigmatically. He glanced away before observing the crestfallen look his words brought to the schoolteacher's face.

"I don't expect you'll be doin' any more drivin' now that you're married," George remarked to Caley as she finally ladled some of the stew onto her plate.

"Why wouldn't I?" she asked with a slight frown of bemusement, still troubled by what he had said about Matt.

"Well, from what the marshal told me," George took his own sweet time about answering, "I don't think he's too much on the idea of havin' his brand new wife gallivantin' all over the countryside."

"Oh?" Her eyes kindled with angry fire, and a dull flush rose to her face. "Just what the devil did he tell you?" she demanded tightly.

"It was at breakfast." He took a bite of corn-bread and rubbed the back of his hand across his mouth. "We got to talkin' about the robbery again, and I said he was dam—er, darn lucky to be alive, and he said you both were, and then I said it seemed to me drivin' a stagecoach was a mighty dangerous profession for anyone, much less a woman, and he said that was the truth of it all right but that you were fixin' to retire."

"*Retire?*" Caley breathed in furious disbelief.

"Would anyone care for more coffee?" Maybelle asked loudly, taking up the coffeepot and rising to her feet.

"I should like some, thank you," said J.D.

"Me, too," Mr. Tate seconded unintelligibly.

"Is that true, Mis—Mrs. Brody?" Eva sought confirmation from the young woman she had long viewed with intense disapproval. "If so, then I should like to say that I think it's about time!" she proclaimed, casting a glance about to make certain everyone was listening. "Heaven knows, it's been bad enough that you have made such a spectacle of yourself in town, but it was never anything but utterly scandalous, the way you spent so many hours alone in the company of men!" She stopped just short of bringing up the rumors she had heard regarding the other woman's "ordeal" on the return trip from Tuscarora.

"I wasn't in the company of anyone," Caley pointed out in a low, simmering tone. "I was too damned busy handling the reins to—"

"Yes, well, now that you've a husband to take you in hand," Eva disdainfully cut her off, "perhaps this nonsense of yours will cease once and for all!"

"Take you in hand," echoed George, then gave a rumble of appreciative laughter for the double entendre. "That's a right good way of puttin' it, Miss Eva."

"Mr. Groat!" Maybelle claimed the honor of calling him down.

"I have no intention of retiring!" Caley declared with searing vehemence, her blue-green eyes flashing. "And as far as my 'husband' is concerned, he can go straight to hell!"

"Trouble in paradise so soon, my dear?" sneered Eva.

"Eva Hartford, either you shut your mouth, or I'll have to ask you to leave my table!" Maybelle snapped angrily.

"Shut my—" gasped Eva, her gaze widening with righteous indignation.

"You heard me!" affirmed the widow. "I don't know what's put such a burr in your saddle, but I will not stand for such mean-spirited behavior at my table!"

Eva clamped her mouth shut and flung her napkin to the table. Rising abruptly to her feet, she treated Caley to one last glare before flouncing from the room in a furious rustle of dark plum silk.

"I'm sorry, Miss Caley," George told her. Visibly contrite, he pushed away his half-empty plate and sighed, "I guess I sort of started the whole thing when I—"

"Why don't we just drop the subject, Mr. Groat," Maybelle advised quietly. She disappeared into the kitchen to fetch more coffee.

Caley acknowledged George's apology with a rather wan smile. Although her appetite had once again fled, she forced herself to eat. She could feel George's and J.D.'s and even Mr. Tate's eyes upon her, but she did not look up until Maybelle came back and resumed her seat at the head of the table. Then, upon meeting the older woman's sympathetic gaze, she felt herself battling the inexplicable urge to dissolve into yet another storm of tears.

"Why don't you stay on after you finish," suggested Maybelle, remembering her own days as a new bride. "The two of us can have a nice talk."

"No. I—I have some business to take care of," Caley declined, hastily returning her attention to her plate.

There were some things she just couldn't talk about, not even to Maybelle. She knew there was no way to explain what she was feeling, no way to make anyone else understand how she could possibly despise Jake Brody the way she claimed to do and yet go absolutely wild with passion in his arms the way she had done last night. The only explanation she could think of was that she had taken sudden and complete leave of her senses—but, heaven help her, *what a sweet madness it was.*

Her thoughts were no less troubled when she headed down to Mr. Ling's later that same afternoon. Tucked underneath her arm was a bundle of soft leather that had once been her cherished buckskin suit. It was sadly in need of cleaning and repair; the latter due to Jake's manhandling, she recalled, her eyes sparking anew at the memory.

They sparked for other reasons as well, foremost of which was the fact that she had seen nothing of her new husband the entire day. It annoyed her that he had left while she was still sleeping; it annoyed her even more that he had taken himself over to Maybelle's for what had apparently been an illuminating breakfast with the regulars. Fueling her anger and resentment was the thought that he cared nothing for her company outside of bed.

Oh, he loved her all right, she told herself with bitter sarcasm as she neared Chinatown. He loved her so blasted much that he could wed her, bed her, and then never give her another thought. Until dark, of course. Yes, by damn, come nightfall he'd probably think of little else.

She was in a dangerous mood indeed by the time she knocked on Mr. Ling's door. Mr. Ling himself answered the knock and graciously welcomed her inside, bowing and telling her in all sincerity how happy he was to learn of her marriage.

"You've already heard?" Caley asked in some surprise.

"Yes, Miss Caley. And I hope you will accept a humble gift."

"Gift? Oh, Mr. Ling, please don't—" she tried to protest.

He was already disappearing through the parted, makeshift curtains. When he emerged again, he was carrying something in his hands. Oddly enough, it was a cup of tea. He offered it to Caley.

"You will please drink this, Miss Caley!" he requested with a broad smile.

"What is it?" she asked, eyeing it dubiously.

"A special tea. Please drink!" he encouraged, smiling once more.

Not wishing to seem rude, Caley took the cup from him and sipped tentatively. The tea was quite warm but not bitter. She quickly drained the cup and handed it back to a highly pleased Mr. Ling.

"You like it, Miss Caley?" His dark gaze was positively dancing with mischief.

"Yes," she replied, then asked in growing suspicion, "What was in it?"

"Only good things," he reassured her, then pronounced happily, "Now you will have many fine babies."

"*Babies?*" Her eyes flew back to the cup in his hands.

"I have a special tea for your husband as well. It is to be used only when you wish to have sons instead of daughters. You would like to take it to

308

him?"

"No! That is, I—no, thank you!" Blushing fierily, she thrust the buckskin suit at him and said, "Please, Mr. Ling, will you see to this for me? And thank you for the tea, but I'm afraid I have to be going now!"

"Come again in two days," he instructed. His eyes twinkled merrily up at her when he added, "I will have more tea for you."

"Thank you," she said weakly. Returning his bow, she murmured, "Goodbye, Mr. Ling," and escaped outside.

"Goodbye, Miss Caley!" he called after her. A soft chuckle escaped his lips before he closed the door.

Her cheeks still burning, Caley traveled back up the street toward Dobe Row. She had been taken completely off guard by Mr. Ling's "gift," and now hurried to put as much distance as possible between herself and the accursed cup—as if by doing so she could somehow alter the fact that the tea was already working its magic on her.

Until now, the thought of children had never entered her mind. She cursed herself for having been so naive, then suddenly realized that the prospect of motherhood was not all that disagreeable. As a matter of fact, she mused in growing wonderment, it was downright appealing.

Children. Her eyes glowed warmly as the idea took root and sprouted to life. She had never had a family of her own. All those years, it had been just her and Paddy, just the two of them going from one lonely western outpost to another. She had always secretly yearned for a sense of permanence . . . for a real home . . . for others to love and be loved by.

Her spirits lifted considerably as she envisioned a future filled with all those things. Of course, she then reflected, there could be no possibility of divorce once she did indeed find herself to be "in the family way". But since her arrogant, overbearing husband had declared a divorce to be impossible to begin with, there was certainly no use in worrying about that.

Her eyes clouded with confusion again. The thought of spending the rest of her life with Jake Brody was unsettling, to say the least.

Walking along with a preoccupied air, she was nearly past *Miss Sadie's* before she realized it. She cast an idle glance up at the bold, red-lettered sign nailed to the front of the building, musing wryly that the place was beginning to show as much wear and tear as the poor girls who worked there. Her gaze was drawn back down to the open doorway. Although it was a good deal brighter outside than within the noisy, smokefilled confines of the ground floor saloon, she had no difficulty in making out the faces of the people inside.

As usual, Saturday had brought with it an endless supply of customers raising hell and willing to pay for the privilege of doing so. Miss Sadie herself was behind the bar, her ample breasts threatening to spill out of the low, rounded bodice of her pink satin gown while she laughed and flirted and poured drinks. Men crowded one another at the bar, sat at tables playing cards or stealing a hand up some painted Delilah's skirts, and kept up a steady flow on the stairs leading to the "gates of paradise" above.

Caley found herself looking for Matt's face in the boisterous crowd. She stepped aside to let two young cowboys make their way outside, then cursed one of them roundly when he offered to buy her a drink. He and his companion beat a hasty retreat, leaving her to peer inside once more.

Finally abandoning her efforts, she released a sigh of defeat and turned to leave. It was at that same, fateful moment that a familiar voice drifted out to her. She spun back around, her gaze widening in shocked disbelief when they fell upon the man who was coming down the stairs with a fallen angel draped on each arm.

Great balls of fire, it was Jake! She shook her head as if to deny it — but the revolting evidence spoke for itself.

The two women were clad in nothing but their lacy undergarments and paper thin wrappers that just would not stay belted. They were all over him. And he seemed to be enjoying every damned minute of it, seethed Caley, judging from the smile on his face and the fact that he made no attempt whatsoever to disentangle himself from their highly seductive grasp.

Her eyes narrowed and blazed with their magnificent blue-green fire. Every square inch of her was filled with righteous, wifely outrage, and it suddenly felt as though someone had plunged a knife in her heart. Pain and anger joined together to send her temper flaring out of control.

She burst through the doorway like a beautiful, avenging tigress. Jake, reaching the bottom step with his two prisoners, saw her a split second before she launched herself at him.

"Caley?" He drew away from the women, his brow creasing in a frown of mingled surprise and worriment. "What —"

"You whoring son of a bitch!" she cried hotly. Bailing her hand into a fist, she brought it smashing up against his handsome chin.

The crowd erupted into an appreciative roar of laughter. Jake's face became a grim mask of barely controlled violence, and his gaze smoldered down into his errant bride's stormy features as he seized her arms in a punishing grip.

"Damn it, Caley, what's going on?" he demanded in a fury-laced undertone.

"That's exactly what *I'd* like to know!" she shot back. Flinging a murderous glare toward the women, she would have given them double what she'd given him if he had not held her back. "Did you and your—your *friends* there have a good time upstairs?" she taunted as hot, bitter tears stung against her eyelids.

"Come on!" he ground out, pulling her none too gently toward the doorway now.

"I'm not going anywhere with you, you four-flushing bastard!" she defied, struggling wildly. Infuriated beyond reason, she was oblivious to the fact that their quarrel was such a public one. Jake, however, was not.

In one swift motion, he spun her about, tossed her over his broad shoulder, and bore her purposefully outside. His actions were met with another round of laughter and cheers of approval from the men in the saloon, as well as several ribald bits of advice on what to do with his redheaded spitfire once he got her alone.

"Put me down, damn you!" hissed Caley when they were outside. She was startled when he did just that.

"Keep your mouth shut and come along peacefully," he warned in a low, dangerously even tone, "or so help me, I'll carry you all the way back!"

Caley knew he was not one to make idle threats.

Feeling more heartsore and full of helpless rage than she'd ever felt before, she clamped her mouth shut and jerked away from him. Jake muttered an oath beneath his breath, then followed after her as she marched furiously homeward.

Chapter XIII

"Somethin' wrong, Miss Caley?" Billy asked as he came around to the front of the building. Caley did not respond, but swept right past him and into the office. His perplexed gaze fell upon Jake. "Marshal Brody? What—"

"It's nothing, Billy," Jake assured him quietly. The merest ghost of a smile touched his lips when he added, "Nothing that a hard head and a steady hand won't cure."

"Huh?"

"Give it a few years," drawled Jake, placing a companionable hand on Billy's shoulder. "You'll understand soon enough." He left the sixteen-year-old staring after him in complete bewilderment as he strode inside.

Caley was already upstairs by this time. She had slammed the door and locked it, still too hurt and angry to contemplate the wisdom of such action. Shadrach, as if sensing the coming storm, immediately took refuge underneath the bed.

"Caley!" Jake's own temper rose to a hazardous level when he tried the door and found it locked. Striving to maintain an iron control over his emotions, he bit back a curse and commanded in a voice of deadly calm, "Open the door, Caley."

"Go back to *Miss Sadie's!*" she retorted, folding her arms tightly across her heaving breasts while she stood and glared at the door through her tears. "And you might as well take your things with you, since you sure as hell won't be sleeping here any more!"

"Damn it, Caley, open the door." His deep-timbered voice held an undeniable warning, but she refused to take heed of it.

"No! I never want to see you again, Jake Brody! Now get the hell out of here and leave me alone!"

Only a short time ago, she recalled miserably, she had actually been thinking about having children with this . . . this *rakehell*. Well, no more, confound it, no more! Their marriage was over with before it had ever really begun. It had been a mistake, she thought while choking back a sob, nothing more than a terrible mistake. But, God help her, she felt as though her heart was breaking in two.

"Caley!"

"Go away!"

There was an awful silence for a moment, followed by a loud, splintering crash when the door was forced open. A breathless cry of alarm escaped Caley's lips as she suddenly found herself staring up into her husband's thunderous features.

"There'll be no locked doors between us, you little hellcat!" he decreed tersely. In two long, angry strides, he was before her, his hands closing about her arms and his gaze piercing relentlessly down into hers. "Now what the devil's set you off this time?"

"You know perfectly well what's 'set me off'!" She brought her own hands up to push at the immovable force of his chest. "I've got eyes, you know!"

"Yes, and you've also got too much imagination for your own good!" While unable to deny feeling a certain triumphant satisfaction for her jealousy, he was still angered by her willingness to believe him guilty—not to mention the fact that she had made her erroneous conclusions so damned public. "What you think you saw is a far sight different—"

"I know what I saw, damn it!" She ceased her struggles for a moment and narrowed her eyes wrathfully up at him. "I saw you with those half-naked floozies, Jake Brody, so don't you dare go trying to deny it!"

"I'm not going to deny it. It's the truth," he readily admitted. "You saw me with them all right, but you didn't bother to let me explain!"

"Explain? What the blazes is there to explain? Hellfire and damnation, I'm not an idiot! I *know* what goes on in that palace of sin over there!"

"I had just arrested those women for robbing one of the men, Caley," Jake ground out. "He filed charges against them only an hour ago. I was taking them to jail when you came along."

"And enjoying every minute of it, from the look of things!" she taunted bitterly. "How convenient for you to have such all-fired *cooperative* prisoners!"

"I've had worse!" he parried between clenched teeth.

"And better, too, I suppose!" she shot back.

"Sooner or later, Caley, you're going to have to learn to trust me," he told her with deceptive calm. "I was only doing my job. And you interfered with that job by letting your heart rule your

317

head!"

"My heart has nothing to do with this!"

"Doesn't it?"

"No! And besides," she went on to demand, "if you really were arresting them, then how is it they weren't even dressed? Just how can you explain that, you lying Texas snake?"

"They refused to put on their clothes, damn it, and I sure as hell wasn't going to do it for them!"

"Why not? No, don't tell me—you're only good at getting women *out* of their clothes!" she charged acidly.

"Sometimes, Mrs. Brody," said Jake in a quietly furious tone, "I could wring your neck."

"No one's forcing you to put up with me!" she pointed out, angrily fighting back another wave of tears.

She didn't know whether to be glad or not when he released her and turned away. A gasp of startlement broke from her lips when he brought his fist smashing up against the palm of his other hand. She expected to hear him let loose with a blistering string of curses, but he remained strangely silent. Staring at his back, she thought about what he had told her—and felt uncertainty creeping into the midst of her fury. She suddenly realized that, more than anything in the world, she wanted to believe him.

"I've never lied to you, Caley," he declared as if reading her mind. He turned to face her again, his eyes glinting dully. "And you're just going to have to take my word about what you think you saw." He resumed his stance before her, but did not touch her. His brows drew together in another frown while he gazed down into the stormy, still fiery-eyed beauty of her face. "What were you doing at Dobe Row, anyway?"

"I wasn't at Dobe Row!" she denied, then bristled when a faint, mocking smile tugged at his mouth. "I was there, of course, but I . . . damn it, I wasn't *there!* I merely happened to be passing by on my way back from Mr. Ling's, and I—"

"And you decided to see what I was up to, is that it?" he finished for her.

"No! I didn't even know you were there! And why the hell should I care what you were doing?"

"Maybe you were feeling a bit lonely." His gaze filled with wry, loving amusement as he watched the telltale color rise to her face. "We didn't get a chance to say goodbye this morning."

Memories of the previous night had made it difficult for him to concentrate on anything else that day. He had forced himself to stay away, knowing full well he'd never be able to leave her once he set eyes on her again. He'd want her too damned much . . . just the way he did now.

The look in his eyes made Caley grow warm all over. She was perilously near to melting against him when she recalled how angry she still was. Drawing herself rigidly erect, she sent him a challenging glare.

"Maybe not," she countered belatedly, "but you certainly had plenty of time to go across the street to Maybelle's and fill everyone's ears with some poppycock about how I was going to stop driving!"

"You are."

"I sure as hell am not!"

"You're my wife, Caley," he reminded her in a voice laced with steel. "You'll do as I say."

"I'll do as I please!" she retorted with a spirited toss of her head. Some of the hairpins were still

319

entangled within the luxuriant mass of auburn curls streaming down about her shoulders; others were lying back on the dust-caked floor of *Miss Sadie's*. "I'm not about to retire, Jake Brody, and you can't make me!"

"I've already talked to Hank and Red. They've agreed to take all the runs from here on out."

"Oh they have, have they?" Her hands curled into fists at her sides while her temper flared to a near explosive level once more. Turquoise eyes ablaze, she lifted her chin to confront Jake squarely and proclaimed in a voice quavering with indignation, "You had no right to talk to my drivers about anything! They work for me, not you, and I'll be hanged if I'm going to sit around here on my backside all the time while they're off — "

"Better that than having your backside shot at or busted to pieces out on the road somewhere!" he decreed bluntly. He took a step closer, his gaze burning down into hers. "No, Caley. I'm not going to let you put yourself in danger like that again. From now on, you're going to hang up your whip and stay home where you belong. I've got other things to think about. I can't be worrying about you. Damn it," he concluded, no longer able to keep his hands off her, "I can't be driving myself crazy with thoughts of you lying hurt or in need of help while I'm back here trying to do the job I was sent to do!"

"I was handling the reins long before you came along, and I'll be handling them long after you're gone!" she declared emphatically. She wrenched herself from his grasp and retreated behind the same rocking chair that had offered such woefully inadequate protection the night before. "Your job is a hundred times more dangerous than mine, and yet you expect me to sit at home with my—my *sewing* while you're out there providing an easy target for any crackbrained bastard who takes it in mind to shoot you!"

"You've still got a business to run," he pointed out with only the ghost of a smile. "But yes, I expect you to let me do what has to be done."

She tried to think of a suitably scathing response, but could not. Words failed her. And to make matters worse, her own emotions betrayed her. Although she knew she should be furious at his high-handed ordering of her life, she was unable to keep from feeling strangely touched by his concern for her welfare. Except for her father, no one had ever cared enough to worry about her. Not even Matt.

Matt. His face suddenly swam before her eyes. But her heart was filled with nothing more than a mixture of pity and remorse. She looked back to Jake—and was startled to feel every fiber of her being come alive. Once again, she became frightened at the depth of her feelings. She found herself wanting to hurt him, to push him away before it was too late . . .

"You want to know what I was really doing down at Dobe Row?" she suddenly challenged, flinging him a look of proud defiance and stubbornly ignoring the warning signal in her own brain. "Well, I was looking for Matt Griffin!"

It was the first thing that had come to mind. Although she should have been satisfied to watch the shadow of pain crossing the rugged perfection of Jake's features, she was not. Quite the contrary, as a matter of fact. She felt absolutely miserable.

"You're lying," he ground out, his blood boiling

321

as jealousy mingled with pain and fury.

"No I'm not! I was looking for Matt, and I—I found you instead!" At least it was partly true, she rationalized inwardly, hating herself for such mean-spiritedness and yet not knowing how to undo the damage she had done.

"So help me, woman, if I thought for one minute—"

"You can think whatever you like!" She dashed impatiently at a tear coursing down the flushed smoothness of her cheek. "I told you it was a mistake for us to get married!" She paused for a moment before delivering the final blow. "Matt Griffin never would have insisted that I give up driving! He is enough of a man to admit—"

"He isn't enough of a man for you, Caley," dissented Jake, his low, deep-timbred voice cutting her to the core. "He never was." His gaze darkened with a savage gleam when he added, "But I am. By damn, *I* am!"

Caley gave a strangled cry of alarm and bolted for the door. Jake caught her, his expression one of grim determination as he dragged her back to the rocking chair. He took a seat, threw her face-down across his knees, and tossed up her skirts.

"Jake!" She squirmed and kicked wildly, but his arm clamped across her waist like a band of iron. "Damn you, Jake Brody, let me go!"

His only answer was to raise his hand and spank her, hard, three times. Then, turning her over, he imprisoned her outraged softness upon his lap and brought his lips crashing down upon hers. She still fought him, but he yanked her arms behind her back and kissed her all the more demandingly.

Caley felt her anger turning into passion. Reason fled as liquid fire raced through her veins. She moaned softly, her lips moving beneath Jake's and her tongue returning the hotly rapturous caress of his. Her arms were released, and she did not hesitate before entwining them about his neck. He stroked one urgent hand downward to grasp the beguiling curve of her hips, pulling her closer, while his other hand smoothed across the buttoned front of her calico shirtwaist to close possessively upon the beckoning fullness of her breast.

The flames of desire rapidly intensifying, Caley did not protest when her husband impatiently tugged her skirts even higher and slipped his hand within the gaping edges of her white cotton, open-leg drawers. She inhaled upon a sharp gasp when his warm fingers found their soft, delightfully appreciative target, and her hands curled tightly upon the granite-hard expanse of his shoulders while she surrendered herself to passion's sweet insanity once more.

With remarkable expertise, his other hand proceeded to liberate the top several buttons of her gown. He swept aside the faded calico, his fingers delving beneath her chemise to brand the satiny, rose-tipped fullness of her breasts. She gasped again when his lips suddenly relinquished hers and trailed a fiery path downward to roam hungrily over her breasts as they swelled above the low rounded neckline of her undergarment.

They were both perilously near to begging for mercy when Jake unfastened his trousers, positioned his flushed, pliant bride so that her silken limbs were straddling the lean hardness of his hips, and brought her down upon his throbbing masculinity.

Caley gave a small, breathless cry as she felt

him sliding within her honeyed warmth. Emboldened by passion, she was not the least bit inclined to object to the shocking fact that they were making love in broad daylight — and in a rocking chair, no less.

She clutched at his strong arms for support, her eyes sweeping closed and her head falling back as she rode atop him. His mouth returned to its intoxicating ravishment of her breasts. His hands curled about her bottom, which still bore a faint redness as a reminder that he was not a man to be crossed, and he urged her forward to meet each fierce yet gloriously pleasurable thrust.

"Oh, Jake! Jake!" whispered Caley, the near painful ecstasy he had created within her spiralling higher and higher. *"Jake!"*

It seemed that he touched her very womb. She cried out again and clasped him tighter, feeling his powerful frame tense beneath her an instant after her own passion reached its wonderful completion.

"Caley," he murmured hoarsely, his arms tightening about her. "Dear God, how I love you!"

She collapsed weakly against him, struggling to regain control of her breathing while he cradled her lovingly upon his lap. It was downright wicked, she mused, the way this green-eyed scoundrel could make her forget everything else. Once again, her traitorous body had named him as its master. And once again, she had welcomed her defeat with an answering fire that no "decent" woman would ever admit to feeling.

Jake reluctantly stood and set her on her feet before him. Crimsoning, she hastened to pull her skirts down, then stole a look back up at his face. His mouth curved into a soft smile, while his eyes glowed warmly down at her.

"The fighting's hell, Mrs. Brody, but the making up's worth every minute of it," he drawled, his voice brimming with wry amusement as he fastened his trousers.

Her gaze fell beneath the loving intensity of his. She raised trembling hands to her bodice, tugging the unbuttoned edges across her thinly covered breasts in a gesture of modesty that even she realized was a bit absurd under the circumstances. Jake gave a quiet chuckle and leaned down to press a roguish kiss upon her lips. She pulled away and fixed him with a sternly quelling look.

"I'll be home late," he announced, already moving toward what was left of the door.

"Going back to your 'prisoners,' are you?" she couldn't resist asking, her eyes kindling anew at the thought.

"I thought we'd settled that." He paused in the doorway and turned to face her again. All traces of amusement had vanished, to be replaced by an unyielding determination once more. "That, and everything else as well," he added quietly. There was little doubt he was referring to Matt Griffin.

"What we . . . what we just did settles nothing!" she insisted, though her words lacked conviction.

"Then we'll have to keep doing it until it does." His eyes held a warning that could not be denied. "Don't even think about contacting Griffin. And don't ever let me catch you hanging around Dobe Row again. I mean it, Caley. That part of town's not safe."

"Not safe?" she echoed in disbelief, her eyes growing very wide. "Well if that doesn't beat all! It so happens, Jake Brody, that I've lived in this town for two blasted years and nothing's ever—"

"Things have changed."

"Oh? And what the hell's changed them?" she challenged with biting sarcasm.

"I have."

On that supremely confident note, he was gone. Caley stared after him, furious and speechless, her eyes shooting sparks but her body still tingling from head to toe from his masterful, splendidly hot-blooded loving.

Saturday night announced its arrival with the usual fanfare of drunken brawls, arguments over card games or women, and even a genuine gunfight or two. But in spite of all that, this particular Saturday night was without a doubt the most peaceful Elko had ever seen. Some credited the new marshal for the sudden lessening of "serious" violence; some blamed it on the weather, which was as stormy and threatening as the previous Saturday's. Whatever the case, things were going along with remarkable smoothness—until shortly before midnight.

That was when Otis Snyder made the biggest mistake of his life.

"Marshal?"

Jake and Dan left off their discussion and turned to look at the man who had just flung open the jailhouse door. Jake strode forward, frowning.

"What is it, Ballard?"

"It's Shorty, Marshal! He—he's been shot!" Ballard pointed a shaking finger in the direction of the saloon. "Down at the Senate!"

Jake took up his shotgun and headed off to investigate. Dan was close on his heels, with the distraught Ballard bringing up the rear. It was already too late by the time they reached the saloon. The place had emptied out, leaving only the bartender and a couple of the women to greet them when they strode inside. Shorty's body lay in a pool of blood near the bar. Jake went down on one knee to check for any signs of life, but there were none. He straightened and shifted his penetrating gaze to the bartender.

"What happened?" he demanded grimly.

"I don't rightly know! Hell, one minute there was a bunch of them jostlin' around here at the bar, and the next — God have mercy — there was Otis Snyder standin' over Shorty with a smokin' gun in his hand!"

"Otis Snyder?" Dan repeated, his eyes widening in startled disbelief. "Are you sure about that?"

"It was him, all right!" Ballard interjected. He looked down at his friend's body and swallowed hard before adding, "Shorty'd gone and gotten himself in a bug-tussle with one of them punchers, and Otis, well, he got caught right in the middle of it! I don't know how he got hold of Shorty's gun, but he did, and then it went off, and then . . . then Shorty kind of just folded up onto the floor!"

"Where's Snyder?" Jake asked the bartender.

"They've taken him, Marshal!" he excitedly proclaimed.

"Taken him?"

"Yes, sir, the whole damn lot of them went pourin' out of here no more'n five minutes ago, draggin' Snyder and sayin' they was plannin' to have a necktie party!"

"Holy smoke, a lynching!" Dan breathed in horror.

"They're headed down to the Hot Hole, Marshal!" one of the women came forward to reveal. Her painted mouth curled into a brief, contemptuous smile. "Somebody thought it would be a good idea to hang the poor bastard down there where folks can get an eyeful of him every time they go to wash."

Jake nodded curtly at Dan. The two of them hurried out into the night, hoping they would arrive in time to prevent an incident that, to the law, at least, represented everything that was bad about vigilante justice.

Ballard stayed behind this time. Moving to stand beside Shorty's corpse, he leaned over the bar and grabbed a bottle of whiskey. He poured himself a drink and, following a time-honored custom, drank to the hope that his friend's departed spirit would find the gates of heaven thrown wide open.

At that same moment, Caley was flying downstairs to answer a loud, insistent knock at the door. She had left it unlocked, telling herself that she sure as hell didn't want to have Jake break it down like he had the other one. Puzzled as to why he didn't just open it himself and come in, she was preparing to ask him just that when she swung the door wide. But it wasn't Jake she found gazing across at her with his blue eyes full of terror. It was Billy.

"Billy!" she said in surprise. "What in the world are you doing here this time of night?"

"It's Pa, Miss Caley!" he burst out in anguish. "They're gonna hang him!"

"Hang him?"

"Is the Marshal here? He wasn't down at the jail and I thought he —" The boy broke off and choked back the sob which rose in his throat.

328

"Please, Miss Caley, is he here?"

"No! No, he isn't! I don't know where he is!" She took hold of his arms and demanded sternly, "Tell me what's going on, Billy! Who is it you think is going to hang—"

"They're gonna do it, Miss Caley! They're gonna do it for sure if the Marshal doesn't stop them!" He drew in a deep, ragged breath and explained, "Someone came to the house and said Pa shot a man down at the saloon! He said they were takin' him over to the Hot Hole and . . . and that they're fixin' to string him up!" He pulled away and drew an old Army pistol from his pocket, his hand shaking so much it would have been impossible for him to hit anything. "I got to stop them before it's too late!"

"Wait, Billy!" Caley instructed, her mind racing. "I'm coming with you!"

She flew back to the counter, snatched up the shotgun she kept hidden there, and hurried to join her frightened young hostler outside. Giving silent thanks for the fact that the thunderstorm had finally passed, she wondered where Jake was. She had been waiting up for him, in spite of her resolve not to do so, and found herself praying that he would get word of the trouble in time. If anyone could put a stop to the lynching, she reflected, Jake Brody could.

"We'll cut across here!" she told Billy, indicating a muddy side street. The boy nodded in silent agreement and followed her lead.

They heard the mob well before they saw it. The awful sounds of bloodthirsty shouts and curses filled the rain-sweetened air, while overhead the moon broke through the clouds to cast an eerie, pale silvery glow upon the terrible proceedings.

"There's Pa!" shouted Billy as they neared the hot springs. Steam curled upward from the two dammed-off pools of water, where many a puncher and miner had washed their clothes as well as their bodies.

Caley followed the direction of Billy's panic-stricken gaze, her own heart filling with dread when she saw that Otis had already been placed atop a buckboard and a rope looped around his neck. The other end of the rope was thrown over the thick, sturdy branch of a tree just above his head. Several of the men in the crowd carried makeshift torches, and someone had already fashioned a sign out of a wooden shingle and nailed it to the tree. It read *Murderer*.

"Stay here!" Caley told Billy.

"No, ma'am!" He shook his head and tightened his grip on the pistol. "That's my pa up there, Miss Caley, and I aim to do what I can to save him!"

Realizing there was no time to argue, Caley started forward. She was approaching the outer fringes of the mob when a shotgun blast suddenly exploded in the air. Her wide, startled eyes flew to where Jake and Dan had just climbed atop the buckboard to stand with Otis.

"There will be no hanging!" decreed Jake, his deep, authoritative voice ringing out while he kept his shotgun leveled directly at the mob. "This man is entitled to a fair trial, and by damn, I'm going to see that he gets it!"

"He killed Shorty in cold blood, Marshal!" a man near the front bellowed. "It don't take no trial to tell us what we saw!"

"Yeah, what do we want to go and turn him over to you for?" someone else snarled. "Hell,

330

you'll just lock him up and feed him three squares a day and make him nice and comfortable, while Shorty's lyin' six feet under!"

"Get the rope off him, Dan," Jake instructed his deputy in an undertone. To the men facing him with such hatred in their eyes, he declared solemnly, "Like it or not, I'm the law here. And this man is my prisoner."

"You and Mitchelson'd best get down from there or we'll fetch some more rope and send you to hell with Snyder!" yet another one of them threatened.

The crowd, some fifty in all, erupted into a roar of approval at that. Caley's throat constricted in alarm. She gazed up at the man who was her husband, as if seeing him for the first time, her heart twisting painfully and her eyes glistening with sudden tears. Unable to bear the thought that he would be killed, she determinedly clutched her gun and began making her way right through the middle of the crowd.

"Let me through, damn you! Let me through!" Using the gun to help her, she knocked aside anyone who stood in her path and successfully reached the front. Billy followed close behind.

"Caley!" Jake ground out, furious to see her in the midst of such danger. Undaunted, she scrambled up onto the buckboard and took a proudly defiant stance beside him.

"Aw hell, Miss Caley, get down from there!" a familiar voice called out.

"This ain't no place for women, damn it!" growled another.

"Go home, Caley," Jake told her in a low, simmering tone meant for her ears alone. If not for the fact that he needed both hands to keep the shotgun level, he would have gladly seized her arm

331

and flung her back down to the ground. "Get out of here. *Now.*"

"No!" She kept her own gun trained on the mob and was not surprised when Billy climbed up to join her.

"Billy . . . that . . . that you, boy?" Otis stammered drunkenly, his bloodshot eyes trying to focus on his son.

"It's me, Pa!" confirmed Billy, raising his voice to be heard above the din. He did his best to keep the pistol steady as he aimed it in the general direction of his father's would-be murderers.

"Caley, I'm warning you—" Jake uttered between tightly clenched teeth. His green eyes smoldered at her refusal, while his own heart twisted at the possibility that she would be hurt.

"I'm not leaving!" she adamantly insisted. She squared her shoulders and proclaimed to the crowd of vigilantes, many of whom she knew by name, "The party's over! There's not going to be any hanging, so you might as well take yourselves on home where you belong!" The men were not receptive.

"Damn it, Miss Caley, you got no place here, even if you are married to the marshal now!"

"What's the matter, Brody—you need a woman's skirts to hide behind?"

"Shoot fire, boys, I do believe we got ourselves a little family reunion of sorts goin' on here!"

"Otis Snyder never harmed a soul in his life!" Caley pointed out angrily.

"Try tellin' that to Shorty!"

"He killed Shorty with his own gun, Miss Caley, and we wouldn't be any kind of men at all if we stood by and let that happen without doin' somethin' about it!"

"He's gonna hang for it!"

"That's for a jury to decide!" Jake decreed once more. Trying not to let his concern for Caley's safety cloud his judgment, he refused to back down. "I'm taking my prisoner to jail," he announced in a cold, clear tone. "Interfere, and I'll not hesitate to shoot."

"I say we kill him now and be done with it!" someone yelled impatiently.

"We've listened to enough gol-darned talk!"

It was then that Jake caught sight of a sudden movement out of the corner of his eye. Reacting with the lightning quick impulses of a man who has lived with danger his whole life long, he transferred the shotgun to his left hand, drew his six-shooter with his right, and at the same time sent Caley tumbling backward out of the line of fire by sweeping one booted foot up behind both of hers.

"Hold it!" he ground out, his gun aimed at a young cowboy whose own revolver had not yet broken leather. While a murmur of stunned disbelief and grudging admiration for his quick draw rose from the crowd, he motioned at the cowboy with his gun and ordered, "Drop your holster and move over here to the front of the wagon."

The other man, who might very well have found himself dead by now, nodded mutely and unbuckled his holster. He did as Jake said, his face pale and his eyes downcast as he turned to face the others.

Caley was helped to her feet again by Billy. Her blue-green eyes ablaze with indignation, she was not of a mind at present to feel gratitude toward her husband for having considered her welfare. But she forced herself to remain silent, and turned her wrathful gaze upon the crowd once more. The air was highly charged with tension, and she was all too aware of the fact that four against fifty presented odds that seemed insurmountable.

"Get going, all of you!" Jake commanded tersely, slipping his Colt back into the holster and resuming his no-nonsense grip on the shotgun. "Anyone staying behind will find himself spending the night in jail!"

Caley watched in breathless anticipation while the men battled indecision. Arguing amongst themselves, they were still wavering between compliance and insurgency when an unexpected source of resolution appeared.

"Do as he says!" ordered the man who suddenly came sauntering from around the corner of the Hot Hole's nearby barn.

"Matt!" Caley whispered in startlement.

"It's Griffin!" said Dan, his widened gaze flying to Jake's face.

Matt's name could be heard on the lips of many in the crowd. He was recognized on sight by most of them, and known by reputation to those who had never had the dubious honor of making his acquaintance. There were none who hadn't heard of Isaiah Griffin and his hell-raising eldest son.

"This doesn't concern you, Griffin," Jake told him in a deceptively low and even tone.

"I've got a right to be here," drawled Matt. His mouth curved into a mocking smile as he drew closer. "Besides, Otis and me are old friends, aren't we, Otis?"

"Matt, what the devil are you doing here?" Caley demanded, conscious of the fact that Jake tensed beside her.

"It looked like you could use a bit of help." He moved to take up a stance in front of the buckboard, then leisurely fired a shot into the air and told the attentive mob, "You've all had your fun, boys! Now do as the marshal says and go on home!"

"But what about Snyder?" one of the men challenged.

"Damn it, Matt, he killed Shorty and—" another tried to protest.

"You heard me! Now go on! I'm buying a round of drinks back at the Senate!" he announced with a broad grin.

The tension eased, and the crowd finally began to disperse. Billy slipped an arm about his father's shoulders and, with Dan's help, got him down from the buckboard. Caley gasped in surprise when Matt's hands suddenly closed about her waist. He swung her down, but did not immediately release her.

"Let me go, Matt!" she whispered stridently, pushing against him. His fingers curled even tighter about her waist.

"What the hell, Mac, I figured I might as well get some kind of reward for taking a stand with you," he murmured with a smile that did not quite reach his eyes.

Jake's handsome face was inscrutable as he maintained a vigilant watch to make certain the danger was truly past. His fathomless green gaze flickered only briefly downward toward Caley, but one glimpse of Matt's hands on her was enough to make his blood boil.

"You can start buying those drinks at the saloon now, Griffin," he prescribed, his voice holding an undercurrent of violence. His eyes still followed the departing crowd, but a tell-tale muscle twitched in the rugged smoothness of his cheek.

335

"Seems to me, Brody, that you owe me thanks for savin' your hide!" countered Matt. He finally relinquished his hold on Caley and turned to face Jake with a sneer. "I should've let them kill you at that. Mac here would make a mighty pretty widow, don't you think?"

"I didn't ask for your help," Jake pointed out. His eyes darkened when he added, "And I'd advise you to leave my wife out of this."

He would have liked nothing better than to have it out with the other man right there and then. But, there were other, more important matters requiring his attention at present. *Soon you black-hearted bastard, soon,* he promised silently. Exerting an iron will over his emotions, he allowed his gaze to meet the scornful blue fury of Matt's.

"Unless you want to share a cell with your good friend Otis," he warned, "you'll be on about your business."

"Hell, man, you can't lock me up," Matt dissented with a low, malevolent chuckle. "I'm just a law-abiding citizen out for a stroll. There's no law against that!"

"Matt, please!" Caley implored, painfully conscious of the underlying rancor between the two men.

"Stay out of this, Caley," cautioned Jake.

"There's no need to rein her in, Brody!" Matt said tersely. He turned and gave Caley a look full of meaning. "Mac and I go way back. Some things won't change, no matter what else happens." His gaze glittered hotly as it shifted back to Jake. "I'll kill you if you ever hurt her!"

"Damn it, Matt, just go!" Caley reiterated, pushing insistently on his arm.

For a moment, she was afraid he would do

something rash. But fortunately, he did not. He flung Jake one last silent challenge, nodded at her, and strode away into the moonlit darkness. She breathed a sigh of relief, her tensed muscles finally relaxing.

"Let's get the prisoner over to the jail," Jake told Dan. He stepped down from the buckboard now and approached the young cowboy who had foolishly tried to draw on him. "Pick up your holster and make tracks. Next time, I won't be so damned forgiving."

"Yes, sir, Marshal!" the puncher exclaimed. Grateful for the reprieve, he bent and snatched up his holster, then lit out for the relative safety of his bunkhouse.

Without a word, Jake took a firm grip on Caley's arm and began leading her along with him to the jail. Otis, still too drunk to realize how near to death he had come, was flanked by Billy and Dan as they each wrapped a supportive arm about his slender frame and hauled him toward the place which had, literally, become a second home for him.

Caley wisely chose not to resist her husband's angrily possessive grasp. She refused to feel guilty for having faced the mob with him, and she couldn't help thinking that her intervention—and Matt's—had averted a very real tragedy. Of course, she mused with another inward sigh, there was also the likelihood that Jake would have prevailed without their unwanted assistance. She had never known a man as stubborn and so committed to the straight course as he was.

"I know you're angry with me, Jake Brody, but I don't care!" she declared in a low, vehement tone as they walked a short distance behind the other three. "When Billy came and told me about—"

"We'll discuss it later," he abruptly cut her off. "Right now, I'm afraid of what I might do to you!"

His fingers tensed about her arm, his eyes gleaming with a savage light. Caley bit back the scathing retort which rose to her lips and settled instead for slicing him a fiery glare.

Upon reaching the jail, Otis was immediately secured in his usual cell. He collapsed upon the bunk, soon dead to the world and snoring loud enough to bring complaints from the prisoners in the adjoining cells.

"Will he be all right in here, Marshal?" Billy questioned anxiously.

"He will," Jake assured him. "Dan and I will stand guard through the night. I'm not expecting any more trouble. But we'll be ready if it comes."

"Does your mother know what happened?" Caley asked Billy. It had suddenly occurred to her that she had seen nothing of Susan Snyder; a circumstance she found odd, given the fact that the woman's husband had very nearly been lynched. Otis was worthless when drunk, of course, but not a bad sort at all when sober.

"No, ma'am. I—I sort of lied to her about it," the towheaded youth confessed, coloring guiltily. "I said I'd gotten word that Pa was in some kind of trouble down at the saloon, but that I'd see he got out of it all right. She's used to . . . well, she's used to spendin' nights without him."

"You'd better go on home and tell her the truth," Caley suggested gently.

"Yes, ma'am. I reckon I'd better."

Thanking them earnestly once more, Billy left. Caley turned to face Jake again, and in so doing

338

finally caught sight of the big, scruffy-looking dog curled asleep in the corner behind the desk.

"Tripod!" she remarked in surprise. She looked to Jake and demanded with a frown, "What's he doing here?"

"He's been here for the better part of a week." He placed his shotgun on the desk in front of him, still battling the desire to beat his headstrong young bride and kill Matt Griffin.

"So that's why I haven't seen him lately," she murmured, feeling as though she had somehow been betrayed. *You old traitor,* she silently accused the dog, though without any true malice.

"He's right taken with the marshal, ma'am," Dan offered in an attempt to lighten the situation. "He followed him in here and just wouldn't go away. We've been feedin' him what's left of the prisoners' meals. I wouldn't be at all surprised if he doesn't just — "

"I want you to see Caley home," Jake broke in to instruct his deputy.

"I can see myself home!" insisted Caley.

"I don't care if you have to drag her there," he went on in complete disregard of her opposition to the idea, "just so long as you make sure she gets there and locks herself in."

"Whatever you say, Marshal," agreed Dan, albeit not too enthusiastically. He pulled his hat on again and moved to Caley's side. "Mrs. Brody?" His eyes were full of cautious entreaty. "You ready?"

"Do I have a choice?" she retorted bitterly, her own eyes flashing across at Jake.

"No," he affirmed. His gaze burned down into hers when he issued one last warning. "I'll be spending the night here at the jail. And you had better be spending it *alone*."

It was entirely unnecessary. They both knew it. But the dangerous combination of love and jealousy had been provoking men to folly since the beginning of time.

"Maybe I'll just invite Dan to stay and keep me company!" Caley taunted in response, two bright spots of color riding high on her cheeks. More hurt by his lack of trust than she cared to admit, she lashed out at him with a vengeance. "Come to think of it, I might as well stop off at the Senate and see if Matt wants to come on over for a visit! Yes, by damn, I'll bet he'd just love to sit back and put his feet up and talk about the old times with me!"

"Go home, Caley," Jake ground out, his hands curling into such tight fists that his knuckles turned white. "Get out of here before I forget my own rule about mixing business with pleasure!"

Caley felt a tremor of fear, but refused to acknowledge it. Instead, warming to what promised to be a full-fledged confrontation, she opened her mouth to say more. She was prevented from doing so, however, when one of the prisoners suddenly called out and claimed to be suffering untold agony as a result of his recent overindulgence down at *Miss Sadie's*.

Caley's wrathful gaze followed Jake as he muttered an oath beneath his breath and disappeared into the other room. She was scarcely aware of Dan's hand lightly touching her arm.

"Come on, Mrs. Brody," he urged, looking more worried than ever. "It's gettin' awful late, and the sooner we get you home the sooner I can get back here and help your husband look after things."

He was surprised, and greatly relieved, when she

340

came along with him. The two of them made their way quickly back to the stage office, running the gauntlet of drunken cowboys and restless horses. Once at their destination, Caley managed a weak smile for the young deputy.

"Thanks, Dan," she murmured, turning to face him as they stood in front of the door. "I can handle it from here."

"The marshal said I was to make sure—"

"I can handle it." Her voice held an unmistakable edge. Dan was not inclined to argue.

"All right, ma'am," he capitulated with a sigh. "I guess I'd better get on back." Giving her a polite tip of his hat, he started to leave, then suddenly paused and said, "Mrs. Brody?"

"Yes?"

"I just wanted you to know I . . . I think Marshal Brody's just about the best damned lawman I ever met." He took his unsolicited testimonial one step farther by adding, "And I think he'd have done just fine without Griffin buttin' in like he did."

"Do you?"

"Yes, ma'am. I do." That said, he nodded down at her and took himself off once more.

Caley stared after him, a soft smile of irony tugging at her lips in spite of her lingering anger. She heaved a sigh of her own and opened the door.

A dark figure suddenly loomed behind her. Before she could react, a hand clamped across her mouth and she was dragged inside.

Chapter XIV

"Shhhh! It's me, Mac!" a familiar voice whispered in her ear.

The hand was removed from about her mouth, and she was released before her struggles had gained momentum. Whirling to face her blond, rakishly attractive assailant in the lamplit office, her eyes sparked with furious recognition.

"*Matt*! Damn your hide, what do you mean sneaking up on me like that?" she demanded indignantly.

"I wanted to talk to you. And I sure as hell didn't think you'd be of a mind to invite me in!" he ably defended himself.

Fixing him with a hard, reproachful look, Caley hastened to close the door and pull the shades. She placed the shotgun in the corner. It never occurred to her to mistrust him; she had known him for so long that granting him a few minutes of conversation seemed a perfectly natural thing to do. She pushed all thoughts of Jake to the back of her mind—or rather, she tried. There was little doubt in her mind what his reaction would be if he knew she was alone with another man, especially *this* man.

"You can't stay long, Matt," she pronounced with a frown. "Now what is it?"

"I came to tell you I'll be pulling out soon." He tossed his hat onto one of the benches.

"Pulling out?"

"Soon as I get a few more things settled, I'm heading back out to California."

"But . . . why?" Moving closer to where he stood beside the counter, she gazed up at him with eyes that were wide and full of stunned bewilderment. "Why, Matt?"

"Don't you know?" he challenged softly. His mouth curved into a bitter little smile. "Hell, Mac, you were the only thing keeping me here."

"But what about your father?" she protested. "And the ranch? For heaven's sake, you can't just run off and leave—"

"None of that's got any hold on me," he insisted. "Besides, it's time I struck out on my own. Ned did it. If he can, then by damn so can I!"

"Oh, Matt," she murmured, feeling sad and guilty and so damned confused that her head ached. She wandered back toward the door. Folding her arms across her chest, she closed her eyes and released a long, disconsolate sigh. "This is all my fault. I've made a mess of everything."

"Maybe," allowed Matt. "But it doesn't have to stay that way!" He swiftly closed the distance between them and turned her back around to face him. "Come with me, Mac!"

"What?"

"I said come with me!" he reiterated, his eyes alight with fierce determination. "You're not Brody's, damn it—you're mine!"

"But I'm married, Matt!" she pointed out, unable to believe what she was hearing. "I can't just go running off with you!" *Nor would I want to,* she found herself adding silently.

"Yes you can! You can come with me right now! We can put all this behind us and make a new start out in California!" Sweeping her up against him, he imprisoned her arms behind her back. He smelled strongly of whiskey, and she could sense the black anger waiting to explode. "I haven't waited all these years to let some other bastard come along and take what's mine!"

"I'm not yours!" she denied hotly, her turquoise gaze searing up into his. "Now let me go!"

"Like hell I will!" he ground out. "I should've taken you years ago! This never would have happened if I hadn't been so stupid and treated you like you were different from other women! You're no different, Mac! Damn you, you're no different!"

"Take your hands off me, you boneheaded son of a bitch!"

She twisted furiously in his grasp and attempted to bring her knee slamming up against the portion of his body she knew to be the most vulnerable. He did not release her, however, but brought his lips slanting down upon hers with punishing force. His arms tightened about her like a vise until she could scarcely breathe.

Instead of fear or even a spark of passion, Caley felt only outrage. She went pliant against him for a moment, making him believe she had surrendered, and was satisfied to feel him releasing her arms so that she could curl them about his neck. She seized advantage of the momentary deception. Her hands crept up to entangle within the thickness of his hair, and she gave a sudden, painful jerk while at the same time tearing her lips

345

from his and kicking at his unguarded shin.

With a blistering curse, Matt let her go. She scrambled back behind the counter, snatching up her whip and raising it high in a gesture of defensive readiness.

"Don't ever try that again, Matt Griffin, or I swear I'll beat the living daylights of you!" she threatened, her bosom heaving and her eyes ablaze with their brilliant, blue-green fire.

"Someday, Mac, I'm going to take that damn whip of yours and burn it!" he vowed between tightly clenched teeth. Swearing again, he retrieved his hat and stalked to the door. He wrenched it open, then spun back around. "I won't leave without you! Get your mind set on going with me, because that's what you're going to do!"

"*No!*" she cried vehemently, shaking her head. "Don't you understand? It's too late now!"

"Not for me it isn't!"

With that, he was gone. Caley flew across to close the door after him, her hands trembling as she turned the lock. She leaned weakly back against the door and thought about what had just happened. But it was her husband's face, not Matt's, that swam before her eyes as they filled with tears.

"Oh, Jake!" she whispered, suddenly wishing he were there to take her in his arms and tell her everything would be all right. It was strange, she realized, to be yearning for the presence of the very man who had caused all the trouble in the first place. But, heaven help her, she could always count on forgetting about the whole world whenever she was in his arms. . . .

She sighed again and headed upstairs. Uncertain whether to be relieved or sorry that Matt was

346

planning to leave Elko, she sought the lonely comfort of her bed and soon tumbled into a mercifully deep and dreamless sleep.

When dawn broke with its usual blaze of color the next morning, she was already awake. Jake had not yet come home. Her eyes were drawn instinctively to the empty place in the bed beside her, and she blushed at the wicked thoughts racing through her mind. One night together, she mused wryly, and then she had been abandoned in favor of Otis Snyder.

Bemoaning the lack of her buckskin suit, she hurried to wash and dress. She was filled with excitement for the day ahead. She was also filled with more than a touch of apprehension, but she staunchly refused to let it interfere with her plans. Nothing was going to keep her from taking the run to Tuscarora. *Nothing.*

"Mornin', Miss Caley!" Billy and Red greeted her in unison when she appeared at the foot of the staircase. Hank was in Carlin with his new wife, just like he'd been more and more of late.

"Good morning," she replied with a smile for the both of them. She nearly laughed when she saw how they were staring at her unusual attire. Wearing a pair of old denim trousers that had belonged to her father, and a plaid flannel work shirt, she knew she looked anything but proper. "Red, I'll be going to Tuscarora today," she surprised him by announcing as she took up her whip and gloves. "I want you to make a run over to Buck Station."

"But, the marshal said—"

"I don't care what he said, I'm going to Tuscarora!" she insisted stubbornly. "Besides, we're both needed, what with Hank away for a couple

347

of days. And there's a load of supplies waiting over at the depot that I've been trying to get to Buck Station for three days now."

"Any passengers?" asked Red, knowing it was useless to argue with her. Arguing with her was the marshal's job now, not his, he mused with an inward grin.

"No. I've only got three heading to Tuscarora. And not much else," she added with a sigh. She turned to Billy. "Everything ready?"

"Almost, Miss Caley. The gear's all in place. I was just fixin' to bring the team around."

"Did you stop by the jail and look in on your father?" She was tempted to ask him about Jake, but did not.

"Yes, ma'am. He was still sleepin' it off. I just hope they'll get all this cleared up soon." He shook his head sadly, then brightened a little. "Oh, and Marshal Brody said to tell you he'd be along soon," he revealed on his way out the door.

Speaking of the devil, thought Caley when Jake appeared in the doorway almost immediately after Billy left. She was dismayed to feel herself trembling at the sight of him.

"Mornin', Marshal," drawled Red. He murmured something about the horses and hurried to leave the newlyweds alone. If there were going to be fireworks, he sure as hell didn't want to be around to get burned.

"Sleep well?" Jake asked his wife softly. His anger with her appeared to have been forgotten.

"Well enough," she answered, her gaze falling before his. Matt's image suddenly returned to plague her.

Coloring guiltily, she opened the schedule book and feigned a great and sudden interest in its

348

pages while Jake tugged the hat from his head and advanced on her. She was acutely conscious of his eyes raking over her.

"Who's watching the jail?" she asked with deceptive nonchalance, refusing to look up.

"Dan. I let him catch a few hours of sleep earlier. Now it's my turn."

"You're not expecting any more trouble about Otis?"

"No." He stood close beside her now, staring down at her bent head while she battled the overwhelming desire to slip herself into his arms. "The night always takes with it any danger of a lynching," he remarked with a faint smile. "Men never seem to have the same kind of courage once daylight takes over."

"So you . . . I expect you'll be wanting to get some sleep now," she faltered, her grip tightening on the edges of the book.

"Care to join me?" he offered in a low, devastatingly vibrant tone.

She finally glanced up at his face—and felt herself growing perilously lightheaded at the familiar look of mingled tenderness and desire in his green eyes. For a moment, she was afraid she would say to hell with everything and go right on upstairs with him and surrender her body to his sweet mastery. But reason prevailed. Reason, and a proud determination to show him she was not to be either bullied *or* seduced into submission.

"I've got work to do," she declined with a frown, obstinately returning her gaze to the book.

"All right. I'll let you off this time, Mrs. Brody," he conceded, his deep voice brimming with amusement now, "because I'm too damned tired to argue." Pressing a sudden, roguish kiss

349

upon her lips, he smiled unrepentantly down into her stormy features. "Wake me at noon, wildcat. I'll be feeling more like my old self then," he assured her, his gaze smoldering with the promise of passion.

"That's what I'm afraid of!" she retorted, turning to watch in spite of herself as he sauntered past her.

Once she heard the upstairs door closing, she slammed the book shut and hurried outside. Billy was hitching up the team, and told her that Red had gone over to the Depot Hotel to see what was keeping the passengers. She glanced up toward the windows in the apartment above, praying that Jake would not become suspicious until after she was well on her way.

Her prayers were answered. Jake was sound asleep by the time she cracked the whip above the horses' heads and drove the loaded stagecoach northward out of Elko. A gleam of triumph shone in her eyes, and she raised her face gratefully to the sun's warmth as the wheels rolled and bounced over the dusty main street.

There was no one riding shotgun on the trip; the day's shipment included only a small amount of mail and gold. The three passengers, all male, were glad of the fact that the weather held. Even the roads cooperated, their slightly damp surfaces ensuring that the coach made remarkable time on its journey to the wild mining town. The four travelers reached Dinner Station in almost record time, ate a delicious if somewhat overly filling meal of fried chicken and potatoes, then set off again across a countryside that was alive with the sights, sounds, and fresh smells of a rain-washed summer day.

Caley was feeling quite satisfied with herself when she drew the team to a halt in front of the station in Tuscarora. Jake had never been out of her mind throughout the day, of course, but she was able to prevent thoughts of him from interfering with her reinsmanship. She found herself wondering frequently about how he would react when he awakened and found her gone. Whatever it was, she reflected with an inward sigh, she knew she'd catch hell when she got home. The prospect caused her to shift uncomfortably on the driver's seat before she climbed down.

"Sorry, Miss McAlister, but we ain't got no passengers for you to take back to Elko with you," the stage line agent told her when she was preparing to leave again.

"It's 'Mrs. Brody', now, Donnelly," she corrected him without pausing to consider the significance of her action. "What happened to the two you had listed in your book?" she queried with a frown of puzzlement. "A Mr. and Mrs. Woulfe?"

"I don't know," Donnelly replied with a shrug. "They never showed up. Guess they figured on stayin' here a while longer."

"Well then, we might as well get her loaded."

She carried the mail pouch out to the coach and hoisted it up to its place beneath the seat. Donnelly, a big man with a full head of hair the color of carrots, filled the empty interior with an array of boxes and packages. He singlehandedly carried the express box out and secured it in place.

Caley, keeping a critical eye on the hostler as he finished tending to the horses, took up the reins again and braced her booted feet against the board. She reached up to settle the hat lower on her upswept auburn tresses.

351

"Here they come, Miss—Mrs. Brody!" Donnelly suddenly announced, referring to the young couple he had spotted hurrying forward along the boardwalk. "That's the Woulfes. Just got married. He won her in a race."

"A race?" Caley echoed in disbelief.

"That's the right of it." The agent grinned broadly. "She took a shine to a city feller from over in San Francisco. Problem was, she'd already given her promise to young Harry Woulfe."

"So they raced horses for her?"

"No, ma'am, they raced themselves. Right here down the middle of town. You'd have thought that foot race was the biggest thing happenin' around Tuscarora since the first strike. 'Course, everyone was pullin' for Woulfe to win. He did."

Caley smiled and watched as the newlyweds, no older than herself, drew to a breathless halt beside the coach. They apologized to Donnelly and then to her for being late, quickly took their places inside the mud wagon, and offered no complaint whatsoever about the close quarters they were forced to share because of the boxes which were taking up fully half of the interior.

"Have a care now!" Donnelly called after them when the coach pulled out.

Caley acknowledged his farewell with a nod. She allowed the horses their lead and kept a steady eye on their progress. But her attention was momentarily diverted when she glimpsed someone who looked very much like Matt leaning negligently against the wall of a building near the stage office.

It is Matt! she told herself in surprise. And he was talking with Ed Tickner. The two of them were part of a group that included four others.

Her eyes widened in even further startlement when she recognized three of the men as the same punchers who had accosted her in front of the Senate several nights ago. She even remembered their names — Buck, Farley, and Hooker.

"What the devil," she murmured, curious as to what Matt was doing with Tickner and the others.

She waited for him to look up and wave, but he did not. He pretended not to see her at all; no easy feat, she mused resentfully, given the fact that the stagecoach was a pretty difficult thing to miss. She could only suppose that he was still angry about what had happened between them the previous night. Well then, so be it, she thought with a frown, her eyes glowing dully.

The return trip to Elko was, fortunately, every bit as expeditious and uneventful as the trip up to the high country had been. Although pleased with the day's run, Caley was not feeling exactly overjoyed to be home again. Her nerves were strung tight when the coach rolled to a stop, and her gaze moved instinctively to the upstairs windows. She steeled herself for the inevitable confrontation with Jake. In truth, she dreaded his anger.

"Is my . . . is the marshal still sleeping?" she asked Billy once the Woulfes had disembarked and headed off to the Depot Hotel.

"No, ma'am. He's gone to Carlin!"

"To Carlin? What for?" Wondering how it was possible to be relieved and disappointed at the same time, she drew off her gloves and pulled the hat from her head.

"I don't know for sure," admitted Billy. "He got a telegram not too long after you left this mornin'. I hated to wake him, but I figured, bein' that it was a telegram and all, I'd better do it. He wasn't

353

too all-fired happy when he found out where you'd gone. But he didn't waste no time in settin' out!"

"He didn't say anything about why he was going?"

"No, Miss Caley, I don't recollect that he did." A sudden smile lit his face, and his blue eyes twinkled mischievously. "But he did say I was to tell you he'd settle with you when he got back!"

"Thanks," she murmured cryptically. She took herself inside and up the stairs, musing with a sigh of disgruntlement that a few more hours of anticipation sure as hell wouldn't help the situation any.

Shadrach greeted her with a characteristic swat on the ankle. She scooped him up and carried him to the back door, where she set him outside with a stern admonition to leave off bedeviling the horses. He tried to dart back inside, but she was too quick for him.

"Carlin," she muttered, still thinking of Jake as she set about peeling off her dust-laden clothes. It seemed there wasn't a minute of the day or night when she *wasn't* thinking of him, she reflected.

She was surprised to feel a twinge of regret for what she had done that day. It wasn't like her to be sorry for defying Jake Brody.

"Great balls of fire, don't go all moony-eyed!" she berated herself aloud. Still, there was something different in the way she felt about him now, something that, strangely enough, made her long to ease the tension between them.

Her gaze softened at the thought, and dread gave way to a more pleasant expectation. She was, after all, every inch a woman. Jake had certainly made her aware of that fact.

Suddenly possessed of a determination to look her best when she faced him, she flung the shirt and trousers onto the floor. She built a fire in the stove and set water on to heat for the luxury of a real, honest-to-goodness bath, then dragged out the large metal tub. Positioning it near the stove in one corner of the main room, she emptied into it a bucketful of cold water pumped from the bathroom and went back for another. The hot water was added just seconds before she hastily drew off her undergarments and lowered herself gratefully into the soothing liquid warmth.

Taking up the cake of lavender-scented soap she saved for special occasions, she scrubbed at every square inch of her skin until it positively glowed with cleanliness. Her hair came next, its flame-colored thickness turning to a dark red as she bent her head forward and used a dipper to pour water over it.

Once she had finished bathing, she leaned back against the cool metal and closed her eyes for a moment. Her thoughts drifted lazily about, from Matt to Jake to various other people and places and things—but they always returned to Jake. Instead of consigning his rakishly appealing image to the devil, however, she surrendered to the desire to keep it before her. A shiver that had nothing to do with the temperature of the water danced down her spine.

There was still so much about him she didn't know, she mused with another sigh. He was at once mysterious and straightforward, a man who did not hesitate to lay everything on the line. *I love you*, he had told her, more than once. And she had refused to believe him.

"Do you believe him now?" she challenged herself in a soft whisper, only to groan inwardly and sink even lower in the tub.

Just then, the door swung open.

Caley felt a sudden rush of cool air upon her bare, glistening skin. She started in alarm, her eyes flying open as she instinctively grabbed the towel and plunged it into the water to cover her nakedness.

"Jake!" she gasped out, blushing crimson at the sight of his tall, muscular frame in the doorway. "I—I didn't expect you back so soon!"

"I gathered that," he countered dryly. His handsome face was inscrutable, but his eyes smoldered with magnificent green fire.

"You could have at least knocked first!" she charged, clasping the towel to her breasts.

"I could have," he readily conceded. With slow deliberation, he closed the door behind him, tossed his hat to land atop the sofa, and advanced on his wife.

"That's close enough!" insisted Caley. Although embarrassed to have been caught in such a highly intimate and vulnerable position, she could not deny feeling more than a touch of excitement as well. She watched, wide-eyed and breathless, as her husband crossed to stand in front of her.

"I seem to recall, Mrs. Brody, having forbidden you to do any more driving," he began calmly enough, though he was battling a powerful combination of fury and desire. His burning gaze raked over her wet, beguiling charms, his loins tightening at the thought of what lay beneath the towel.

"Just as I recall having told you I had no intention of giving it up!" she retorted with a flash of spirit. Her long hair was smoothed away from her face, which was becomingly flushed from a good deal more than the water's warmth. "Now get out of here and let me finish my bath in peace!"

Her eyes grew round as saucers when, instead of offering a response, he moved to take a seat in the rocking chair. He tugged off his boots.

"What in tarnation do you think you're doing?" she demanded.

"I don't just think it, wildcat," he replied in a low, vibrant tone. He stood and began unbuttoning his shirt. "I could use a bath myself."

"Well you'll have to wait!"

"I've waited long enough." He removed his shirt and started on his trousers.

"Surely you don't mean you're going to—" she started to ask in shocked disbelief, only to break off and turn beet-red as he pushed his trousers downward. She hastily closed her eyes and swallowed hard, telling herself that this wasn't the way she had envisioned things at all—*not at all*!

Opening her eyes again, she realized that Jake was actually planning to join her in the tub. As a matter of fact, he had already lifted a foot and brought it down between the two of hers. She hurriedly stood, clutching the wet towel about her.

"You—you can't do this!" she protested in a small, tremulous voice. "The tub isn't big enough for the both of us!"

"Isn't it?"

He took a seat, seized her about the waist, and forced her back down into the soapy water. She gasped as the towel was yanked from her grasp. It landed in a sodden heap on the floor.

"Jake, stop it!"

Disregarding her protests, he leaned back against the tub and pulled her forward between his bent knees until her naked curves rested atop his lithe hardness. His strong, manly arms imprisoned her

357

upper body, while his taut thighs, one on each side of her hips, ensured that she could not wriggle free.

"Now what was that you said about the tub not being big enough?" he teased, anger having been vanquished by passion.

"Damn it, this is . . . well it's downright *indecent*!" she cried, blushing anew and pushing in vain against the bronzed immovability of his chest. To make matters worse, she could feel his manhood throbbing beneath her.

"Then we'll be indecent," he murmured huskily, gathering her even closer. "Every damned chance we get."

His hand crept upward to entangle within the wet abundance of her hair, and he pulled her head down toward his. She squirmed atop him, which only served to arouse him further, and then found herself being kissed with such bold, sensuous persuasion that an answering passion coursed through her like wildfire.

Soon, he urged her farther upward and tasted of her satiny, rose-tipped breasts, his mouth and tongue working together to drive her wild with longing while his hands roamed over her trembling curves with an intoxicating fierceness that provoked a near painful ecstasy deep inside her. She thrilled to his tempestuous lovemaking once more, and was far beyond reason when his hands clasped her well-rounded hips and lifted her for his ultimate possession.

"Oh, Jake!" she whispered hoarsely, her velvety passage accepting every hot, undeniably masculine inch of him. The final blending of their bodies was achieved with perfection, leaving the two of them wonderfully lightheaded and gasping for breath when it was over.

A short time later, after Jake had carried his beautiful and thoroughly loved bride to the bed, they lay entwined beneath the covers and discussed — calmly, for a change — what had happened that day.

"I was furious when I found out you'd gone," Jake told her, frowning at the memory. "If not for that telegram, I'd have come after you and thrown you across my saddle!"

"Why *did* you go to Carlin, anyway?" she queried, hoping to steer the conversation away from such dangerous ground.

"The sheriff there had some news about the robbery."

"You mean the first one?" She raised up on one elbow and peered down at his face. When he nodded, she asked, "Well, what did he say? Does he know who did it?"

"Maybe," was all Jake would tell her. His eyes darkened at the thought of what he had learned that day. He had suspected it all along; the break he had been waiting for had finally come.

"What do you mean, 'maybe'?" she demanded. "Hell's bells, does he know or doesn't he?"

"You'll find out soon enough, Caley," he decreed, knowing full well how upset she'd be once the truth was out. "For now, you're just going to have to trust me to do my job." He pressed her head back down upon his shoulder and trailed his warm fingers down across the silken curve of her back. "Speaking of which, I'll be leaving in the morning. But I should be back in a couple of days."

"Where are you going?"

"You'll find out —"

"I know! I'll find out soon enough!" she answered for him, her eyes kindling with exasperation.

"I'm sorry, my love," he responded quietly, "but I can't tell anyone just yet."

My love. The endearment was particularly captivating on his lips. Her heart filled with pleasure, and her pulse leapt anew. But a sharp gasp broke from her lips when a large hand suddenly bestowed a hard, familiar smack on her naked backside.

"What the devil was that for?" she demanded indignantly

"You'll get far worse than that if you ever defy me again, Mrs. Brody!" promised Jake, his deep-timbred voice laced with steel. "Either do as I say and stay put, or I'll have to remove all temptation from your path."

"Oh? And just how do you propose to do that?" she parried, raising up again to fix him with a narrow, challenging look.

"I'm your husband. Under the law, what's yours is mine. That means I have the right to dispose of the stage line any time I please."

"But you—you can't do that!" she sputtered in disbelief.

"I can and will," he assured her grimly. "You're welcome to keep the business, so long as you leave the driving to Hank and Red."

"But I *like* driving! Damn it, Jake, I'll go crazy sitting around here—"

"I can't imagine you ever 'just sitting'," he quipped with a faint smile of irony. Once again, he pushed her head back down and swept her supple curves into even closer contact with his lithely muscled hardness. "No, Caley, you're going to have to obey me in this. God knows you don't do it in anything else," he added, his voice tinged with loving amusement.

"I told you before, Jake Brody—if you wanted a woman who'd let you run roughshod over her, then you married the wrong blasted person!" she shot back, yet knew herself defeated.

"I married the right person," he confidently maintained. "But hell, woman, who cares about wrong or right when it comes to what we have together." His hand smoothed back down to the beckoning roundness of her hips while his eyes gleamed with a passion that always smoldered just below the surface.

"You do!" she retorted. That was the truth of it all right, she thought, her eyes sparkling with mingled annoyance and admiration. He was the most straight-arrow man she'd ever known. "And I suppose you'd still claim to love me even if I . . . even if you didn't like what happens between us in bed?" she then dared. It was difficult for her to think clearly with his fingers gently kneading her flesh.

"They're tied together, Caley," he answered with a soft, crooked smile. "It's because I love you that I like what happens. And I guess the same holds true the other way around."

She had no response for that—partly because what he said could not be argued with, and partly because his other hand had slipped beneath the covers to close upon one of her breasts. A warm flush stole over her as his light caress sent shivers down her spine.

This time, however, she was not content to give herself passively over to his splendid mastery. No indeed, it was time he learned that she, too, was capable of exerting the power with which nature had endowed her . . . the power which *he* had enabled her to know how to put to such good use.

Jake was surprised when she suddenly drew away. Surprise turned to delight when she flung back the covers, lowered her body atop his, and pressed a boldly entrancing kiss upon his mouth. He smiled against her lips, then rewarded her audacity by wrapping his strong arms about her delectable curves and deepening the kiss.

Moments later, he frowned in protest when she raised her head and pushed herself up a little. He would have forced her back down, but she drove all thought of complaint from his mind by trailing her lips purposefully downward. She covered the magnificent, hard-muscled expanse of his chest with a series of light, tantalizing kisses, even going so far as to swirl her tongue about the twin peaks of flesh that were like hers and yet so vastly different. Jake's handsome features tensed, and his eyes darkened with passion.

But Caley was not of a mind to show him mercy yet. Further emboldened by a new, heady sense of dominance, she seared a fiery path lower. Jake's fingers threaded within the damply curling thickness of her hair as she covered the flat planes of his stomach with another provocative rash of kisses and dipped her tongue within the irresistible target of his navel. Then, she moved lower still . . .

Her eyes lit with wholly feminine triumph when she heard his low groan of pleasure. She gasped in the next instant, however, when he suddenly brought her sliding upward upon his searing hardness.

"Damn it, wildcat, no more!" he ground out,

though his voice held only desire instead of anger.

Imprisoning her within the warm circle of his arms again, he rolled so that she was beneath him and claimed her lips with his own in another fiery possession. She entwined her arms tightly about his neck, straining up against him and moaning low in her throat as passion's fire blazed between them once more.

By the time Jake reluctantly bid farewell to her and took himself back to work with the stated intention of being home before midnight, Caley was feeling much too contented to think about anything save the man who had taken her by storm and turned her life upside-down. She stretched lazily in the bed and smoothed a hand across the spot that still bore a lingering indentation from his virile, hot-blooded frame. Her beautiful eyes were softly aglow.

Heart, mind, body, and soul—none would ever be the same again, she mused with a deep sigh of satisfaction. And she was not in the least bit sorry.

Chapter XV

"Now you know I can't tell you that, Mrs. Brody," said Dan. He shook his head and reiterated, "No, ma 'am, I can't tell you. If the marshal had wanted you to know, he'd have told you himself."

"Why the devil is it such a big secret?" Caley demanded, frowning in suspicion. She leaned forward across the desk and fixed him with a narrow look of scrutiny. "What is it you and Jake are hiding? If it has something to do with the robbery, then I have a perfect right to—"

"You'll just have to wait till he gets back," the deputy refused to budge.

"Blast it, Dan Mitchelson, you're every bit as stubborn as he is!" she burst out in exasperation, straightening abruptly and folding her arms beneath her breasts.

"Yes, ma'am. I take that as a compliment," he replied with a grin.

Caley rolled her eyes heavenward and breathed another curse. She spun about, marching from the jail and back outside into the morning sunshine. Jake had ridden away only two hours ago, and yet she felt as though he'd been gone for days already.

"Men!" she muttered, her turquoise gaze bridling with irritation. Pleasure replaced irritation when she heard someone call her name and turned to see Ned Griffin striding toward her. "Ned!" He, at least, had done nothing to raise her dander. She greeted him with a warm smile. "What brings you to town this early?"

"Peterman sent me in for supplies," he answered, raking the hat from his head and brushing her cheek with his lips.

He was the only man she had ever allowed to treat her with any degree of familiarity—*until now,* she thought as Jake's image floated across her mind again. She did her best to ignore the blush stealing over her and linked her arm companionably through Ned's.

"Come on then. I'll walk you down to the mercantile."

"Been to pay a visit to that husband of yours?" he asked, nodding back toward the jailhouse.

"No." She heaved a long sigh of dissatisfaction and confided, "He's gone riding off to only God knows where, and left me here to wonder if he'll make it back alive!"

"You care an awful lot about him, don't you, Caley?" The thought gave him only a slight twinge of pain. He and Jake Brody had settled the air between them some days earlier.

"Care about him? Why should I care about him? Great balls of fire, he's the most flat-out infuriating, arrogant, overbearing man I've ever known!" she denied a bit too vehemently.

"You always were a hardheaded little cuss," opined Ned with the privilege of long acquaintance. He gave a low chuckle. "It's sort of comforting to know some things haven't changed."

They had reached the mercantile by now. Caley was about to bid him goodbye when they both caught sight of the pretty, raven-haired woman who was riding past. Two young boys, one in front and one behind, were perched atop the large gray mare with her.

"Why, that's Elena Larronde!" murmured Caley, half to herself. Turning to Ned, she was surprised to observe a sudden, pained expression crossing his features. *So that's the way the wind blows.* "I believe the two of you have met already," she remarked dryly.

"We have. And that's the whole problem," he declared with a frown. His eyes followed Elena as she guided her mount farther down the wide, busy street. "I wonder where she's headed."

"There's only one way to find out." She took his arm again. "Walk me back home and we'll keep an eye on her."

"I can't," he declined regretfully, his gaze suffused with a dull glow. "Peterman's expecting me back before noon. And to tell the truth, Caley," he went on to confess, "the last thing she'd want is for me to try and talk to her. She made that clear the last time."

"I can't believe she meant it," insisted Caley. "Why, any girl would be proud to have someone like you—"

"Not her," he disagreed, shaking his head. "Her father doesn't hold with anyone who isn't the same as them."

"So you're just going to give up without a fight?"

"I didn't say that." His mouth curved into a crooked grin. "I just don't think now's the time to make my move. Some things take a while, you

367

know. Not everyone can work the whole rest of their lives out as fast as you and Marshal Brody did."

"I'm not sure that's the right way to put it," she commented in a voice brimming with irony, "but I will say this, Ned Griffin — don't go wasting too much time, or else you'll find yourself no better off than you were before!" She had always thought he could benefit greatly from the love of a good woman; she prayed that Elena Larronde would not break his heart instead.

"He who hesitates is lost, is that it?" quipped Ned. His blue eyes twinkled across at her.

"Exactly!" She smiled and continued on her way, leaving him to stand alone on the boardwalk for a few moments longer before he finally forced himself to go inside the store.

It was only a quarter of an hour later when Caley received not one, but three unexpected visitors. She had just finished removing a disgruntled Shadrach from atop her desk when she glanced up and saw them.

"Miss Larronde!" she proclaimed in surprise. Her eyes traveled downward to the two little boys who stood peering cautiously at her from behind the protective barrier of their aunt's skirts.

"I—I am sorry to interrupt you, Miss McAlister," Elena began hesitantly, "but I did not know where else to go!"

"Is there something wrong?" Caley asked, her gaze full of genuine concern as she hurried forward.

"I am afraid so," the other woman admitted, though she did so with visible reluctance. Her face was quite solemn, and her dark eyes shone with a troubled light. "Our camp was attacked again last

368

night."

"Dear God, was anyone hurt?"

"My brother," Elena answered with a nod. "But it is not a deep wound. Our wagon was burned, and more of our sheep were killed. The men wore masks to cover their faces," she finished with a tight-lipped expression of contempt.

"Those cowardly bastards!" Caley ground out, her eyes kindling with righteous fury. She couldn't help but wonder if Isaiah and Matt were involved this time as well. "Have you told Deputy Mitchelson about this? If not, I'll go down to the jail with you right now and we'll get this—"

"No." The younger woman shook her head. "My father would not permit it. And he refuses to leave. He knows they are trying to frighten us away. But it will not work." Her own gaze was full of angry determination. "I myself would not have come," she explained, "but . . . but the little ones must have protection from the rain." It was obvious that the proud reserve which had been instilled in her since birth made it difficult for her to ask anyone for help.

"I'm sorry about what happened," Caley declared sincerely, her heart stirring with compassion. "I'll be glad to help any way I can. First off, we'll find you a place to stay."

She would have offered to let them stay with her, but knew that such an arrangement would be impossible. The apartment upstairs was too small to accommodate three other people, she told herself, and there was also the unavoidable matter of Jake. That he would disapprove of having company, she had little doubt.

"But where?" asked Elena. "We have tried the hotels. They will not take us. They have said they

369

do not rent rooms to Basques," she related with only a trace of bitterness. In truth, she had grown accustomed to such intolerance. "That is why I have come to you, Miss McAlister."

"You did the right thing. I know just the place. It's the boarding house across the street," she supplied, giving a nod in that general direction.

"How can you be sure—"

"Maybelle O'Grady isn't like the others," Caley assured her, then added, "And besides, I happen to know she still has at least one empty room available. It used to be my husband's."

"Your husband's?"

"I'm Mrs. Brody now." Strangely enough, the name was beginning to seem downright familiar.

"You and the marshal?" Elena asked her in wide-eyed astonishment.

"Me and the marshal," she confirmed, a wry smile tugging at her lips. "Now come on. We'll go on over to Maybelle's and see what we can do about getting the three of you settled before dinnertime."

"But—"

"No buts!" insisted Caley. She smiled again, her hand moving to ruffle the hair of each little boy in turn. "The two of you are welcome to come over here and see me any time you want," she told them, satisfied to watch their faces brighten. "I've got a cross-tailed old cat hiding over there behind the counter. He could use some reminding now and then that he's not really human after all. You boys look like you could do a good job of it." Their shyness all but disappeared at the prospect.

Maybelle, of course, ended up being every bit as kind and understanding as Caley had said she would be. She immediately took Elena and the boys under her wing, fussing over them like a mother hen as she set about preparing Jake's old room. They responded to her warmth and even went so far as to let her coax them into sitting in the kitchen for a mid-morning snack of milk and cookies.

Caley, promising to return later, left them in the widow's capable hands and headed back down to the mercantile. Just as she had hoped, Ned was still there. He was helping the store's owner load the wagon with the supplies he had just purchased, and he smiled in mild surprise when he caught sight of her.

"Decide to do a little shopping yourself?" he asked, stepping leisurely down out of the wagon bed while tugging off his hat.

"I thought you might like to know Elena Larronde's putting up over at Maybelle's," she informed him.

"Maybelle's?" He frowned in bemusement. "What for?"

"Someone took it in mind to pay them another visit last night. They lost more of their sheep, and their wagon was burned. Miss Larronde's brought the boys into town to stay for a while." She wasn't surprised to observe the dull, angry color rising to his face, nor the fierce gleam in his eyes. "I don't like to think it, Ned, but there's a possibility—"

"Damn it, Caley, it's more than a possibility and we both know it!" He settled the hat on his head again and declared grimly, "I'll need to borrow a mount if you can spare one."

"I can spare one," she assured him, having already guessed what he was planning to do. "I'm as riled about it as you are, Ned, but don't you think it might be better to wait?"

"Wait? What for? Hell, sooner or later some-one's going to get killed! No," he concluded, shaking his head while a shadow of pain crossed his attractive young features, "if Pa and Matt are behind this like I think they are, then I've got to try and talk some sense into them before it's too late!"

"Well if you're set on riding out there, I'll have to go with you!"

"No. This is something I have to do by myself."

"Things are bad enough between you and your father without—"

"I'm going alone, Caley," he determinedly insisted. "You stay here and look after Miss Larronde and those boys for me."

"For you?" she challenged with an arch look, only to watch as Ned's color deepened.

"I figure you're probably the only person in town she knows."

"Not for long." She smiled briefly and said, "Bring the wagon on down to my place. I'll look after everything until you get back."

"Thanks."

"That is, if you *get* back!" she then added, her brow creasing into a frown. "Isaiah's liable to skin you alive if he thinks you're siding with the sheep-men against him!"

"I've been skinned before," countered Ned, his gaze darkening at the memories of a lifetime of abuse. His expression became even grimmer, and his voice held a discernible edge when he vowed, "But never again. Never again will I let him lay a hand on me."

Caley's pulse leapt in alarm at the thought of what might happen, but she knew that further argument was useless. She resisted the impulse to

372

ride after Ned when he left town a short time later. There were some things, she realized, that had to be worked out between a father and son all by themselves. She could only pray the two of them didn't kill one another.

She saw Elena and the boys again at dinner. From outward appearances, at least, they were faring quite well in Maybelle's care. The regulars were delighted at the prospect of having three new pairs of ears to bend with their stories and gossip. Eva Hartford insisted that the children be enrolled in school without delay to prevent their becoming wild heathens, J.D. Worthington III offered to show them around town once they were settled, George Groat made the boys laugh, and even the laconic Mr. Tate joined in by mumbling something about being more than happy to arrange credit for them at the mercantile.

In spite of the fact that she was frequently irritated by them, Caley felt her heart swelling with pride for her friends' unreserved acceptance of the newcomers. Faults and all, she mused wryly, there was no denying they were a fine bunch of characters.

The day wore on. After retrieving her buckskin suit from Mr. Ling—and declining the offer of another cupful of his "special" tea—Caley busied herself at the office. She tried, but failed miserably, to prevent her thoughts from straying to Jake at every turn, and was glad when Ned finally rode back into town. She hastened out to greet him as he swung down from the saddle.

"Did you see him?" she questioned anxiously. There was no need to clarify who *him* was.

"I saw him all right," confirmed Ned. It was obvious from the tone of his voice that things had not gone well. Looping the reins over the hitching post, he faced her with an angry, tight-lipped expression. "He didn't even try to deny it was his doing, Caley. As a matter of fact, he was almost boasting about it. He said he'd do the same to any other wooly-tenders who tried to push in on the range. It sure as hell didn't seem to bother him any when I pointed out he was endangering the lives of women and children!"

"What about Matt?"

"Matt wasn't there. But I'm sure he had a hand in it, too. He always does."

"Jake's not going to let them get away with it," said Caley, a knot of dread already tightening in her stomach at the thought. "Even if Elena's father refuses to press charges this time as well, he's not going to let them get away with it."

"I know," Ned agreed quietly. "But he won't face them alone, Caley. I'll be right there with him."

"So will I," she vowed. Her blue-green eyes sparked with the light of determination. "So will I."

Darkness settled over the desert, the nighttime bringing with it a cool breeze and a deep, cloudless sky full of stars. Caley remained at Maybelle's longer than was her usual custom—partly because she wanted to talk to Elena, and partly because her own place seemed lonely without Jake. She would never have believed it possible that she would miss him so much; life was anything but peaceful with him around. But still, she certainly didn't look forward to spending the night alone in that old iron bedstead of hers with only Shadrach for company. A cat was a poor substitute for the

374

warmth of a man's body beside hers, especially when the man was Jake Brody and the body was so sinfully pleasing.

"You're welcome to stay here if you want," offered Maybelle, her eyes full of understanding as she sensed her young friend's reluctance to leave.

"Why on earth would I want to do that?" Caley responded with a frown. She wandered back across the warmly lit parlor to take up a stance behind the sofa. "I've got a home of my own, haven't I?"

"Yes, and you've got a husband of your own, too," the widow pointed out, "only he's not here and you seem a little—"

"I'm fine!" insisted Caley. She even managed a smile, albeit a weak one. "For heaven's sake, Maybelle, I'm a grown woman. And I've lived by myself ever since my father died."

"Yes, but things are different now."

"No they're not!" she stubbornly denied.

"I can see why Marshal Brody finds it difficult to put up with you!" retorted Maybelle. She shook her head and sighed, returning her attention to the sewing in her lap. "The two of you are even better suited for one another than I thought. But not so much that you don't have the whole town talking about your fights."

"I don't know what you mean!" lied Caley.

"We've all got eyes. Ears, too. And you leave your windows open."

Caley blushed fierily. Wondering just what the blazes *else* the whole town was talking about, she compressed her lips into a tight, thin line and returned to the window. Elena had already gone upstairs with the boys, and even the regulars had decided to call it an early night.

"Maybe he'll be home tomorrow," Maybelle offered gently, observing how the other woman's gaze was fastened on the street outside once more.

"If only I knew where he'd gone," murmured Caley.

"The waiting's always the hard part. I guess men are born to roam and women to wait."

"Well not *this* woman! I have no intention of spending the rest of my life sitting at home while Jake Brody goes traipsing off to wherever he pleases!"

"I don't see that you have a choice. It's part of his job to track down and arrest desperadoes, isn't it?"

"Maybe," she grudgingly allowed. "But, hell's bells, I don't even know if he's tracking desperadoes or . . . or sitting in a saloon somewhere with a fancy, fat-chested trollop on his lap!"

"Come now, Caley, you know he isn't that kind of man," chided Maybelle, trying hard not to smile.

"Do I?" She whirled to face the older woman. "I don't even know who I am anymore! Two weeks ago, I was Caley McAlister, driving stagecoaches and answering to no one! And now, now I'm Mrs. Jake Brody, the wife of a lawman who expects her to trust him no matter what and—"

"But that's what love is all about!"

"What the devil does love have to do with this?"

"Everything!" pronounced Maybelle. Setting aside her embroidery, she rose to her feet and joined Caley at the window. "You're in love, my dear."

"Don't be ridiculous!"

"How else can you explain what's been going on? I've known you a long time, Caley," the brunette remarked with an affectionate smile. "And you've not been the same ever since Jake Brody came to town. You weren't in love with Matt Griffin; everyone could see that. But you *are* in love with your husband, and it's high time you faced up to it."

"But I—I don't want to be in love!" cried Caley, hot tears starting to her eyes. Maybelle's words had touched her to the very core, penetrating her well-guarded heart and forcing her to see things she didn't want to see. Life had taught her to be cautious; love was taking that caution and throwing it to the winds. "I don't want to love Jake! I don't want to love anyone!"

"Why not? What are you afraid of?"

"Of being like other women! Of being a prisoner to my own feelings, of being weak and—!"

"You'll never be weak," Maybelle insisted with another smile. "But you are a woman, Caley. Nothing's ever going to change that. You're a woman, and Jake Brody's a man, and if you can't see how wonderful it can be, then I wash my hands of you!"

"Oh Maybelle, I don't know what to do!" she sighed, releasing her grip on the lace curtains and meeting the widow's perceptive gaze. "I just can't seem to—" She broke off at the sudden look of surprise on Maybelle's face. "What is it?" she demanded, her eyes flying to the window again. "Did you see something?"

"Yes," Maybelle answered breathlessly, still unable to believe the evidence of her own eyes. "Your husband!" It was dark, but not so dark that she hadn't been able to make out the faces of the two horsemen. The lamplight, streaming outward from that very window, had fallen upon them as they had ridden past. "He's back, Caley!

377

And he's not alone!"

"He's back?"

She was out of the room before Maybelle could tell her the rest.

Sure enough, she spotted Jake and another man reining their mounts to a halt in front of the jail. She raced across the street and down the boardwalk, her heart soaring at the knowledge of his safe return. It wasn't until she was nearly there that she realized there was something familiar about the other man. She hastened her approach, only to observe with a mild frown of bemusement that, while Jake had already swung down from the saddle, the second rider still sat astride his mount. His hands were tied behind his back.

"Jake?" she called out. She watched as he turned his head toward her. But it was the other man's face which caught and held her startled gaze. *"Matt!"* she gasped.

"Hello, Mac," he said, his mouth curving into a brief, humorless smile. His eyes, glinting coldly, followed her while she came forward.

"What are you doing here, Matt? What's going on?" Her gaze was full of alarm and confusion as it flickered downward to his bound wrists.

"Ask *him!*" Matt ground out, jerking his head toward Jake.

Caley swiftly moved to her husband's side. He secured the reins before meeting her gaze. She was dismayed to view the grim set of his features.

"What is it, Jake? What's happened?" she demanded.

"I've arrested Griffin," was all he would say. His green eyes were unfathomable, but she did not fail to detect the tightly controlled fury in his voice.

"I can see that!" she retorted impatiently. "But,

378

why? Because of what happened to the Lar-rondes?"

"The Larrondes?" He shook his head. "No, Caley. This has nothing to do with them."

"Then *why?*"

"Later," he decreed quietly. Leaving her to stare at him in angry frustration, he untied Matt's hands. He then drew his gun from the holster and commanded, "Dismount and get inside, Griffin."

"You're making a big mistake, Brody!" snarled Matt.

"The only mistake was yours." His gaze smoldered dangerously. "Now get inside!"

Caley watched as Matt reluctantly obeyed. She followed close on the two men's heels when they moved inside the jail. Dan was seated at the desk, his booted feet propped up on the desk as he leaned negligently back in the chair. Caught off-guard when the door was flung open, he swung his feet to the floor and stood with such haste that the chair clattered backward against the wall.

"Griffin!" he burst out. His widened eyes flew to Jake. "I didn't think you'd find him so soon, Marshal!"

"Damn it, *what is all this about?*" Caley demanded in growing aggravation.

Still, no one bothered to enlighten her. While Dan hastened to unlock the door leading to the other room, Jake silently motioned his prisoner forward. He proceeded to lock Matt in the cell adjacent to Otis Snyder's.

"I thought you'd appreciate being next to your good friend," Jake told him with a faint, sardonic smile.

Otis, meanwhile, woke up and raised his head. His bleary, red-rimmed eyes narrowed in scrutiny, then widened in disbelief when he saw the new prisoner.

"Matt Griffin?" Although still feeling hung over from the night before, he managed to pull himself into a sitting position on his bunk. "What the hell you done now, boy?" he muttered with a scowl in Matt's direction.

"Come morning, you stupid son of a bitch," growled Matt, his fingers curling about the bars as he ignored Otis and glared murderously across at Jake, "I'll be out of here and you'll be dead!"

"Don't count on it." He turned and walked away.

"You're a dead man, Brody!" Matt called after him. "Once my father gets wind of this, he'll bring the whole county riding down on you! And by damn, I'll make you sorry you ever tangled with me, you bastard! I'll make you pay with your hide, do you hear?"

Matt's threats struck not a single chord of fear in Jake's heart; only contempt. He closed and locked the connecting door, his handsome face inscrutable as he returned the keys to the desk. He was fully prepared to face Caley's wrath, and she did not disappoint him.

"Why did you arrest him, Jake? What's he done? And why didn't you tell me what you were planning to do?" she leveled the first barrage at him. Her eyes were twin pools of liquid, blue-green fire, and her whole body was fairly quaking with anger. She stalked forward to confront him across the desk, while Dan looked on uneasily. "I want some answers—now, damn it!"

"Sit down, Caley," Jake ordered with maddening calm.

"Sit down? I most certainly will not! I'm not

380

going to do one blasted thing until—"

"*Sit down.*"

He had used an identical tone of voice with her under similar circumstances once before. It achieved the same results now as it did then. Though Caley eyed him furiously, she sat down.

"All right, I'm sitting!" she pointed out with an ill grace. "Now tell me what the devil's going on!"

"I knew you weren't gonna like it none, Mrs. Brody," interjected Dan. "That's why I didn't want to—" He blanched at a fierce, quelling look from her. "Think I'll step outside." He did so.

"Are you sure this doesn't have anything to do with the sheepmen?" Caley asked Jake suspiciously.

She watched as he began reloading his shotgun. Oddly enough, in spite of her annoyance with him, she experienced the sudden urge to soothe the faint, tired lines from his face. Realizing that he must have been in the saddle all day long, she wondered if he had even stopped to rest.

"Griffin's been charged with armed robbery, Caley," he finally revealed.

His eyes met hers, and he swore inwardly. He hated being the one to cause her pain, but there was no way around it. He had known this day was coming. He had known it, and yet he hadn't counted on loving her so much that he cursed his own duty.

"Armed robbery?" she echoed, frowning in bafflement. "You mean, like a bank, or a—"

"A stagecoach," he finished for her. "He was leading the men who robbed Hank's stage. And he was leading them again the day they tried to rob yours."

"*What?*" She leapt to her feet, shaking her head

381

in a vehement denial. "I don't believe it! It isn't true, damn it, it isn't true! Matt Griffin would never—"

"He did, Caley," insisted Jake. His piercing gaze burned down into the wide, stormy depths of hers. "He did."

"How can you know that?"

"I have proof."

"Proof? What possible proof—"

"The Senate's bartender got another one of those marked coins a couple of days ago. Only this time, his memory had improved enough so that he could tell me who had given it to him."

"That proves nothing!" she protested. "Why, Matt could easily have gotten that coin from someone else!"

"There's more, Caley," he cautioned her.

"More?" She waited impatiently while he lowered the shotgun to the desk and pulled the hat from his head.

"I found part of a spur when I rode out to investigate the first robbery," he continued, tossing the hat down beside the gun. "Griffin turned up in Carlin the next day to order a new pair of spurs. He liked to get them custom-made, with a special kind of rowel. The same as what I found."

"That still doesn't make him a road agent!" she insisted. "There could be a perfectly simple explanation for all this!" She flung about and folded her arms tightly across her chest. Breathing a curse, she whirled to face him again. "That's pretty flimsy evidence, Jake Brody!" she charged indignantly. "No jury's going to convict a man because of a coin and a pair of spurs!"

"Maybe not," he allowed with only the ghost of a smile. "But I also have a witness."

"A—a witness?"

"That's what took me to Carlin yesterday. The sheriff there sent word about a man found lying unconscious near town last week. Someone had apparently left him there to die." Moving around the desk, he stood before her and raised his hands to close gently about her arms. "He was one of Griffin's men, Caley. And it was my bullet in his chest."

"How do you know that?" she asked, swallowing a sudden lump in her throat.

"Because he talked. He was delirious for a while, and it wasn't until two days ago that he could be questioned. His name's Sutter. He's young. But not too young to know what he was doing. Griffin had warned him to keep his mouth shut. He threatened to come back and finish the job if anything was said. But Sutter did talk, Caley."

He released her, his features tensing as he turned away and resumed his stance behind the desk. Caley stared at him as if transfixed. Her emotions were in utter chaos, and her head spun dizzily. *This can't be happening,* she told herself. Surely it was a nightmare from which she would soon awaken.

"It seems Griffin was double-crossing him," she was only dimly aware of Jake continuing. "He still hadn't received his share of the take from the first robbery. And when he had the bad luck to get shot, Griffin told him he'd just keep holding on to the money. It was because of that he decided to take his chances with the law. That, and because he also happened to be wanted for murder back in Virginia City."

He paused for a moment and met her gaze

383

again. White-hot rage flared anew toward the man who was responsible for her pain. But she had to hear the truth. Once and for all, she had to see Matt Griffin for what he really was. And God help him, he couldn't help being relieved that the other man would be out of her life forever.

"The sheriff promised to try and strike a deal on Sutter's behalf if he gave evidence against the others," he told her somberly. "I'll be bringing him back here to testify." He didn't add that the sheriff had placed the wounded man in protective custody; there was a very real possibility that one of the other robbers still at large, or even Isaiah Griffin, would try to get to him before the trial.

"I don't believe it," Caley whispered raggedly. She looked away and shook her head again, feeling sick at heart. "Matt . . . Matt would never do anything to hurt me!" *Dear God it can't be true*, she thought, tears welling up in her eyes. *Not Matt. Not Matt!*

"Go home, Caley," Jake instructed in a low, distant tone, his eyes glinting dully. "I'm sorry you had to find out this way, but there's nothing—"

"Why didn't you tell me you were going after Matt?" she demanded reproachfully. "Was it because you didn't know if it was all going to hang together? Or *maybe,*" she accused at a sudden thought, "just maybe it was because you were afraid I'd try to warn him! That's it, isn't it? You didn't trust me!"

"I trust you. Except where Matt Griffin is concerned!" he admitted. His gaze burned down into hers once more. "I know how much he means to you. And I know you'd do just about anything to keep him out of trouble. But this is one time you can't help him, Caley. This is one time he's going

384

to pay for what he's done!"

"Innocent until proven guilty—isn't that the way it goes?" she countered with an angry toss of her head. "Only it won't get that far! Damn it, Isaiah won't let you get away with this! Whether Matt's guilty or not, his father's not going to stand by and do nothing while you—"

"He has no choice."

"Isaiah Griffin makes his own choices!"

"Go home, Caley," Jake reiterated with deceptive calm.

"Not until I've seen Matt!" she demanded. "I'm going to talk to him and—"

"Like hell you are!"

"It won't do any harm just to let me see him!" she insisted, the fire in her eyes blazing hotter. "I've got to talk to him, Jake! I've got to know if it's true!"

"It's true all right," he ground out, trying unsuccessfully to keep his personal feelings out of it.

"Then I need to know why he did it! Don't you understand? I need to know *why*!"

Jake resisted the urge to sweep her into his arms and kiss her until all thought of Matt Griffin was driven from her mind. More than anything, he wanted to hold her and never let her go, to make her realize what he had known all along—that she was his and no other man's.

But she was right, he told himself reluctantly. She needed to talk to Griffin. Whatever the man was, whatever he had done, he was a part of her past that had to be resolved. And even if the only thing she heard was a denial, it was necessary for her to hear it from Griffin himself. He knew she'd never rest until she did.

His gaze narrowing imperceptibly, he removed

385

the keys from the desk. Without a word, he unlocked the door and stepped aside to let her pass. But he seized her arm before she could do so.

"Five minutes, Caley," he decreed, his voice holding an undercurrent of raw emotion. "Five minutes, and then you'll leave."

She nodded in silent acceptance. Feeling more uneasy about the meeting with Matt than she cared to admit, she pulled away and moved through the doorway.

Matt's face lit with mingled surprise and relief when he saw her. He gripped the bars again, his blue eyes glittering hotly.

"Mac! Damn it, Mac, what's been keeping you? You've got to get me out of here!"

"Get you out of here?" she echoed in bewilderment. She glanced toward Otis Snyder as she traveled past his cell, only to note that he was sleeping soundly again. "How the devil am I supposed to do that?" she asked Matt in a hushed tone.

"You've got influence with Brody, don't you?" he challenged with bitter sarcasm. He reached out and grasped her hands, pulling her forward so that her face was mere inches from the scowling fury of his. "That bastard's gone too far this, time! You've got to get word to my father right away! Tell him—"

"I'll get word to him," she agreed, frowning, "but not so he'll get you out of here." She tried to pull away, but he held fast. Heaving a disconsolate sigh, she said, "Jake told me everything, Matt."

"He told you nothing more than a pack of lies!"

"Are they lies?" she demanded sharply. She searched his familiar, rough-hewn features for the truth, fervently praying that he would be able to deny the charges. "Did you rob Hank's stage, Matt? Did you try to rob mine?"

"No!" He let her hands go as if the contact had suddenly burned him and spun away. "Hell, Mac, I can't believe you're even asking me that!" he bit out. He flung about to face her again, and she felt a pang of remorse when she glimpsed the angry recrimination in his eyes. "We've known each other for ten years, *ten years*, damn it, and in all that time I've looked out after you better than anyone else could've done! There's too much between us for you to believe I'd ever do anything to hurt you!"

"But Jake has evidence!" she reminded him, still trying desperately to sort things out. "He said there's a man in Carlin who—"

"I don't give a damn what he said!" Matt declared furiously. He stalked forward again and fixed her with a hard, unwavering look. "I didn't do it, Mac! That so-called 'witness' of his is nothing but a lying son of a bitch! I don't know why Sutter's out to get me—but I know why Brody is!"

"What are you talking about?"

"You know damned good and well what I'm talking about! Brody hates me because of *you*, because he knows you'll always be mine! That's why he's doing this, Mac! He knows I'm innocent, but he wants me out of the way!"

"That—that isn't true!" she stammered, her eyes wide and filled with horrified disbelief.

"It is true!" he maintained in a tight, simmering voice. His hand shot out to close about her wrist in a bruising grip. "But it's not going to matter much longer! I'll be out of here soon, Mac, and then we'll be free of Brody!"

"Free?" she repeated dazedly, her stunned gaze

387

meeting his again.

"You know as well as I do that Pa's not going to let me rot in jail! And you know he's not going to let this thing go all the way to trial, either! No, Mac, like I told that soon to be *ex*-husband of yours," he reiterated with a savage tightening of his features, "I'll be out of here by morning and he'll be dead!"

"No!" she whispered. Her eyes clouded with dread. Surely such a thing couldn't happen, she reasoned with herself. Jake would never let any prisoner of his be taken. Why, he'd die first!

He'd die first. The words sunk in with chilling effect. That was the whole point of Matt's threat, she realized. The whole, terrifying point.

She felt a sharp pain in her heart. Suddenly, she knew that she could not bear to let anything happen to the man she had married. And she also knew what she had to do to keep him alive.

"I don't want anyone to get hurt, Matt!" she said breathlessly. Her mind was racing to formulate a plan. "Promise me that no one will get hurt!"

"How the hell can I promise that?"

"You can and will!" she demanded, lowering her voice even more as she leaned purposefully closer. "If you want out of here, you'll do exactly as I say!"

"I knew you'd come through for me!" Matt told her with a low, triumphant laugh.

"Shut up and listen!" She cast a narrow look toward Otis, but was satisfied that he was still asleep. Her bright gaze shifted hastily to the doorway before she turned back to Matt and disclosed to him in a tone of quiet determination, "I'm going to go back out there and get the key."

"How?"

"Let me worry about that! You just be ready to take off when I get back!" She cast another worried glance toward the door. "Remember what I said, though—no one's to get hurt! Once you're outside, get on your horse and ride like hell for California! Don't ever come back, Matt!"

"I'll be back for you!" he declared, still refusing to admit defeat where she was concerned.

"No!" She shook her head firmly. "No, Matt, you can't do that! I won't go with you! I told you before, it's too late for us!"

"Then why are you helping me?" he asked with a deep frown of puzzlement.

"Because . . . because you've been a good friend all these years!" she finally blurted out. "And because I know there's a chance you really are innocent!"

That was true enough, but it wasn't the main reason. She couldn't think of a way to explain it to herself, much less to him. There was certainly no time to stop and analyze things now. Later, she promised herself. Right now, she had to get Matt out of jail before it was too late—before Isaiah Griffin came riding into town with the fire of vengeance in his blood and murder on his mind.

She turned away and started back toward the door. Pausing for a moment, she squared her shoulders, gathered her courage about her, and prayed that she was doing the right thing. Then she stepped into the other room to face Jake again.

His gaze fastening on her as she approached him, he holstered the six-shooter he had just finished reloading. Her eyes fell beneath the intense scrutiny of his when she drew close. She knew he was waiting for her to speak, and she was dismayed to feel herself coloring guiltily. The silence stretched between them.

"He denies it," she revealed at last. Her voice was remarkably steady under the circumstances. *Great balls of fire, how am I going to go through with this*? she lamented, but knew there was no other way.

"I expected him to," replied Jake. Although he could tell she was troubled, he attributed it to Matt's arrest.

"Matt seems to think you're doing this because of me," she disclosed. She forced herself to meet his gaze. "Are you?"

"No," he answered truthfully. His eyes were full of such warmth as they traveled over her upturned face that she found it difficult to breathe. "I can't deny there's no love lost between Griffin and me. But I'm only doing my job, Caley. He broke the law."

"What about Isaiah?"

"What about him?"

"He'll kill you, that's what!" Her eyes flashed anew, and she made one final attempt to make him see reason. "Damn it, Jake, he'll kill you if you don't—"

"It's nice to know you have so much confidence in my abilities," he drawled, his gaze brimming with ironic amusement. Her concern stirred his heart, and his spirits suddenly felt lighter. The journey to Tuscarora and back had been a hard one, but seeing her again made him forget how tired he was.

"This isn't a joke!" she pointed out angrily. "It's a matter of life and death—*yours!*"

"I have no intention of making you a widow."

390

He drew her close now, his strong arms slipping about her tense body. "No, Mrs. Brody, you'll not get off that easily," he vowed softly. "When I said 'till death do us part', I meant in about fifty or sixty years."

"What if I asked you to let him go? Would you do it for me?" she appealed. She was clutching at vain hopes and she knew it.

"No, Caley." He frowned and shook his head. "Not even for you. Nor would you want me to. It would be going against everything I believe in. I've sworn to uphold the law, no matter what the cost. And besides which, I'll admit to having a personal interest in seeing Griffin pay for his crimes. He endangered your life," he reminded her, his voice underscored by vengeful fury once more. "He and his men nearly killed the express guard. They nearly killed us."

She could put it off no longer. Steeling herself for what lay ahead, she swayed against him and raised her arms to curl about his neck. A faint smile touched her lips.

"I'm sorry, Jake. I—I guess you're right," she murmured with a deceptive air of capitulation. Once again, she found it difficult to look him square in the eye.

"He'll get a fair trial," Jake assured her. If he suspected anything was amiss, he gave no indication of it. "So will the others after I round them up. For now, my job is to make sure Griffin stays behind bars. I'm afraid Dan and I will have to stand guard through the night again."

"So you are expecting trouble?"

"I may be stubborn, but I'm not without sense," he remarked mockingly, then sobered. "I know it's come as a shock to you. I'm sorry I couldn't tell you before now. I've known about him for a long time, Caley. That's one of the reasons I wanted you to stay clear of him. Maybe now you'll understand."

She nodded mutely and strained upward on tiptoe, hugging him tighter. *Forgive me, Jake*, she implored in silent contrition. *But it's for your own good*.

"Would you . . . would you mind walking me home?" she requested in a small voice. "I'm not feeling just real well right now."

"What's wrong?" he demanded. Setting her away a bit, he frowned down at her in loving concern.

"It's because of all that's happened, I suppose," she murmured weakly. Her face was flushed, which only lent credence to the lie. Well, she rationalized inwardly, it wasn't a total lie—she *did* feel sick inside at the thought of what she must do.

"Come on then," he said, slipping an arm about her shoulders. "The best place for you right now is bed."

She allowed him to lead her outside. Dan was still in front of the jail. He quickly straightened from where he had been leaning back against the log wall.

"I'm taking Caley home," Jake told him. "Stay inside and hold ready. I'll be back shortly."

"Yes, sir, Marshal!" the deputy eagerly concurred. He tipped his hat to Caley, then stepped inside and closed the door.

They started off toward the stage office. Caley was glad for the silence between them, for her mind was once again racing to think of a way to keep Jake at home long enough for her to carry out her plan. That she could somehow get past

Dan, she had little doubt, but she'd never even make it back to the jail unless she made sure her husband was out of the way first. She needed only a little time. A few minutes would do the trick. Just a few minutes . . .

Fate intervened. The solution to her dilemma arrived in the form of gunshots suddenly erupting down at Dobe Row.

"Damn!" muttered Jake. He and Caley were almost home by now, and he turned to her with a frown. "I've got to see what's going on," he announced, his gaze flickering briefly toward the red-light district. "I'll look in on you on my way back to the jail."

"All right."

She battled the impulse to call after him as he left her. Her eyes, full of warmth and anguish and determination, followed him for several long moments. Once he was well away, she spun about and flew back down the boardwalk.

Chapter XVI

Dan Mitchelson had just settled back in the chair again when the door burst open. He leapt to his feet, seizing hold of the shotgun and leveling it defensively at the intruder.

"Mrs. Brody?" he exclaimed in startlement. His eyes grew very round. "What are you—"

"Jake needs your help!" she told him breathlessly. "He's down at Dobe Row!"

"But I'm supposed to stay here and guard the prisoner!"

"Damn it, Dan, he needs your help now!" she reiterated in a voice tinged with rising panic. "Please, just go!"

"I'll go!" he finally acquiesced. "You stay here and keep an eye on things for me!" He thrust the shotgun into her hands and headed out the door.

"I will!" she agreed. "Now hurry!"

She watched as he went running across the darkened street. Then, her eyes glowing purposefully, she closed the door and hurried over to the desk. She was satisfied to find the keys right where Jake had left them. Snatching them up, she moved to unlock the door. Her fingers were trembling and her heart pounding fiercely as she swung the door open and flew to where Matt waited with hard-eyed impatience in his cell.

"Hell, Mac, I didn't think you were ever coming back!" he complained, scowling darkly.

"Shhhh!" she cautioned, nodding toward Otis Snyder. Otis lay on his bunk with his back to them. He was snoring quietly for a change. "We don't want to chance waking him up!" she whispered to Matt.

"Where's Brody?"

"Dobe Row!" she answered, working feverishly to find the key that would unlock his cell. "But he could be back any minute!"

"And Mitchelson?"

"With Jake!"

She tried yet another key, and breathed an audible sigh of relief when it turned in the lock. Matt swung the barred door open. Grabbing Caley's arm, he pulled her along with him into the other room.

"Head for California, Matt, and don't look back!" she urged him.

"Not California, Mac—Tuscarora!" he corrected. He released her and took up the shotgun she had set atop the desk only moments earlier. It was immediately discarded, however, when he caught sight of his own guns hanging on the wall. He seized his holster and hastily buckled it on. "He won't be looking for me there again!"

"Tuscarora?" she echoed, frowning as she watched him check to make sure his guns were still loaded. "No, Matt, you've got to get out of the state!"

"Not without you! I'll be back for you, just like I promised!" He swept her close with one arm and gave her a quick, hard kiss. "Tell Brody it's not

396

finished yet!" he bit out.

"Damn you, Matt Griffin, it *is* finished!" she cried vehemently, pushing him away. "I'm married now and that's the way it's going to stay! Now get the hell out of here and don't ever come back!"

"You won't regret helping me out of this, Mac!" he vowed. "I'll make it up to you!"

"I already regret it!" she retorted, shoving him toward the door. "Now get going!"

Casting her one last warm look full of meaning, he did as she said. He checked first to make sure the coast was clear, then hurried outside to his mount. He swung up into the saddle and prepared to rein about.

Caley stepped onto the boardwalk, gazing at her longtime friend in mingled sorrow and mistrust. She didn't want to believe him capable of doing what Jake had said he'd done. But guilty or not, she couldn't bear to think of him spending the rest of his life in prison—or having it cut short at the end of a rope.

"Take care, Matt!" she choked out through sudden tears. It was difficult to believe she would never see him again.

"Tell Pa where I've gone!"

Spurring his horse, he rode away. Caley watched him disappear into the night. She drew in a deep, ragged breath, feeling emotionally drained and not at all ready to face Jake's wrath. He would be furious, she knew. No, he would be *beyond* furious. And heaven help her, she was suddenly uncertain whether she had done the right thing after all. . . .

The reckoning was soon upon her. Wandering back inside the jail, she sank wearily down into a chair and closed her eyes. Otis Snyder's voice drifted out to her from the other room.

"Miss Caley?"

"Yes, Otis?" she called back, paying him little mind.

"You want I should keep that part about Tuscarora a secret?"

Her eyes flew open at that. *Otis*! Great balls of fire, she thought he had been sleeping!

She came out of the chair like a shot and raced back to his cell. He was sitting upright on his bunk now, his features looking more drink-ravaged than ever and his eyes still painfully bloodshot. His mouth curved into a wan smile when he saw her.

"Howdy, Miss Caley."

"Otis!" She hurried forward, her fingers curling about the bars while she demanded anxiously, "Otis, what did you hear?"

"Enough, I guess," he offered with a slight, noncommittal shrug.

"Listen to me, Otis!" She fixed him with a stern look, her voice full of exaggerated patience as if she were speaking to a child instead of a grown man. "You can't tell anyone what you heard, do you understand? You can't tell anyone!"

"Not even the marshal?"

"Especially not the marshal!"

"Well now . . . that don't seem right," he murmured, frowning at the notion. "My boy told me it was the marshal saved my life last night."

"Matt Griffin was there, too!" she reminded him. "Damn it, Otis, he helped you out and now you've got to do the same for him!"

"I'll have to think on it, Miss Caley." He lay back down and noisily cleared his throat.

Caley gazed at him in perplexity, wondering how

she could make him keep quiet about what he knew. If he told Jake, then Jake would track Matt down, bring him back to town, and the whole thing would start all over again. Her efforts would have proven entirely futile. And Jake would be in as much danger as ever.

"*Caley*?" a deep voice rumbled out from the front room.

"Dear God, Jake!" she whispered.

She whirled about, her face paling and her turquoise gaze filling with dread. Before she could move, he was there. She cursed the impulse to run.

Jake's eyes gleamed with savage fury as they took in the sight of Matt's empty cell—and his wife's guilty but proudly defiant countenance. He towered menacingly above her, his hands shooting out to grasp her arms and yank her close.

"Damn it, woman, what have you done? Where's Griffin?" he demanded in a low, smoldering tone.

"He's gone! He's gone, and I'm glad of it!" she declared, unflinching beneath his wrath.

"Why?" His fingers dug into her soft flesh, while his gaze darkened with thunderous rage. The pain of her betrayal cut him to the core. "Why did you do it, Caley?"

"Because there was no other way!" she cried hotly. "Because you'd have gotten yourself killed and—"

"It was because of *him*, wasn't it?" he ground out. "This didn't have anything to do with me! You wanted to help Griffin! I should have known! By damn, I should have known!"

"No, it wasn't like that!" She shook her head in furious denial, while tears stung against her eyelids

399

once more. "It wasn't because of Matt!" she insisted truthfully. "I did it for you! Isaiah would have killed you!"

"Isaiah Griffin was my concern, not yours! Don't you understand what you've done? It's more than just a mistake in judgment—it's a criminal offense! You broke the law, Caley!"

"And I'd do it again!" she proclaimed with a brave show of unrepentance. Inwardly, she was still plagued by terrible doubts, but she refused to back down. "I swear, I'd do it again!"

A tremor of fear shook her when she glimpsed the violence in her husband's penetrating gaze. She found herself abruptly released. Clutching at the cell bars for support, she watched as Jake's handsome face became a grim mask of determination.

"Where's he gone, Caley?"

"I—I don't know!" she lied, only to feel the telltale color staining her cheeks.

"Yes you do! Now tell me!" he commanded in a tone that was whipcord sharp.

"I don't know, damn it!"

"I'm warning you, Caley! Either you tell me, or—"

"Marshal!" Dan suddenly called out from the jailhouse doorway. "They're comin', Marshal!"

Jake left her without another word. She stared numbly after him, both her mind and emotions in complete turmoil. Her wide, luminous gaze moved instinctively to Otis Snyder. He was peering at her with a dispassionate expression on his face, but she could have sworn she read something akin to reproach in his eyes.

Breathing an oath, she turned to follow in Jake's furious wake. Her pulse leapt in alarm when she neared the front door and heard another, all too familiar voice. *Isaiah*! She hastened outside to take her place beside a dangerously silent Jake and a nervous, watchful Dan.

Isaiah Griffin, still astride his horse, turned his head and looked down at her. There were nearly a dozen other men with him, all of them armed and fully prepared to do his bidding.

"Isaiah, what are you doing here?" Caley demanded, though she already knew the answer.

"I've come for Matt!" he announced curtly. Even in the darkness, he was an imposing figure.

"But—how did you know he was here?" she asked with a frown of puzzlement.

"Ed Tickner told me!" His gaze narrowed and blazed murderously as it traveled back to Jake. "You've gone too far this time, Brody! Matt's done nothing!"

"That's for a jury to decide."

"You think I'm going to let it come to that? No Griffin's ever stood trial and I'm going to make damned sure no Griffin ever does! Now bring him out! Bring him out, you bastard, or I'll—"

"Don't threaten me," Jake cautioned with deadly calm, "unless you want two Griffins to have their day in court."

He and Dan were both armed with shotguns, and there was little doubt in Caley's mind that they would not hesitate to shoot the first man that made a move toward the jail. She couldn't let things go any farther.

"Matt's not here!" she blurted out to Isaiah. Her willingness to impart such information earned her a furious, quelling look from Jake, but she stubbornly disregarded it and went on to reveal, "He's gone, Isaiah! He—he broke out only a short time ago!"

401

"Broke out?" He eyed her closely for a moment, then was apparently satisfied that she was telling the truth. His rancorous gaze sliced to Jake again. "Maybe you 'arranged' for him to escape," he suggested with a sneer. "Hell yes, maybe you knew I'd be coming and you figured it'd go easier all the way around if you let him out. Is that the way it was, Brody?"

His words were laced with scorn. Several of the other horsemen smiled contemptuously, and Caley felt another sharp twinge of guilt. She was sorely tempted to tell Isaiah of her part in the escape, but sensed that it would only make matters worse.

"It makes no difference how it happened," Jake replied in a clear, steady tone of authority. "I'll be going after him. And I'll bring him back."

"You do, and I'll see you in hell!" vowed the tough old cattleman. He leaned forward in the saddle, his grip tightening angrily on the reins. "You've been making trouble ever since you came here! Well no more, by damn, no more! I've already sent word to the governor—you'll be on your way out of here for good this time tomorrow!"

"You're wasting your time, Griffin," said Jake. His own eyes glinted coldly. *"And mine."*

"Please, Isaiah, go home!" Caley implored, moving to his side. She tilted her head back to cast him a look full of entreaty. "Matt's gone now! There's nothing more you can do!"

"He may be gone, but I'm not going to let him have this hanging over his head from now on! It's got to be cleared up!" His gaze softened a bit when he told her, "You know Matt couldn't have done it, Caley. I'll grant you he's a wild one, but he'd never stoop to thieving. And he'd never bring

402

hardship on *you*!"

"I know!" she declared, though she didn't know at all. "I know he wouldn't, but—"

"That's enough, Caley," Jake decreed quietly. "Now get back inside."

"Why, you puffed-up son of a bitch!" growled Isaiah, his anger fueled by what he perceived to be the other man's insolence. "Who the hell do you think you are to go telling her what to do?"

"I'm her husband," he answered with deceptive equanimity. In truth, he was tensed for action. His eyes never left the group's leader.

"What kind of a fool do you take me for, Brody?" taunted Isaiah, curling his lip in a gesture of disgust.

"It's the truth!" Caley hastened to intervene once more. "I . . . we were married last week!"

For a moment, it appeared Isaiah would strike her. Jake would have killed him if he had.

"So, you've gone and done it." His voice was edged with pain and disappointment as well as fury now. He hadn't seen Matt in days; he couldn't help but wonder if it was all tied together somehow. "All right then. You've made your choice. You've sided with him against us!" he accused Caley, flinging her a hard, vengefully wrathful look.

"No! I'm not against you!" she denied. "I just—"

"Thank God your father's not alive to see how low you've sunk!" he pronounced like the embittered old man he was. Then, for the last time, he fastened his gaze on Jake and warned, "You better hope you don't find my boy, Brody. The only chance you've got of staying alive is to let it drop here and now. Because, so help me, even if you do

403

find him and bring him back, I'll not let that badge of yours keep me from cutting you down!"

With that, he jerked on the reins and rode away. The other horses thundered after his, stirring up a cloud of dust to be borne aloft on the cool night breeze. Dan stared expectantly at Jake and waited for him to speak. So did Caley.

But he didn't speak. He simply turned and strode back into the jail. Caley and Dan exchanged mutual looks of bewilderment, then followed after him.

"What you plannin' to do now, Marshal?" asked Dan on his way inside, only to find that Jake had returned to the other room to question the one remaining prisoner. Caley offered up a silent prayer that Otis wouldn't talk.

He did, of course. He told everything he knew, and then some. Even if she hadn't heard him "spilling his guts", she would have known by the look on Jake's face. There was no mistaking that look.

"I'm riding to Tuscarora again," he informed Dan as he emerged into the front office again. For his wife, he spared only a passing furious glance.

"You really think he'll head back up there?" the deputy asked with a dubious frown.

"I do." He crossed to the door.

"Jake?" Caley sought to detain him, and was rewarded when he finally turned to face her. She blanched at the savage gleam in his eyes. Musing wretchedly that she had never seen him so angry, she swallowed hard and faltered, "I . . . I . . . please Jake, don't go!"

"I have to, Caley." Damn it all, he was tired and hungry, and so enraged and hurt by her betrayal that he couldn't trust himself to go near her. "You didn't really think I'd let him go, did you?" he challenged with a faint, mocking smile.

"I didn't know what to think!" she confessed in a burst of emotion. Her eyes were glistening with unshed tears, and she suddenly looked so vulnerable and forlorn that Jake was tempted to relent in his anger. "I didn't think about breaking the law, or about what would happen once it was done—I just wanted to help you stay alive!"

"And you wanted to help Griffin stay alive."

"No! I mean, yes, I did, but that wasn't why—"

"I'll find him, Caley," he vowed, his gaze burning across into hers. "He'll pay for what he's done. And I'll deal with *you* later."

She hastened to the doorway to watch as he strode outside and mounted up. Her heart twisted painfully at the sight of his grim, tight-lipped features. She would have given anything at that moment to soften his gaze, to ease the awful tension between them. She knew she had only herself to blame. But the knowledge didn't lessen her pain—or his.

"Jake!" she impulsively called after him when he rode away. He didn't look back. She stared after him, her eyes full of misery, until he disappeared into the silvertoned darkness.

Dear God, what have I done? she thought in growing trepidation. She may have saved him from the father, but there was a very real possibility she had just sent him off to be killed by the son. Matt would not hesitate to spill his blood. Of that, she was sure.

"How could I have been so stupid?" she murmured aloud. There were no answers. Only the terrible certainty that she could do nothing but wait.

* * *

"Perhaps you would like to come to Mrs. O'Grady's with me?" suggested Elena.

"No," Caley replied, shaking her head. "Thanks just the same. But I—I don't feel much like facing everyone right now."

Reading the compassion in Elena's dark gaze, she managed a weak smile. She was grateful for the young woman's company. Jake had been gone nearly twenty-four hours now, and there had been no word. The waiting was even more difficult than she had expected; so much so, that she had been unable to conduct business with any degree of success throughout the day. Not since the death of her father had her spirits been so low.

"It is getting late. I should go now," Elena announced reluctantly. Concerned by her new friend's absence at all three meals, she had taken Maybelle's advice to pay her a visit following supper. The widow had expressed a mutual desire to know how Caley was faring, and had offered to see that the boys were well entertained during her absence. "Are you sure you would not like something to eat?"

"No, thanks," Caley declined once more. Her mouth curved into another brief smile. "Don't tell Maybelle, but Billy brought me a sandwich from home this afternoon. Besides, I think I'll just stay here and try to get some sleep. It's hopeless, of course, but I might as well give it a try." She released a long, disconsolate sigh, then asked at a sudden thought, "Would you like to come upstairs for a while? I've already put some coffee on to boil, and I . . . well, I'd like it if we could talk. I know it's late, and you've got the boys to see to,

406

but—"

"I am certain Mrs. O'Grady would not mind," Elena opined solemnly, though her brown eyes were alight with merry humor. "She said I was to remain as long as I pleased. And as for Martin and Pierre, they have never been treated so well."

Shadrach was fortunately not there to fly at them when they stepped into the living quarters. He was, however, following his usual custom of sitting on the back stoop and meowing resentfully. Caley offered Elena a seat, then hurried to let him in.

"He doesn't take too well to strangers, I'm afraid," she cautioned Elena as the cat bounded inside. "But he'll keep his distance."

He hadn't kept his distance with Jake, she suddenly recalled. *Jake.* His face swam before her eyes again. She would have surrendered to the impulse to ride up to Tuscarora, but knew he might return at any time. She hadn't counted on the hours stretching into days. Tomorrow, she promised herself. If he wasn't back by tomorrow, she'd go looking for him.

Forcing her attention back to the present, she noticed that Shadrach was settling himself contentedly on Elena's lap. Her gaze widened in surprise.

"I suppose he does not consider me a stranger," Elena remarked with a quiet laugh. She stroked his thick white fur. "I had a cat once. I was no older than Pierre then. My mother and I, and my brother and sister, had just come to America to join my father. He was herding in the San Joaquin Valley, in California." She smiled softly at the remembrance. "We were very poor, like all *Euskaldunak* when they first come, but we did not mind."

"Is that where you were living before you came here—in California?" asked Caley. Glad to have something to take her mind off Jake, if only for a short while, she sank down into the rocking chair.

"Yes. We would have remained, but my father was told it was better to bring the sheep into Nevada now."

"I spent most of my life in California, too." She and Matt had first met back in Sacramento, she reminisced sadly. But she didn't want to think of Matt.

"And will you live in Elko now, you and your husband?" queried Elena.

"I—I don't know," she admitted, frowning slightly. Jake had never mentioned his future plans, and she had never thought to ask. So far, their married life had consisted of one stormy—or passionate—confrontation after another, with little time for discussion. "There are a good many things I don't know," she murmured, half to herself.

Silence fell between them for a few moments. Caley stared toward the window in a preoccupied manner, while Elena fastened her gaze on the cat and allowed her own thoughts to wander. When she spoke again, she was dismayed to find herself putting into words the question which rose in her mind.

"Have you seen Mr. Griffin of late?"

"Who—Matt?" Caley asked in guilty startlement.

"No! No, I . . . I mean the younger brother," faltered Elena. A dull flush of embarrassment crept up to her face.

"Oh, Ned," said Caley, her brow clearing. "I haven't seen him in a couple of days." She subjected the other woman to a sudden, close scru-

408

tiny. "Has he been to see you yet?"

"To see *me*?" Her color deepened. "No, he has not!"

"Don't you want him to?"

"Why, of course, but my father—"

"What in tarnation does your father have to do with it?" Caley demanded in gentle exasperation. "Ned doesn't want to court your father. He wants to court you."

"But it is impossible!" protested Elena. She set Shadrach on the sofa beside her and stood, wandering to the window. "Even if I wished it, my father would never allow him to do so!"

"Why not? I certainly can't blame him for being bitter about what's happened, but Ned had nothing to do with it! He's as fine a young man as ever lived, and—"

"You do not understand." She shook her head and turned back to Caley. "Among my people, there is a saying, 'What was good enough for my father is good enough for me.' We are taught to have the deepest respect for the *aintzinekoak*, the ones who have gone before. Their ways are our ways. It does not change," she concluded unhappily.

"Maybe something will happen to change it!"

"No. But it does not matter. From what I have seen, Isaiah Griffin bears a deep hatred for us."

Caley could not deny that. Isaiah had never been known for his tolerance, nor for his ability to accept change. Jake had been right about that, she now realized. Jake had been right about so many things . . .

"I will be married next year," she became aware of Elena proclaiming.

"Married?" she echoed in surprise, then watched

409

as the raven-haired beauty nodded.

"To a young man from our village in the old country. Our families have arranged it." There was a catch in her voice, and Caley's heart stirred at the shadow of distress crossing her features. "I have not seen him since we were children together."

"You can't really mean to go through with it!"

"I have no choice."

"Of course you have a choice!" insisted Caley. She rose to her feet as well now and joined Elena at the window. "Everyone has a choice! For heaven's sake, no one can force you to marry someone you don't want to marry!"

Her words burned in her own ears. Realization struck her like a bolt of lightning.

It was true. Great balls of fire, it was true! She hadn't been forced into marriage with Jake Brody; she had married him because she wanted to. Plain and simple, she had wanted to!

And why the devil had she wanted to? came the next inevitable question. Was it merely because his very touch set her afire, because he made her feel things she had never thought it possible to feel? Or was it because—

Because you're in love with him, her mind's inner voice finished for her.

"Why the devil didn't I see it before?" she whispered, temporarily forgetting she was not alone. Her heart soared and her blue-green gaze sparkled with exaltation. *She loved Jake Brody.* "I've been a fool," she murmured, "a blasted fool!"

"What?" Elena questioned in puzzlement.

Caley met the other woman's wide, inquisitive gaze and smiled. The smile quickly faded, however, as joy was replaced by an apprehension even more intense than before. *Dear God, was it al-*

ready too late? she wondered, her eyes clouding with dread. Had she finally found the one man who was perfect for her in every way, only to lose him? Fate couldn't be so cruel, she told herself vehemently. By damn, it couldn't!

"What is it, Caley?" Elena asked, frowning worriedly now. "What is wrong?"

"I can't stand it any longer!" Caley burst out. "I'm going after him!"

"Who?"

"Jake!" She whirled about and disappeared into the bedroom, her fingers already working to unbutton her bodice.

"But you must not do that!" Elena tried reasoning with her. She followed and stood in the doorway while Caley hastened to exchange skirts for buckskin trousers. "It is too dangerous for you to ride alone at night! And your husband will surely return—"

"If he does, then you can tell him where I've gone! He'll check at Maybelle's first, anyway!" She flung the bodice aside and started on her skirt.

"But it is so far and—"

"Hell, I could find my way to Tuscarora in my sleep!" Caley assured her. "And I know how to take care of myself!" Stepping out of the skirt, she virtually yanked off her undergarments and drew on the fringed leather suit.

"Would it not be better to wait until morning?" Elena pointed out.

"I've waited too damned long as it is!" she exclaimed. "I should have followed my instincts and ridden after him last night!"

"What if you cannot find him?"

"I'll find him," Caley vowed determinedly.

Elena was forced to admit defeat. She moved

411

out of the way when Caley strode back into the main room to resume her place in the rocking chair and draw on her heavy traveling boots.

"You've done me more good than you'll ever know, Elena!" she declared. "Tell Maybelle I'd appreciate it if she'd send word to Billy Snyder—he'll look after things until I get back."

She stood and paused to embrace the other woman for a moment, then caught sight of Shadrach. He was still curled up on the sofa.

"Let the cat out for me tomorrow, will you? He's liable to get a bad case of cabin fever without anyone here to torment!"

"I will look after him," Elena promised, then urged with heartfelt concern. "Please, Caley, you will be careful?"

"As careful as I always am!"

She was already on her way to the back door when the sound of a dog's barking drifted up from the stables below. Her brow creased into a sudden frown, for she was certain it was Tripod she was hearing. Unlike most dogs, he seldom barked. Maybe on half a dozen occasions in all the time she had known him, she recalled absently.

"What the—" she murmured, preparing to investigate.

Her gaze widened with sudden alarm when she heard someone climbing up the stairs outside. She reached down to withdraw the knife concealed in her boot. Before she could shout a warning to Elena, the door crashed open.

"*Matt*!" she breathed in stunned disbelief when her eyes fell upon the man framed in the doorway.

"I told you I'd be back!" he declared triumphantly.

"But what—what are you doing here?" She retreated a few steps, her incredulous gaze shifting to the man who followed him inside. It was the swarthy, hawk-eyed puncher named Buck. His lips curled into a scornful smile. A tremor of fear shook her, but she didn't have time to worry about him at the moment. She looked to Matt again, her pulse racing. "Hellfire and damnation, Matt Griffin, don't you know Jake is looking for you? If he finds you here—"

"You think I'm afraid to face him?" Matt challenged tersely. His hand shot out to close about her wrist, and the knife clattered to the floor. "If he finds me, so much the better! The bastard couldn't have taken me before, if he hadn't sneaked up on me in that saloon in Tuscarora! He won't be looking for me here! Hell, this is the last place he'd expect me to turn up! Now come on! We're wasting time!"

"I'm not going anywhere with you!" She tried to pull free, but his grip tightened with bruising force. "Damn you, Matt, let me go!" she demanded. "I told you, I'm married now!"

"And I told you I wouldn't leave without you!" he countered in a low, furious growl. "You're coming with me, Mac! Even if I have to tie you across a saddle, you're coming with me!"

"No!" She fought him as best she could, but he yanked her forward and imprisoned her with his arms.

Buck, meanwhile, caught movement out of the corner of his eye. Leaving Matt to struggle with Caley, he gave chase to Elena as she whirled and headed downstairs to seek help.

"Not so fast, you little bitch!" Buck ground out, catching her about the waist. A sharp, breathless scream broke from her lips, and she twisted vio-

413

lently within his grasp.

"Let me go!" she cried. "Let me go, you coward! *Zakhurra*! Yankee dog!"

His strength was far superior to hers, and she found herself tossed roughly over his shoulder. He bore her back upstairs, where Matt still had his own hands full with Caley.

"Let's get out of here, damn it!" he snarled.

Disregarding Elena's furious protests, Buck hurried outside. Matt had lost all impatience. He balled his hand into a fist and brought it smashing up against Caley's chin. She crumpled, unconscious, into his arms.

He carried her down to where he and Buck had left their horses tied. Tripod was waiting at the foot of the stairs. In an effort to protect Caley, he lunged at her captor. Matt cursed and gave him a brutal kick, sending him tumbling back into the corral. The horses there snorted and pranced about in agitation, while the injured dog cringed out of the way of their hooves.

Buck tossed Elena up onto his mount and swung up behind her before she could escape. Clamping an arm about her waist, he yanked her back against him.

"Open that mouth of yours again, and I'll break your jaw!" he threatened close to her ear.

Matt had no choice but to place Caley facedown across his saddle. He gathered up the reins and was preparing to mount when a familiar voice sounded behind him.

"Hold it, Matt!"

He spun about to face his brother. Ned stood a few feet away, his revolver drawn and his eyes glinting with righteous fury.

"This has gone far enough!" he told Matt.

414

"How the hell did you—" demanded Matt, only to be cut off.

"I know you better than anyone, remember? Soon as I heard what had happened, I rode into town. I figured you'd be back; that's why I've been keeping an eye on Caley's place!" Tripod's barking had alerted him to the trouble. He had expected Matt to return for Caley. But he hadn't expected to find Elena Larronde involved as well. His gaze narrowed wrathfully. "You're going to let Caley go, Matt, and you're going to tell your *friend* there to let the other woman go, too!"

"The hell you say!" Matt sneered, then warned, "Get out of here, Ned! Get out of here before I forget we're brothers and put a bullet in that thick skull of yours!"

"I'm liable to forget the same thing!" He raised the gun a little more and cast a quick, cautious glance toward Buck. "Now let the women go and be on your way!"

"You yellow-livered son of a bitch!" Buck suddenly ground out, his fingers tensing about his own six-shooter. Elena jabbed him in the midsection with her elbow and slid halfway down from the saddle. Buck caught her, but at least she had succeeded in momentarily diverting his attention from Ned.

"Don't shoot, damn it!" ordered Matt. He rounded on his brother again and taunted contemptuously, "You won't kill me! You've never killed anyone!"

"I'll do whatever it takes, Matt," Ned replied in a low, steady tone. "I don't want to kill you, but I will if I have to."

"No," Matt disagreed, shaking his head while at the same time edging closer. "No, you don't have

415

enough guts! And besides, neither Pa nor Caley would ever forgive you. You'd have to live with that the rest of your life. God knows, you've always been too damned soft for your own good."

"And you've always been too hard."

"Maybe. But we're still brothers. That ought to count for something." He continued advancing, his gaze locked in silent combat with the younger man's. "Put down the gun, Ned. Put it down, and I'll forget this ever happened."

"But I won't, Matt."

"All right then." He stood directly in front of Ned now. His eyes filled with a savage light. "Damn you to hell, you had your chance!"

Before Ned could move to stop him, he whipped his gun from the holster and brought it crashing down against the back of his brother's head. Elena's scream was cut short when Buck's arm tightened cruelly about her. She watched in horror as Ned staggered against the wall of the building next door, then fell heavily to the ground.

"Why didn't you just go ahead and kill him?" Buck demanded angrily.

"Shut up!" Matt bit out. Eyeing his brother one last time, he finally mounted up. He took control of the reins with one hand and held tight to Caley's still unconscious form with the other. "If you're going to bring *her* along," he cautioned Buck, glaring malignantly at Elena, "you'd damned well better keep her quiet!"

He spurred his horse into a gallop, riding northward beneath the endless, starlit sky. Buck followed close behind.

Chapter XVII

Jake swung agilely down from the saddle. He'd had no more than four hours' sleep in the past two days, and only that after losing Matt Griffin's trail for a while that same morning. He had tracked him to Tuscarora—and now all the way back to Elko. There was little doubt in his mind why Griffin had chosen to risk coming back.

Caley. Refusing to let himself think the worst, he hurried inside the stage office and up the stairs. A lamp still burned in the main room.

"Caley?" he called out, his deep-timbred voice edged with raw emotion. There was no answer.

He conducted a quick but thorough search of the other rooms. Other than clothing strewn all about the bedroom, he found nothing amiss. Then, he noticed the back door standing ajar—and Caley's knife on the floor. He strode outside, his eyes scanning the darkness below until they fell upon a shadowy figure lying on the ground beside the lodge. Within seconds, he was kneeling beside Ned. Tripod limped over from the stables to whimper softly down at the injured man.

"Ned?" Relieved to discover his pulse still strong, Jake shook him with firm insistence. His one thought was to find Caley. "Wake up, Ned!" he urged.

Ned's eyelids fluttered open. He groaned, moving a hand to the back of his head as Jake pulled him into a sitting position.

"Is . . . is that you, Brody?" he stammered out weakly.

"It's me. Your brother's taken Caley, hasn't he?" demanded Jake, still hoping he was wrong.

"Yes," Ned confirmed his fears. "I tried to stop them, but I—I couldn't do it." He cursed his own weakness.

"Them?"

"Matt had someone else with him. A dark, ugly bastard!" he recalled. "He took Ele—Miss Larronde!" His head finally began to clear, and he climbed to his feet with Jake's help. "They couldn't have been gone long! And Caley didn't go with Matt willingly!" he added, as if sensing the other man's inner turmoil.

"How do you know that?"

"Because she was unconscious when he rode away with her across his saddle!"

Jake's green eyes smoldered with a lethal combination of rage and vengeance. Lurking in the back of his mind throughout the night and day had been the suspicion that Caley had planned to go with Griffin all along. He hadn't wanted to believe it; in his heart, he knew she wasn't that devious. Headstrong and rebellious, perhaps, but not devious. Still, the seed of doubt had been planted when she had helped Matt escape. *All doubt was gone now.*

"Did you see which way they headed?" he asked Ned grimly, his blood boiling at the thought of her in the other man's clutches.

418

"No. But Matt spends a lot of time up at—"

"Tuscarora," Jake finished for him. His rugged features tightened.

"He'll be expecting you to look for him there, won't he?" Ned questioned with a frown.

"I think that's exactly what he wants."

He turned and strode purposefully back to the front of the building. Ned hesitated only a moment before following, with the dog close on his heels.

"I'm going with you!" he insisted.

"No," replied Jake, his tone one of undeniable authority. "I'll travel faster alone."

"I've got just as much reason as you do to find them! More, if you count Elena!"

"Damn it, man, you're hurt!" He mounted up again and met Ned's determined gaze. "Stay here and tell my deputy what's going on."

"I'm coming!" Ned repeated stubbornly. "It doesn't matter what you say—I'll go on my own if I have to!"

Jake had neither the time nor the inclination to argue any further. He gave the other man a curt nod.

"Get your mount. I'll meet you down at the jail."

Ned hastened to obey. He retrieved his horse from where he'd left it tied nearby, swung up into the saddle, and rode after Jake. Tripod gazed toward the jail with his large, doleful eyes for a moment, then lay down in front of the stage office as if to wait for Caley's return.

Following a brief conversation with Dan, Jake and Ned were ready to leave. Jake's weariness had long since vanished. His heart twisted painfully at the thought of Caley in danger, but he knew that

419

the only way he'd be able to find her was by maintaining an iron control over his emotions. It was no easy task he had set himself. He loved her more than he would ever have believed possible . . . more than life itself.

Caley. Offering up a silent, fervent prayer for her safety, he reined about and watched Ned do the same.

For the third time in two days, he set a course for Tuscarora. Matt Griffin would pay, he vowed inwardly while Caley's beautiful face swam before his eyes. *The bastard would pay*.

Caley sat rigidly erect in the saddle, trying to hold herself as far away as she could from Matt. But avoiding contact with him was impossible. Grateful at least for the fact that she was no longer riding face-down, she tightened her grip about the saddlehorn and cast a swift glance back toward the couple on the other horse.

She cursed the fact that Elena had been taken as well. Although she had encountered Buck only once before, she sensed correctly that he was the sort of man who would stop at nothing, not even murder, to get what he wanted. Her suspicions about Matt had only been further aroused as a result of his association with Buck.

Oh, Jake! her heart cried out to her beloved. She knew he could be in Tuscarora at that very moment, or back in Elko, or even somewhere in between. That he had not found Matt, she was certain, just as she was certain he was still alive.

He would come after her, she reflected with a ragged intake of breath. He would come after her, and he would kill Matt. It was inevitable. Her

420

throat constricted tightly at the thought, but she drew courage from her newly realized love for him. She closed her eyes and prayed once again, with every fiber of her being, that he would be kept safe.

Matt had spoken only rarely to her during the wild flight across the rugged, night-cloaked countryside. She had thus far refused to answer, even when they had stopped to rest the horses. They were approaching Tuscarora now, and she was surprised to hear his voice sounding close to her ear.

"I've got something big planned, Mac!" he boasted. "Something that'll mean you and I can live in high style the rest of our whole damn lives!"

Although tempted to ask him what the "something big" was, she remained silent and unyielding. He was angered by her continuing obstinance, but he said nothing more until they had reached the outskirts of town. The lights of the saloons and gaming halls twinkled brightly in the near distance, and Caley knew they would not grow dim until a new day dawned.

"I'm going to have to leave you for a while," Matt told her. The tone of his voice gave every indication of his annoyance with her. "You and the little *senorita* will have to stay out of sight!"

She tensed, but still said nothing. He muttered an oath and suddenly drew his mount to a halt. Buck did the same.

Caley struggled as Matt pulled her down. She opened her mouth to scream, hoping that someone would hear, but he gagged her with his kerchief before she had uttered a sound. Though she kicked and struck out at him, he managed to tie her hands behind her back.

421

"Sorry, Mac, but it's your own fault for being so damned stubborn!"

Her eyes, blazing with the blue-green fire that was like no other, hurtled invisible daggers at his head. She looked and saw that Elena had met with the same rough treatment. Seething with outrage, she was tossed unceremoniously back up into the saddle.

"I can't take a chance on Brody finding us just yet!" said Matt, resuming his place behind her. He gathered up the reins again and spurred his mount down the hill. "I don't know why the hell you're acting this way, Mac, but I'll be damned if I'm going to let you ruin everything!"

Minutes later, they drew to a halt in front of a two-story wooden building situated just off the main street. Buck dismounted and carried Elena inside. Matt swung down and reached back up for Caley. Hot, angry tears were glistening in her eyes, and she delivered a forceful kick to his stomach before he managed to haul her into his arms. He was forced to endure several more blows from her booted feet as he spirited her quickly inside the building.

The lamplit room filled with laughter when Matt appeared with his furiously struggling burden. Caley's fiery gaze traveled over the faces of the four men who were so obviously amused by her plight. Ed Tickner was among them, as were Buck's two friends, Farley and Hooker. The fourth man was a stranger to her, but she recalled having seen him with Matt in Tuscarora a few days earlier.

"Looks like you could use some help there, Matt!" remarked Elko's former sheriff.

Glaring at the others, Matt spun about with a curse and bore Caley up the stairs. He finally set her on her feet in a room containing a bed, a chair, and nothing else. The only source of light was a single window, where the moon's pale, silvery glow crept in through the glass.

Buck had just thrown Elena down upon the bed, and his lustful gaze raked over her while Matt yanked the gag from about Caley's mouth.

"Get downstairs!" he ordered the other man, then threatened Caley, "Keep quiet, Mac, or I'll have to put it back!" He untied her hands and frowned as she stood rubbing at her chafed wrists. "I didn't want it to be this way, damn it!"

"What in blazes did you expect?" she finally retorted. "I told you I didn't want to come with you! You had no right, no blasted *right* to do this!"

He opened his mouth to answer, but angrily clamped it shut again. Seizing her arm, he forced her relentlessly along with him into the darkened, empty room next door. She jerked free and confronted him with all the force of her outrage and resentment.

"I could kill you myself, Matt Griffin!" she stormed. "Don't you realize what you've done? You've kidnapped me, and that innocent girl in there! I'm Jake Brody's wife, and he's not going to—"

"To hell with Brody!" Matt ground out. "He'll be out of the way soon enough!"

"Wha—what do you mean?" she stammered breathlessly, her heart leaping in sudden fear.

"I mean, damn you, that I'm going to kill him!"

"*No!*" She launched herself at him, but he captured her wrists before she could strike a blow.

"You and me, Mac!" he told her, yanking her arms behind her back and pulling her close. "It's always been you and me! I've waited ten years, *ten years*, but I'm not going to wait any longer!"

"It's too late!" Even in the darkness, she felt scorched by his hot, possessive gaze. "I belong to Jake now, and what's more, I—"

"Brody may have had you, but you're mine! I'll make you forget you ever knew him! I'll brand that body of yours with mine until you think of no other!" he vowed in a low, simmering tone. "By damn, I've kept my hands off you all this time! I've left you alone and taken my pleasure elsewhere—all because I thought you were saving yourself for *me*, for when we got married!"

"Let me go, Matt! You're hurting me!" she cried out sharply, wincing at the pain shooting up her arms.

"Even the robberies were for you!" he went on to confess. "I wanted the money for *us*, Mac! I wanted to get free of the old man once and for all, so you and me could get a start of our own back in California! I'm sorry you had to get involved, but it was the only way!"

"How could you do it, Matt?" she demanded reproachfully, facing the truth about him at last. She took a shuddering breath. "Those were my coaches! You nearly killed that express guard, and you nearly killed me!"

"That was Brody's fault! If the son of a bitch hadn't started shooting, no one would've gotten hurt!" He abruptly released her and flung away with another blistering curse. "He killed two of my men! And—"

"And you left another one for dead outside of Carlin!" charged Caley. She met his gaze unflinchingly when he rounded on her again. "I tried telling myself it couldn't be true! I didn't want to believe you could do something so vile! You've changed, Matt! The Matt Griffin I used to know wouldn't have robbed stages, or even attacked a sheepherders' camp the way you did!"

"I'm the same Matt Griffin all right!" he insisted bitterly. "You just never bothered to find out!" Stalking forward, he grasped her arms and fixed her with a narrow, fiercely deliberate look. "I've always been there for you, Mac! You could always count on *good old Matt*! I never asked for anything in return! But I'm asking now, damn you, I'm asking now! Once this last job is finished, you're going with me!"

"What are you planning to do?" she was almost afraid to question. "What is this 'last job' you keep talking about?"

"We've been planning it for weeks," he told her, calming somewhat. "Ed Tickner's been in on it all along, but I had to bring in the others after—"

"After you tried to rob my stage!" she finished for him.

"It wasn't supposed to happen like that!"

"Are you planning to try it again? Is that what all this is about?"

"No! No, I'm through with stages. I've got bigger things in mine." He paused for a moment, his eyes traveling over her in the smoke-scented darkness. "We're going to rob a train."

"A train?" she echoed in shocked amazement.

"It's been done before!" he pointed out defensively. "Hell, Mac, it'll mean we never have to worry about money the rest of our lives! There'll be enough to set you up in one of those fancy houses on Nob Hill in San Francisco, and—"

"You're only going to get yourself killed! Even if you did manage to get away with it, Jake would

425

hunt you down!"

"I'm going to settle with him before I leave Nevada!" Matt declared, his fingers digging into the soft flesh of her arms again.

"No! No, Matt, I won't let you hurt him! I'll kill you first!" she vowed passionately.

She fought him like a veritable tigress now, her fists pounding at his chest and her feet delivering a series of painful kicks to his unguarded shins. He tumbled her roughly down to her back on the floor and straddled her, yanking her arms above her head.

"Why, damn it?" he ground out. "Why does Brody matter so much to you?"

"Because I love him!" she declared, tears coursing freely down the flushed smoothness of her cheeks. "I love him, Matt! I didn't mean to fall in love with him, but I did! And so help me God, I'm not going to let you hurt him!"

Matt's face became a tight mask of savage fury. He let her go and climbed to his feet. She hastily pulled herself up to her knees, her flame-colored tresses streaming wildly down about her face and shoulders.

"Get out now, Matt, while you have the chance!" she pleaded in a voice fraught with anguish. "Get out before it's too late!"

"It's already too late—*for Brody*!"

He spun about and left. She heard him moving down the stairs to speak with the impatiently waiting members of his gang. Dragging herself upright, and feeling bruised all over, she returned to the next room to check on Elena. She closed the door softly behind her.

"I'm sorry I got you into this mess!" she whispered as she hurried to kneel on the bed and loosen the other woman's bonds. "We've got to find a way out of here!" She removed her gag, then gripped her shoulders and queried anxiously, "Are you all right, Elena? Do you think you can ride?"

"I—I am all right!" Elena confirmed with a nod. She was only a trifle unsteady on her feet as she and Caley stood beside the bed. "I know we must escape, but how?"

"I don't know!" admitted Caley. "But there's got to be some way!" She flew across to the window and tried to open it, only to discover that it had been nailed shut. "Damn!" she muttered beneath her breath. Whirling about, she told Elena, "Maybe there's a way out in one of the other rooms!"

She moved back to the door and eased it open. Peering cautiously outward, she motioned to Elena to follow. They crept down the narrow landing to the room at the front of the building.

Downstairs at that same moment, Matt was giving final instructions to his men.

"Farley, you head east with Hooker. Tickner, you and Davis ride out by the smelter."

"What about you?" asked Ed. His gaze shifted to Buck. "Don't tell me you and *him* are sticking together?"

It was no secret that the two men had been at odds with one another from the very beginning. The only reason Matt had allowed Buck to accompany him back to Elko was because he needed a backup and the dark, lean puncher was the handiest with a gun.

"We'll be heading out separately," Matt replied with a noticeable edge to his voice. "We'll meet where we planned, just this side of the tracks at the bend near Carlin. Stay out of sight, and don't let yourselves get followed. All of you got that straight?"

"We got it," answered Hooker. "But what if the train ain't on time?"

"Then we'll wait, damn it!" snarled Matt.

"What about the women?" This came from Buck, whose hawkish gaze drifted up toward the ceiling. "Who's going to keep an eye on them?"

"No one! They'll stay put!"

"Well now, it didn't look to me like they was real willin' to do that," offered Davis, a young man with a squint and an annoying habit of letting loose with a stream of tobacco whenever the mood hit him.

"I don't give a damn what it looked like to you!" sneered Matt. "You just worry about being on time!"

"Let's go, Davis!" urged Ed. He pulled on his hat and shifted the holster a little lower on his wide hips. "See you all at the rendezvous, boys — or in hell!" he pronounced with a deep rumble of laughter.

"No one said anythin' about women bein' mixed up in this," Davis muttered on his way out. He spat on the floor and disappeared through the doorway after Ed Tickner.

"He's right," Farley gathered enough courage to speak up. "Davis is right. The law'll be hot enough on our trail without bringin' the women into it!"

"Get going!" Matt ground out.

Farley's eyes widened with alarm, and he hastened to obey. Hooker followed at a more leisurely pace. That left only Buck and Matt.

"You want some help?" Buck offered mockingly,

casting another glance overhead.

"Shut up and do as I said!"

"Seems to me you been sayin' too damned much!"

"I'm giving the orders here, you bastard!" Matt reminded him furiously, his gaze burning across into the other man's. "I'll take care of the women! Now get going!"

"Sooner or later, Griffin," promised Buck, "you and me are gonna have it out. And then we'll see who's givin' the orders!" Compressing his lips into a tight, thin line of anger, he stalked outside.

Matt turned and climbed back up the stairs. He scowled darkly when he saw that neither Caley nor Elena were where he had left them. Moving along the landing with slow, measured steps, he was satisfied to discover them in the front room. They had been trying to pry loose the wooden planks which boarded up the window, and they were just about to abandon their futile efforts when Matt suddenly appeared in the doorway.

"It won't do you any good."

They both started in alarm at the sound of his voice. Caley whirled to face him.

"Let us go, Matt!" she demanded. "Damn it, you can't do this!"

"Don't try anything, Caley," he cautioned tersely, "unless you want the little *basco* there to get hurt!"

"You—you wouldn't do that!" she countered, though her voice lacked conviction. As she was beginning to realize, he was capable of just about anything.

"I would," he assured her. He began pulling the door to. "Stay put and keep quiet. I've left a man on guard below, and he's got orders to shoot

429

anyone trying to come in—or out!" he lied with effective gruffness.

"Matt! Please Matt, don't!" she cried hoarsely, racing forward.

But it was too late. She stared at the door in helpless fury as Matt slammed it and turned the key in the lock. It was almost pitch black in the room now, and the air was positively stifling.

"What are we going to do?" Elena asked with a telltale catch in her voice.

"I don't know," sighed Caley. "But I'll think of something." Her own spirits plummeted at this latest cruel twist of fate, and she choked back the sob which rose in her throat.

Jake! Dear God, what was going to happen to him? She had to think of some way to get out . . . she had to find him and warn him!

Despair threatened to overwhelm her. She closed her eyes and buried her face in her hands. Elena moved to her side.

"Marshal Brody will find us!" she said, striving valiantly to give them both courage. "He will find us!"

"That's what I'm afraid of," murmured Caley.

She hugged Elena close for a moment, then began pacing about the room while her mind raced feverishly to think of another plan. It was her husband's welfare which concerned her; not her own. She would think of some way to help him. After all, she told herself with a renewed burst of proud defiance, she was Paddy McAlister's daughter—and by damn, she would *not* give up!

Matt quickly returned downstairs and took up his hat. Preparing to leave, he leaned over to blow out the lamp.

430

"I've done some thinkin', Griffin."

He jerked his head up to see Buck smiling malevolently across at him from the doorway.

"What the hell are you doing back here?" he demanded, his blue eyes glinting harshly. "You're supposed to be on your way to—"

"That's what the thinkin' was about," drawled Buck. He came all the way inside and nudged the door shut behind him with his booted heel. "I've decided I don't much like this plan of yours, Griffin." Though his manner was almost indifferent, his dark gaze held the inescapable promise of violence.

"Damn you, you're in too deep to get out now!" Matt gritted belligerently. His hand edged down toward his gun. "On your way, you bastard, before I—"

"You don't scare me," Buck declared with another faint smile. He walked slowly forward, his eyes never leaving Matt's face. "Anyhow, I always knew it'd come to this sooner or later."

"What are you talking about?"

"You and me. Right from the first, when I threw in with this plan of yours, I had it in mind to take over. I figured I'd wait till we pulled it off, then make my move. But now . . . well now, I've decided to cut my losses and get out. You see, Griffin," he concluded, his eyes filling with malignant humor, "I don't give a damn about the rest of you sons of bitches, but I don't much like the idea of gettin' my own neck stretched."

"Hell, man, I never took you for a coward!" sneered Matt. His fingers curled about the handle of his gun, his whole body tensing for action. "We can settle things between us later! And none of us will get killed if we just stick to the plan!"

"That's another thing. This plan of yours—the more I think about it, the less I like it. Seems to me you've got it fixed so *you're* the one gets away with the money and the rest of us stand to lose!"

"It'll work out for all of us," insisted Matt, "just as long as you've got the guts to go through with it! Now I'll give you one more chance," he then offered, begrudgingly aware of the fact that the job would be almost impossible to pull off without the other man's help. "Get going now, and I'll forget about this. You've got my word on that!"

"Your word?" echoed Buck. He gave a snort of disgust. "Your word ain't worth piss! No, I'm stayin' right here." He cast another significant glance overhead. "And when I do go, it won't be empty-handed," he vowed. His hawkish gaze locked with the vigilant fury of Matt's again. A slow smile, even more sinister than before, spread across his swarthy features. "I ought to get somethin' for my troubles."

"You can take the girl! You can do whatever you like with her—only wait until after we've finished the job, damn it!"

"I don't want the *senorita*," said Buck. He paused for a moment and inched even closer. "No, Griffin. She ain't the one. The others can have her for all I care. It's the redhaired bitch I'm after!"

"Why, you—" Matt bit out, drawing his gun at last.

Buck was ready for him. He balled his hand into a fist and brought it smashing up against Matt's chin with brainrattling force. Matt fell heavily back against the table, the gun slipping from his grasp.

The lamp crashed to the floor and broke. Oil streamed freely across the boards. Chasing it was a

432

river of fire. Flames leapt upward, and smoke began filling the room.

Buck had just drawn his own gun and leveled it at Matt, intending to kill him and then go upstairs to fetch Caley. But the fire changed his plans. Cursing, he holstered his gun again and turned to flee. Matt was on him in an instant, dragging him back.

"Not so fast, you double-crossing bastard!" he growled, jerking him about to retaliate with a hard, punishing blow of his own. Buck staggered backward, then came at him again.

"Get used to the heat, Griffin—you'll burn in hell soon enough!"

"No, by damn, *you* will!"

His blue eyes gleaming triumphantly, Matt fired the gun he had just drawn from the other man's holster. Buck gave a sharp howl of pain and clutched at his chest. His eyes widened with stunned disbelief as he looked to Matt. Finally, he crumpled to the floor.

Upstairs, Caley and Elena had once again been trying desperately to loosen the boards at the window. They had just become aware of the acrid smell of something burning, when the unmistakable sound of a gunshot tore through the darkness of their prison.

"Jake!" breathed Caley, her first thought of him. She spun about, but Elena's hand closed upon her arm.

"It is on fire!" the younger woman cried, pointing downward to where smoke had begun rising from cracks in the bare wooden floor. "Caley, the building is on fire!"

"Dear God!" she whispered in dawning horror. Flying to the door, she raised her fists and began

433

pounding on it with all her might. "Help! Some-one, please help!"

"Caley!" It was Matt's voice.

"Matt!" she called back, torn between relief and dread. "Matt, get us out of here!"

"I'm coming!" He unlocked the door and flung it open. His face was blackened from the smoke, and his hair was singed as a result of his frantic dash up the stairs to save the only woman he had ever loved.

"Oh Matt, what's happened?" asked Caley. "Is Jake—"

"No!" he denied, shaking his head. "We'll have to get out from up here!" Striding forward, he grasped her arms and revealed, "The fire's spread too far!"

"But the window's boarded up!" she pointed out. "And we can't—"

"Stand back!" he ordered, roughly setting her away.

Elena hastened to her side, and the two of them watched as he moved to the window and lifted a foot to kick at the boards. Smoke was pouring up from below, making their eyes burn. Coughing, they clung to one another and prayed for deliverance from the flames which had now crept up the walls to bathe the room in a horrible, ever-intensifying golden glow.

"Hurry, Matt!" screamed Caley. Terror gripped her heart, and tears streamed down her face while she thought of Jake. *Please God, don't let it be too late*!

There was a loud, splintering crash as Matt succeeded in kicking the boards free.

"Come on!" he yelled, holding out his hand for Caley.

434

She and Elena raced forward. Matt seized her about the waist and swung her out the window. She found her footing on the tin roof of the porch, then helped Elena out as well. A crowd had gathered in the street below, and a woman screamed when she caught sight of them.

"Look!" she cried, pointing up at Caley and Elena. "Help them, for the love of heaven, somebody get them down!"

The first floor was completely engulfed by the raging inferno now. Smoke billowed forth, choking the cool night air while the flames leapt higher and higher. The horrified onlookers, streaming out of the nearby saloons, watched helplessly while the building burned. They had no means with which to fight the blaze, no fire wagons or bucket brigades. And even if any of them had wanted to try, there was no possible hope of winning, for the fire had already grown too intense.

"Jump, Caley!" Matt shouted above the fire's roar. He was still inside, his hands gripping hers.

"Matt! Please, Matt, get out!" she urged frantically. She could see the flames shooting up behind him. "Matt!"

"Go on!" He tore his hands from hers and pushed her away from the window.

She turned and clutched at Elena, the two of them stumbling across the roof. The people below yelled at them to jump. Panic-stricken, they hesitated.

"Caley!"

Through her tears, she saw the man who suddenly forced his way through the crowd.

"*Jake*!" She blinked hard, scarcely able to believe the miracle. "Jake!"

"Jump!" he bade her, holding his arms ready to

catch her. "Come on, Caley—now!"

"Elena!" Ned Griffin called out as he, too, came running to the front. "Jump, Elena!"

Elena immediately drew courage from his presence. She let go of Caley and hurled herself downward. Ned broke her fall, his arms wrapping about her. He lost his balance, but others helped prevent them from tumbling to the ground.

"Caley!" Jake yelled again. She cast one last, anguished look back at Matt.

"Go on!" he reiterated. "I'll be right behind you!" He swung a leg over the windowsill, but suddenly discovered that his other foot was caught. Although he tried frantically to pull it free, he could not.

In that split second of time, Matt Griffin sensed the inevitable. His eyes were brimming with a mixture of fear and regret as they fastened on Caley.

"Caley! Dear God, Caley, *jump*!" Jake commanded hoarsely, his heart standing still at the sight of her in such danger. He was oblivious to the heat and smoke as he raised his arms toward her.

She hesitated no longer. Moving closer to the edge, she steeled herself and finally obeyed her own instincts. Jake caught her. His strong arms enveloped her, and he swiftly bore her to a safer distance from the flames.

"Jake!" she choked out when he set her on her feet. "Matt's still inside!" She lifted a trembling hand. "He-he's still up there!"

Looking back, he tensed. Matt was framed in the window, his body outlined by the fire's terrible light.

"Stay here!" he ordered.

He left her and hurried back toward the building. But it was too late.

Suddenly, there was a loud crash. The entire second floor collapsed, plunging downward in a magnificent burst of flames. Matt disappeared in the midst of the conflagration.

"*Matt!*" screamed Caley. She raced instinctively forward, only to be detained by Jake.

"It's too late!" he told her. "He's gone, Caley!"

"No!" she whispered, shaking her head in a futile denial. "No!" She stared dazedly at the ghastly sight before her. The tears which now sprang to her eyes had nothing to do with the smoke. A deep sorrow crept over her, and she collapsed weakly against Jake.

"I'm sorry, my love," he murmured close to her ear, his arms tightening about her. "It's over, Caley. It's over."

The crowd surged forward again, watching in awestruck silence as the fire set about consuming what was left of the building. Elena hastened to Caley's side. Ned followed close behind. Like the others, they remained silent.

Caley clung to her husband, her heart full of both sadness and profound relief. *Jake was safe.* And she was in his arms, where she belonged. She closed her eyes and swayed against him, grateful for his strength and his courage . . . and, most of all, for his love. Never again would she doubt him, or herself.

Then, fate played out one final, cruel trick.

Without warning, Buck reappeared. He staggered around from the rear of the building, one hand clutching his chest while the other grasped the same gun Matt had used to shoot him only minutes earlier.

Something within Caley made her aware of impending danger. She opened her eyes just in time to see Buck raising his gun toward Jake. Her pulse leapt in renewed alarm.

"Jake!" she cried out a shrill warning.

"I told you I'd get even with you, Brody!" rasped Buck.

Jake spun about, placing Caley protectively behind him. His whole body tensed for action. Beside him, Ned stood ready to respond as well.

"It's no use," Jake told the wounded outlaw, his manner deceptively calm and steady. "Shoot me, and you're a dead man."

"Then I'll see you in hell!"

Caley screamed as Buck took aim. But he never had a chance. Jake easily beat him to the draw.

The bullet pierced his heart. He fell dead at last, his blood draining from his lifeless body while the flames danced triumphantly beside him.

"Oh, Jake!" breathed Caley. She flung herself against his broad chest once more and wound her arms about his neck, holding him as though she would never let him go. "I love you!" she declared with all her heart and soul. "I love you!"

"I know you do, wildcat," he murmured, his green eyes brimming with that intoxicating mixture of tenderness and warm amusement she knew so well. "And I love you."

She pressed even closer while his arms tightened about her with fierce yet gentle possessiveness. Ned and Elena looked at one another and smiled softly.

The first rays of the dawn glowed upon the horizon, signalling an end to the long, terror-filled night . . . and the beginning of a new day.

Chapter XVIII

"Is it true, Miss Caley?" asked Billy. "Is it true you and the marshal are leavin' town?"

"Yes, Billy." She smiled and closed the schedule book, then placed it behind the counter. "At the end of the month. My husband feels it's time he went home."

"Home? You mean, to *Texas*?" The idea apparently struck him as preposterous.

"That's what I mean all right," Caley confirmed with a soft laugh. "Jake plans for us to start a ranch of our own. I guess he's had enough of keeping the peace for a while." *And so had she.* Thank the Lord, she added silently, no longer would she have to spend each day wondering if the man she loved would still be alive come nightfall.

"But—what about this place? And the stage line?"

"I was going to tell you later." She came forward and took his hands in hers for a moment. "It so happens, Billy Snyder, that you're going to have new bosses."

"I am?"

"You are. I've signed the business over to Hank

439

and Red. God knows they've earned it."

They hadn't wanted to accept, of course. Claiming that she was being far too generous, the two of them had been downright bullheaded about it. She had remained adamant, however, and had pointed out truthfully that she would never have been able to keep things going the past six months without them. In the end, they had come around to her way of thinking—although it had required Jake's help in getting them there.

"You mean I'm gonna work for Hank and Red?" Billy's youthful features beamed with pleasure at the prospect. "Well I'll be damned!" he breathed in wonderment.

"You'd better not let your mother hear you talking like that," she cautioned, her blue-green gaze alight with indulgent humor. "By the way, how's your father doing?"

"Better than he's been in years," Billy was proud to report. "Once that murder charge against him was dismissed, he sort of became a different man. He's gone back to work, and Ma thinks it's gonna last this time. I hate to say it, but it looks like nearly gettin' lynched was the best thing that could've happened to him. It sure enough seems to've scared the livin' daylights out of him. He hasn't had a drink ever since."

"I'm glad to hear it." She gave him another warm smile before suggesting, "You'd better go on home now. I'll see you in the morning."

"Yes, ma'am!" He headed for the door, but suddenly drew to a halt and turned back to face her. "Miss Caley?"

"Yes, Billy?"

"There's something I been meanin' to say." He paused and looked down for a moment, gently

440

clearing his throat. When he raised his eyes to hers again, she was surprised to glimpse the emotion contained within their bright blue depths. "I'm sorry about Matt Griffin, Miss Caley. And about old Mr. Griffin, too."

"Thank you, Billy," she replied quietly, touched by his heartfelt expression of sympathy. "Good night." She watched as he pulled on his hat and left.

Thinking of Matt still brought her a twinge of pain, but she knew time would lessen it. Isaiah's pain would never ease, she mused with an inward sigh. The news of Matt's death had hit him even harder than anyone had expected. He was a broken man now, a mere shadow of his former self. Instead of seeking revenge, he had retreated within himself, and would be returning to California within a few days' time.

Ned would be running the ranch from now on, and she couldn't help but think the arrangement was going to work out for the best — especially for Ned, who was making remarkable progress in his efforts to convince Bertrand Larronde of his worth as a suitor for Elena. His part in her rescue certainly hadn't hurt matters any.

She was glad Ed Tickner would be standing trial. He and the four other would-be train robbers were locked up down the street in the jail, right where they belonged. It was only after he had brought them in that Jake had mentioned his plans to return to Texas. A new start for them both, he had said. And a real home, all their own.

A faint smile tugging at her lips, Caley wandered to the doorway and gazed out upon the familiar bustle of Main Street. Twilight had recently settled over the land, bringing with it the promise of yet another star-filled night. She found it difficult to believe that less than a week had passed since Jake had brought her home from Tuscarora. In so many ways, it seemed long ago. . . .

Another sigh escaped her lips, and she was about to return inside when her eyes suddenly fell upon the dog ambling toward her on the board-walk.

"Tripod!" Her gaze shone with affection. She bent down and smoothed a hand across his large, perennially scruffy head. "Maybe you'd like to come to Texas, too, you old rascal!" she murmured.

"He's welcome to, so long as he sleeps outside," remarked Jake, sauntering forward. His eyes twinkled down at her. "Since we've got to take that devil cat of yours, we might as well bring someone to keep him in line."

"No," she declined with visible reluctance. She shook her head and rose to her feet. "I don't think he'd want to leave. And Elko just wouldn't be the same without him around to keep an eye on things." She met Jake's warm gaze. "What are you doing home so early?"

"Is that any way to greet your husband, Mrs. Brody?" he challenged in a low, wonderfully vibrant tone of voice.

Before she could respond, he swept her into his arms and kissed her—right there in front of God and everybody. She melted against him, of course, and didn't think to blush until after he released her.

"Shame on you, Marshal!" she chided with a mock frown of disapproval. "What will the neigh-

442

bors think?"

"The truth," he replied, smiling unrepentantly. "They'll think I'm so damned crazy in love with my wife that I can't keep my hands off her."

"Then we'd better get inside before we shock them any further!"

In mutual and completely willing accordance with that suggestion, they went upstairs together. Jake bent his tall frame into the rocking chair and pulled Caley down upon his lap.

"Are you sure you won't mind leaving?" he asked, growing solemn for a moment.

"Not at all," she reassured him. "I'll miss Maybelle, and some of the others, but I won't mind too much. After all, I'll be with you." She entwined her arms about his neck and rested her head contentedly upon his shoulder. "I never thought I could feel this way about anyone, Jake."

"And how is that?" he queried, his green eyes brimming with loving amusement again as he pulled her even closer.

"Like I'm only half a person without you." She raised her head and gazed up at him with all the love in her heart. "I still can't believe it's finally happened to me. Deep inside, I always wanted to find someone to love. And someone to love me back."

"Well you've found him. I love you, Caley, and I'll never let you go," he vowed quietly.

"I'll never try to get away," she promised, giving him a soft, teasing smile that stirred his heart and made his pulses leap with desire.

"Look at me like that again, wildcat, and you'll find yourself in bed before supper," he warned huskily.

"There's something I want to know first."

443

"And what's that?"

"Who is Smitty?" she queried, remembering the name on the telegram he had received that morning. The telegram had officially relieved him of his duty as a United States Marshal, effective on the last day of the month—the day they would leave to build a new life for themselves in Texas.

It was Caley's turn to grow warm all over as she watched her husband's mouth curve into a roguish, utterly devastating smile.

"You've been reading my mail, have you?" he accused without any trace of displeasure.

"It's a wife's duty, isn't it?" she retorted saucily, then demanded once more, "Who is Smitty?"

"I can't tell you," he replied with maddening evasiveness.

"Great balls of fire, why not?"

"Because his identity has to remain a secret. It goes with the job."

"Is that so? And how do I know *you're* really who you claim to be?"

"Because you trust me."

She couldn't possibly argue with that, and they both knew it. Besides, she mused, her eyes glowing with passion's fire, she didn't feel like arguing. No indeed, that wasn't what she felt like doing at all.

Taking her fate in her own hands, she sent Jake another thoroughly captivating look just like the one he had warned her about. It achieved the desired results.

"This will be the fourth time this week we've been late for supper!" she pointed out breathlessly as he stood and began carrying her toward the bedroom. "Everyone will talk!"

"Let them," he drawled. He lowered her to the bed and covered her body with his own. His gaze burned tenderly down into hers. "I love you, Caley."

"I love you, too." She smiled again at a sudden thought and said, "Maybe I should pay a visit to Mr. Ling before we leave town."

"Mr. Ling?" echoed Jake. A slight frown of bemusement creased his handsome, sun-kissed brow. "What for?"

"Oh, you'll find out," she answered with a touch of secrecy all her own, thinking of Mr. Ling's special tea. "And I hope it's soon."

It would be. But, for now, there was only Jake. His hands had already begun working their magic. She gave a low moan of surrender as his lips claimed hers in a kiss of sweet, splendid mastery that sent her passions spiralling heavenward.

Her heart had found a home at last. And before them both lay the bright golden promise of tomorrow.

EXHILARATING ROMANCE
From Zebra Books

GOLDEN PARADISE   (2007, $3.95)
by Constance O'Banyon
Desperate for money, the beautiful and innocent Valentina Barrett finds work as a veiled dancer, "Jordanna," at San Francisco's notorious Crystal Palace. There she falls in love with handsome, wealthy Marquis Vincente—a man she knew she could never trust as Valentina — but who Jordanna can't resist making her lover and reveling in love's GOLDEN PARADISE.

SAVAGE SPLENDOR   (1855, $3.95)
by Constance O'Banyon
By day Mara questioned her decision to remain in her husband's world. But by night, when Tajarez crushed her in his strong, muscular arms, taking her to the peaks of rapture, she knew she could never live without him.

TEXAS TRIUMPH   (2009, $3.95)
by Victoria Thompson
Nothing is more important to the determined Rachel McKinsey than the Circle M — and if it meant marrying her foreman to scare off rustlers she would do it. Yet the gorgeous rancher feels a secret thrill that the towering Cole Elliot is to be her man — and despite her plan that they be business partners, all she truly desires is a glorious consummation of their vows.

KIMBERLY'S KISS   (2184, $3.95)
by Kathleen Drymon
As a girl, Kimberly Davonwoods had spent her days racing her horse, perfecting her fencing, and roaming London's byways disguised as a boy. Then at nineteen the raven-haired beauty was forced to marry a complete stranger. Though the hot-tempered adventuress vowed to escape her new husband, she never dreamed that he would use the sweet chains of ecstasy to keep her from ever wanting to leave his side!

FOREVER FANCY   (2185, $3.95)
by Jean Haught
After she killed a man in self-defense, alluring Fancy Broussard had no choice but to flee Clarence, Missouri. She sneaked aboard a private rail car, plotting to distract its owner with her womanly charms. Then the dashing Rafe Taggart strode into his compartment . . . and the frightened girl was swept up in a whirlwind of passion that flared into an undeniable, unstoppable prelude to ecstasy!

Available wherever paperbacks are sold, or order direct from the Publisher. Send cover price plus 50¢ per copy for mailing and handling to Zebra Books, Dept. 2781, 475 Park Avenue South, New York, N.Y. 10016. Residents of New York, New Jersey and Pennsylvania must include sales tax. DO NOT SEND CASH.

LOVE'S BRIGHTEST STARS SHINE
WITH ZEBRA BOOKS!

CATALINA'S CARESS   (2942, $4.50)
by Sylvie F. Sommerfield

Catalina Carrington was determined to buy her riverboat back from the handsome gambler who'd beaten her brother at cards. But when dashing Marc Copeland named his price—three days as his mistress—Catalina swore she'd never meet his terms . . . even as she imagined the rapture a night in his arms would bring!

BELOVED EMBRACE   (2941, $4.50)
by Cassie Edwards

Leana Rutherford was terrified when the ship carrying her family from New York to Texas was attacked by savage pirates. But when she gazed upon the bold sea-bandit Brandon Seton, Leana longed to share the ecstasy she was sure his passionate caress would ignite!

ELUSIVE SWAN   (2061, $3.95)
by Sylvie F. Sommerfield

Just one glance from the handsome stranger in the dockside tavern in boisterous St. Augustine made Arianne tremble with excitement. But the innocent young woman was already running from one man . . . and no matter how fiercely the flames of desire burned within her, Arianne dared not submit to another!

SAVAGE PARADISE   (1985, $3.95)
by Cassie Edwards

Marianna Fowler detested the desolate wilderness of the unsettled Montana Territory. But once the hot-blooded Chippewa brave Lone Hawk saved her life, the spirited young beauty wished never to leave, longing to experience the fire of the handsome warrior's passionate embrace!

MOONLIT MAGIC   (1941, $3.95)
by Sylvie F. Sommerfield

When she found the slick railroad negotiator Trace Cord trespassing on her property and bathing in her river, innocent Jenny Graham could barely contain her rage. But when she saw how the setting sun gilded Trace's magnificent physique, Jenny's seething fury was transformed into burning desire!

Available wherever paperbacks are sold, or order direct from the Publisher. Send cover price plus 50¢ per copy for mailing and handling to Zebra Books, Dept. 2781, 475 Park Avenue South, New York, N.Y. 10016. Residents of New York, New Jersey and Pennsylvania must include sales tax. DO NOT SEND CASH.

HEART-THROBBING ROMANCES BY KAY MCMAHON AND ROCHELLE WAYNE FROM ZEBRA BOOKS!

DEFIANT SPITFIRE (2326, $3.9
by Kay McMahon
The notorious privateer Dane Remington demanded Brittar Lockwood's virtue as payment for rescuing her brother. But onc he tasted her honey-sweet lips, he knew he wanted her passiona and willing rather than angry and vengeful. . . . Only then woul he free her from his bed!

THE PIRATE'S LADY (2114, $3.9
by Kay McMahon
Shipwrecked on Chad LaShelle's outlaw island, lovely Jennif Gray knew what her fate would be at the hands of the arroga pirate. She fled through the jungle forest, terrified of the outlaw embrace—and even more terrified of her own primitive respon to his touch!

FRONTIER FLAME (1965-3, $3.9
by Rochelle Wayne
Suzanne Donovan was searching for her brother, but once sh confronted towering Major Blade Landon, she wished she'd nev left her lavish Mississippi home. The lean, muscled officer mac her think only of the rapture his touch could bring, igniting th fires of unquenchable passion!

SAVAGE CARESS (2137, $3.9
by Rochelle Wayne
Beautiful Alisha Stevens had thanked the powerful Indian wa rior Black Wolf for rescuing her as only a woman can. Now sh was furious to discover his deceit. He would return her to h people only when he was ready—until then she was at his bec and call, forced to submit to his SAVAGE CARESS.

UNTAMED HEART (2306-5, $3.9
by Rochelle Wayne
Fort Laramie's handsome scout David Hunter seemed determine to keep auburn-haired Julianne Ross from doing her job as a r porter. And when he trapped her in his powerful embrace, th curvaceous young journalist found herself at a loss for the wor to tell him to stop the delicious torment of his touch!

Available wherever paperbacks are sold, or order direct from th Publisher. Send cover price plus 50¢ per copy for mailing an handling to Zebra Books, Dept. 2781, 475 Park Avenue Sout New York, N.Y. 10016. Residents of New York, New Jersey an Pennsylvania must include sales tax. DO NOT SEND CASH.